IMAGINE THAT

MARK FINS

 OLD FARM
PRESS

ISBN: 978-0-692-57245-0 (sc)
ISBN: 978-0-692-55902-4 (hc)

Library of Congress Cataloging-in-Publication data is available on file.

— To Mom and Dad

IMAGINE THAT

PART ONE

CHAPTER 1

Bayside, New York
Summer 1957

I ran out of the shed. My heart pounded. I could barely catch my breath. Thoughts raced through my mind in a way that terrified and confused me. The image of my dad and his red, angry face kept replaying in my mind. I saw his clenched teeth and fist in the air. I thought for a second it might come down on me. I remembered his voice, as loud as thunder, and the horrible words, "What the hell is wrong with you!"

I kept running. I tried to get as far away from his voice and angry face as I could. I passed the front of our duplex and ran around the corner to 210th Street hoping none of my friends would see me. I didn't want to tell them what had happened. I wanted to forget about it, get my mind on to something else. But after running all the way down the street and back again, the red-faced image of him still was there. I slowed to a walk and felt my head bend as if the weight of all my bad thoughts was too heavy for it. I watched the ground and noticed that my new black Keds sneakers seemed to move out in front of me on their own as I struggled to figure things out.

I guess what I did was dumb, even though it didn't seem dumb at the time. I suppose taking matches from the kitchen drawer and lighting a few of my army guys and a couple of my plastic Jeeps and tanks on fire using my dad's workbench in the shed was a stupid idea. But I had such a good reason. I needed to make a realistic scene like what I'd seen on the newsreels during the intermission at the Bayside Cinema, where me and my friends went on Saturday afternoons. For a second, I thought maybe God had sent a message to my dad and told him to scream at me for lighting American tanks and Jeeps on fire. But I wasn't doing that. I mean I was, but I was pretending that they were Nazi tanks and soldiers, not Americans, so that it wouldn't be a sin or crime or anything bad.

Still, I felt my dad was wrong to yell at me. And I didn't really believe God was behind it. To me, a dad should never shout at a son, and a son should never shout at a dad. They should always explain things calmly to each other and be nice like the Beaver's parents, Mr. and Mrs. Cleaver, on TV. I know it's possible to be that way. In fact, that's how my dad used to be with me. It's true that he got a little upset with me a couple of weeks ago when I lit some firecrackers with a few of my friends in the woods when we were pretending to be in the Battle Of The Bulge, but nothing even close to the way he was today.

I finally felt my breathing getting easier, slowing, and my heartbeat coming back to normal, not such big thumps. I felt thankful. All I needed to do now was to figure out what I could do that would be fun instead of causing me so much worry. It didn't seem fair that kids like me who were only eight years old should be afraid. Someone should make a law that kids should have as much fun as they can until they're really old and have to get a job and get married.

I discovered a long time ago that I could get away from bad thoughts and into a better mood by pretending to be someone else. My favorite person to pretend with is Jeffrey, my best friend who lives across the street in a red-brick duplex just like ours. Just this morning before it got really hot, we went to the Little League diamond and took turns pretending to be Mickey Mantle hitting homers into the upper deck of Yankee Stadium. We ran around the bases and yelled stuff like "Holy Cow, that one is going into outer space," just like our favorite radio announcer, Phil Rizzuto, did. Just remembering how much fun we had, and how Jeffrey's blubbery body seemed to jiggle as he ran around the bases was enough to make me laugh inside and feel a little bit happier.

I made my way back to 211th Street and thought about catching up with Jeffrey or one of my other neighborhood friends. On my way, I walked past my neighbor, Sharon Silverbloom, and her girlfriend Lilly from up the street. They were drawing boxes for hopscotch with thick sticks of pastel-colored chalk. Every so often one of them would stop and hop or do a cartwheel.

A little farther up the street I passed Mr. Shapiro, who was in his driveway wearing sunglasses and a Yankee cap. He was washing his bright red Ford Fairlane with a hose and a big, soapy sponge. Kids in the neighborhood secretly joked about his car and called it "Shapiro's fire engine" because of how red it was and how clean he kept it. He was listening to his brand-new transistor radio. I heard the word "Russians" as I moved past him, and noticed how just that word was enough to make him wince and shake his head.

When I finally caught sight of Jeffrey, he was way up the street near the McBride's house. He saw me at almost the same second I saw him. He waved his toy rifle, a sure sign he wanted me to come over right away. He was wearing a kid-sized GI helmet and Army gear. I noticed that the McBride brothers, Gerard and Brian, were on their hands and knees right next to him looking down at something on the sidewalk.

His voice called out excitedly, "Marco Polo! Come here! Quick!"

Jeffrey always made up lots of crazy names for people. Instead of calling me Mark, he liked to call me names like Marco Polo or Marcus Aurelius. Sometimes, he even said hilarious stuff like "Hark, it's Mark," which always got everyone laughing.

I hustled up the street until I was right next to him. I noticed that his hair was glued up with so much butch wax that I could see little chunks of it between the globs of hair closest to his forehead. His freckled face was lit up with excitement.

"Look at this!" he said excitedly, pointing to the ground and then dropping to his knees for a closer look.

I got on my hands and knees and finally saw what all the excitement was about. Gerard and Brian were busy pounding a huge colony of ants with rocks that were about the size of golf balls. The ants had been swarming over a half-eaten popsicle, but were now racing in every direction. Gerard was making excellent explosion, rocket, and missile sounds as he and Brian tapped hundreds of them to death.

We were talking about it and making up stories of how they were really Nazis getting what they deserved when Mr. McBride appeared on his front steps across the street. Wearing a dirty white undershirt and suspenders over his great big belly, he looked fierce next to the big American flag that blew gently in the breeze next to his front door.

"What are all you kids doing?" he said in a voice that naturally boomed.

Mr. McBride was really big. Gerard once told me he was six foot two and weighed more than 230 pounds. He had a scruffy kind of face that had a lot of little holes in it that you could see if you dared to get up close to him. It made him look extra tough and scary. Mr. McBride had been a Marine in World War II but was now a fireman. It was a little hard to imagine him sliding down a pole with his enormous belly, but maybe he just went down the back stairs or something. Gerard and Brian looked up at him at almost the same second, but it was Brian who got his words out first.

"We're killing ants and pretending they're Nazis," said Gerard, getting to his feet.

Mr. McBride thought for a couple of seconds and then surprised us with a laugh and a wave of his hand. "Oh yeah? Good.

Kill 'em all. Then, get the Japs and Commies when you're done. But before you do, where the hell is your brother Patrick?"

"Don't know, Dad," said Gerard, looking like he was almost standing at attention.

"Well don't just stand there; get off your asses and go find him. Check with everyone on the street. Try the Goldberg kids first, and then try 212th Street. Tell the little shit if he isn't home in five minutes to clean up for dinner I'm going to bury my foot in his ass. You hear?"

We all watched in awe as Mr. McBride patted his stomach as if to see how big it was, before turning to go back inside. We were all used to his cussing and found it a little funny that he never tried to cover it up for us.

I found myself watching the front of the McBride's duplex for several seconds after Mr. McBride went back inside. It made me wonder. I turned and looked at Gerard and Brian, who were looking at each other and seemed to be trying to figure out who should look where for Patrick.

"Is your dad really going to bury his foot in your brother's ass?" I asked.

Jeffrey was the first to laugh out loud, and then the McBrides followed until finally Gerard explained. "No, he just says that. He doesn't actually do it."

"Why does he say it, then?" I asked.

"I dunno," said Gerard. "My mom says he's always mad about everything and that cursing and talking like a tough guy makes him feel better."

"What's he mad about?"

"I don't know. My mom says he's mad about the war, his job, and not having enough money."

I thought about what Gerard said. "So he's not really mad at you when he says all that stuff? And he isn't really going to kick anyone in the ass?"

Jeffrey was standing and listening and shifting his weight from side to side.

"Nah, he just says that stuff to get us to move quicker."

"Did he ever make a fist at you or scream at you or say, "What the hell is wrong with you?" I asked.

For a few seconds everyone was quiet. No one said a word. Then I noticed them all staring at me as they slowly shook their heads. I got the sense that they were beginning to wonder about me and why I asked those kinds of questions. I felt myself getting really embarrassed, so to change the subject as quickly as I could, I said, "I can go to 212th Street and help you look for Patrick." It seemed to work. Gerard nodded and we all split up.

As I started toward 212th Street, my mind went back again to what happened in the shed. It was so hard to stop thinking about it; it kept making its way back into my mind. I knew I was still worried. I knew my dad was definitely going to be talking to me about it when dinner time came, and I had no idea what might happen after that. I felt the knot in my stomach getting tighter as I went to look for Patrick. I was ready to look for him for as long as it took. I was in no hurry to go home.

CHAPTER 2

I found myself sitting across from my dad in our living room. He had ordered me to sit on the couch and pulled up a chair so that he was right in front of me. He seemed even bigger and scarier sitting so close. I watched his lips move as he mouthed words like "fire," "permission," "matches," and "dangerous," but for some reason I could barely understand him. I knew his message was never to start a fire again, and that I'd be punished if I did, but beyond that, it was like being in the front row of the cinema with a giant movie screen with a humongous tense face and moving lips on it. The face had bent eyebrows and sharp, serious eyes and it was still making me nervous even though there wasn't any fist in the air or thundering voice to break my eardrums. Even while I watched him on the movie screen, I wondered if something was happening to him that was making him turn into a different kind of dad. It crossed my mind that maybe Martians were behind it, using their special powers to change him. Or maybe he'd eaten a special poison fruit or vegetable that no one else had ever seen or known, except for other crazy people, and it was slowly changing him. On the other hand, maybe it was simpler than that. Maybe he just didn't love me as much as before.

The clatter of pots and pans brought me back to earth. My eyes flicked toward the kitchen and I saw Mom, a pot holder in her hand, stirring something that was sizzling in a skillet. I knew not to allow my eyes to wander for more than a second or two, because the red-faced thunder-monster on the movie screen was still in front of me. A few more moments went by and I was distracted again by the great smell of frying peppers and onions as they made their way to my nose. I felt my mouth water and my stomach growl. I risked another glance at Mom and watched her lift the lid off one of the pots, lean over, and take a taste with a big wooden spoon. With her long, dark hair and white, flowered apron around her waist, she always looked graceful and pretty to me, but especially so when she was moving pots and pans around on the stove.

My eyes returned to the giant face and I looked back at it uncomfortably. For a second I thought about Mom and how odd it was that she stayed completely out of what was going on. She just kept cooking, as if pretending she couldn't hear a thing that Dad was saying. I didn't mind, though. We all knew that the Jewish tradition in our house made Dad the boss. That was because Sephardic men like my dad, who brought home all the money, were the ones who got to make up almost all the rules. My mom, who was Ashkenazic, didn't always agree with his rules, but she didn't interfere because she knew it would cause a big argument. Instead, the two of them worked out a system of imaginary departments like in a department store so that my mom could be the boss too. My mom's departments made her the boss of cooking and cleaning and caring for the kids, and my dad's departments were things like making money, mowing the lawn, fixing things that broke, and punishing the kids when they were bad. The most important rule about the department system was they were not allowed to go into each other's departments no matter what.

For a few seconds, while I looked back into my dad's eyes, my mind accidently wandered again. By the time I realized he'd asked me a question and was waiting for my answer, it was too late to think back and remember exactly what he'd said. I tried, but I couldn't, so I did my best and just said, "What?"

He stared back at me, then in an annoyed tone, said, "Have you been listening to what I've been saying? And do you understand what I am saying?"

I nodded and looked right back into his eyes and wondered if I had just told a lie.

He looked at me for a few more seconds and finally said, "Okay, go upstairs and get ready for dinner." His face relaxed a little and for the first time in a very long time I was able to take a really deep breath.

I went upstairs to my room, sat on the edge of my bed, and began to think about what I could do to get away from bad thoughts before getting called for dinner. As I glanced around the room looking for ideas, my eyes settled on my favorite stuffed animal, an all-black Scottish Terrier I had named Blackie. Mom had given him to me for my birthday. She'd attached an envelope with a card in it and on the envelope she'd written, "Happy Birthday, Mark Lemon". The 'Lemon' was a joke because when I was little and couldn't pronounce stuff, I told people my last name was Lemon instead of Leonard.

Blackie was a favorite of mine from the first minute I owned him. At night, just before going to sleep, I liked to hold him up over my head and talk to him about all sorts of things, including things that only dogs would know about, like how it felt to be pulled around on a leash all day, and why so many dogs liked to pee on fire hydrants.

I grabbed Blackie and plopped back down on my bed to have a talk about everything that happened today and maybe get some good dog advice. But as soon as I held him up, one of his red glass eyes fell out. It was the same glass eye that had fallen out twice before. Those other times I just screwed it back in and hoped it wouldn't happen again. But this time I decided he was going to need surgery in order to fix it once and for all. I knew without it he would have a hard time playing with other dogs or finding his food bowl. And the thought of him wandering around half-blind all the time would make us both really sad. I know because we talked about it.

I went to my desk and pushed all my army guys out of the way—bazooka men, machine gunners, grenade throwers and snipers—and lay Blackie down on his side. Imagining myself to be Dr. Mark Leonard, the world's most famous dog doctor, I told Blackie what I was going to do ahead of time, just like the doctor at the hospital did with me before taking out my tonsils. When Blackie was ready, I pinched his nostrils together and made him go unconscious. Then, using my pillowcase, I carefully wiped the area around his eye so it would be clean. The nurse who helped me knew I didn't always remember the exact name of the operating tools that were on her silver tray, but she knew what I meant when I asked for sculples, crinklers, and dog-skin chubbers to do each step of the operation. Finally, after imagining a complicated ten-hour operation, I gave the glass eye an extra-hard twist and got it screwed in tightly. Then I took a pencil from my desk and pretended it was a needle, like the kind doctors use when they give you a shot, and carefully stuck Blackie in the butt with it. A few seconds later he started to wake up. At first, he was groggy. But when he realized he could see perfectly out of both eyes he got so excited he ran all over the room barking and wagging his tail before jumping on me and licking my face about a hundred times.

Mom's call from downstairs and the smell of steak and onions stopped my imagination fast. I put down Blackie, went into the bathroom, rinsed my hands, and raced downstairs to eat.

At the table were my two sisters, Bonnie, who was 12, and Arlene, who was only a year-and-a-half. Dad stayed in the living room and was reading from a stack of papers that he must have gotten from his open briefcase on the floor next to his chair.

As soon as I sat down, Bonnie stuck her tongue out at me to show me that she hated me and that the war that had been going on between us since I was really little was still going. I stuck my pointer finger up my nose and left it there, hoping to make her throw up when Mom jumped in and put an end to it.

"I don't want any trouble from you two. Do you hear me?" she said pointing to each of us in turn. "This is exactly why your father can't digest his food and has to wait for you to be finished before he can sit down. I want the first shift to concentrate on eating and getting along."

Without another word I looked away from Bonnie and began scooping steak, potatoes, and fried onions and peppers onto my plate. I knew there would be plenty of other chances to make Bonnie's life as miserable as she tried to make mine.

Arlene was in her high chair with a bib around her neck. She was mostly unaware of everything except for the bits of food Mom occasionally put on the tray of her high chair. It was fun to watch Arlene eat. Nothing went into her mouth without some of it smearing across her face. When we all laughed and pointed at her, she didn't even know how to be embarrassed so she laughed and pointed back at us, often excitedly pounding her plate with her little hands and knocking stuff all over the place.

In between gulps I glanced into the living room at my dad, who sat in his lounge chair half buried in business papers, a strange look of worry on his face. I remembered how just a couple of weeks ago I was still able to go right over to him and climb onto his lap. Back then, no matter how busy he was, he made room for me by adjusting all of his worry papers to make sure I could fit in snuggly between his chest and right arm. Without a word he would continue reading and thinking, from time to time stopping to lean down and sniff the top of my head. Sometimes I'd reach up and feel his scratchy whiskers and smell his aftershave lotion. My dad's lap was one of the best places in the world, and I realized how much I missed going there. But the more I thought about it, the more I wondered if I would ever be able to go there again. Not because he wouldn't let me, or because I didn't want to. I was just too scared of him to imagine ever doing it again.

CHAPTER 3

The next evening, a Monday, I put on my bathrobe and pinned a paper with a great big red "S" on the front of it. I started throwing crayons at myself to make it seem like bullets were bouncing off my steel chest, just like Superman, when I heard Dad's car pull into the driveway. I moved to the doorway of my room where I could see downstairs to the front door. The first shift had already eaten, and Mom had warned us to be quiet, since it was a work night and Dad had already called to say he'd had a rough day. She moved to the front door, and got ready to take Dad's coat as soon as he came in.

The door opened and he slowly entered, looking tired and upset. Mom gently pulled on one sleeve and then the other to help him take off his coat. I thought how different he looked compared to the pictures I once saw of him when he was a drill instructor in the army. In those pictures his shoulders were back, he was tan, and he was standing up straight. You could see his six-foot-tall body and muscles rippling right through his T-shirt.

He went into the bathroom and I heard the water rushing as he washed his hands. When he came out Mom walked him to his seat at the table and he sat down.

A little worried, I decided to be brave and move closer. I really wanted to understand, or at least get clues to why he was always looking so tired and upset. If it was Martians that were changing him I wanted to be able to learn about it. I knew he would be talking to Mom about his tiredness and a bunch of other stuff, so I decided to be a spy and find out whatever I could. I got out of my Superman outfit in a hurry and put on my army pants, jacket, and helmet. Then I grabbed my toy rifle and crawled out of my room on my stomach, first to the top of the stairs and then down to the landing just like the GI's did in Iwo Jima.

The landing made a good spying nest, and I could see my dad from the side and my mom facing him.

When he finally spoke, his voice sounded hoarse and defeated.

"Al told me he caught a guy punching in a friend's time card today. The guy wasn't even scheduled to work."

Al is my dad's brother. They are in a new business together. It's a factory. They take tubes that are made out of brass and bend them into different shapes with big machines. Then they sell them to plumbers.

"Al fired the guy on the spot, but the union steward overrode him because he said it was accidental. The guy pretty much laughed in our face."

I watched Dad pause again and take a sip of water.

"Later, the freight elevator broke down. Trucks were lined up trying to make deliveries and we couldn't receive them. This is the wrong type of elevator and the wrong kind of building for this business. That's why everything is always breaking down and everything takes much longer than it should. It wasn't meant for this type of freight or storage. Everything is inefficient. We didn't have a clue when we bought the place."

For a few seconds it was quiet. Then, he continued.

"We got two more code violations from the State. Our insurance premiums are going to go through the roof. I can't believe how tough New York is on business. You would think they would appreciate the jobs we provide."

Mom began to scoop salad into his salad bowl.

"Can I see the mail?" he asked.

Mom looked up surprised. "How about after you eat," she said gently.

"I'd rather get everything done before I eat, so I can relax after."

"Irving, I don't think it's such a good idea. Mail and bills always upset you. Maybe you should get some food in your stomach first."

"It's all right."

"Why don't you work on the salad. The kifteh and Spanish rice will be ready in two seconds."

Kifteh is one of my dad's favorite Sephardic foods. They're weird-tasting, golf-ball sized things made out of leeks. Mom learned how to make them from my dad's mom, Grandma Bessie. Grandma Bessie learned how to make them from her mom while growing up in a country called Turkey.

"Well, let me see the mail while I wait."

"How about right after dessert."

His voice got much louder. It scared me. "What's going on? Why can't I see my own mail in my own house?"

Everything got quiet. Mom went into the kitchen and came back with a small stack of mail and handed it to him while carefully sliding the salad bowl closer to him. But after tearing open several envelopes without taking even one bite, he stopped and looked at one piece of mail in particular.

"How much did the installation of the dishwasher cost? This bill is nuts. How long did it take the repairman to do it?" he asked, looking up at Mom.

Mom went back into the kitchen and didn't answer.

"Did you at least ask him ahead of time what he was going to charge?"

"Irving," she said, calling over, "please have dinner first and then I'll explain. You're like a time bomb right now."

Dad looked around the room as if he wanted to pick a fight with a wall or a lampshade. It was creepy to watch.

Mom came back from the stove and began loading rice, kifteh, and roast chicken onto his plate. I didn't know what was going to happen, but my heart started to beat faster, until finally, thankfully, he started to take a few bites and stopped asking questions. I relaxed enough to take a deep breath and let it out as Mom sat down near him at the table.

"Do you know what I think about on days like today?" he asked more softly.

Mom just looked at him, but I could tell she was glad to see him calming down.

"I think about what a mindless fool I was to drop out of college." He shook his head back and forth in disgust. "I was a good student. I was a year and a half into it and getting good grades. I could have been a professional—a lawyer, an accountant, even a doctor, maybe. Pop was so proud of me when I was going. He would have put his last dime toward my education. He was devastated when I dropped out. And now, here I am, 15 years later, being punished in the business world for being such a fool."

Mom gave him a fresh paper napkin and filled his water glass.

Dad cut off a piece of chicken and chewed it slowly for a long time before swallowing.

There was a short silence.

"It worries me to no end that we borrowed Pop's last $25,000—money he worked for his whole life. There's no more after that. God only knows how we'll ever pay it back. And if we fail, I become a slave for someone else."

Mom put her hand on his arm.

"You won't become a slave. You'll make it. We'll make it. You're a smart man. You'll find a way. Let's just take it one day at a time. Right now the bills are getting paid, the kids are eating well, and we have a roof over our heads. And—I've got ice cream and strawberries for dessert."

Dad nodded.

I started to think about how it would be if Dad had to become a slave. It worried me as I recalled pictures in my Hebrew books that showed slaves working for the mean Pharaoh guy who was the boss of Egypt. I remembered the drawings in our Passover Haggadah, too, of Egyptian guys with weird-looking hats and no shirts and little short skirts holding whips, while poor skinny Jews way down below in muddy pits were being worked to death mixing mud and straw to make bricks by hand. I wondered if it could actually happen to Dad and then to our whole family. I'd have to make bricks, too. But then I realized my dad must be exaggerating. He had to be, because everyone knows in the United States of America, everyone is free, except maybe bad guys, and besides, no one makes bricks that way anymore.

Dad put his fork down carefully. Everyone in our family knew when he did that it meant he was getting ready to say something important.

"Look Bea," he said, getting her attention, "that option I was talking to you about—remember? Al and I are going to drive the DeSoto up there for another look on Saturday. It'll be another overnight. Can you book a room at that Putnam Motel for me? If you can, try to get the lowest rate."

Mom paused for a very long time, and then slowly nodded.

In that instant, I knew something was going on that I didn't understand. This particular grown-up secret had come up a few times before, but it never sounded quite this important. When I asked Mom about it last time, she said it was a business trip Dad was going on with my Uncle Al. But this time there was something about the way Dad said it, and the way Mom got quiet for such a long time right after, that made me think it might be an extra-important secret. I made a note in my head, because now that I was beginning to understand some of the reasons why Dad was always being sad and mad, I knew if I was ever going to help him be happy again, and be like the old Dad, I would have to be a very good spy and learn as much as I could about everything that was going on—even the sneaky stuff that moms and dads like mine do behind their kids' backs and never tell you about.

CHAPTER 4

The next morning, when Bonnie wasn't around, I sneaked into her room and tore out a few blank pages from her spiral notebook. I went back to my room, sat down, and tried to write a letter to my dad's union. I tried a whole bunch of times to write it in my very best penmanship and make it sound as nice as possible so that the union people wouldn't be mad at Dad, and he wouldn't be mad at them. I just wanted them to understand how upset and nervous they were making him and how it was making our whole family nervous and worried. It seemed like a great idea when I started writing, but every time I read it back, it sounded dumber and dumber. I ended up crumpling up about a thousand pieces of paper before giving up.

Late in the day, just before dinner, I was up in my room on my bed holding Blackie up over my head and telling him about why Yogi Berra was the best catcher in baseball, when Bonnie appeared in the doorway holding up her notebook. After raking back her blond hair with her right hand and adjusting her headband, she pointed an accusing finger at me and then used the same finger to point to her notebook.

"Did you go into my room and tear out sheets from my spiral

notebook?"

"Yeah, so what? I needed some paper to write an important letter. And Mom said she's going to buy you a new notebook as soon as school starts." It was actually a fib, but not a lie, since I knew I could convince Mom to do it.

Bonnie opened the notebook and began writing little notes on the edge of one of the pages. A long time ago she had told me that the notes she made while we talked were transferred to a big list called "The Master List" and it was kept in a secret hiding place. She told me that when the time was right she was going to give the Master List to a judge she knows.

Even though I was almost certain she was bluffing, it somehow worried me enough to make me search the house from top to bottom to try and find it. But I didn't find a thing. Instead, I had no choice but to watch her slowly etch my crimes onto paper while she read them aloud.

"Going into my room without permission...hmm...that's an infraction."

I hated the way she said and did stuff, and I hated that stupid word 'infraction.' It was one of her special big words that she'd looked up in the dictionary just to drive me crazy.

"Let's see," she said under her breath, but loud enough for me to hear, "touching my spiral notebook without permission—another infraction. And um...tearing out pages without permission— that's a huge infraction, really two. You leave me no choice. These are going to have to be transferred to The Master List."

"You're a liar. There's no such thing as a Master List." I tried saying it with confidence.

"There sure is," she said much more confidently then I had.

"Then where is it?"

Bonnie made a face of disgust. It was the kind of face that let me know she wished I'd never been born. "Do you think I am going to tell you where it is? Do you think I'm stupid? I would never do that. You'll know very, very soon though, because it's almost ready for the judge to see it."

"What judge?"

"I told you before. He's a judge that lives in the back part of the White House. He talks to the President almost every morning and sometimes even at night when there are lots of people to punish."

"You're making it up."

"Why would I make up something about such a serious thing having to do with the President of the United States of America?"

"Because you're an idiot, that's why."

Bonnie began to write and murmur again. "Called…me… an idiot…on…August the—"

"If there is a judge, what's his name?" I challenged

"The name of the judge?" she repeated.

"Yeah."

"Judge Thomas Copperfield."

Her answer startled me, especially because of how quickly she answered. It began to worry me, especially because it sounded like the kind of name that could possibly be the name of a real judge.

Still trying to sound confident I said, "How do you know him, then?"

"From a friend of a friend who you don't know."

"Oh yeah, what's their name?" I asked. But my voice cracked, giving away how much it was beginning to worry me.

Bonnie fidgeted with her charm bracelet and casually looked around the room. "Mary Farnsworth. And that is all I am going to tell you."

I couldn't get over how quickly she came back with that name, either. And like the first name, it sounded like it could be another real person's name.

Bonnie looked at me with a serious face and nodded the truth of what she was about to say.

"He specializes in cases like yours."

I had a brief thought about how great it would be if I could get Bonnie thrown in jail for something, but such imaginings were interrupted by Mom's piercing voice filling the house.

"First shift! Now!"

The call to dinner actually felt like a relief from Bonnie torturing my mind, but better still, it was a chance to get some revenge because Bonnie was a lousy eater, and Mom and she were always going at it over what she wouldn't eat. Dinner time was my chance to show her up and let her see how much I enjoyed her suffering because of food. Their fighting began almost immediately after we sat down.

"Why aren't you eating your mashed potatoes?"

Bonnie looked up at her and away. I made sure she could see me gobbling up my portion of mashed potatoes with huge satisfaction, a fake grin plastered on my face like that creepy-looking cat in *Alice In Wonderland*.

"Well?" Mom demanded.

"There's lumps in it," Bonnie complained.

"No, there are absolutely no lumps," Mom replied. But to be sure, she went over to the pot on the stove, lifted the lid with her right hand, and took a swipe with her left pinky finger, which she brought to her lips. "They're fine," she said. "Smooth as silk."

I could tell Mom was getting more disgusted with her. She prided herself on her cooking. Bonnie turned away and seemed to shrivel a little. "Mine are lumpy," she said in a whiney voice.

Mom banged down the lid and whirled to face Bonnie. "Eat them anyway. Lumps won't hurt you if there are any. And what about the corn that's also sitting on your plate?"

"I don't like the corn, either."

"Why? What's wrong with the corn? You had corn before."

"It's too yellow."

"Too yellow? What kind of *mishigas* is that?"

"Also, it touched the mashed potato."

"So what! So what if it touched!"

"I don't like it when they touch. I like them to be separate."

"Meshuggeneh! It's going to touch once it's in your stomach anyway," said Mom, putting her hands in the air.

Bonnie didn't move. Her head was down. She finally peeked up at Mom. "I think I might throw up if you force me to eat either of them."

Mom paused. There had been a time when Bonnie had followed through with her threat and that one time was enough to remind Mom she'd better not push too hard. Instead, she picked up Bonnie's plate and with a scowl on her face began scraping the mashed potato and corn onto my plate without even asking. The whole time, she mumbled a whole bunch of insulting Yiddish words like shlub and nudnick in Bonnie's general direction. It was a fabulous victory for me. To make it even sweeter, I started in on the extra food, and made sure to say "yum" and "mmm...delicious" to stick it to Bonnie a little extra before getting a kiss on the head from Mom for being such a good, cooperative boy.

Mom dismissed the first shift and Bonnie and I went to different parts of the house. When I remembered that tonight was allowance night, I got very excited. I had saved up some money that I got for doing chores around the house. I knew if I added my allowance to it I'd have enough to buy a whole new bag of U.S. army guys to add to the army of guys I already had, and make a huge, humongous battle. I might even have enough money to buy some tanks and jeeps to replace the ones I burned in the shed. There was still time to get to the five and ten before it closed. All I had to do was ask Mom. But when I did, I got the worst answer I could ever imagine.

"Sorry, allowance is your father's department."

"But Mom," I complained, "I really need to buy some new army guys for a huge battle I've been planning." But she didn't even answer.

"Mom, you're not being fair. I'll pay you back. I'll even do extra chores for free," I said. But she didn't budge. I kept at it. "Why are you being so mean?" I said, getting much louder.

"Sorry, it's not my department."

I raised my voice even louder. "If you were really sorry, you'd change your mind and not just say..."

I was shocked when her answer cut me off and came back even louder.

"I said no! End of subject."

I stopped in my tracks, surprised at how loud she'd shouted and yet curious about the sound of fear that seemed to be part of it.

"Do you want me to get into a big argument with your father? Because that is exactly what will happen if I do what you're asking. Do you understand? It's how it works in this family and there's no debate about it. He's in charge of allowance, and I'm not."

It was hard to think of the next thing to say, so I didn't say anything. Still feeling badly but glad that I tried my best, I wrote a note to my dad asking for my allowance and left it on the kitchen counter in case he got home after I went to bed.

When I went to bed that night, Mom's nervous words were in my head. It reminded me of a time long ago when I had managed to convince her to do something that wasn't in one of her departments. My dad got mad at her and raised his voice way up. Mom went around for hours without talking to him. It was one of the worst feelings in the world to see them both upset and angry over something that was my fault. I even worried that they might get divorced like one kid I knew at school who said his mom and dad always fought before his dad moved out. Even though Mom almost always gave in to Dad to get things back to normal, I could tell she was upset and not herself for hours afterward. It was something I definitely didn't ever want to happen again.

CHAPTER 5

The next morning, with my dad already off to work, I raced downstairs and found my allowance right on the note I'd left. Together with the money I'd been earning clipping weeds and washing the car, I had enough to buy a whole bunch of new army guys. An hour later, after returning from the store, I was really excited as I imagined a hundred different ways the battle might happen. I went to the basement playroom and made my old army guys join forces with my new ones, setting them up across the floor, on windowsills, behind the TV stand, and even in the cracks of the cushions and couches. I even managed to use some of my leftover cowboys and Indians, who had decided to join the fight against the evil Nazis.

Pausing to make sure each guy was in exactly the right position, it suddenly came to me how thirsty I'd become. I called on both sides to have a five-minute truce and then climbed the stairs two at a time in search of something to drink. In the kitchen, I was about to yank on the refrigerator door when my eyes were distracted by the sight of a pack of matches lying alongside my Grandpa Abraham's white Yahrzeit candle on the kitchen counter. I froze at the sight of them as something strange started to go on inside me. It was as if Dad were staring at me and wondering whether I'd take them or not. I knew he'd warned me not to play with matches, and yet here I was, thinking about going against what he'd said. It was as if his ghost was telling me to choose between listening to his mean voice warning me not to have fun or choosing to have an imaginary battle that might be one of the best of all time. I felt a tiny swell of uncomfortable feelings, including being mad at him for not being fun anymore and for talking angrily to me and Mom. With hardly another thought, I grabbed the book of matches and shoved them into my pants pocket and pushed everything else out of my mind.

It all happened in less than ten seconds—the time it took to gulp down a big glass of orange soda and let out a giant burp. Still not sure why I would do such a risky thing, I started back toward the downstairs playroom. By then, I must have known how sneaky I was being, because I didn't even look up at Mom, who was busily vacuuming the living room carpet as I went by. Instead, I made my way downstairs, tiptoeing on the bare linoleum steps until I saw the battle layout again and imagined ways I could make it even more exciting.

It came to me that maybe I could light a match each time there was a pretend explosion. Or maybe I could light one and pretend it was a missile or a rocket, like the Russians used in the battle of Stalingrad.

Without another thought, I pulled one of the matches from the book and scraped the head along the brown scratchy stripe on the side of the pack. When the flame was about halfway up the stem, I blew it out and thought about what to do next. I could feel myself getting more excited by the second, and I decided to do the same thing again, except to make it extra exciting, I decided to wait until the flame was almost touching my fingertips before blowing it out. It would be like a close call in a battle against a charging enemy. I lit another one and watched for a few seconds as the flame came closer and closer to my fingertips, but again, just past halfway, when I began to feel the heat, I reacted with quick whipping motions of my wrist until it was out, leaving a trail of smoke behind it. The trail of smoke reminded me of the flaming planes of the kamikazes that I'd seen in the newsreels—the ones that had been hit by our anti-aircraft guns and had spun around and around until they fell from the sky, leaving long, winding trails of thick, black smoke behind them before crashing into the ocean.

Feeling more excited, I decided to light a piece of paper from the playroom's trash container and let it burn for a while before beating it to death with a rolled-up newspaper that I'd found nearby. My plan was to surprise the enemy with my new, never-before-seen weapon that I had invented —a "firewhacker." My story was that it was the only Allied anti-fire weapon of its kind and it was for battles when the enemy sent fire at us. I got ready to use my firewhacker to give enemy flames a good beating if they dared to try and get out of control. As I tightened my grip on it, I tried not to be distracted by the smoky haze that was building up in the playroom and instead concentrated on defending myself and the United States of America against the evil enemy flames that were about to come to kill us.

I tried the firewhacker a couple of times with a few small pieces of paper, and each time I lit one I was able to put out the flames by using fierce whips of my hand and arm. With each victory I felt proud of myself for defeating such a dangerous enemy.

I imagined myself receiving a medal for bravery and being called to the White House for a ceremony for the most important war heroes of World War II. I compared it to the feelings our American soldiers must have had when they won their battles.

I came up with the idea that it would be an exciting challenge to give the enemy fire in the trash container a full 20-second head start before fighting back. It was the longest time I had ever allowed a fire to go without trying to control it, but confident in the firewhacker as my secret weapon, I lit a small piece of paper and began my count.

I held back as long as I could, but when I got up to 16, I saw with a surge of fear that the fire was spreading to other papers in

the trash container much faster than I'd thought possible. All at
once smoke was billowing and my confidence vanished as small
flames turned into larger ones that began leaping above the rim of
the wastebasket. As I beat on the flames with my firewhacker they
appeared to weaken for a second or two, but then, to my horror,
they bounced right back and grew even stronger. I blew on them
over and over, but each burst of wind from my straining, puffed
cheeks only made things worse. I continued pounding away with
my firewhacker, hoping and praying it would make a difference.
But it didn't. The flames only grew stronger. Horrified and in fear
I would lose the battle, a new, frightening truth came to me—
my secret weapon was just a rolled-up newspaper. Frantically, I
thought about where I could get some water. But there was none
downstairs and I knew it would take much too long to get it from
upstairs. I pounded on the flames with all my might until my arm
felt like it was turning to rubber. Still I kept on, praying only for
enough time to figure out what to do. But the flames wouldn't
cooperate. Instead, they seemed to almost reach up from the trash
container to catch onto something else. Sparks were everywhere
and soon flames were licking their way toward the TV stand. I
worried that the TV might catch fire next, yet it was too heavy to
move and I didn't have time. With another surge of fear I worried
that the mysterious wiring inside the TV might mean it could
explode like a bomb if the fire got too near it. With my heart
pounding, I did the only thing I could—I ran upstairs in a panic
and yelled to my mom.

"Mom! The house is on fire!"

Mom turned off the vacuum cleaner. At first she just stood
there as if wondering if she'd heard me right. But the look on my
face must have convinced her without the need for more words.
Seeing her moving toward me, I raced back downstairs and she
followed. By the time she was halfway down the steps we could
both see a real live fire burning in the trash container and reaching
out toward everything near it.

"Oh my God!" she said in disbelief.

A second later she began to bark orders. "Mark, get the mop and stick it in the toilet until it's soaking wet. Bring it to me as fast as you can. Then bring pitchers of water from the sink. Hurry!"

As I ran back upstairs to do what she said, I looked over my shoulder and saw her struggling to pull the TV stand away from the hungry flames. On my way back downstairs, she yanked the wet mop out of my hands and began punching at the flames with it, making sure to smother some of the lit papers that had fallen over the side. All around her on the floor and floating in the air were ruby-red cinders. She raced upstairs past me to get water, calling over her shoulder as she did.

"Don't get near the fire. I'll do it. Just follow me and fill up the containers and put them on the floor. I'll do the pouring. Keep bringing them to me."

I did exactly what she said and raced back upstairs. I pulled out pitchers and vases from the cabinets and filled them at the sink as fast as I could as Mom battled the fire below. Each time I came with a jar or vase filled with water, she grabbed it from me and doused the fire as best she could, working the mop to suffocate some of the more dangerous flames. Several times she passed me on the stairs to get more water faster. Up and down we went, trying to be careful not to bump into each other on the steps as we filled, carried, and spilled the water on the trash container and the smoking papers that were all over the floor. It took about seven trips up and down the steps by both of us before I could see that Mom had it under control. My heart continued pounding as I looked at her. With her chest heaving and out of breath, she looked all around. My army guys and tanks were knocked over and scattered everywhere. The basement was a stinking, smoky, watery mess.

With the fire no longer a threat, I felt a few seconds of relief. But it didn't last. Instead, I began to sense a new, different kind of fear as I watched Mom focusing her eyes on me. I backed as far away from the trash container as I could and wished and prayed to God that I could become invisible and disappear through the basement's cement walls. But it didn't work. Mom's eyes narrowed and with her hands and arms, she began to almost swim through the haze of smoke toward me, occasionally coughing as she came closer. I could see by her expression that she was looking for some kind of an answer. I watched nervously as her expression hardened and I just knew she was putting everything together in her mind. Looking right at me and squinting, she asked in a scarily calm voice, "Mark, did you do this?"

Petrified, I managed to nod my head.

"But why?" she said, unable to keep her voice from rising. "Why did you do it? What were you thinking?"

I didn't know how to answer. How could I say it was my idea of an experiment or tell her that it was a battle and I was using a secret weapon for the Allies? It was pretend. Everything I did came out of my imagination. It was hard for grown-ups to understand. Even I didn't completely understand. So I told her the honest truth: "I don't know."

"What do you mean you don't know?" she said, her voice rising even more.

Now I really didn't know what to say. I gulped but couldn't seem to swallow.

"Why did you do it?!" she yelled. "Why? Why? I want an answer. Now!"

I gagged on my words. Shaking, I told her the truth as best as I could.

"I wanted to see if...I could...put it out."

She looked at me as if she couldn't believe what I'd just said. I could tell that even though she was very, very upset she was struggling to understand.

We both knew she would have to tell Dad about this, and the idea of it scared me to death. Mom's eyes were watering and she was near tears.

"Go to your room!" she shouted, her voice cracking.

I stood, frozen, looking at her, wishing I could talk, wishing I could explain. But all I heard was her voice suddenly screeching at me.

"Now!"

I ran upstairs to my room, jumped onto my bed, grabbed Blackie, and buried my face in my pillow and began to sob. It was all my fault—everything. I had really upset Mom. I had made a horrible mess. I was almost definitely going to get screamed at by Dad. And the chances of ever making him happy again or liking me again or saying he loved me again, seemed to be close to zero.

CHAPTER 6

From my room, I could hear Mom moving all over the house opening windows and spraying some kind of nice-smelling stuff to get rid of the smoky stink that still lingered everywhere. Finally, I heard her come up the basement stairs one last time and go into the kitchen, and soon the familiar sound of clattering pots and pans began. Before long, I could smell the strong odor of onions and garlic frying and I just knew it was Mom's way of covering any smells that might still be coming from the basement. When it was time for the first shift to eat, she told Bonnie and me to eat quickly without talking and then she served us our dinner without another word. When I finished eating, she pointed for me to go back to my room.

The sounds of Dad arriving home finally came, and the knot in my stomach grew worse than ever. I waited until I could hear him at the dining room table talking to Mom, before inching down the stairs to the landing. I could smell one of Dad's favorite Sephardic dishes, spinach boulemmas. I had the feeling, especially since she didn't serve them to the first shift, that she had made them to cheer Dad up, so that when she told him what I'd done, maybe he wouldn't kill me. But as he took a few bites, he seemed unaware of how good it tasted.

Instead he went on angrily about business. "They make it impossible to get anything done. I can't get rid of a single person, no matter how lazy and incompetent they are, without running into union work rules."

There was a strange silence.

"What's wrong?" Dad finally asked.

"Nothing," Mom said. "Finish eating."

"Is it the kids?" Dad asked urgently. "Are they okay?"

Mom couldn't hide her look of dread.

"Irving. They're fine. Finish eating."

"I'm in no mood to wait, Bea. I'd rather hear it now."

Mom let out a sigh.

"First, let me check to see if there's a mole in the CIA."

As soon as I heard her say it, I knew she was going to check to see where I was and find out if I was listening. So I quickly made my way back to my room.

Now out of sight, I could only hear Mom's footsteps as she moved toward the living room to check and see if I was in my spying nest on the landing. But then her footsteps went back to the dining room and it sounded for a time like normal dinner talk started up again, although it was much harder to hear. But then, all talk seemed to stop and I couldn't hear a thing. That's when I realized they must be whispering to each other. As time went on Dad's whispering grew louder.

"He did what?" I heard him say.

But there was only the faint sound of Mom whispering to him, until I managed to make out words like "fire," and "trash container".

It got quiet for a long time. Then I heard something I couldn't quite understand, until my dad's voice got much louder than regular talking and I heard Mom say, "Shush."

"What the hell is wrong with him?" he said, his voice rising above her whisper. His tone sounded very scary.

Mom said something back to him, but I couldn't make it out.

"Never mind the business about his imagination. His

imagination will get him and the rest of us killed."

I heard the creak of a chair followed by the sound of footsteps pacing as he said, "I warned him last time. In fact, I warned him twice."

Mom answered him weakly in a whisper that was so soft I couldn't make out a single word.

"I was very, very clear," said Dad. "Do you remember what I told him the last time? The time he lit a fire in the shed?"

Between them, the whispering became so loud that I could hear more of what they were saying.

"He's gotta get the strap for this," Dad said.

"I don't know," said Mom. "It doesn't feel right."

"How else are we going to convey the message?"

There was no answer from Mom, and I began to panic. The strap? My dad was thinking about giving me the strap? I could hardly believe it. I'd never, ever gotten it before. But I'd heard about it from my cousin. He said that Dad and my uncle both got the strap from my grandpa when they were kids and did something very bad. It sounded horrible.

I heard some whispering by Mom, but it was uncertain sounding. Dad cut her off. "What? Do you think I like the idea? It makes me sick. But it has to be done. Pop always said it would come down to this with boys."

"Irving, I just don't think it's the right idea."

"You have a better one?" he snapped.

"No. I didn't have brothers and my dad wasn't the strap type. This is your family's way, but still I don't—"

I could almost picture Dad pointing his finger at her as he said, "Stay out! This is not your department. This is hard enough."

Everything went completely silent and I grew really afraid, my ears straining to make out words, sounds, or anything that would help me understand what was going on or what I needed to do. Then I heard footsteps—big ones. Seconds later, the door to my room flew open and my father stood there like a giant, with the buckle part of a belt wrapped around his fist. His face looked red and angry and it seemed to almost quiver in a way I'd never seen before.

"Get over here and bend over!" He pointed to the end of the bed.

I burst into tears and my body started shaking so hard that I felt like I couldn't move. "Now!" he thundered.

Somehow I managed to get myself to the place he ordered me to go to and I got on my knees and bent over like he said.

"Didn't I tell you specifically not to light fires or play with matches unless your mother or I are around?" he boomed.

Terrified and ashamed, I looked back over my shoulder and saw him lean back just like when Whitey Ford starts to pitch a baseball, before whipping his whole body forward.

Before I could answer I felt the sting of the strap on my butt and cried out. It was as if ten bees had stung me all at once. I felt my stomach turning inside out and noticed that my tear-filled eyes were blinking like mad.

"Do you know what could have happened?" he thundered.

I couldn't say anything. I didn't know what he wanted me to say or how to answer.

Whap!" came the next hit, feeling as sharp as the one before.

"Am I getting through to you?"

"Yes!" I screamed, my eyes and cheeks flooded with tears.

Whap!

"Do you understand that fire is dangerous and not for little boys to play with?"

"Yes, yes, I do."

"Or do you need…"

I was expecting another lash, because of the way each question seemed to be followed by one, but to my surprise it didn't come. I turned and looked over my shoulder at Dad, and through the blur of my tears, hiccups and sobs, I saw that he had stopped short and had watery eyes, like the kind people have just before they start to cry. I didn't understand it. I was the one being hit. So why were his eyes watering?

He turned and walked out of my room. I was sure he was going to slam the door, but instead he closed it quietly without a word.

Sniffling and crying and as confused as I'd ever been, I slithered onto my bed and crawled under the sheets. I curled up into a ball, afraid for myself and yet wondering what had happened to the dad I loved. I knew what I did was wrong and bad. But still, I had to wonder if someone had given him a pill that was changing him into someone else? This was not the same dad who moved aside all of his important business papers so I could sit up on his lap no matter how busy he was. This was not the dad who would let me feel his scratchy whiskers and smell his aftershave lotion. It wasn't the dad who cracked jokes and took me to Coney Island, and even once to Yankee Stadium. The dad I loved taught me how to ride my bike and played catch with me. The dad I loved called from work when I got sick and asked Mom how I was. He worked hard all day long at his factory so we could have money to buy food and pay for things. He was a good dad, and crazy as it sounds, I still believed it somehow. But I also didn't know what to do. And I didn't know how I would ever feel safe again. I couldn't see myself cuddling up with him. I was too afraid. And just like with Humpty Dumpty, I didn't see any way that things could be put back together again.

CHAPTER 7

Almost a whole week had passed since the strap punishment. I mostly put it out of my mind and tried to be happy every single minute of every single day. The summer was the perfect time to do that. In my neighborhood, summer was like one big, wonderful dream filled with excitement and new things to learn and do every day. Best of all, it seemed to go on forever.

Everyone in the neighborhood was excited about Mickey Mantle and the Yankees. Mickey was hitting homers like crazy, and it looked like the Yankees might win the pennant again. People were still talking about the homer he hit in Baltimore that went 460 feet.

Jeffrey, the Goldberg kids, the McBrides and a ton of other kids from the neighborhood found a million things to do. We went swimming. We caught grasshoppers and traded baseball cards. We played games like Parcheesi and chess on our front steps, and stickball in the street. We bought ice cream from the Good Humor truck and went to the movies to see films like Frankenstein and The Bridge on the River Kwai. Later, we acted out the best scenes. We dressed in our army clothes and had battles where we fought and died for The United States of America and freedom. When we died we whispered our final words and vowed to be best buddies forever. We ate watermelon and sold Kool-Aid to the construction workers on 210th street—five cents for a small and ten cents for a large. We told great war stories and shared dirty jokes and tried to act, and make faces, like Jerry Lewis, the funniest guy on earth.

I wished the summer would go on forever. But the early signs that it wouldn't came when all the mothers on the street began blabbing about how they had to start shopping for school supplies and clothes for their kids. It was a sure sign that summer was almost over and all the fun was going to end very soon. I tried not to think about it because it made me sad. But also, I knew when it finally did come to an end, me and lots of other kids on 211th Street would be going back to the special prison for kids known as school.

For me, what was even worse, was that I was going to have to go to Hebrew school right after regular school. Hebrew school was torture because the rabbis and teachers always tried to get you to learn to read, write, speak, and understand Hebrew, a language that every Jewish kid knows they will never use even if they live to be a million years old. In Hebrew school there aren't any sports or games, and it's in a rickety old building with only a couple of small windows that only let in tiny amounts of fresh air. I think the Hebrew school people chose small windows on purpose so kids like me wouldn't be tempted to jump out of them and kill ourselves. This year, I was going to have to go three times a week and I knew it was going to be terrible. But the thing that made everything much worse in both regular school and Hebrew school was that I was actually in the wrong grade.

When I was not even in kindergarten, Mom and Dad heard about a thing called an "advanced track." It was meant for really smart kids and I guess Mom and Dad talked it over and decided it would be good for me to be in with older, smarter kids. They signed me up for it and told me to lie about my age if anyone asked. So even though I was only four at the time, Mom made me promise to tell everyone I was five. After a while, when I started to do really badly in school, I stopped thinking about the difference in my age and instead began to think I just might be dumb, since I barely ever knew what was going on in class. School became really hard and I battled the clock every minute, forever squirming in my seat and praying for the minute hand to finally move. That's why I was nervous and worried that this year would be even worse than last year. This year, I would not only be an eight-year-old that everyone thought was nine, but right after regular school prison I would have to go to Hebrew school prison.

CHAPTER 8

From the very first day of fourth grade, I hated P.S. 205 and my new, witchy teacher, Miss Pelman. She was a gray-haired, ugly old woman with a horrible, crackly voice like the bad witch from The Wizard of Oz and she had a long nose and small, mean eyes. But worst of all was her breath and body odor. She had the pukiest smell coming from her that I'd ever smelled in my whole life. It was worse than the smell of a garbage can with rotted meat and vegetables in it. Someone, sometime, must have told her how bad she smelled because she tried to cover up the stink with tons of disgusting perfume. I took the desk at the very back of the fourth row behind four other kids because I thought it gave me the best chance to avoid being called on, and also, it was the farthest away from her stinky smell I could get.

Miss Pelman stood at the front of the room next to some words she had written on the blackboard that I'd never seen before. She quickly told everyone their meanings and used them in a boring sentence that didn't help me understand them any better at all. Then, almost as if floating on a broomstick, she moved around the classroom and studied each kid with her mean little eyes to see which one she could turn into a rat using her special witch magic.

"If anyone has a question about the meaning of any of these words, now is the time to ask," she said, with her voice cracking. "I don't want to have to go over them again later."

The room went silent and everyone just stared ahead. To everyone's surprise, one brave kid made the mistake of raising his hand.

Miss Pelman seemed to almost take it as a challenge.

"Yes," she said, faking a smile.

"Um, the second word. What did you say that meant?" he said.

Miss Pelman closed her eyes and let out a big, fake sigh. She opened her eyes and pointed a bony finger at the boy and spoke in a scolding voice.

"Well, if you had listened the first time, we wouldn't need to go over this again, now would we?" she said.

From then on, everyone understood that they'd better not ask questions. And after that, hardly anyone ever did.

The first few days of school passed, and each day I went up to my room and tried to do my homework so I wouldn't get in trouble with the witch. But in no time I was lost and needed help. I went to Mom, while she was moving stuff from our brand-new dishwasher into the cabinets, and asked, "Can you help me with my homework?"

Mom looked at me for a few seconds and then looked back to the dishwasher and the counter where a few bags of groceries were waiting to be put away, including a quart of ice cream. Then came a crash followed by the sound of Arlene crying from the living room. Mom darted towards her while calling back to me in a frazzled voice. "See if Bonnie can help you, or maybe you can ask Dad after dinner when he's had some time to relax."

Of course I didn't seriously consider either of those two choices, because I couldn't stand Bonnie, and ever since the strap, I tried not to get too close to Dad. In the end, I did the best I could by myself, filling up the spaces with dumb answers so that the witch would at least think I tried.

Each day at school I couldn't wait for recess when, for 15

minutes, twice a day, I was allowed to run free and feel alive. In those minutes, happiness returned and the world didn't seem like such a bad place. But 15 minutes wasn't really a very long time, so when the bell rang and recess was over, it was as if the school building itself was saying, "Back to your cages, you wild dogs!" But instead of being wild dogs, everyone returned to class like weak little lambs, each kid following the kid in front until the red brick prison had collected us all.

This was a brand-new school for me and I noticed right away it was hard to get into a group. I couldn't even count on meeting up with a single friend from 211th Street because the McBride brothers went to a Catholic school and Jeffrey and the Goldbergs had a different recess time.

Most of the time I just walked or ran around by myself looking for a chance to make friends with someone. But most kids were either playing tag or throwing a rubber football. A few other kids were flipping and trading baseball cards. There didn't seem to be any way in without acting creepy.

There was one afternoon, though, when I overheard a conversation that was kind of interesting. Some kid with buck teeth and squinty eyes was telling three other kids about someone who went over Niagara Falls in a barrel and survived. The other kids, who had him sort of surrounded, were making fun of him and obviously didn't believe him. But instead of changing his mind or being embarrassed, the kid went on and told another whopper about the same guy, except this time the guy supposedly walked across Bell Boulevard blindfolded without getting hit by a car. He said the guy was an amazing daredevil and did stuff like that all the time. I thought about some of the stuff this kid was saying, and my first thought was to ask my dad about it. But then I remembered everything that had happened and realized I was still too afraid to go near him. And besides, he was coming home so late I hardly saw him anyway. That's when I realized that something else was bothering me—something besides Ms. Pelman and school. I thought more about it and was finally able to figure it out. I was lonely.

CHAPTER 9

On Friday nights, our family ate together because it was the Sabbath. I liked that the dining room table was covered with a beautiful white tablecloth. I liked using special silverware and fancy plates. And I especially liked how the room glistened from the crystal wine glasses, silver candleholders, and long-stemmed candles. But the thing I was most happy about was the peaceful look on my dad's face as he sat at the head of the table. It reminded me of how he used to be. Maybe it was because he came home an hour early instead of three hours late. I only know, when he relaxed it made everyone else relax, and it made me happy.

My dad wasn't real religious like his dad, even though he read all of the prayers on Friday nights and went to synagogue on the High Holidays. He didn't go to services on Saturday and he didn't keep strictly kosher, but he liked a lot of Jewish traditions and he definitely believed in God.

I wasn't so sure about God. I didn't like that you couldn't really talk to Him and get answers. Also, I once had a yellow parakeet named Lucky who would stay perched on my finger or shoulder when I took him out of his cage. He was my only pet. One day he got sick and I was really worried. I prayed to God for him to get better, but instead of getting better I found him a couple of days later dead at the bottom of his cage. After that, I just couldn't be sure about God, even though I always wondered why there was a whole synagogue full of people on the High Holidays who prayed to Him.

As we stood around the table waiting for Dad to read the Friday night prayers from his old, wine-stained prayer book, the spectacular smell of Mom's chicken soup simmering on the stove made my stomach growl. I glanced at the challah on the table and then looked all around the room. Everything was perfect until my eyes accidentally met Bonnie's. As if by instinct, she stuck her tongue out at me and pulled it back in her mouth faster than a lizard catching a bug. To get even, I coughed the word "Jerk" under my breath and once again stuck my pointer finger up my nose, until Bonnie looked away in disgust. Mom saw what was going on and gave us both our usual warning.

"I don't want any trouble from either of you two on Shabbos," she said looking at each of us in turn. "Do you hear me? Shabbos is a time of peace."

After dinner, we all left our dishes on the table for Mom to bring to the sink while Dad stayed in the dining room and read after-dinner prayers. I decided to set up some of my army guys and tanks and mortars and direct them at him while he was praying. From my view of him on the floor, he seemed as big as Godzilla and that made shooting him with pretend missiles kind of cool. I started to make a lot of different sounds like gunfire, missiles, and explosions, and after a while he noticed what I was doing. To my great surprise he cracked a smile.

As soon as he did, it reminded me of rain delays at Yankee Stadium and how the sun would sometimes break through the clouds making everyone happy and excited because the fun was going to start again. That's how it was for me the instant I saw him smile. I moved closer, but not too close, and asked him all the questions that had been building up in my mind.

"Dad?"

"Yeah, Zeendala?"

It was a very good sign when he called me Zeendala because it meant something like "sweet little boy" in Yiddish. He learned the word from Mom because she was Ashkenazic and knew that language. Dad, being Sephardic, knew a language called Ladino that was a mixture of Hebrew, Spanish, and a bunch of other languages, but he didn't use it very much. In addition, Mom would also call me Mark Lemon sometimes, when she wanted to let me know she loved me, so I never minded.

"Dad, could a guy jump over Niagara Falls in a barrel and live?"

Dad closed his prayer book. Still smiling, he moved toward the living room and sat down in his big chair. With a wave of his hand he invited me to come over. I followed him and sat on the couch next to his chair and waited. I think he noticed that I didn't climb up on his lap like I used to, but he didn't say anything.

"Niagara Falls, huh? Well, I don't know, but I doubt it."

"Yeah? How come?"

"For one thing, it would be a very long fall. And even if a person survived the fall, the weight and power of the water pressure would be tremendous, not to mention how freezing cold the water is up that way."

I had no time to waste. Dad was in a good mood and was being like his old self. Remembering another conversation from the schoolyard, I asked, "Dad, can a crocodile eat 200 pounds of food in a day?"

He smiled and thought about it. "The truth is, I don't know. Maybe we should take a look in the encyclopedia and find out."

For the next half hour we both learned about crocodiles, lizards, and reptiles. With every word, I was aware of how much I was loving it. And yet, as much as I wanted to believe that everything was back to normal, I knew it wasn't. Underneath, I was still scared of him. I thought how great it would be if he were like this all the time from now on and forever.

CHAPTER 10

In the schoolyard during recess, I spied a kid I had been wondering about who was in Miss Pelman's class. He had neatly combed hair and wore wire-rimmed glasses. He was always very quiet in class. Out in the schoolyard he seemed to prefer to be by himself. Like me, he wandered around a lot. Today he had his arms folded and was leaning against the chain-link fence. I decided to take a chance and move a little closer. When I did, I noticed he had freckles and a skinny body like mine. He was a little shorter than me and wore a white shirt with a stiff collar. He seemed to be the kind of kid who had parents that made him be clean a lot. He looked a little out of place compared to all of the kids running around, throwing and catching footballs. I remembered that his name was Stuart Young because he always said "Here!" when Smelly Pelly took attendance in the morning and called out his name. Now and then he rubbed his back against the fence as if he had fleas. When our eyes met he seemed to recognize me, but then looked away as if he didn't want to stare too much. I decided to move closer still.

When I was right next to him, I asked, "Do you like school?"

He turned and looked me over for a second or two before

answering, "Not really."

His glasses reflected the sun and I had to move so I wouldn't have to squint from the glare. He had a chipped front tooth and more freckles than I first thought.

"Do you like Miss Pelman?" I asked.

Stuart shook his head.

"Do you think she smells?"

He nodded.

"Me too," I said.

"She should take a shower and use a lot of soap," Stuart said.

"She should take two showers," I added.

Stuart laughed. "She smells worse than a fart."

I laughed and thought that maybe I had made a friend. "She smells worse than dog poop," I offered.

Stuart's smile got bigger, and he giggled as he paused to think up the next thing to say. "She smells like vomit on top of dog poop," he said.

I could sense he was watching me closely now. We both knew it was my turn. I didn't want to disappoint him so I said, "She smells like a vomit sandwich with dog poop and cow manure mixed with pig snot, and she has ass breath too."

We both started to laugh hysterically. Stuart held his nose and made a disgusted face, and that made me laugh even harder. Our laughter was so strong that every time one of us had a chance to say more, we couldn't, because we would crack up again.

"No, no, she smells like a…" And there was even more laughing.

It took a long time before we finally calmed down but when we did, I felt really good. We talked and talked and I was surprised to learn how much Stuart knew about the Yankees and war movies. He even had a sister that he always got into fights with just like me and Bonnie.

The morning recess went by in a flash and soon we were back in class. I wanted to keep talking to him and have more fun, so I got the idea to stand my book up in a way that allowed me to hide my head behind it so I could send him special messages and make funny faces without Miss Pelman seeing me.

Even though he tried to look straight ahead and pay attention to Miss Pelman, I could tell he really liked what I was doing. A couple of times he almost burst out laughing, but somehow he managed to look away in the nick of time.

It was probably stupid for me to think that my trick of hiding my head behind my raised book would last for long or fool anyone, especially when I realized that a missing head was probably a pretty easy thing for a teacher in the front of a classroom to notice.

Still, it came as a shock when the voice of the wicked witch pierced the air. "Perhaps Mark Leonard, who evidently likes to hide behind his textbook, can tell us what eight times twelve is?"

I felt my blood surge as shame filled my body. In a second it was as if the whole class had turned around to stare at me. Miss Pelman stood at the front of the classroom. Behind her was a blackboard full of math problems. In her hand she had a wooden pointer stick with a rubber tip that she used to point to each problem. When I didn't answer, she moved toward me bringing a wave of stink with her as she did.

"Umm," I heard myself say.

"Ummm," she hummed sarcastically.

Except for a single glance at Stuart, I looked straight ahead. But in that single glance I could see he felt bad for me.

"We are waiting for you, Mark Leonard. Do you know how much eight times twelve is?"

I didn't answer. I couldn't. I didn't know the answer.

She moved back to the blackboard and pointed to another problem "Well, how about nine times nine?" she said. Hearing nothing back from me, she moved her pointer again. "Okay, Mark Leonard, do you know what eight times seven is?" I knew I was choosing between being completely silent or risking a guess. If I guessed and was wrong, it would bring me even more embarrassment in front of a whole classroom full of kids.

"Well, Mark Leonard, it appears as though you are not paying attention at all in this class. Perhaps you need to be left back a grade to catch up. These are third-grade multiplication tables, and this is the fourth grade. You are supposed to know the answers to these problems. How are you going to move on in math if you don't even try? Now stop hiding behind that book and pay attention. I will talk to you more after class."

I felt hot and uncomfortable. Miss Pelman had known what I was doing all along and had taken my only good hiding spot and exposed it for everyone to see. It was as if she had pulled my pants down and left me naked for everyone to laugh and point at. Also, I was worried about what she said about getting left back. Being left back was about the worst shame a kid could have. It was like wearing a sign on your head forever that said "Dummy." As much as I found school hard, as much as I found it a struggle to even pay attention, I knew getting left back would be terrible, especially for Mom, who wanted so much for me to be a good student and grow up to be someone like Einstein, who was Jewish and a genius, or Jonas Salk, the Jewish guy who had just found a cure for polio.

In the yard, during afternoon recess, Stuart said he felt bad I got picked on. I felt so much better when he said it, that soon we were blabbing about everything that didn't have to do with school. At one point, after getting really excited talking about different war movies we'd seen, Stuart said, "Hey, did you see that war movie about the Japanese prison camp—the one with a really mean Japanese colonel who put the British officer guy in a little metal hut and made him almost die from the heat?"

"Yeah," I said. "That was The Bridge on the River Kwai, wasn't it?"

"Yeah, that's right. That was a great movie," Stuart said.

"Yeah. It was. Did you see the one about Midway Island where the good guys were shooting down a whole bunch of kamikazes?"

"Yes! I loved that! That was incredible! I loved seeing the bad guys' planes twirling around and around with their tails on fire, and thick black smoke trailing behind them until they crashed into the sea," Stuart said.

I thought it was so neat how we'd seen the same films and loved the same scenes, and the more we talked about them the more I began to think about something. I remembered the box of wooden matches at home in the drawer next to the Yahrzeit candles and how, on Friday nights, after striking a match and lighting the candles Mom would shake out the match with a whipping motion of her hand and wrist. Then, right afterward, she would throw the burnt-out match into a trash container, leaving a trail of smoke behind. In thinking about it, it reminded me of what Stuart was talking about, and how, in a way, it looked like a real plane on fire with smoke trailing behind it. And just like that I thought how great it would be if I could be the one to show him a miniature version of one of his favorite scenes.

But before I could even think about it further, the thought of the strap punishment came into my mind and I felt a shudder. I knew I would be in an unbelievable amount of trouble if I got caught using matches again. For a while, the sting of the strap and Dad's scary, angry face was all I could think about. I felt terrified. But I also felt mad that I was being forced to choose between obeying a person with an angry, maniac face and crazy screeching voice, or giving a good friend, my only school friend, a special one-of-a-kind imagination present.

Also, as I managed to think more about it, I could see how different my idea was compared to all the other times when I got into trouble. If I followed through on what I was thinking, I wouldn't be lighting anything else on fire. I would only be lighting the matches themselves and then making them go out. It seemed like a big difference. In fact, it seemed completely different.

That night I went over it again and again in my mind and weighed everything, finally deciding to use them as part of a plan to be a good friend and make a good friend. Confident that I had considered everything, I tiptoed downstairs, opened the drawer and grabbed a handful of wooden matches as fast as I could and made my way back upstairs before any other thoughts could get in the way. The only thought I allowed was what I would do if something went wrong. I decided that if things went really badly, I would try to live at Stuart's house in disguise, or at the police station, or the library, or possibly under the bleachers at Yankee Stadium—any safe place where Dad wouldn't be able to find me. One thing was certain. I wouldn't be able to go home.

CHAPTER 11

At P.S. 205, the kids in the higher grades used the second and third floors of the school and had to walk down a wide, winding stairwell to leave the building for recess. Smelly Pelly's classroom was on the second floor.

Stuart and I looked for each other when we got out of class for recess. When I found him, I put my finger to my lips to let him know I had a secret to share.

"Do you want to see some kamikazes in flames crashing into the sea?"

"Yeah," he whispered, eyes excited.

"OK, go down to the first floor and wait by the stairwell until all the kids are outside and I'll show you."

Stuart did what I said, and I went up to the third floor. I looked down the stairwell and waved to get his attention. He put his head all the way back and waved up at me. A few minutes later, with the building empty, I called down to him in a loud whisper. "OK, start firing!"

Stuart did his best to make the sounds of an anti-aircraft gun firing. I took out an unlit wooden match and held it out over the railing and pretended it was flying by. I could see him way below holding his two fists together and shaking them as if firing an anti-aircraft gun. As I moved along the edge of the railing, I spoke like Colonel Saito in The Bridge on the River Kwai, with my best Japanese accent, showing pride and hatred as if I were the commander of the Japanese Air Force.

"Kamikazes will dive down onto all Americans and blow up all the ships in Pearl Harbor! Americans are cowards! Americans have no shame! Americans have no honor!" I said, doing my best to remember the words from the movie while working myself up into a rage.

Stuart, like every good American soldier, increased the rat-a-tat-tat sound of his anti-aircraft gun while I matched him with the sound of machine-gun fire coming from my Japanese Zero.

We imitated the sounds of roaring plane engines, gunfire, exploding bombs, and screeching near misses. The scene was even better than I'd imagined, and I knew it was time to go to the next step.

"Oh, my plane is hit," I called, still using a Japanese accent. "My plane is on fire. I must be a kamikaze now. I will dive down onto American aircraft carriers and blow them to bits!"

I dragged the match head along the scratchy cement surface between the tiles lining the stairwell and it flared wonderfully, releasing the smell of sulfur and a puff of smoke that lazily drifted into the air. A second later I dropped the flaming wooden match over the railing and watched it go down the stairwell, leaving a smoky trail behind it, just like the kamikazes that Stuart and I had seen on TV and in the newsreels. It looked as real as I had ever hoped.

Stuart looked up in amazement. I could see he was as excited as I was, as if he had been the one to shoot it down. He yelled out a giant "Neat!" to let me know how much he loved it.

The echo from the stairwell made our gunfire and sound effects seem all the more real as I lit match after match and plunged them over the railing. In the back of my mind I tried to be aware of anything that might happen that might get us into trouble, and I began to think for the first time that lighting a match, even though I wasn't lighting anything on fire, might be something that people would think was bad—especially school people.

All the doors to the classrooms were closed, and I knew if I heard so much as a squeak of a door opening I was going to run down the stairs at the speed of light.

But the sound of Stuart's great rat-a-tat-tat machine gun getting more and more consistent got me even more excited. Now he's got it, I thought. It was the scene we had talked about on the playground, and now we had it right in front of us. As a haze built up all around me and burnt matches littered the first floor next to Stuart, only the feel of my palms getting sweaty and the spooky silence of the empty school made me finally pause. In all, I had dive-bombed about six or seven kamikazes when I was shocked to see the door to the girls' bathroom open. A blond, fifth-grade girl with pigtails, dressed in a plaid skirt and white blouse, stepped out.

At first, looking down and wiping her hands with a paper towel, she didn't notice me. But then, as she looked up and saw me standing by the stairwell, a frozen look on my face and a haze over my head, her eyes narrowed. The next thing I knew she became like a sniffing dog, intent on finding out where the haze and smell of sulfur was coming from. When she peered over the railing and saw Stuart, her mouth dropped open. Moving past me, with a hand-over-hand motion, she made her way down the stairwell, craning her neck to figure out what was going on. When she began to move more quickly, I knew she was heading to the principal's office.

I ran after her. "Don't tell!" I begged, putting my hands together in prayer.

She didn't answer, quickening her pace instead.

"Please! Please! Please!" I begged as I ran down the stairs alongside her.

"Stuart!" I yelled. "She's gonna tell!"

"Oh no!" he said. "Beg her not to!"

"I did, but she won't listen!"

A second later Stuart yelled, "Run outside!"

Without thinking, I bolted down the stairs and out into the schoolyard and met up with Stuart seconds later. We looked for the largest group of kids and tried to blend in. Shaking with fear, we crouched by the chain-link fence. I looked at Stuart, hoping he had some idea of how to get us out of the mess we were in, but all I saw in his eyes was the same fear I was feeling. The thought of my father finding out about what I'd done gave me a rising sense of terror, and I began to wonder if it was time to run away and live somewhere else. That's when I realized all at once how much I was going to miss Mom and Arlene and Blackie, my poster of Mickey, and all my toys and soldiers, my cowboys and Indians, and all of my friends on 211th Street. I realized how stupid I was to think that it would be possible to run away and live at Yankee Stadium under the bleachers. It was probably freezing cold there at night, and the food places would be closed. I didn't have any money to buy hot dogs and pretzels to live on anyway. And how would I get in? Those ticket people always made sure no one got in without a ticket.

Minutes later we heard the bell ring. We got up and tried to mix in with all the other kids as they streamed into the school. We were still hoping to be invisible, watching in secret horror as a few kids stopped near the stairwell and began to sniff the air. It was so different from the smell of the fresh outside air that I wondered how it would be possible for anyone not to notice it. Just then a kid called out, "Smoke! I smell smoke. Do you smell it?"

"Yeah! I do!" said another. "It smells like matches. Hey, look here, on the floor. Here's one!"

Teachers gathered and began sniffing the air and looking all around with concern as they tried to figure out what had happened. Stuart and I walked by them, making our way up the stairs to our classroom. We took our seats and barely glanced at each other. Instead we just looked down at our desks. I began to relax ever so slightly as the harsh, grinding sound of moving desks and chairs and shuffling feet felt strangely familiar and comforting. I thought how glad I was to hear the sounds of boredom and of nothing in particular happening. If only it would last.

When class started, I sat up as straight as I could. I tried to be like the other students and listen to what Miss Pelman was saying. I prayed to God for help and promised in a silent prayer never to do anything bad again for as long as I lived. My heart thumped as I wondered if we had somehow escaped. I knew only a miracle could have made the girl change her mind and not tell the principal about what she saw. In my prayers I decided that this would be my new life. True to God, I was going to be different than before. I felt like I finally understood why all the Jews in the synagogue prayed so hard, just as I was praying now. If their lives were anything like mine, they must have needed lots of help. In fact, maybe, as with me, God was the only possible hope for them. With each passing minute I was more and more grateful for my new life. To show my appreciation for it, I was now even thinking of raising my hand to answer a question if the chance came.

After 15 minutes of the best student behavior of my life, my good luck ended. It came to a screeching halt when the door opened and a teacher stepped inside our classroom with the blond girl by her side. I looked at them both for a second as the girl looked over all the faces in the room. I turned my head away in a last, desperate attempt to avoid being recognized. But seconds later I heard a voice call out sharply, "Him!" I turned slightly and saw her dagger-like finger pointing right at me.

I couldn't even bring myself to fake surprise. Instead, I just felt the blood drain from my face as the finger kept pointing. She scanned the room again and her gaze locked onto Stuart. Pointing again, she added, "And him."

I looked up at Miss Pelman in complete desperation. Witch or not, right now she seemed like the only one who might have enough power to save us, although I could not imagine any way in the world such a thing might happen. But it didn't matter. She put her chalk down and looked at the teacher and the girl next to her. A few seconds later, with a flick of her wrist, Miss Pelman motioned for Stuart and me to leave her classroom and go with the teacher.

I don't remember walking to the principal's office or how I ended up on a chair in his office facing his desk. I don't remember anything about the room or when Stuart was separated from me. I only knew I was numb.

When the principal, Mr. Washington, sat down to face me in his clean, nicely pressed white shirt, blue tie, and gray suit, I found his face easy to look at. It didn't have any creases in it like the kind you see when someone is mad at you. He was handsome, and I think he must have been about my dad's age. He probably did a lot of sports because he didn't seem to have much fat on him anywhere. I could smell his cologne and it reminded me of the way Dad smelled when he was nice. Mr. Washington looked at me almost as if he wanted to get to know me, like our family doctor when he examined me. When he finally spoke, his voice sounded serious but not angry. "Bringing matches to school is a very dangerous thing. It's dangerous for the schoolchildren and everyone in this building. Do you know that?"

I nodded and began to sniffle and sob. I wasn't sure why I was crying. It was probably because I'd been feeling more and more scared since the girl discovered us. I couldn't find my way into my imagination either and so I couldn't be John Wayne and not be afraid of anything or anyone.

"Do you have any more matches with you?"

I nodded.

"Give them to me."

I reached into my back pocket and took out the last two wooden matches I had and handed them to him.

He looked at them and then back at me. "Is this all you have?"

I nodded.

He paused for a time, maybe thinking about the best way to say something. "Mark, what were you thinking when you lit the matches and threw them down the stairwell at Stuart?"

Hearing the mention of Stuart's name made me realize

he'd already been talked to. I knew if he told the truth to Mr. Washington, it would be clear that it was me who brought the matches, me who lit them, and me who threw them down the stairwell. I thought about Stuart and felt badly that he was going to be in so much trouble for this. I thought about the heroic guys in the combat movies I'd seen, guys who gave up their own lives to save another guy's life. I saw the honor in that.

"I don't know," I answered.

The answer was as truthful as I could be, because the real reason—shooting down pretend kamikazes to win the war—wasn't something that was going to make sense to Mr. Washington.

"Stuart said it was your idea to light the matches and that he didn't know you were going to do it. Is that true?"

This was my chance to give up my own worthless life for someone who deserved better. I nodded, unable to speak.

"So Stuart didn't light any of the matches?"

I shook my head.

"None at all?"

"No," I finally managed. "He didn't. Are you going to tell my mom and dad?"

Mr. Washington thought for a time before answering softly, "Yes, I have to."

The words rang in my ears. I could see the end of my life coming into view. There was a long pause. His face still looked kind, but it didn't seem to matter anymore. My terror overcame me and I blurted out my greatest fears while sobbing uncontrollably.

"My dad...is going...to...hit me with the strap...for this. Then...Mom...is...going to...send me...to reform school."

Mr. Washington studied me. I looked back at him but couldn't keep looking into his eyes because I was too scared. Instead, I looked around the room and glanced at pictures and plaques and things on his desk. I heard his grandfather clock make a few soft chimes and I turned to look at it before returning my attention to him. Our eyes met and he began to speak.

"Mark, I am going to have to suspend you from our school

until we can figure this out. I would like for you not to think of this as a punishment, but rather, something I need to do to protect the rest of the children in my school until I decide what should be done. Do you understand?"

Sure, I understood. My life was over, just as I thought, but I nodded since I wasn't able to speak.

"Good," he said. "Do you have anything you want to say?"

I shook my head, all the while thinking I wanted to get myself under control like the brave guys in the movies who never cried. But I couldn't do it. Instead, I burst into tears and said, "I don't want…to…go to…reform…school. I don't…want to…get…the strap…from my dad."

Mr. Washington looked back at me and spoke to me in a kind voice. "I am going to talk to your parents. You won't go to reform school and you won't get the strap."

Maybe, I should have been relieved to hear Mr. Washington say that. But instead, I became suspicious and wondered if he was telling me the truth. After all, how could he say such a thing or promise it? Maybe, he could convince Mom not to send me to reform school and that would be great, but how could this average-sized, quiet man be so sure he could stop Dad from doing anything he pleased to his son? Mr. Washington didn't know Dad. Mr. Washington didn't know anything about the stupid ways Sephardic dads like mine punish their kids and don't say "I love you". I looked at him closer and wondered about him. Did he like to say nice things no matter what was going to happen? Was he just making it all up to make me feel better? I didn't have to think about it for long. I knew Dad. I knew what I'd done. The strap was coming and it would take a miracle to stop it.

CHAPTER 12

As I walked home, I could not remember a time in my entire life when I felt so unhappy and worn out. I couldn't even get my imagination to help me be someone else. All I wanted to do was go to sleep. The world around me was as dead as if the sun had gone and it was suddenly winter.

I thought of what might happen when I got home. I could picture Dad wrapping the buckle end of the strap around his fist and shouting, "Goddamn it! When are you going to learn?" I could see his powerful body arching back and then lunging forward. And I could almost feel the sting of the strap on my butt and hear myself cry out.

It hurt to think about it. It hurt to think that maybe he wasn't going to love me anymore and that maybe I didn't deserve to be loved—by him or anyone. I was sliding into sadder and sadder feelings when all of a sudden I began to notice something different happening inside me. It's hard to explain, but I only know that after so much worrying and being afraid, I began to get a completely different feeling. It was a feeling of..well..not caring.

A thought came to me as if brought by a cloud floating by, that if I were dead, I wouldn't have to worry about any of this. Not the strap, or my father's angry face, or Miss Pelman, or math, or getting left back—or anything.

As I went over these strange new thoughts I began to feel almost protected by them. I began to think about the heroes in the movies and how they were so unafraid of dying, how they were so brave they didn't seem to care what happened to them. Their attitude was, if they suffered while trying to reach their goals, well, it was just the price they had to pay. And if they died trying, they could go to heaven knowing that they had given it their best. That's what made them heroes. And that was how I always wished I could be.

My thoughts paused briefly when I realized I was approaching Bell Boulevard, the same street that the schoolyard storyteller had talked about. It was the street that the daredevil had crossed blindfolded without being hit by a car.

As I thought more about it, I could see that there were two kinds of heroes: the soldier who risked his life for his cause, and the daredevil who risked his life to be famous and feel glory. Both were willing to pay any price if they failed. Both would feel proud that they tried, or they would die proudly, satisfied in the last seconds of their lives that they had made the bravest choice they could.

It came to me that I might end up proud of myself if I succeeded at a daredevil feat like walking across the boulevard blindfolded. On the other hand, if I ended up dead, nothing would matter anyway.

My mind seemed to want to go in its own direction, as thoughts of being a hero or a daredevil and the traffic and the feeling of not being loved all mushed together into a glob until I realized I was standing on the sidewalk looking out onto Bell Boulevard thinking about the next thing I was going to do.

Traffic came and went. At times the boulevard went from being busy to no cars driving past for a half-minute or so. I hoped, if I decided to do what I was thinking about doing, I would be lucky and go forward when there was no traffic.

I stepped off the curb and stood between two parked cars that were a good distance from the regular crosswalk. I sensed that I blended in with the long rows of cars on the boulevard, especially since I wasn't much taller than the trunk of the car in front of me. I thought about squinting to see what being blindfolded or blind would be like, but I decided not to, since I knew it was like cheating. Instead, I shut my eyes tightly to be true to my new code of honor and leave no doubt that what I was about to do would be true to myself. Besides, who ever heard of a daredevil or soldier hero cheating?

I stepped out farther so my right hand touched the trunk of one parked car while my left touched the hood of another. As my heart began to beat faster, it occurred to me that if I waited much longer, full-blown fear might stop me from doing what I was planning and I wouldn't have a chance to be a true hero ever again. If that happened, I would probably feel ashamed and afraid for the rest of my life. I knew I had to decide, and I knew it had to be now. Panicking, I made a last-second deal with myself. I wouldn't try to cross the entire boulevard, but instead would just take two giant steps out into the street like I did when I played Simon Says.

I waited several seconds, my ears straining to hear if the boulevard had gone silent while my eyes remained tightly shut. Hearing nothing I took a couple of deep breaths and told myself, "Go!" I lurched forward, taking two giant steps straight out from between the cars and onto the boulevard. But before the second step was finished, I felt my foot come down on something that was not pavement. A tiny part of a second later I opened my eyes to see that my foot had landed on the running board of an older car that was whizzing along the boulevard. In an instant I felt myself spinning like a top as my body bounced off the fast-moving side of the sedan. Still spinning, I hit the ground and heard the horrifying screech of brakes. Dazed but unharmed, I jumped up and ran back across the sidewalk and onto a front lawn. I could feel blood pumping madly through my body and my heart was beating so fast, it felt like a bongo drum being pounded by hands that moved like lightning. I saw the screeching black car that grazed me come to a full stop and the door on the driver's side shoot open. The driver, a thin man with glasses and a mustache, jumped out. Two other cars came to a screeching stop right behind him and had to swerve to avoid hitting his car. He was in such a rush to get to me that he didn't even close the door behind him. With an expression of terrible fear, he ran toward me.

Behind him, the heads of two grown men and a lady appeared above the roofs of their cars like popping popcorn as they stepped outside and stared at me and the man running toward me. All had stunned, disbelieving expressions on their faces. Then, voices seemed to come from everywhere.

"Did you see that?"

"He almost hit him."

"I think he did hit him, but he looks okay."

"The kid went out into the street without looking. He just walked straight out."

"Yeah, he shot out from behind a car. I wouldn't have been able to see him if it was me."

"Is he all right?"

"He looks okay—just scared. The guy was going too fast."

A lady in a red skirt shook her head while covering her open mouth with her hand. More cars slowed behind them and stopped until a whole bunch of people were looking at me. The driver of the black car was now bent at the waist and holding out his arms as he came toward me. I could see that he was shaking and panting. For a second I thought he might be coming after me to kill me. But then I realized he was as terrified as I was.

"Are you okay?" he asked, panting, his voice cracking.

His words shocked me. I couldn't believe that the first thing on his mind was whether I was okay or not. I realized I had not given any thought to how the person who ended up running me over might feel if my plan to survive this daredevil stunt didn't work out. They might get arrested, sent to jail, or be punished in some horrible way. I'd thought only about myself. My thoughts became even more of a muddle when I saw him throw off his sunglasses to get a better look at me. In the same trembling voice, he said, "You're okay? You're not hurt? You're all right? You're not cut?"

I realized in an instant that he was a kind man who wasn't going to come after me for the terrible thing I did and so I said, "Yeah, I'm fine. I'm fine."

He looked up and down at my whole body, probably to see if there were bruises or signs of blood I didn't know about. On legs that felt like rubber, I kept backing away as he inched closer. Seeing how scared I was, he stopped moving closer and gave me a final once-over.

Then he did something I will never, ever forget. He fell to his knees on the lawn and began to cry in a way that I had never seen or heard a man cry. It was like a wail. He looked up at the sky, clasped his hands together in prayer, and began to bob back and forth as he shook them. Then, he unclenched them and began to cross himself while saying in a weak and crackling voice, "Our Father, who art in heaven..."

With so many people looking on, I was surprised that not one of them blamed me or pointed at me or called me a jerk for doing such a stupid thing. That's when it came to me. Being a kid was, well, kind of sacred. "Sacred" was a word Dad explained to me once when he was talking about the Torahs in the synagogue and why, when the rabbi marched around holding one up, we all tried to touch it with our prayer books and kiss it. I could see from the look on all the faces around me that somehow, no matter how dumb a kid might be, good people like this man and the others who looked on, believed that killing a kid was the worst thing a grown-up could do. It made me feel sorry. In fact, I was so sorry that I decided right then and there, if I was still alive after Dad got home and gave me the strap, and still alive when Rosh Hashanah came, I would read the prayer that asked God to write this guy's name into *The Book of Life* so nothing bad would happen to him for a whole year—and maybe even longer if I remembered also to pray for him next year. And even though this guy definitely wasn't Jewish, I would still make sure to read the English translation so he would live at least one more year without anything bad happening to him or his family.

CHAPTER 13

When I got home, the first thing I saw was Mom slumped sideways on the living room chair. I knew just by the exhausted look on her face that Mr. Washington had called and told her everything. It made me feel so terrible to see her that way that I almost wished she would yell at me or send me to my room or even throw something at me. But instead, she did nothing.

I stood in one place for a long time and watched as she pushed down on her chair and struggled to get up. I knew when she had to try a second and third time to do it, that all her energy had been drained from her. When she finally got to her feet, she spoke softly in a voice that sounded hoarse and defeated. "Go upstairs to your room."

I turned and started to slowly climb the stairs when I turned and asked, "Are you going to send me to reform school?"

She looked back at me, closed her eyes, and took a couple of deep breaths. Then, without opening them, she shook her head ever so slightly and whispered, "No."

Once in my room, I knew it would be a long, long wait for Dad to come home and whip me to death, and so I knew I needed to keep my mind busy thinking about other things to pass the time. Not surprisingly, one of the things I thought about was death row.

Earlier in the summer, Brian McBride had learned all about prison and death row from our genius friend Dave-the-Brain who lived one street over on 212th Street. One night after a game of stickball, Brian told a bunch of us kids all about it. He told us about the electric chair too—like how many volts it had, how many were needed to kill someone, and how long it took for people to die.

One of the things he told us was that just before someone got electrocuted, they got to choose anything they wanted for their last meal. Jeffrey said if it were him, he would want a whole pepperoni pizza with extra pepperoni and cheese, while the McBride brothers went back and forth between cheeseburgers and French fries and extra-crispy fried chicken with mashed potatoes and gravy. But when I tried to figure out what I would have wanted, I realized I would have been too nervous to enjoy any food, no matter how good it was, if I was going to be electrocuted right afterward.

Another thing Brian said was that all the convicts on death row were given permission to call the state's governor and ask one last time if they could be forgiven and maybe even go free if they promised never, ever to do anything bad again. That was called their "appeal" and if the governor said "no" it meant there was nothing else that could save them from getting fried, except for the Supreme Court or God. Brian said that the Supreme Court usually said "no" and I knew for myself that God didn't really seem to hear prayers very much and might not even be real.

As I lay there in my death row room comparing my situation to the situations of real death row guys in real prisons it made me wonder if all death row guys were actually bad, or if some of them might be nice guys like me who got confused sometimes and did bad things once in a while but were really nice underneath.

But thinking about this stuff made me so exhausted that soon I fell asleep.

I awoke sometime later to the sound of our front door opening. Through bleary eyes, I looked at my Yankee baseball clock to see how long I had been sleeping. The miniature baseball bat hands showed that I had been asleep for more than two hours. I tried to make out from the sounds coming from downstairs what was going on. Because it was so quiet, I figured Bonnie must be finished eating and was probably doing homework in her room or down in the basement playroom and Arlene was probably with her or asleep in her room.

It took a while for my head to clear, but when it did, I could make out bits and pieces of a conversation. I slid out of bed and crawled sniper-like out into the upstairs hallway and then down to the landing, staying as flush to the floor as I could until I was positioned well enough to see a good amount of the front part of the house.

I saw Dad seated as he looked up at Mom. "What's with you? You've got that look on your face," he said, cutting into his stuffed peppers.

"Eat your dinner first," she said, before nervously glancing away.

"Bea, what's going on? You look like you got run over."

At first Mom acted as if she didn't hear him and then perhaps thinking better of it, she said, "First finish your dinner. Try the couscous and vegetables. I sprinkled in a little extra turmeric and cumin."

Dad stopped eating. I heard the clink of his fork being put down and watched as he turned toward Mom. He spoke slowly, "The peppers are fine. They're always fine. In fact, they're delicious. My mother taught you well. Now what's bothering you? Is it the kids? Are they all right?"

Mom looked away.

Just then the phone rang. After a few rings, Dad looked at the phone and then at Mom, since she was normally the one to answer it at dinner time. Mom looked at it, too, and I could tell by the way she hesitated that she didn't want to answer it. I was sure she wanted to make sure Dad had a full stomach before doing anything else. But it kept ringing and ringing until she finally gave in.

"Hello?"

There was a pause and then I heard her say, "Yes, Mrs. Young, this is Mark's mother." There was another pause and then I heard Mom say softly, "Yes," and a little bit later, "Yes, yes, I know."

I realized it was Stuart's mother and my heart felt like it stopped. I knew this couldn't be good.

There was another, much longer, pause and I knew by the amount of time that went by that Mom was being talked to in a way that didn't give her a chance to talk back. It was odd and a bit spooky to think that Mom's normal spunkiness had disappeared. It could only mean one thing: she agreed with what was being said.

"Yes," she said again. "Uh-huh. Yes, I understand."

But then, all at once, as if some mysterious line had been crossed, her tone changed sharply and she lashed out. "He's not a bad influence! He's a child, just like Stuart!"

I appreciated Mom defending me like she was, even though I could easily understand how Stuart's mom could think what she was thinking. At the same time, I was worried about Dad hearing everything.

"I am going through a hard time, too, Mrs. Young. We are all very upset about this."

There was a pause as Mom listened again. I knew Dad was wondering what this was all about. By the sound of her voice, I sensed Mom was trying to keep Dad from figuring out what was being said, but by now it was too late.

"Mrs. Young, I've listened to everything you've said and agree with most of it. I…" Mom stopped short, obviously cut off. "Mrs. Young…I am…trying to tell you." Then finally, "That's not true, Mrs. Young. Mr. Washington called me also. He was not trying to set fire to anything. They were lighting matches. There's a difference."

Mom stepped back into view, pulling the phone cord as far as it would go while she listened. A second later she pulled the phone away from her ear and winced. Her expression told me that she'd been yelled at. At first, trying to calm Mrs. Young, Mom spoke softly.

"I know. I know," she said. "What do you want from me, Mrs. Young? What do you want me to do?" Then, louder, Mom demanded, "Tell me!"

There was a pause and a strange silence filled the house. Defeated, Mom moved back out of view into the kitchen and for a few seconds said nothing. Then I heard her say, "I'll tell him. Yes. I'll tell him. Yes. Under no circumstances. Yes, I am sure Stuart is a good boy—and so is my Mark."

I heard her hang up the phone and saw her as she stepped out of the kitchen and back into view. I could see she wasn't allowing her eyes to meet Dad's. Dad turned back to face the wall again. When he finally turned his head to look at Mom, it was as if the blood had drained out of it. He looked all white and a little gray.

Mom went back to her seat at the table.

"What happened with Mark?" he asked, in a calm, almost spooky voice.

"I made date ma'amouls," she said, sounding like a dazed salesman. "They're almost ready."

"What happened with Mark? I heard you say something about lighting matches. And also Mr. Washington—as in Mr. Washington, the principal?"

Mom took hold of Dad's arm below his elbow.

"Irving, I don't want you to give him the strap."

Dad looked down at her hand and carefully removed it. They looked at each other without saying a word and I could feel my fear growing as I held my breath. But there was something else going on, something I could hardly believe, that gave me hope. It was what my mom had just said. Even though I doubted Dad would listen to her, I clung to the tiny bit of hope coming from my mom's words. She didn't want Dad to give me the strap! I had to say it in my mind again and again. Mom didn't want Dad to give me the strap! The other time she had disappeared because it wasn't her department. But now, could she be changing her mind? I was so confused, because on the one hand I needed someone to help me, but on the other hand it was very risky for her to go into Dad's department, especially at a time like this.

"Are you going to tell me what went on, or am I going to have to find out for myself?" said Dad.

For some reason I began to think of that machine that has a needle on it that measures when earthquakes are coming.

Mom finally let out a long sigh and the words slid out of her mouth as if coming down the slide at our playground. "Mark was suspended from school today for lighting matches."

Dad turned away from her and looked back at the high part of the wall. It was weird to watch, because a second later, it was as if he were talking to it. "Unbelievable. Un-be-liev-able, damn it."

"Irving," Mom said, putting her hand back on his arm. "No strap. Promise me."

"What the hell is wrong with him?" he whispered scarily.

"Irving, have some ma'amouls. Calm down. I have vanilla ice cream. We can deal with it afterward."

I could tell Mom was confused and afraid. She went to the oven and pulled out a tray of ma'amouls, grabbed the ice cream out of the freezer and brought it near his plate even though Dad hadn't finished eating his main course. The feeling in our house was way off. Even Bonnie felt it, because soon she climbed the basement stairs and moved off to the side. She was waiting like we all were when Dad turned to her and said, "Where is your brother?"

Mom cut in. "He's in his room. He's asleep."

My father looked at Bonnie and said, "Go upstairs and see if he's awake."

The second I heard him say that, I silently bolted up the stairs and down the hall, jumped into bed, and closed my eyes. I could hear Bonnie climbing the stairs quickly. She rounded the corner and looked down the hall into my room to see me with one arm hanging over the edge of my bed and my body sort of crumpled up. With so much practice dying and being dead with my friends, I felt pretty sure I could fake sleep as well.

Bonnie came toward me carefully. Closer and closer she came, putting her face right next to mine, her breath intentionally blowing on me to either wake or annoy me. I knew she hoped I was faking so she could watch me be tried, convicted, and electrocuted.

But I stayed with it, until she left, went back downstairs and announced, "He's pretending to be asleep, but he's awake."

I crawled back toward the stairs and down toward the landing while vowing to get even with her someday for saying that.

"Exactly what did he do?" Dad asked.

Mom again put her hand firmly on Dad's arm without saying a word. A moment later, she put her other hand on his arm as well. My dad bent his head and shook it slowly. It was as if he was saying that his mind couldn't handle that one extra piece of news.

"And the call?"

Mom answered like someone who didn't want to answer but had to. "I guess this boy Stuart was involved. The call was from Stuart's mother. She wanted to let me know that Stuart had never been in any trouble before. She said Mark was a bad influence and told me she didn't want Mark playing with Stuart ever again."

Instead of shaking his head, my father nodded.

"Who brought the matches?" he asked still looking down.

"Mark brought them."

"Where did he get them?"

"From the drawer, the same place as last time."

There was another long pause.

"So he ignored me? I gave him the strap last time, and he still ignored me."

"Irv," she said softly. "I don't think that's what's going on. Mark has impulses and does things before he even thinks."

My father made a face as if he had just eaten something very sour. "Where the hell did you get that from?"

"From Mr. Washington. Irving, he made sense. He talked to Mark's teacher. She thinks the same thing."

"Baloney," he whispered. "He took the matches either the night before or the day of school, right? That means he planned it. And don't give me this 'impulsive' business or any other psychiatrist nonsense."

One of Mom's hands slid off Dad's arm and her expression changed completely. "I don't like it when you talk to me that way," she said.

Dad fired back, "And I don't like it when you say foolish things about a serious subject."

Those words were Dad's way of letting everyone know he didn't like Mom interfering in his department and that when the earthquake finally erupted, there would be no survivors.

"Irving. No strap!" she insisted, putting her other hand back on his arm.

He yanked it away and pointed a finger at her, his voice now booming, "This is not your department!"

"Yes, it is!" she insisted, raising her voice back at him. "My children are my department!"

"It...is...not...your...department!" he thundered.

Lowering her voice, she tried again. "Irving, will you please, please listen to me for a second?"

"Listen? Why? What brilliant thing are you going to tell me?" he yelled.

"Mr. Washington doesn't think Mark is a bad kid. He said his teacher says he's always daydreaming. They both think Mark is in the wrong grade. We made a mistake—a big one. Being a grade ahead of his age group is too much for him. He can't focus. He's too young." I could see she was gripping Dad's powerful arm the whole time.

"You're a genius, you know that? You're telling me he's in the wrong grade and that's why he's lighting fires? That makes no sense—zero. But maybe you have a future in psychiatry. One conversation with George Washington and you're qualified to be a psychiatrist. And Mark? Are you saying he's going to be held back?"

"You're not listening to me." she pleaded. "He can't keep up."

"A lot of good that information will be when he burns the city down. Can you guarantee me with that imagination he isn't going to do that? That he won't hurt himself or someone else?"

Mom bent her head for a second and seemed to search for an answer. "Irving, you're mad at the world and you want to take it out on your son. I don't have to be a psychiatrist to see it. Anyone can see it."

Ignoring what she said, he yelled again, "Can you guarantee that he won't?"

"No, I can't. But hitting him isn't going to help. It will just make everything worse."

"Oh no? We'll see about that."

He pulled his arm away, throwing her two-handed grip aside easily. His hand moved toward his belt buckle and he began to unfasten it.

"Irving!" she shouted as he started to get up from the table. "No!" He was still rising when she shouted again, "Will you listen to me?"

He pointed a finger at her and thundered, "This is not your department, goddammit!"

"Irving, the last time you hit him you came downstairs nearly in tears. You knew something was wrong with it. The wisdom inside you stopped you from taking it further. Now you want to go back and make an even bigger mistake? It doesn't make sense. You're not making sense."

Dad pointed his finger at her and almost touched her nose with it.

"It's not your department!"

"To hell with departments!" she shouted. "And to hell with you and your stupid Sephardic ideas about beatings and punishments! This is your son! This is who you're supposed to love, even if you can't say the words. You're supposed to protect him, not hurt him."

Dad headed toward the stairs unmoved by what Mom said, but Mom followed him. As afraid as I felt for myself, I was beginning to feel even more afraid for Mom. I backed away from my place near the landing because it was too close to the front lines. From my fallback position, I could see Mom sitting at the bottom of the stairs, blocking the steps with her arms. Dad, towering over her, shouted at her in a voice like claps of thunder, "Get the hell out of the way!"

"No!" she shouted back, still somehow holding her ground, like a cat snarling back at a dog ten times its size.

"Don't make me…"

"Don't make you what?" she challenged. I could tell that tears were coming to her eyes and her voice was cracking. "You gonna hit me too? Is that part of the tradition too? Is this so your father and grandfather will approve? Why don't you put on your stupid fez so we can have the whole experience!"

"You don't know when to quit, do you?"

"You are going to turn him into an angry kid! That's all it will do," she said, choking back tears.

I could hear Bonnie sobbing. Seconds later, Arlene began shrieking as she toddled down the hallway. The sound was so loud and sharp it made my eardrums feel like they were going to burst. I grabbed her as she went by and pulled her toward me and pressed her face against my chest and began to rock her back and forth as she cried and screeched while I patted her head.

"You don't know what you're talking about, damn it! There are ways things have to be done and they aren't done by women. It doesn't work that way. So don't give me any bull about being an angry kid. He'll be a disciplined kid if you get the hell out of my way and let me do my job."

"Disciplined, huh? Is that what you are right now?"

"Never mind that. My father gave me and Al the strap plenty."

"And it worked, huh? You're not an angry man? You're not out of your mind right now, scaring your children to death?"

In that instant, something changed. Dad's face reminded me of this boxer I once saw on TV who got punched in the face really hard. He tried to pretend it was nothing and that he could take it, but everyone could see he wasn't the same after it. Like the fighter, Dad tried to pretend it didn't bother him, and instead tried to cover it up with another sonic boom. "Get the hell out of the way!"

"No!" she screamed at the top of her lungs, matching Dad's thundering voice. I could see her cheeks streaked with tears and mascara. "Get out!" she shouted, pointing toward the door. "Get out of this house right now!"

This was the end of our lives, I thought. Now we weren't going to have a mom and dad together anymore. And it was all because of me. I watched in horror as Mom twisted off her wedding ring and threw it at Dad as hard as she could. It hit him in the chest, bounced off, and rolled under the couch.

Amazingly, like a second big blow, this one stopped him in his tracks. Horrified, I knew it meant that the fight wasn't just about me anymore. It was about "being married" stuff too. It got strangely quiet and I started to hope and pray the worst might be over. Dad backed away, shocked and stunned. He looked around and began to talk as if there were other people in the room. I could tell he was mostly talking to himself.

"I've got a union on my back that makes sure all the new hires slow down and do as little work as possible. I've got a son who tried to burn down his school today, and I've got a wife who won't let me do my job and who thinks maybe she should become a psychiatrist."

He moved toward the dining room. I changed my angle to see him better. With Arlene clinging to me, I watched in shock as Dad began to throw plates and dishes and silverware against the wall.

A glass salad bowl shattered as it hit. Dad usually loved salad with oil and vinegar dressing, but now pieces of lettuce were stuck to the wall, slowly curling and then falling to the floor. The force of the dish hitting the wall made me realize his tremendous power. Next came the pitcher of juice and the platter of stuffed peppers. Smash! Smash! Then came the couscous. And then the tray of ma'amouls followed by the half-gallon of ice cream. Smash! Splat! Still not satisfied, he looked around for something else.

Mom just watched him from her seat at the bottom of the staircase without saying a word and without trying to stop him.

She knew, and I knew, these were only things, and that breaking things was better than breaking kids.

Finding nothing more to throw, and needing to show us how extra mad he was, he took hold of the table, and with a mighty heave turned it over with glasses, dishes, and silverware still on it. It made a loud, crashing sound as it hit the floor. Striding across the living room, he grabbed a sweater from the closet, stomped over to the door, opened it, and left, slamming it behind him.

Bonnie and Arlene rushed to Mom and threw their arms around her while they cried, hiccupped, and sniffled uncontrollably. Mom kept shaking her head and whispering to herself, "I should have never taken that call."

Even though I was crying, gagging, and hiccupping, and my vision was blurred with tears, I crawled along the living room carpet like a U.S. Marine in the jungle, staying as low to the ground as possible. I was on a desperate mission to find Mom's ring. After squeezing my head and body under the couch, I crawled forward and groped around in the dark. Pushing aside a ball, a long-lost toy, and a couple of lost army men, I finally found the gold ring. Backing out from under the couch, I crawled to Mom, took her hand, and started to force the ring onto her ring finger. She didn't resist. Once it was on, she pulled me closer to her and kissed me on the head while I hugged her. Speaking in a soft voice, hoarse from straining, she said, "What are we going to do with you, Zeendala? What are we going to do?"

I looked up at her, tears streaming down my face, and said in a choked voice, "I'm sorry... I'm sorry... I didn't mean to make Daddy go."

That night in bed, the house a wreck and my dad gone, I found myself thinking and wondering about God again. After the kind of day I had, it was beginning to seem like God just might be real after all. For one thing, I didn't get the strap tonight, and if I had gotten it, it might have turned into one of the worst things ever. Wasn't that a miracle? And wasn't it a kind of miracle that Dad didn't hit Mom? And what about the way she saved me from him by going into his department? Weren't those miracles too? And what about the miracle that I didn't get killed crossing the street? I could see now, as I thought it over, if I'd been even a little bit farther out into the street, I would have been a goner.

On the other hand, I wondered how the "Our Father" man who cried and prayed on the lawn fit into all this. If God helped me, did He have to make that man so scared? It didn't seem fair for God to use him to save me. Or was that maybe a punishment to the "Our Father" man for something else he did that was bad?

And what about the whole business of walking out into the middle of a big boulevard with my eyes closed? God didn't make me do that. I walked out there because I made up something stupid in my head and did it. So maybe, just maybe, if there was a God, maybe He let people do stupid things if they wanted to. If that was His idea, I could sort of see the point of it. After all, even though He was God, maybe He couldn't go around to every single person and talk to them about what they were planning to do. Maybe, there were too many. Or maybe He figured out that the next best thing was to let people do whatever they wanted so they could learn from their mistakes. Unless, of course, they got killed. That's the part I couldn't figure out.

CHAPTER 14

The next morning after Bonnie left for school, Mom told me we were going to take Arlene with us to a park near our house. It was a sunny day and the air was fresh and crisp, but the thought of my missing dad was like a cloud blocking the sunshine. Mom and I were both quiet during the walk there. To show Mom I was a good boy and wanted to be helpful, I offered to push Arlene in the stroller. She let me.

We were the only ones at the park, and I volunteered to push Arlene on the swings, too, being extra careful not to be wild and push her too high. Later, when she was in the sandbox near Mom, I took a turn on the swings, pumping my legs back and forth until I was going as high as the swing would go because I wanted to feel what it was like for those kamikaze pilots when they dove their planes down on their suicide missions. I was glad I was only imagining it and didn't have to blow myself up to feel what it was really like.

Every so often, I looked over at Mom, who was deep in her thoughts sitting at the edge of the sandbox watching Arlene playing with her pail and shovel at her feet. Every few minutes, Mom looked down and twirled her wedding band around and around. And every time she did, it made me worry.

Dad was gone. I wanted him to come back, even though he scared us all to death.

Things were moving around in my mind. They were mostly confusing thoughts about Dad, Sephardim, and straps. But for some reason, there were many other thoughts too. Like about Blackie and how I loved him, and how glad I was that I made him be able to see. And there was Mom's Yahrzeit candle for my Grandpa Abraham who died and who I never got to know. I thought about Stuart and how his mom told Mom I was a bad influence and how losing him as a friend forever was all my fault. Feeling sad, I got off the swing, picked up a stone, and threw it side-armed like I would if I were trying to skim it on water.

"Mom?"

She looked up and watched as I found another smooth, flat stone on the ground and flung it. "Yes?"

"Did your dad ever give you the strap?"

Some time went by without an answer, so I stopped what I was doing and turned and looked at her. When our eyes met, she shook her head.

"Um, did your dad love us?"

Mom sighed. "My dad was crazy about you."

"He was?"

"Yes, he was."

"I was only a year old when he died, right?"

Mom nodded and closed her eyes, and I knew she was remembering him. "Yes."

I turned away and looked for another stone and found a really good one. I brushed off a little bit of the dirt that was on it, knowing it would make a good skimmer.

"Did he say he loved me?"

Mom was taking a long time between answers and I couldn't figure out why, but finally she said, "He loved you to bits."

"So, he said it? You remember him saying it?"

Mom didn't answer right away. Instead she seemed to be

studying me. Finally she said, "He showed it in every way."

"Yeah?"

"Yeah."

I thought more about the confusing things in my mind that were getting sorted out with each question.

"But do you remember him actually saying it—saying 'I love you'?"

Mom looked at me but didn't answer.

"Shouldn't people say it to each other so they'll know for sure?"

Mom hardly moved. It seemed like her jaw had dropped a little. She did manage a couple of slow, thoughtful nods that told me she understood and agreed with me.

"Some people have trouble saying it. Some people just show it. It's all the same. When you are loved by someone, you can tell."

It was good to know, but I wasn't sure I agreed.

"I think they should say it while they're alive, because once they die, how will the person they loved ever know for sure that they did?"

It looked like Mom wanted to say something but couldn't. So I picked up another stone and whipped it side-armed.

When we got back from the park, Mom told me to play in the backyard. I had to go by way of the front door because the huge mess from the night before was still there in front of the sliding-glass door that separated the dining room from the backyard patio. Mom seemed to have no plan to do anything about it.

Once in the backyard, I put the picture of the dining room out of my mind and pretended to be the Lone Ranger on his horse, Silver. I held a stick between my legs with my left hand and slapped my right side with my right hand as if I were slapping Silver's side to make him gallop. I galloped all around yelling, "Hi-ho, Silver!"

When I stopped to catch my breath, I was completely startled by the strange and almost unbelievable sight of Dad from inside the sliding-glass door of our house, holding a sponge in one hand and a bucket in the other as he began to wipe down the inside glass. His hair was messy, he hadn't shaved, and he looked like he hadn't slept all night. He must have been watching me through the glass for a while, because as soon as he noticed me looking at him he stood up and looked back without moving. At first my heart beat faster, since I couldn't be sure about his mood. But as the seconds passed, I began to relax, watching his expression change from a blank stare to the slightest of smiles. I looked back without being able to figure out how anyone felt about anything or what I should do. Yet it only took but one lift of his hand and our old, special "hi" sign to give me hope. A smile formed on my face and before I knew it, my hand was rising and I was waving back the "hi" sign too. He looked at me for a while longer as I stood squinting into the sunlight. I don't know what he was thinking as he stared at me, but something told me to just be still and let him look. Just then, to my surprise, Mom came into view behind him holding a broom and a dustpan. With no expression on her face she kneeled down alongside him and began helping him clean up the mess. I was amazed as I watched them. Without a word they just handed each other what they needed and kept their concentration on what they needed to do. It was as if they had an invisible referee talking to them, saying "Don't talk or fight; just clean up and start over."

I stood without moving a while longer. I had to keep telling myself that we'd all survived and no one was dead and no one got hit and we were still a family. I felt a surge of relief that was bigger than Niagara Falls. Feeling like I might cry from happiness, I thought to myself, "Thank you, God. Thank you for keeping us all together."

CHAPTER 15

Mom made a bunch of phone calls to the school and in one conversation, I heard her talk about my record and whether my being suspended, or the reason for it, would go on it. She sounded pleased to learn that it wouldn't. But the odd thing was that she didn't seem to be pushing for me to get unsuspended and back into school. In fact, even when she talked to Mr. Washington on the phone, she didn't mention it at all.

The night after the big fight, I overheard a conversation between my mom and dad about sending me to a special kind of doctor. Mom wanted me to go, but Dad said he didn't believe in doctors who were "head shrinkers." Since I didn't want to get anywhere near someone who might do something like that to me, I was glad Dad came out on top in that discussion, even though Mom said we should at least try one session.

I don't think Mom wanted to cross Dad again and risk another battle so she agreed, saying only, "Maybe we can consider it another time." Dad didn't answer her, but at least he listened and didn't get mad. Instead, they both agreed to just keep an extra-close watch on me until they figured out what to do next.

To keep her end of the bargain, Mom started doing the stupidest and most annoying stuff, like peeking her head into my room about a million times a day to see what I was doing. Even though I understood what she was doing and why, it drove me crazy. I even noticed her sniffing the air a lot, like some kind of grizzly bear or bloodhound. Other times she would call out my name in the middle of the day for no reason if things got too quiet.

"Mark?" she would yell from downstairs.

"Yeah?" I would answer.

"What are you doing up there?"

"Nothing. What are you doing down there?"

"Nothing. Are you playing?"

"Yeah. I'm playing. Are you cooking and cleaning?"

"Yeah. What are you playing with?"

I wanted to tell her I was playing with an atom bomb to let her know how annoying her snooping was, but then I decided, with everything that had happened, she might not think it was funny.

It was two nights later, in the middle of my sleep, when I was awakened by the sound of Mom and Dad whispering in their bedroom. I looked at my clock and saw it was almost one o'clock in the morning.

Grown-ups never seemed to realize whispering is actually easier to hear than talking sometimes—especially at night, and especially by kids. Einstein probably knew why, but I only know it was true. That's why I didn't even have to get out of bed to hear their words. I knew from the slight difference in their voices that they were both lying down in their big bed and talking up toward the ceiling. Both of them took extra-long pauses and did lots and lots of sighing as they spoke.

"I've been doing a lot of thinking," said Dad. "Times are changing. I'm used to certain ways of doing things, even thinking about things—many are like what my father did and his father before him. I need time to sort it all out."

Mom didn't say a word. It was a very good sign, because it meant she liked what he said, or she agreed with what he said, or something just as good.

There was another very long pause and then Dad switched over to his business voice.

"Bea, this move we've been planning, it's set. It needs to happen. It's the only way. Are you set?"

There was a long pause and I heard Mom sigh. "Yes, I'm set. It's for the family, isn't it? That's the most important thing."

I didn't understand the last part, but it sounded very, very important to know about. What was "set"? What "move" was Dad talking about? And why was it the most important thing?

CHAPTER 16

A couple of days passed and I was surprised at how normal things became. Dad came home and ate quietly while Mom sat near him and served him just like before. When Dad spoke to me, he was careful to say things in a nice tone. It was as if he were trying out a new way of being nicer to me and everyone. I began to feel less afraid and I started to feel lucky to have a forgiving mom and dad. Of course I couldn't really know what Dad was thinking and whether he would ever be tempted to use the strap on me again, because he never said he wouldn't. But at least for now, I think we were all happy enough to just feel the house was safe again. I wondered if moms and dads with kids on death row were as forgiving to their kids as much as mine were.

Something else that was odd, but great, was that Mom and Dad didn't seem to have a plan for me to go Hebrew school. They must have agreed Hebrew school wasn't a good idea right now. I was so thankful I even thanked God in a quick, made-up prayer, just in case He was real or had something to do with it.

There was one other thing going on that was kind of creepy. There had been a bunch of secret conversations between Mom and

Dad where they mentioned things like "The Putnam Motel," and "Plan B," and a place called Worcester, Massachusetts.

Making things even more spooky were new telephone conversations Mom kept having with a mysterious Melanie something-or-other. Whenever I came into a room and she was on the phone with Melonhead, which is what I started to call her, she would end her conversation in a hurry and promise to speak with her the next day. And every time I asked who it was, Mom would say, "Oh, nobody."

"Nobody" was a sure sign Mom was hiding something and didn't want to talk about it. But I'd heard the name Melanie so many times I wanted to find out once and for all who it was and what she had to do with us.

I'd seen bits and pieces of a new TV show called Perry Mason about a super-smart lawyer. The whole boring show happened in a courtroom, and no one ever got shot and nothing ever got blown up, but I have to say, it did give me some cool new ideas about how to talk to people so I could squeeze secrets out of their heads. Since Mom was keeping the secret of Melanie from me, it seemed like it might be a good time to use some Perry tricks on her to find out who Melonhead was. I waited till she was finished putting away some dishes, and then I sprung my trap on her.

"It must have been somebody," I said.

She looked at me for a second and started to walk away. "No, it wasn't."

I followed her and said, "I'll bet you wouldn't testify under oath that it was 'nobody.'" She stopped and turned her head toward me and smiled. I smiled back since I knew a gigantic Perry thing had managed to come out of my mouth. She pinched my cheek and kissed me on the head to let me know she thought I was cute, but that it was the end of it. Of course, I couldn't just let it go since I still wanted to find out who Melonhead was.

"Well?" I said.

"Well, what?" she said.

"Who was it? Was it Melonhead?"

"Okay, it was Melanie."

Wow, I thought. It worked! Without skipping a beat, I raced ahead. "Who is she? Why is she always calling here?"

"I am not going to answer that, and you have to stop asking. Enough already."

But I was excited about my new discovery.

"Is she a criminal? Is that why you're protecting her?"

Mom grabbed me by the collar and pulled me into a different room. Then, with a half-smile she told me to buzz off. I thought about following her to see if I could corner her and get her to swear on a Bible, but I knew she wasn't going to go for it.

As it turned out, I found out almost all the answers to the new mysteries the very next day. While I was running around in the backyard pretending to be a famous racecar driver, Mom placed herself in front of me. I stepped on my brake and made a long, loud, screeching sound, so I could come to a stop and not crash into her. When I did, she put her hands on my shoulders as she often did when I was still in my imagination and gently turned me a bit so I was facing her directly. Looking me right in the eyes with a voice that could not cover up her sorrow, she said, "Go visit all your friends. Tell them goodbye. We're moving."

Every last bit of my pretending vanished and I stood there in frozen disbelief.

"What?" I said.

"We're moving."

"What?" I asked again.

Mom looked at me and sighed, and I could see her eyes were watering as she tried again to help me. "We're moving."

"Moving where?" I asked as I tried to understand what this meant and how life was going to change.

"To Massachusetts."

I'd heard that name once before but only once. I think it was when one of my teachers was talking about different states in the United States and that was one of them. I didn't know much about other places, just my own neighborhood and Bayside, where I lived.

"Where's Mass…a…tooshis? Are we going to move back here later?"

"No," she said, looking sad.

"What about Jeffrey and Peter and Gerard and his brothers… and the Goldbergs and Shapiros and the other kids on the street? Will I ever see them again?"

She paused and I knew that a pause right now could not be good.

"Maybe someday."

My questions poured out.

"How far away is it? When do we have to leave? But Mom, I like it here." I felt my stomach getting tighter. I realized how much I loved this street and all the kids on it. "When? When do we have to leave?"

"Tomorrow," she said.

"Tomorrow? Why do we have to leave tomorrow? Why can't we leave in a month?" I felt more desperate with each second. "Why so soon?"

She closed her eyes for a second and let out a long sigh. "Daddy is moving his business and he's afraid some of his workers might throw rocks through our windows."

What she said made no sense to me. Yet, there was nothing I could say or do. "In Massa…chu, do they have any kids there?"

"Yes, I am sure they have kids there."

She smiled slightly and it made me almost angry to see it. Right now I didn't think anything was cute, nice, happy, or funny. I just couldn't understand how something could come out of nowhere and turn my life upside-down like this.

"Can't we call the police if someone throws rocks? Can't we move to a different house near this one? We could…uh…put up those…uh…boards on the windows—like when there's going to be a hurricane."

Mom looked straight ahead but said nothing. I could tell she felt really bad.

"I don't want to go," I said.

"I know," she whispered, closing her eyes. "I don't want to move either." She pulled me close and gave me a hug and kissed me on my forehead. "Now go tell your friends."

I pushed open the backyard gate and walked to the street feeling like a zombie as I made my way to each of my friend's houses one by one.

Jeffrey asked me a lot of the same questions I asked Mom. In the end, he got sad and quiet, like he was getting ready for me to be gone by acting like I was gone already. But then he managed to say, "That stinks." And then, looking really sad, he said, "Let's write to each other forever."

I looked into his eyes at one point and I knew in that instant how much he meant to me and how I was going to miss him.

"Yeah," I said trying to sound hopeful. But I had a sinking feeling it might not turn out that way.

I walked home after saying goodbye to everyone I could think of and then for some reason began to feel like I was floating.

Early the next morning, a great big moving van came and parked in front of our house. Four moving men came in and packed everything we owned: all of our clothes, dishes, shoes, toys, dolls—everything. When they finished packing, it was late morning. Afterward, the workers carried out our couches, chairs, and other furniture, and put it on their giant truck along with all of our other stuff. When the house was completely bare, I stood in the living room in disbelief. Finally, taking one last look around, I walked out the front door onto the sidewalk and looked up and down the street. A thousand great memories of all the fun I had came to me in a second and I felt like crying. Was that it? Was all of the fun of living on 211th Street, the best place in the world, the best place in the universe, gone forever?

By late morning, I found myself squeezed into the back seat of our car with Bonnie at one window, me at the other, and Arlene between us. We were on our way to a place called Worcester, which Mom said was a city in Massachusetts. She showed me where it was on a map, but it didn't make sense to me and I was too numb to care.

I struggled to think if anything good could possibly come from this. But the only thing I could come up with was that maybe, just maybe, after we moved, Dad might be able to be happy again since he was finally getting away from the union and his building and elevator problems and all the bad rules that made it hard for him to run his business in New York. I tried to be happy for him. I tried to think this was even a good idea. But as we pulled away I couldn't help but think that I might never see Jeffrey, the McBrides, Peter, the Shapiros, or Stuart or any of my friends again. Not a single one. Not ever.

PART TWO

CHAPTER 17

While on the way to Massachusetts, I began to think a lot about what it would be like to be all alone on Mars. I knew a little about Mars because during the summer, kids on 211th Street had talked all about it. Everyone had gotten interested in what secret weapons the Martians might have and what kind of creatures they might be. No one was sure if they had two heads or three, or how many arms they had, and whether their eyeballs could shoot killer rays. Nobody knew for sure what was true and what wasn't until Dave-the-Brain straightened everyone out. Dave told us that with no oxygen or water and freezing cold temperatures, there probably wasn't anything or anybody that could live on Mars.

Even though I was pretty sure Dave was right, I imagined myself in a rocket ship on my way there anyway. I breathed on the window of the car imagining it to be a space capsule and drew pictures in the mist, noticing how, over time, the license plates on all the cars and trucks that went by seemed to be changing from mostly New York ones to Connecticut ones and finally to ones from Massachusetts.

Bonnie asked a lot of questions about where we were going

and what the new place would be like. Like me, she had less than a day to say goodbye to all her friends. She had cried a lot with some of her girlfriends on the street but especially with her best friend, Doris.

Four and a half hours later, with only a couple of short stops in between, we turned onto Roxbury Street, a street with great, big leafy trees. Right away I noticed the houses were much bigger, older, and farther apart than houses on 211th Street.

I got out of the car and stared at the big old house we were going to live in. It was two stories high and had a slanted roof. There was a garage in the backyard that wasn't connected to the house and it had a rusty old basketball hoop over the garage door. The front and back lawns were much bigger than lawns in Bayside, and Mom, who'd been reading about houses in a book on the way up, said the house was a Victorian. But the thing I noticed was that there wasn't a single kid or grown-up on the street, even though it was the afternoon.

When Mom and Dad said we were renting the house from someone called a landlord, I worried it might be someone we would have to pray or bow down to, like in the Middle Ages when there were kings and lords and rulers and everyone had to bow down and say "Your Highness" and "M'lord" and stuff. I was glad to find out our landlord was named Sidney and he wasn't any kind of lord, and he mostly just liked to play golf, drink beer, and collect rent.

Once inside, I could see the place was big—more than twice the size of our duplex in Bayside. My room had smooth, hardwood floors that were going to be great for setting up army men and equipment for huge battles. Another good thing I figured out was that if I ran down the hall in my socks as fast as I could and grabbed on to the doorjamb as I turned the corner, I could drop to the floor and slide across a good part of my room just like Mickey did when he was stealing bases.

Next to my bed was an ugly, metal thing Mom told me was a radiator. It made loud, annoying, knocking sounds every time it went on. The only good thing about it was that after a while, it made a hissing sound and steam would shoot out of a hole. I was able to tie one of my army men onto the end of a pencil with a rubber band and pretend he was a Nazi general and stick him into the steam and scald him to death.

The walls in the room were purple. Mom said they were atrocious. The ceiling had white paint that was old and peeling and there were brownish rings on other parts of the ceiling that Mom said were water stains.

Later on, when I went outside, Mom told me not to wander off too far and make sure to stay on the street. I went down the street a bit to see if there were any kids to play with and see what the end of the street looked like, but all I saw were other, big old Victorian houses like ours. The only one that was different was the house at the very end of the street. It was gigantic and didn't look like a Victorian. I could only make out the front because the rest of it was surrounded by really high stone walls. The walls were at least as tall as a basketball rim, which I knew was ten feet high, and the entrance had great big white pillars that were like the kind Samson pushed apart to make the temple cave in and kill all the Philistines.

The house was two stories high and I counted ten huge windows across the top floor, all with black shutters. As I peeked through the iron front gate I could see the same number of giant windows on the first floor too. At first, I guessed the place was as big as three regular Victorian houses, but when I got to the very end of the street, I was amazed to see the house actually wrapped around the corner onto another street. With the second part looking at least as big as and maybe even bigger than the first part, I realized I was looking at my first mansion.

It seemed odd because I always thought mansions were far away from other houses and all alone on hills with huge front lawns and a bunch of servants sitting in big rooms inside and barely talking. This house sat right in the middle of a neighborhood. Well, at least it was kind of a neighborhood, even though I hadn't seen one single other person yet, let alone a kid.

I started to walk back down the street toward my new house and remembered how Dave-the-Brain had said there was no oxygen on Mars and that all living things needed to have oxygen to survive. That's why I tried cupping my hands and bringing them to my mouth each time I breathed so it would sound like I was breathing through a mask that was connected to a tank of oxygen. I knew how to do it perfectly, because I had watched the show Sea Hunt every Saturday morning in Bayside.

I peeked into the backyards on the other side of the street as I walked, looking for almost anything: a swing set, bicycle, baseball bat, or basketball hoop—anything that would be a clue to where I could find another kid. But here on Mars, there didn't seem to be any at all.

CHAPTER 18

It was the beginning of fall, and most of the leaves were still on the trees and just beginning to change color. We'd been in the new house for almost a week and I was getting used to it. Although Mom was on the phone just about every day calling different people about getting me back into school, so far nothing had happened.

Dad was still coming home late from his new factory and didn't have time to play with me or my sisters. But at least he didn't seem upset or angry like before. He was just very tired. I kept my fingers crossed that his better mood would last and his business would turn out good.

The neighborhood was still as quiet as could be. I had walked up and down the street and around the corner about a thousand times and hadn't seen a single kid. That's why, when Saturday came and Mom told me my cousins were coming over, I was really glad to hear it. They had moved to Massachusetts like we did and Uncle Al had told Mom they were having a hard time getting used to everything, just like we were. In their conversation, I heard the name Melanie and finally figured out that Melonhead was the person who helped sell our house. They said she was called a real estate broker.

With my Aunt Jenny and Uncle Al chattering with Mom and Dad in the living room and kitchen, and my cousins playing board games and telling jokes, for a while I felt like I was back in Bayside.

Dad seemed relaxed as he listened to Uncle Al go on about his kids, the different synagogues that were available, the house he was renting, and how much he liked the new workers at the factory. My dad nodded a lot and just listened until the subject of business expenses came up. The second it did, my dad jumped right in and gave his opinion.

"The one thing that's killing us is overtime. Even early on I can see we're paying way too much time-and-a-half to get a regular day's run completed. We're not as efficient as we need to be. There has to be a better way to pay the machine operators than by the hour. We need to provide them with some kind of an incentive to get things moving, but I have no way of knowing what the production expectation should be."

And that's when it happened. The words I had been looking for, for so long, seemed to pour out of Dad's mouth just for me.

"I'll tell you what would put a smile on my face and that's fixing this time-and-a-half issue so the overtime is reasonable, and of course making sure we don't ever have a labor problem like in New York. Everything else, I think we can live with."

The two of them took some time out to sip and eat quietly. I stayed and watched them a while, but there was so much buzzing in my head after hearing Dad say what would put a smile on his face, that I went outside to think about it. I lay down on a lawn partly covered with giant leaves and looked up at the sky and thought about Dad and his problem of paying too much overtime and wondered how I could help him. But right now, I didn't even know what overtime was, so I knew I had a lot of work to do.

I held up a giant maple leaf to the sun, and with the help of the light streaming through, I was able to examine all of its little veins as a tiny caterpillar inched its way along the leaf's outer edge. I put my eyes up really close so I could see all of its gazillion little legs and feet and somehow got reminded of something Dave-the-Brain once said about numbers. He had said that there were more stars in the universe than grains of sand on earth.

At first, I didn't believe him, because even a handful of sand was probably millions of grains. A whole beach would have been trillions and trillions and all the beaches in the world would have to be gazillions. For the first time ever, I doubted what Dave said. But since he was an honest kid, as well as a genius, I thought maybe he just remembered it wrong or something.

When Dad came out onto the back porch and saw me lying on the grass, he surprised me by speaking in a friendly voice.

"Hey, Zeendy, what are you doing there?'

I smiled because he called me Zeendy. Then I looked over at him through squinting eyes, as he put a paper bag of trash into the metal trash-can near the garage. While still holding up the leaf and glancing at the caterpillar I decided to ask him a question, just like I used to, before he started being grouchy and angry.

"Dad, how many legs does a caterpillar have?"

He stopped what he was doing for a second.

"Hmm. That's a good one. Can't say I know."

He went back inside and came out with another bag of trash and put it in the metal container as well.

"Dad?" I asked. "Do you think there are as many stars in the universe as there are grains of sand in the whole wide world?"

Dad stopped what he was doing and looked at me, hardly moving, when I noticed a slight smile crossing his face.

"It's possible. Who told you that?"

I answered casually. "Dave. Dave-the-Brain."

"Tell you what. Next time we go to the library, we can look it up. How's that?" he said, just before going back inside.

I would have loved to have gone to the library with Dad, but he didn't say when, and I knew he was too busy to go anytime soon. I knew we would, though, because if he said he'd do something he always did it, but just not today.

The fresh air felt really good, and for a while I just thought about all the different things I was curious to understand, like how to solve Dad's business problems and find out if it was true about how many stars there were. But soon I became sad again as I thought about how many more cool facts Dave might have given me and how many more laughs and good times I might have had with Stuart, Jeffrey, the McBrides and everyone else in the neighborhood, if only I still lived in Bayside. I looked around at the trees and leaves and back to the one leaf with the caterpillar on it and put it down. I was lonely. So lonely, in fact, I wasn't even in the mood to pretend.

CHAPTER 19

Three weeks had passed since the end of summer, but with all that had happened, it seemed much longer. Mom and Dad spoke about whether I should go to public school again and be in the right grade or to a private school, which would cost a lot of money but might be better for me. They said there were still some problems to figure out, like getting me tested to find out how far behind I was and what to do about my "fascination problem," which Mom was careful not to talk about with the school people.

Most days I walked to the end of the street in my army helmet and jacket with a couple of plastic grenades on my belt, and on other days I wore a cowboy shirt, boots, and a belt with a holster and a six-shooter in it. Today, because I was looking for a good war, or at least a good battle, I wore my World War II stuff and carried a stick to use as a rifle. Every so often I stopped, wheeled around, and shot snipers who were way up high in bedroom windows or crouched behind big, leafy maple trees.

I had just finished shooting two deadly snipers when I noticed something very different down the street. A real, live kid was standing across the street in front of his house wearing an army helmet. Even though I could tell he was much younger than me, maybe only five or six, it was the first kid I'd seen on Mars and so I got excited.

The kid was short and had a roundish body and he kept looking toward me without saying a word, so I crossed the street and walked up to him. When I got right next to him I lifted up my stick and aimed it at him. "Hands up!" I ordered.

To my surprise, nothing happened. All he did was look back at me without as much as a single word or motion. I tried again, but all I got was a wide-eyed look. That's when I realized this kid wasn't ready for a serious pretend battle. So I asked, "What's your name?"

At first he didn't say anything. Then, weakly, he finally answered, "Anthony."

"Right. Can you cross the street by yourself?" I asked like a drill sergeant.

He shook his head. "Uh-uh."

I was about to leave when a big man in great, big overalls appeared from behind the house. He had on a long-sleeved, plaid, flannel shirt, and heavy, rubber boots covered with mud. He held a rake in one hand as he came closer. With just a single look I was sure it was this kid's father because they had the exact same round faces. When he smiled I noticed he was missing a couple of teeth.

"You must be the new kid. My name is Vincenzo. Anthony is my son." He put his hand on Anthony's shoulder. "Anthony says you're out here every day with your guns, always pretending, and he wants to pretend too. You're a big kid to him so he wants to be like you and pretend like you."

I looked back at him not knowing what to say. His thick accent made it hard to understand him. "I live in that side of the house over there," he said, turning and pointing with the rake handle.

As I looked over, I realized he lived in only one part of the house.

Vincenzo's hands and arms moved all over the place while he talked.

"Anthony's not in school because he doesn't talk. He doesn't raise his hand and he doesn't play with other kids. I'm looking for a special school while his aunt teaches him at home. So far I didn't find any place for him. Everything costs a lot of money and I don't have it."

It was funny to watch Vincenzo talk because, whenever he talked about hearing, he put his hand up to his ear and cupped it and sort of stretched his neck out. When he started to talk about thinking, he pointed to his head and tapped it with his pointer finger. Also, he said "dem" instead of "them" and "I no have" instead of "I don't have".

"Sometimes I think maybe he doesn't know what's going on. All I know is, you came along and now he doesn't shut up. I think to myself, if he wants to make believe then fine." Vincenzo stopped talking for only a second before starting right up again and using the rake handle again as a pointer.

"I take care of Mr. Hawkins' house. Anthony doesn't have a mother. When he was born she died. Mr. Hawkins is in the great big house on the two corners. I do the garden, the mulch, and the lawn and I make everything look beautiful with nice flowers and bushes. I make it as beautiful as when I lived in Italy. Also, I fix anything that breaks. Mr. Hawkins is a special man and he likes the way I fix things."

Vincenzo put all his fingertips on his right hand together, brought them to his lips, and opened them like a blooming flower while making the sound of a kiss. "I make it so beautiful. That's why we live here right across the street, because it makes it easy for me to be close to work and home. Most of my work is for Mr. Hawkins."

I looked over at Anthony. He was smiling. Then I looked back at Vincenzo, my head pounding from how hard it was to understand him, and asked, "Is it okay for him to cross the street?"

Vincenzo thought for a second before answering, "If you look both ways two times and you're sure no cars are coming you can take his hand and cross the street."

I thought about it, but it didn't sound quite right, so I said, "Mr. Vincenzo, I'm General Mark and Anthony is Captain Anthony, so when we pretend, I can't hold his hand."

"I see," said Vincenzo, considering and then laughing at himself. "I'm so stupid," he said, hitting his forehead with the palm of his hand. "What kind of a general is going to hold the captain's hand? You're right. How about looking two ways two times and then you can tell him if it's okay to cross. Okay?"

"Okay."

"Good," said Vincenzo. "Good." Vincenzo patted us both on the shoulder and then leaned over and kissed Anthony on the head like Mom always does with me. Anthony seemed to like it. Vincenzo went back into the house, and I looked at Anthony, who still had not said a word. I wondered if he ever would.

"Do you want to cross the street?" I asked.

He nodded.

I looked up and down the street two times like I promised, and told Anthony it was okay to cross. A moment later, he raced across the completely empty street.

"Okay" I said, getting a little hopeful, "We have to go on a mission to my backyard, and we have to crawl through the hedgerows of Normandy and be snipers and kill Nazis. Are you ready?"

For a while, we just looked at each other. But a few seconds later, my heart sank when he shook his head. Being a sniper was such a good idea, and the weather was beautiful. I could feel how desperate I was to play with someone—anyone—even this kid. So I tried again. "Do you want to do something else?"

And again, after several seconds, he shook his head.

Frustrated, I asked him if he wanted me to cross him back over to the other side of the street. When he nodded, I did. But to make him feel better since he was only a little kid, I decided to give him a medal. Saluting him I said, "Captain Anthony, you fought bravely today. A lot of American lives were saved because you crossed the battlefield and fought bravely. I am going to give you the Medal of Honor." I picked up a leaf and pretended to pin it to his chest. I was surprised when he raised his hand and put it to his forehead in salute. "Dis…missed!" I commanded, and stepped back. Then I turned sharply, and headed home without looking back.

Dad and Mom settled into the living room after dinner and talked in a whisper. I got to a good new spying place where I could see them both clearly and they couldn't see me.

"Oy, Irving, where did you take us?" said Mom. "The stores close at 9:00 p.m. here. The whole city shuts down as soon as it gets dark. People make fun of my accent. Mark is so lonely he imagines he's on Mars. He pretends to need oxygen every few seconds, and he inhales it through an imaginary mouthpiece."

Dad laughed for a second, and took out the newspaper, splitting his time between the paper and Mom. "I feel like that every day," he said, glancing over at her.

Mom only half smiled. "Very funny."

"How's it going with the school system?" he asked as he opened up the entire paper before folding it over twice to get to the page he wanted.

"I got a call from the Truant Officer in Bayside about Mark not being in school. He said in cases where the family moves to another state, they contact the public school in the new location."

"Did you tell him we're having him tested, and we're looking into private schools too?"

"Yes. He said the paperwork takes a few days, and then we should expect a visit from someone around here if Mark is not enrolled somewhere."

Mom paused and then went on. "Another thing, I called City Hall to find out about garbage pickup. They put me through to Sanitation and do you know what they said?"

Dad lifted his nose above the paper and looked at her.

"They explained that 'up here' there's a difference between garbage and trash. Trash is papers and 'burnable materials,' and garbage is like banana peels and food waste. Garbage gets picked up twice a week by the city, and trash goes into that 55-gallon metal drum in the backyard— the one behind the garage. I asked them what happens to the trash barrel when it's full. You're not going to believe what they told me."

Dad didn't answer, but he was definitely paying attention.

"They said we're expected to burn it!"

"Burn it?"

"Right. Burn it."

Dad thought about this, then went back to his newspaper. "When you burn the trash, make sure Mark isn't around."

Mom made a face. "How am I going to do that? He's around all the time now."

"I don't know. Try to figure something out."

"Oh, great! So this is my department?"

Dad had a blank look on his face. "What can I tell you? I don't have any good ideas right now. I'm on overload."

There was a brief silence and Dad bent his head to think. "Anything else?"

Mom didn't need to think for long. "Yes, actually. One of the things the fellow at City Hall said was that once the leaves really start falling in earnest they should be put in piles and burned right on the street. That's how they get rid of them around here."

"Should I guess why you are bringing this up?"

Mom paused for only a second. "Irving, I think we're making a mistake if we don't get someone for Mark to talk with. The issue is still there, and we can't assume just because we've moved it's going away any time soon. Especially with these…eh…new opportunities."

Dad shook his head. "Bea, I told you what I think. I'm still not for it. It's expensive as hell and it just goes on forever, with session after session and no clear results. I've talked to people about it. In the end, he'll come home with real problems from all of the shrink talk. Give me some more time on this. I'm thinking about a way to do this that we can agree on."

Mom didn't seem convinced, but she didn't want to start a fight, so that's where their conversation ended.

CHAPTER 20

The next afternoon I went to the far end of our yard, got down on my stomach, and, with a stick that I pretended was a rifle, I began crawling on my elbows through the leaves, shrubs, bushes, and hedges that separated our yard from the neighbors' yards. I crawled for a long time, being careful to stay as quiet as possible, so that I could keep the advantage of surprise on the Nazis.

After a while, the plants and bushes became so thick it was hard to know where I was. I didn't know if I had crawled in a straight line or veered off into some strange new land near the hedgerows of Normandy. For a time, I thought about trying to stand up, or turning back towards home, but the excitement of my mission as a deadly sniper was so exciting, I stayed down and inched forward.

A few minutes later, my movement was blocked by a large stone wall that appeared right in front of me. Brushing aside twigs and leafy branches that nearly covered me, I reached out and felt the wall's surface. Rising to my knees, and then to a standing position I ran my hand along it to get a better sense of it, looking up to see how high it was and then marveling from another angle how long it was.

There were a few places where the cement between some of the stones had fallen out, and I wondered if I might be able to get enough footing from those holes to climb up and see what was on the other side. By using a tree branch that was leaning against the wall, and some cracks in the wall that helped me to get some footing, I made my way to the top, where I felt a smooth, flat, stone surface that reminded me of our patio in Bayside. Finally at the top, I was able to see the other side. What I saw made it hard for me to believe my own eyes. There, spread out in front of me, was a huge lawn and garden that looked like a picture of The Garden of Eden from a Bible storybook. The grass was dark green and neatly cut. Flowers and neatly trimmed bushes were everywhere and I couldn't see a single weed or anything that was out of place.

A stone walkway made out of the same kind of flat, blue slabs of stone that were on top of the wall led to the side of the house and to a couple of round-shaped patios where there were tables and benches made of stone and a few folding wooden lawn chairs. There was even a bird feeder and a round, stone bird bath. In rows near the back wall were hundreds of ripe tomatoes hanging from dozens of tomato plants. A row of tall pine trees ran along the back wall. The house closest to me was gigantic and looked like a mansion, while another smaller house in the distance seemed more like an oversized shed, even though it was bigger than any shed I'd ever seen.

I threw my trusty stick onto the ground and then pushed myself away from the wall until I felt my feet land on a mound of soft, spongy soil and grass. I rolled as I landed to break the fall. When I stood up and looked around, the Garden of Eden seemed even more beautiful than before, now that I was in the middle of it.

It didn't take long for my imagination to tell me that being a sniper was just too slow and quiet for such a beautiful place. Wide-open spaces like this made me want to run like a deer. Soon I was imagining myself on a horse galloping all over the Wild West. My stick became a bow, then a spear, and later a rifle as I galloped all around shooting everyone and everything in sight.

I don't know how long I was doing this before finally stopping. I only know it would have gone on much longer if I'd not been startled by the scary sight of a tall, thin man in a kind of sport coat walking toward me. As he got closer, I began to get nervous. My instincts took over and I looked around for a possible escape route.

There was a closed gate at the far end of the yard and I wondered if I could outrun this guy if I had to. But then I thought, what if it was locked and I couldn't get over it? What would I do if he caught me and wanted to kill me for coming into the yard? Maybe because things were so different here in Massachusetts they could do that and it wouldn't be against the law. I whispered, "Oh God," and just as I did, it was as if God Himself answered, because the man in front of me stopped in his tracks.

"Young man, I am Tilden. I am in the employ of Mr. John Hawkins. Mr. Hawkins requests the honor of your presence in his study."

I didn't have any idea what to say and felt scared to death. I only knew that this tall, thin guy looked a lot like one of those waiters at bar mitzvahs who walks around serving mushrooms and wieners on tooth picks from a silver tray. He stood unmoving while waiting for me to answer, but must have finally figured out that I needed help. With one of his eyebrows going way up, he said, "Which means he would like to meet you."

Feeling a tiny bit more relaxed, I held my hand up to block out the afternoon sun so I could study this guy a little more. I kept wondering how he managed to stand up so straight all the time while letting his hands hang at his sides. Then everything dawned on me at once. I must be in the backyard of the giant Hawkins' mansion that Vincenzo, Anthony's father, had talked about. The more I thought about it, the more certain I was.

But I also began to feel embarrassed as I thought about how the whole Hawkins family might have been watching me running around and pretending all this time. I looked back at Tilden and realized he was still waiting for an answer. The more I looked at him, the more he seemed like one of those English butlers I'd seen in some old movies. Since I'd never heard of scary or evil butlers, I decided to take a chance. Shrugging my shoulders, I finally said, "Okay."

"Very well, young man, and now if you will impart your name I will be pleased to introduce you."

I shrugged my shoulders again. "Mark. Mark Leonard."

"Please be so kind as to follow me into Mr. Hawkins' study where he will meet you shortly."

Tilden turned and marched toward the house and I followed. Once inside, he adjusted the curtains so the glare of the sun was less strong. Motioning with his hand, he let me know he wanted me to sit on one of the big leather chairs. I climbed onto it, rubbed the armrests, kicked my feet, and looked all around as he left.

A great, big desk made of dark wood was in front of one wall. Against another wall were high shelves filled with about a million books. There was a fireplace that had a stack of firewood next to it, and on one side of the fireplace were some iron tools— a little broom and shovel, and a little pointy iron stick that hung on a kind of holder for clunky iron things. The desk was cluttered with papers and a couple of open books. There was a quill pen in its own holder. Next to the desk was the biggest globe I'd ever seen on its own floor stand. It must have been almost three times as big as a beach ball.

There were a few pictures on the wall over the fireplace. One picture had the name John Hawkins underneath it and it showed a man in a wheelchair shaking some other man's hand, while a whole bunch of dressed-up people watched. The same guy was in another picture, only he was much younger in that one, with a woman and three little kids. I figured it was probably his family.

Suddenly, the double doors to the room opened and a white-haired man in a wheelchair, a lot older than Tilden, wheeled himself through the doorway. He had a nice smile that made me want to trust him right away.

"Thank you so much for coming," he said cheerfully.

It is him, I thought. It was the guy in all the pictures on the wall. This was Mr. Hawkins.

"You're welcome," I said.

Tilden stepped forward and motioned to me with an open hand. "Sir, this is Mr. Mark Leonard." Turning to Mr. Hawkins, he made the same motion. "Mr. Mark, this is Mr. John Hawkins."

I thought it was so neat the way Tilden introduced us. It made me feel comfortable and grown up. Mr. Hawkins was watching me. When our eyes met, he said, "I noticed you on the back lawn running about and playing in a way that made me think you might be doing some imagining."

I nodded.

"I take it that you like to pretend."

I nodded again.

"Me too," he said.

As I thought about what he said and tried to picture it, it seemed funny—a guy who was as old as a grandpa, pretending—but I didn't say anything.

"Well, I hope I am not embarrassing you when I tell you that I watched you for quite a while out there in the yard."

I was a little embarrassed, but he was so nice about me climbing over his wall and jumping in his yard that it made me feel calmer.

I shook my head to let him know I wasn't too embarrassed.

"Good," he said with the same smile. "I want to tell you something." He paused as if trying to figure out the best way to say it.

"What?" I asked.

"Well, you see," he said, motioning to Tilden, "Tilden is my servant, but he is also my good friend. It was Tilden who first discovered you on our grounds, and it was he who called my attention to you."

I was still a little uneasy, but I didn't panic because I was interested to know what he was going to say.

"May I ask you a question?"

I liked the way he was talking to me, as if I were a good friend, so I nodded.

"Did you ever make a bet with someone?" he asked.

I nodded.

"Good," he said. "I made a bet with Tilden about you."

"About me?"

"Yes."

"What did you bet?"

Mr. Hawkins cleared his throat and took a sip of water from a glass that was on a little table right next to him. After a few long seconds, he put his glass of water down and looked directly at me again. "I think I know what you were doing when you were pretending. Tilden didn't think you were doing anything in particular, but I'm pretty sure you were."

I smiled. This whole thing was about me and so far I liked it. I could tell Mr. Hawkins wanted me to tell him something, and I liked that I had the answer he needed.

"I would appreciate it if you would tell us, more specifically, what you were doing, and if it is what I guessed, then I will win the bets."

I found myself smiling even more.

"How many bets did you make?" I asked.

"Three," said Mr. Hawkins, whispering as if he were giving up an important secret.

"How much were the bets for?" I asked, kicking my feet.

He answered in a whisper and cupped his mouth as if it were top secret. "A quarter."

I looked at Tilden but couldn't figure out what he was thinking. He kept the same stone-faced expression.

I remembered when I used to bet a dime on the Yankees with my grandpa, and I wondered if this was the same kind of bet between Tilden and Mr. Hawkins—just a little money thrown in to make it more interesting.

"So, will you tell us?" he asked.

I paused, thought about it, and shrugged. "Sure."

"Wonderful!" he said, clapping his hands together.

Mr. Hawkins adjusted himself in his wheelchair. Then he raised his arms and pretended to pull back on the string of a bow just like I had done on the lawn. He let his fingers fly apart, just like I had, to show he was letting go of the arrow.

It was a little funny to see him do it, but he got it right so I answered, "I was shooting my bow and arrow. I was an Indian."

"Exactly!" said Mr. Hawkins with a big smile. He glanced at Tilden, whose expression was now slightly sour.

Mr. Hawkins turned to me again, even more excited. "Next, I think you did this," he said imitating me. "You held your stick this way."

Again, it looked funny to see him do it, but I wanted to tell him what I imagined since he seemed to like it.

"That was when I got hit by the arrow. It got me in the heart and I died."

"Exactly! Wonderful! Yes! A wonderful imagination!" he said, slapping the arm of his wheelchair in delight. "Now here is the last one." He glanced at Tilden briefly. "Tilden would never have been able to get this one and it took me a while, but I think I figured it out." He slapped the side of his wheelchair with his right hand while holding his left hand in a fist out in front of him.

"Um, that's when I had to hold on to the reins of my horse, Silver, with this hand so I wouldn't fall off, and I slapped him on his side to go faster with my other hand. Later, I pulled back my bow and shot the bad Indian from my horse."

"Exactly!" he said as if hitting a bull's-eye. "Absolutely correct!" he said, with growing laughter.

Tilden moved forward, put his hand into his pocket, and took out a small handful of change. He selected three quarters, placed them on the table next to Mr. Hawkins, and then turned and started to leave the room.

"Ah, Tilden, you're a good sport," said Mr. Hawkins, calling after him and laughing. "You have no imagination, Tilly, but you're a good sport." When Mr. Hawkins finally stopped laughing, it got really quiet and I began to wonder what would happen next. I could feel myself hoping I could stay longer and I realized how much it helped my loneliness to be around someone new and friendly. To my surprise, Mr. Hawkins' eyes met mine and I swear it was like we had read each other's minds. We both smiled.

"Would you like to see some more of my house?" he said.

I nodded right away.

"Can you stay for lunch?"

I nodded even more quickly.

"Good," he said. "Just follow me."

As he wheeled himself toward the door, he called out, "Tilden, could you check with Rosa and find out what she's planning for lunch? I think it's going to be American chop suey with fresh tomatoes from the garden."

"Very well, sir," said Tilden from a distance.

Mr. Hawkins looked at me. "Will that be okay?"

I nodded again.

"Mr. Mark," said Mr. Hawkins, "may I have your phone number so I can call your mother and tell her where you are and make sure it's okay for you to have lunch with us?"

I nodded, but I forgot to say the number because of how much was going through my mind.

Mr. Hawkins waited for a while and then smiled. "And that number is?" he prompted.

"Oh yeah. It's BA9-6659."

"Hmm. That doesn't sound like an exchange or a number from around here. Did you move here recently?"

I nodded. "We used to live in Bayside. Now we live here in Massachusetts."

"I see. And is that a new number or your old number?"

"If we have a new number, I don't know what it is."

"That's quite all right. Tilden will find it. Isn't that right, Tilden?" called Mr. Hawkins.

"Indeed it is," answered Tilden from another room.

"While Tilden is looking for your number, let's go into my armor room."

"What's an armor room?"

Mr. Hawkins' eyes lit up and he smiled as if he had a really good secret. "Oh, you'll see."

I walked alongside him as he pushed the big wheels of his chair until we entered a huge room. At first it reminded me of one of those ballrooms you sometimes see in movies about the South, where all the ladies get dressed up in gowns and jabber about who they hope to dance with and stuff.

But all my thoughts about ballrooms flew out the window when my eyes fixed themselves onto a truly amazing sight. There in front of me was a row of more than 20 sets of steel armor lined up against the wall. From head to toe, it was steel everywhere. All that was missing was the knights inside them. But it hardly mattered. I felt like I was dreaming as I walked closer to them. There were shields next to some of the suits of armor with pictures of lions or eagles on them. One even had a lion with wings and sharp bird's claws. There were also swords and long spears of some kind, and a big steel ball on the end of a thick, heavy chain. The steel ball had spikes and was connected to a short stick. Breathless, I asked, "Are these knights in shining armor?"

"Yes," he answered. "Well, not exactly knights, but this is the armor they wore."

"Can I touch one?" I asked, moving toward a particularly shiny piece.

"Yes, you may. Just be careful."

I moved to the middle of the line and carefully touched a knight with a shiny steel warrior helmet. As I moved my hands around the face piece, Mr. Hawkins explained, "The main part around the head is called the helm, like a helmet. The piece in front of the face is called a visor and the part around the neck is called the bevin."

"Is this a museum and also your house?" I asked while still in awe.

Mr. Hawkins smiled. "Well, no, but I think someday I will give these pieces to a museum."

"These are amazing," I said.

"Yes, they are. Do you know that when I was your age, I loved to imagine myself wearing one of these and being a warrior knight?"

"You did?"

"Yes, I certainly did."

"Oh wow," I said. "It must have been neat to imagine being a warrior knight."

"Yes, it was."

I walked around the room slowly, looking at each piece as Mr. Hawkins pushed on the wheels of his chair. At the end of the room, Mr. Hawkins wheeled out in front of me while I thought to myself that nothing on earth could be more amazing than what I'd just seen. But I was wrong. When we entered the next room, I saw two knights in full armor on huge, armored horses, holding out long spears as they charged toward each other. It was as if they were frozen in time a second before crashing into each other. The top piece of one of the knight's helmets was as high as one tall grown-up standing on the shoulders of another tall grown-up. The two gigantic horses had brightly colored blankets over their backs and sides, and over their heads they had their own steel armor, just like the knights that rode on them.

"Wow!" I said in a long, breathless whisper. "Wow!"

Walking around them, I studied every detail—amazed at how they seemed to take up the entire room. Only the sound of Tilden's voice from another room interrupted my thoughts and made me remember where I was.

"Sir, I have Mrs. Leonard on the line," he said.

"Very good, Tilden," said Mr. Hawkins. "I'll pick it up in the ballroom."

A few seconds passed. I barely noticed Mr. Hawkins moving out of the room to answer the phone until I heard him say, "Mrs. Leonard? This is John Hawkins, your neighbor down the street. I'm in the house on the corner of Williams and Roxbury. We've had the good fortune to meet your son, Mark. He dropped in on us a while ago, and he appears to be enjoying himself as much as we are enjoying him. I thought I might ask you if it would be all right to have him join us for lunch."

After a pause, he continued. "Yes, that's right. Hawkins... Well, he seems to have climbed over our wall and landed in our backyard...No, not at all. It was our good fortune. He is a fine lad. I can tell already."

For a time everything was quiet. But then, I heard Mr. Hawkins say, "Certainly!" and a second later he called out to me. "Mark, it's your mother on the line."

I walked back to the ballroom and was still thinking about the knights when Mr. Hawkins handed me the phone. Almost as soon as I put the receiver up to my ear, Mom started asking me a whole bunch of her worry questions, which were followed by a whole bunch of her safety questions. I had no choice but to answer every single one of them. When she finally let me go, I gave the phone back to Mr. Hawkins and went back to the room with the knights on horseback and my jaw dropped open again, as I heard Mr. Hawkins finishing up the call, "Yes, five p.m. will be just fine. And, oh, Mrs. Leonard, please do come by sometime. I would very much like to meet you and welcome you to our neighborhood. I would come to you myself, but I am a bit restricted." There was a pause and then, "...yes, yes...Goodbye."

I heard the phone hang up and then Mr. Hawkins called out.

"I'll bet you're in the exhibit room with our knights and chargers. Am I right?"

"Yeah," I said, sounding as if I were dreaming.

Mr. Hawkins wheeled into the room, clapped his hands together and called out, "Mark, I was right. Rosa's planning to make us American chop suey for lunch. I can smell it already."

As I turned to look at him, I noticed another empty wheelchair off to the side of the room. Curious, I moved toward it and pointed. "Is this your wheelchair too?"

Mr. Hawkins stopped and looked up. "Yes, it's my old one."

"You have two?" I asked.

"I have three, actually. I have one upstairs as well."

"How do you get upstairs to use it?"

"I have a lift—an elevator."

"Oh. But why do you have so many wheelchairs?"

Mr. Hawkins considered this for a time. "Well, I suppose that even though the old one doesn't work quite as well as this new one, I am still somewhat reluctant to dispose of it. You see, it served me well for many years and I feel a certain loyalty to it."

Even though he was probably as old as my own grandpa, I got the feeling just from what he said about his wheelchair that he could be a true friend, like the guys in the movies you would fight and die for, and they would fight and die for you.

"Can I sit in it?"

"Why, certainly."

I sat down and began to get the feel of it, examining the great big wheels and foot stirrups.

Just then, a cheerful woman in an apron, who looked to be about my mom's age, came out into the hallway. Her skin was the color of cocoa and she had a nice smile, dark eyes, and black hair that she wore in a long braid.

"Si, señor. Muy bueno," she said. "Cuántas personas? How many?"

I didn't understand all of her words, but I could tell she was mixing up her English and Spanish.

"Tilden!" Mr. Hawkins called out. "Will you be joining us?"

"Thank you, but no," he called back. "I am not as fond of American chop suey as you are, so perhaps I will fix myself a sandwich later. I would like to read the newspaper in any event."

"As you wish," said Mr. Hawkins. "As you wish." He turned to Rosa. "It will be three. Tres."

"Excellente," she said. Then, sort of correcting herself, she said, "Berry good," and went back toward the kitchen.

Mr. Hawkins followed her and I tried to follow using his old, loyal wheelchair. But the wheels were hard to turn, and I was barely able to move forward. Mr. Hawkins must have noticed because he stopped and turned to face me.

"Well, Mr. Mark," he said with a smile and a kind of light in his eyes, "it appears as though we might do well to get a phone book or two to help boost you up a bit."

It was a good idea. In no time Rosa was back with three big phone books and I was propped up on my new wheeling machine and able to move right along.

"Let's go out on the patio," said Mr. Hawkins. "We can eat out there. It looks like a glorious day."

When we got to the patio, we pulled up close to one of the stone tables and looked out onto his backyard. Mr. Hawkins' eyes got squinty and he took in and blew out extra-large breaths before letting out a sigh. A few minutes went by with neither of us talking, so it seemed like a good time to ask Mr. Hawkins a few questions I'd been thinking about.

"Mr. Hawkins, how much money do you have?"

Mr. Hawkins didn't answer right away, but for some reason he smiled before scratching his head. "Oh, quite a bit, I imagine."

"Do you have a million dollars?"

His smile got even bigger, even though he seemed to be trying to hide it.

"Oh, I expect I do. I would have to talk to my accountant to be sure, though."

"How did you get so rich?"

His face, and especially his eyes, told me he liked my questions.

"It's a long story, but I had a factory—still do, actually."

"My dad works in a factory too," I said excitedly.

"Well, then, there you go."

"Yeah, but he doesn't have as much money as you. He even had to borrow from my grandpa. He worries about it a lot. It makes him sad and nervous. He doesn't want to lose it all and become a slave. Are there still slaves anywhere?"

"Haven't seen a single one. Have you?"

I shook my head.

My mind drifted back to the room with all the armor. "Mr. Hawkins, what did the knights do with their big spears and their horses?"

"Do you mean their lances?" he corrected.

"Yeah, their lances."

"Well, they had what was called a joust."

"What's a joust?"

"A joust was like a contest." He lifted up both of his hands and pointed them at each other as if to help with his explanation. "People who lived in castles hundreds of years ago would have tournaments, which is a series of contests, and one of the contests was jousting."

"What did they do with their long spears—I mean lances?"

"Well, the knights wore armor and carried a shield and a lance. They got on their chargers and rushed toward their opponent and tried to knock them to the ground."

"What are chargers?"

"That's what they called their horses because they charged toward one another on them."

"You mean they would go straight at each other like in your room with the giant horses and knights?"

"Precisely. The only difference is that there was usually a separating wall between them. Otherwise, the exhibit shows them pretty much as they were, a second before contact."

"Wow."

"Yes, it must have been quite something to see."

"Yeah." I said trying to picture it. "It must have been quite something to see."

"Sometimes knights would joust for the affection of a lady," Mr. Hawkins said, "like the beautiful Guinevere."

I didn't know what "affection" was, but it didn't seem too important, and besides, I had a really good idea.

"Do you want to have a pretend joust with me?"

"Pardon?" said Mr. Hawkins, looking up at me.

"A joust. Do you want to have one?"

For a few seconds, Mr. Hawkins was completely silent. But then he seemed to gradually get more interested.

"How would we do that?" he asked, "As you can see, I might

have difficulty mounting a horse. And even if I could, where would we get one?"

"We don't need a real horse. You can use your pretend horse that you're already sitting in and I can use mine."

Mr. Hawkins looked down at his wheelchair and then up at me.

"I see," he said, sounding more interested.

"Do you have armor we could use?"

He tapped his lip, thinking. "I do. In fact, I even have a kettledrummer's armor, which would be perfect for a boy. It's mostly upper-body armor, but perhaps I could fit out the rest with a couple of other pieces from upstairs. I think there's a set in the attic."

"What's a kettledrummer?" I asked.

"It was a boy who beat on drums that were shaped like kettles before and during battle. They rode on horses like the knights but didn't fight."

This was so cool.

"How shall we do it?" Mr. Hawkins asked.

I loved that he was asking my opinion about everything. It was just like having a good friend my own age—actually, it was even better.

In no time at all we worked out how to have our joust. On Mr. Hawkins' orders, Tilden got the armor from up in the attic, and Vincenzo helped me suit up. He propped me up extra high with a few extra phone books so that I could turn the wheels of my chair more easily. Next, brooms and mops were padded with pillows and pillowcases and taped so that they were like firmly cushioned lances. In no time at all we were ready to joust.

CHAPTER 21

I learned pretty quickly that Mr. Hawkins had a great imagination. Every time I thought of something good to do, he found a way to make it even better.

He got Rosa involved by setting up a long straight-back chair and covering it with cloth and lace. It was up on a platform and looked like a throne. On it was a beautiful bouquet of flowers. Mr. Hawkins even started calling her Guinevere when she came dancing into the room. Her hair was up and sparkly stones glittered from her made-up crown. She looked around to make sure me and Mr. Hawkins were ready.

As soon as the cloth was dropped, Mr. Hawkins and I charged each other. Our mop lances grazed each other's shield and chest armor as we passed by. Laughing out loud, I heard myself and my echo as if I were inside a tin can. Bubbling over with excitement, I raced to the opposite end of the ballroom to prepare for another charge.

From time to time, Mr. Hawkins called Tilden for help and despite Tilden's slightly grumpy face he always helped Mr. Hawkins do what he wanted. Vincenzo had been pulled in too. He'd only wanted to show Mr. Hawkins some new bulbs for the garden and instead had been told to help me suit up, pad the mops, and be ready to help me.

With each pass I could hear Mr. Hawkins laughing, too, just like an excited kid. "Ha ha!" he cried, sounding like he was having the most fun he'd ever had. "Again," he commanded, lifting his mop higher for another go-around.

After three or four times of charging each other, we ended the contest with a bunch of pokes to each other's armor and shields as we sat alone in the middle of the ballroom. Finally, in the middle of one of my loudest laughs, Mr. Hawkins poked me in just the right spot and my wheelchair flipped over and I fell out with a crash. I got up off the floor, feeling like the Tin Man from The Wizard of Oz and lifted my visor, hysterical with laughter, and watched as Mr. Hawkins took off his helmet and threw up his arms in victory.

"Glorious knight," he said, "I trust you have not suffered any injuries. Are you all right?"

"I'm fine, O knight of steel," I said, trying to talk over my laughter.

It took a good 15 minutes for everyone to catch their breath and let things quiet down. Rosa changed back into her regular work clothes and made hot cocoa for all of us, and Mr. Hawkins invited everyone into the sitting room to sip in front of the fireplace, where firewood was crackling. Looking at Vincenzo, Mr. Hawkins motioned for him to bring over a few of the big, comfy chairs that were in different parts of the room. I would have helped, but they were too big and bulky for someone my size to carry.

For a while, everyone sipped and talked and laughed about the joust. Mr. Hawkins told us all a few things about how life was back when all of this kind of stuff went on, and it was very interesting. Tilden was the only one who didn't join us, and Mr. Hawkins seemed okay that he didn't.

Soon after, Rosa said she needed to clean something in the kitchen, and Vincenzo said he had to go outside and finish pruning one of the trees in the backyard.

I barely remember them leaving, though, because of how

distracted I became by the crackling fire. At one point, I actually got out of my chair and stepped closer to it. I must have been staring for quite a while, because I didn't even notice that the only remaining people in the room were me and Mr. Hawkins. My eyes were fixed on the little jets of orange and blue shooting out of one of the logs, while other parts just smoldered and crackled.

Mr. Hawkins' voice jarred me, even though it wasn't loud. "Hey there, Mark. You see that iron poker off to your left? Can you give that top piece of wood a poke and push it back a bit? Then throw on another small log."

I found it hard to believe Mr. Hawkins was asking me to do such a thing, but I guess to him it seemed normal. With some excitement, I took hold of the iron poker and did my best to do what he'd asked. I felt kind of grown up by the time I finished and couldn't help but notice how the fire seemed to be relaxing me and how it seemed to make nice thoughts go in and out of my mind like floating leaves on a breezy day.

I guess one of those floating thoughts turned into words, because I was surprised to hear myself say, "Mr. Hawkins, have you ever been suspended?"

I didn't turn to see his expression, but instead continued to look at the fire.

I heard him clear his throat, and that's what finally made me look over at him. He was studying me.

"Let's see. Well, uh…off hand I can't exactly recall. Do you mean 'suspended' from school?"

"Yeah," I said dreamily, now turning back to look at the glowing, red chunks of wood near the bottom of the pile.

"I see," he said thoughtfully. "No. Can't say I have."

I knew he was wondering about my question, but I couldn't seem to pull my attention away from the fire, and before I knew it, another question floated in. "Did anyone ever tell you that you were a bad influence?"

There was a long silence. It was so long, in fact, that I finally turned and looked at him.

Still, he took a while before answering. "Oh sure—many people in fact. But they didn't know what they were talking about."

For some reason, his answer made me light up.

"Really?"

"Absolutely. Who is to judge such a thing anyway?"

I thought about his wonderful words and began to smile. It was as if a great weight had been lifted off me.

"Yeah," I repeated. "Who is to judge such a thing?" I nodded over and over again.

Time flew by and before I knew it, it was 5:00 p.m. and I was yawning and trying extra hard to keep my eyes open as I sat at a bridge table and sorted through a 1,500-piece jigsaw puzzle with Mr. Hawkins.

He must have noticed my yawning because he said, "Hey, young fella, maybe it would be a good idea for you to rest on that nice, comfortable hallway couch until your mother gets here."

I had no idea how much time had passed when I woke up. I only knew I was groggy and my stomach was growling. I sat up halfway and looked down the hall at Mr. Hawkins' grandfather clock and realized I had been asleep for more than an hour. Remembering that Mom was supposed to pick me up, I began to wonder where she was. Propping myself up a bit more, but still bleary-eyed, I adjusted myself so that, when I looked ahead and to the side, I could see Tilden and Mr. Hawkins in the study. They were almost like a silent movie to me, but I was able to hear them a little because the doors separating us were made of glass and were opened slightly.

Mr. Hawkins was looking toward Tilden, who was sitting in a big leather chair. He spoke to him softly as if he wanted to be careful not to wake me. "What'll it be, my friend?"

Tilden picked up a newspaper from the table near him. "How about brandy?"

"Excellent choice," said Mr. Hawkins as he struggled to rise out of his wheelchair with the help of a cane.

Tilden immediately began to rise to help, but Mr. Hawkins

waved him off.

"No. It's all right, Tilden. As you can see, I am full of adventure today."

Tilden's face soured slightly. "Speaking of adventure, sir, Dr. Reed will be here to see you at nine-thirty tomorrow for your bi-weekly physical. I should advise you that he will ask if there have been any side effects to the new medications, particularly the nitro tablets. You may recall we agreed to make a list of any other physical complaints or symptoms you might have. He will no doubt ask if you have had any abnormal rhythms. I shall not involve Dr. Reed in today's shenanigans, as I am quite sure he would disapprove wholeheartedly. Although duped into taking part, I must assume a certain measure of responsibility, since I was the one who wheeled your absurd charger down the ballroom floor."

By now Mr. Hawkins was out of his wheelchair and standing shakily, propped up only by his cane. He steadied himself, hobbled over to the cabinet, opened one of its doors with his free hand, and took hold of a half-full bottle.

"And what shall we say to Dr. Reed of the two bruises on your side as a result of today's absurd joust?" said Tilden.

Mr. Hawkins smiled. "You needn't mention anything about any bruises, Tilden. I earned them honorably in a manly contest, in which I was victorious by the way, and see no need to involve a young physician into my private affairs. It is enough that I have you forever nipping at my heels."

I watched Mr. Hawkins try to balance his cane, the bottle, and two large glasses as he moved back toward his wheelchair. Finally seated, he sighed and said, "Tilden, I thought I'd serve you tonight as a way of saying thank you for going along with me today. I know you were uncomfortable through most of it."

"It was odd, sir."

"Maybe so, Tilden," said a smiling Mr. Hawkins, "but it was an absolutely wonderful kind of odd."

Mr. Hawkins poured two glasses of brandy and handed one to Tilden. They each swished the liquid around for a while and put the glasses up to their noses. Mr. Hawkins took a sip and said, "You know, Tilden, so many years ago when I had the builders erect the walls around this grand house, I did so because my accident left me feeling weak and vulnerable. The outside world had become too intrusive. Life seemed to grant me no quarter and there seemed to be no place I could escape to to find peace. I remembered thinking if only I could make a beautiful lawn and garden, adorn it with flowers and shrubs and all things natural, and seal it with ten-foot walls, perhaps within that space I could begin the healing of my troubled soul and, eventually, find peace."

I could see Tilden was listening carefully, only moving to take a sip now and then.

"The odd thing, which appears to be part of today's learning, is that it can just as readily keep out that which brings joy."

Even though I was still groggy, I could tell it was an interesting thought, a grown-up thought, and one I actually understood.

"Well, isn't that why we read newspapers and good literature? To bring in what we want and keep out what we don't?"

Mr. Hawkins leaned back and carefully sipped his brandy, not directly answering Tilden. Reaching into a nearby drawer, he pulled out a box of cigars, handed one to Tilden, and began unwrapping one for himself. Running its entire length under his nose and drawing in its scent, he said, "The best Cuban cigars they make."

"Yes," said Tilden. "But perhaps it is time to forego this little pleasure, considering the state of your health, sir."

Ignoring Tilden, Mr. Hawkins answered. "Today, knights on chargers with lances were unable to bring me down, so perhaps a few puffs won't either."

"Compliments of your friends at Worcester National Bank, no doubt."

"Yes, yes indeed."

Mr. Hawkins leaned back in his chair and smiled.

"You know, Tilden, when our little friend Mark scaled our formidable walls to join us, I observed that he could have remained in his imagination all day long without missing a beat."

Mr. Hawkins' face seemed to light up more and more as he spoke. "It was as if he could make a conscious decision when to leave and when to return. It was as though he could simply choose the place and time and decide within that context who he wished to be. It is his own magnificent way of—I don't know—transcending time and place. And he can do it on a moment's notice. Imagine being able to come and go to wherever you please, whenever you want, as whomever you wished to be."

I smiled to myself. Mr. Hawkins was the first grown-up in a long, long time to say my imagination was a good thing. All I ever heard from teachers, and even Dad that night when I spied on him, made it seem like it was a bad thing. By the way Mr. Hawkins was speaking, I got the feeling he didn't just think it was a good thing, he thought it might be a great thing. I decided then and there, that from now on I would be proud I liked to imagine stuff, even if it got me into trouble sometimes. The world was much more interesting when you used your imagination, and meeting Mr. Hawkins was actual proof. After all, if I hadn't been imagining myself being a sniper in the hedgerows of Normandy, and later, a cowboy and an Indian, I don't know if we would have ever met, just like he said.

CHAPTER 22

The next morning I raced into the bathroom to take a shower. While the water was hitting my face and I was shampooing my hair, I began singing "Peggy Sue." I tried to make my voice quiver the way Buddy Holly did when he sang the words "Peggy Sue ooo-ooo-ooo-ooo." I loved singing in the shower because it made my voice echo and sound really good.

When I was out and all dressed except for my shirt, Mom came to my room with a big stack of clean laundry and plopped it down on the end of my bed. She looked down at the empty floor and said, "No battles today?"

"No. Truce until midnight."

She nodded like she understood.

"Mom, how did I get home from Mr. Hawkins' house?"

"Daddy carried you home."

I thought about it and remembered it, sort of, but I had thought it was just a dream.

"He did?"

"Yes. You were out like a light. Mr. Hawkins called to tell us you were asleep, and so Dad ran a few errands before picking you up."

Boy, Dad was pretty strong to carry me all the way down the street. For a second I wondered if he pretended to be a GI and imagined me to be a wounded buddy that he had to get out of the jungle on Okinawa. That's what I would have imagined.

Mom was moving all around, changing sheets and collecting trash. "Take the end of the sheet and pull it out," she said.

After changing some more pillowcases and sheets and stripping the beds, I could see Mom was on her way to turning me into her slave, so the first chance I got I raced out of the room and downstairs to eat.

I was well into my bowl of Wheaties when the phone rang. I heard Mom go to the upstairs line and pick it up. I stopped eating and moved closer to the stairs so I could hear what she was saying, thinking that if it had something to do with Melanie or some other secret person, I wanted to know about it as soon as possible.

"Yes, thank you for getting back to me, Mr. Adams," said Mom.

Everything grew silent as Mom listened.

"The transcript from New York?" she said with a voice that sounded concerned. "You mean it got lost somehow? Gee, I was really hoping to have Mark enrolled somewhere by now. Could we at least arrange to see the school while we wait for the paperwork to be sorted out, perhaps even begin the required testing?" There was another pause. Finally, she said, "That will be fine. I will note it on the calendar, and I will follow up with the school in Bayside, since this is really taking too long. Yes. Yes. Thank you."

Just as Mom hung up the phone, the doorbell rang. I went to open it and was surprised to see it was Aunt Jenny. She gave me a big smile as soon as she saw me, and that's when I figured out she must be here to babysit Arlene.

"Hi there, Markala," she said happily. Then, stepping back and pretending to be shocked, she said, "Oh, my goodness, look how you've grown."

I smiled and held the door open for her because she was always nice to me and I was always glad to see her. She had a big, wide smile and nice teeth. As she entered, she gave me a couple of light pats on the shoulder. "What a nice young gentleman you are turning out to be."

I accepted her pats and even a kiss because I knew she loved me. I was lucky. I had good aunts and uncles. None of them were drunks or stupid, like in my friend Eddie's family in Bayside.

Minutes later, I was bouncing out of the house and skipping sideways down the street toward Mr. Hawkins' house while Mom walked behind me. She was curious about Mr. Hawkins and wanted to meet him. I looked for Anthony on the way, but he wasn't standing in his usual spot. When we got to Mr. Hawkins' house, Mom did the same thing I had a few days earlier. She stopped and gazed at the mansion and walked all the way to the end of the street before following it all the way around the corner. "My God," she said, "it's enormous."

By the time she got around to looking at me, I was already on the front step and ringing the bell. When the door opened, Tilden stood there as straight as a flagpole. With a slight bow, he said, "Ah, Mr. Mark. Good morning. I trust you slept well last night." Then he turned to Mom. "And good morning to you, Mrs. Leonard."

I could tell by the look on Mom's face, she was surprised by Tilden. At first I thought it must be because she never went to any kind of politeness school, like Tilden must have, to learn to talk and act like him. Still, she sometimes surprised me at how smart she could be and how she could figure out the right thing to do in almost any situation.

"Good morning."

Tilden opened the door wide and stepped back. "Won't you come in, Mrs. Leonard? Mr. Hawkins is looking forward to meeting you. He is with his doctor at present, but they should be finished in five to ten minutes, I expect. Won't you make yourself comfortable in the sitting room?"

Looking at me, he said, "Would Mr. Mark like to continue to work on the puzzle while Mr. Hawkins is occupied?"

I looked at Mom and she nodded.

"If you will follow me," Tilden said.

Mom looked around as we walked down the hallway but then stopped when we passed the entrance to the ballroom. Tilden stopped and turned to wait for her. It seemed like he was used to people slowing down when they saw the armor room for the first time. Mom nodded like she was telling herself something. She looked at Tilden, then at me, and said, "Well, this certainly explains a lot about why you like to play here."

Tilden walked a few steps and motioned to the right—"The game room." Then, turning to look at Mom, he motioned to the left—"The sitting room. Mrs. Leonard, please make yourself comfortable. There are some magazines on the table near the light stand should you wish to read while you wait."

Mom entered the room and found a comfortable chair by the fireplace.

"Would madam like some tea?"

"No, thank you." Mom said politely.

Tilden nodded, bowed, and left the room.

I kept watching Mom. I could tell by the way she twisted her neck all the way around and tilted her head way back to look up at the high ceilings and paintings on the walls that she had never, ever seen a house like this.

I went into the game room and got up on Mr. Hawkins' old loyal wheelchair by the puzzle table. After putting one or two pieces in place, I was surprised to hear voices coming from a room that sounded as though it were right next to me. I quickly figured out that there was an entrance from the game room to this other room but that it was covered by a heavy curtain and blocked by a big chair that was pushed up against it. As soon as I recognized Mr. Hawkins' voice, I climbed down off the wheelchair and up onto the big chair to better hear what was going on. Then, like a sneaky spy, I pulled the curtain back a tiny bit and watched and listened.

Mr. Hawkins was sitting in his wheelchair with his back to me. His shirt was off and he was speaking with someone who must have been his doctor, since he had a black leather bag and one of those special stethoscope things. The doctor placed it on Mr. Hawkins' back and chest every few seconds and kept saying the usual stuff like, "Deep breath now," and "OK, now let it out." But when the doctor put the scope over Mr. Hawkins' heart, it seemed like he left it there and listened for a long time. I heard the sound of a newspaper rustling and that's when I realized that Tilden was in the room with him, just out of view.

After removing the scope, the doctor took the two plug parts out of his ears and looked sternly at Mr. Hawkins. "John, are you taking your medication? In particular the blood pressure medication?"

Mr. Hawkins looked annoyed. "Yes, of course."

"Not always," interrupted Tilden.

Mr. Hawkins lifted his hands as if to say, Thanks a lot, Tilden.

"Well, often enough," he said. But then, after a few seconds of Tilden and the doctor remaining quiet, he finally added, "Okay. Okay. I will try to do better."

"John," said the doctor firmly, "I hear some irregularity. More than usual."

"What did you expect to hear? Beethoven?" It sounded sorta like a joke, but nobody laughed.

I guessed the doctor was a little older than Dad but definitely much younger than Tilden. "John, I don't like what I am hearing through my stethoscope. You need to moderate the alcohol, and you need to be careful about overexertion. Do you hear me?"

Mr. Hawkins put his hand up to his ear and cupped it. In an old lady's crackly voice, he said, "Whaaaat? Did you say something about over-insertion?"

The doctor looked irritated but couldn't help but smile.

"Yes, well, I can see that this is all one big joke to you, but I need to tell you, John, that you are playing with fire if you don't heed my warnings. You could be looking at the big one or perhaps a stroke if you don't take the medications I've been prescribing. Also, you need to be more serious about controlling the booze and cigars."

When the doctor left, Mr. Hawkins put his shirt back on and wheeled himself out of the examination room. His frown changed to a smile, and when he saw Mom he sort of lit up. "Good morning, Mrs. Leonard. I am so glad you took me up on my offer. It is so nice to meet you."

"It's nice to meet you, Mr. Hawkins," said Mom, rising to her feet and then sitting back down as Mr. Hawkins smiled and waved for her to be seated. "You have an interesting, and, if you don't mind me saying, rather overwhelming home."

I couldn't hear what Mr. Hawkins said back to her, and at first I didn't know why. But then I realized Tilden had gently closed the glass doors to the game room and was about to do the same thing with the glass sitting-room doors. Grown-ups always do annoying stuff like that, and I always have to figure out ways to get around it.

I waited a few minutes before gently nudging the game room doors back open—just enough so Tilden wouldn't notice. Luckily for me, Tilden didn't completely close the glass doors in the room where Mom and Mr. Hawkins were, so I was able to hear them pretty well. For extra cover, I turned out the light in the game room and moved onto one of the big comfy chairs that was closer to the entrance of the room. I curled up almost into a ball and found an angle that was sharp enough so I could stay pretty much out of sight while seeing and hearing everything they said and did. I purposely left the little light on at the puzzle table in case I was discovered. That way it would look like I was taking a little rest in the corner chair. To make things more interesting, I imagined I was spying on Mom and Mr. Hawkins for the United States of America because the safety of everybody in the world depended on what I found out.

"Thank you," said Mr. Hawkins with a smile. "I must admit I have heard that before, and so it certainly must be true. I guess I am a boy at heart, a boy who wants lots of room to play, like your wonderful boy Mark, I think."

Mom smiled. "That's such a nice thing to say. He's been so lonely since we moved here, and yesterday, although exhausted, he went to sleep very happy after visiting with you."

"I am glad to hear that, very glad indeed. I should tell you, I had just as good a time as he did."

Mom smiled again. "If you don't mind me asking, what is it that you did together yesterday?

"Not at all," said Mr. Hawkins. "We spent most of the day using our imaginations. We had a great time making believe. He seems to be quite gifted in that way."

Mom seemed unsure when Mr. Hawkins said it. "I never thought of it quite like that. To be honest, sometimes I wonder."

"Yes. It is quite remarkable. And he has a lovely disposition to go along with it. I think, too, that he has a wonderful heart and is quite kind."

Mom seemed lifted by his words.

"Thank you, Mr. Hawkins. He is kind, except to his older sister, of course."

"Of course," said Mr. Hawkins with a wink.

They sat quietly for a time and then out of the blue Mr. Hawkins said, "If I am not intruding, Mrs. Leonard, may I ask why Mark is not in school?"

I felt a surge of worry go through me. I feared that their conversation might be headed toward all of my secrets about school and what happened. Mom seemed caught off guard by the question, too, but only for a moment.

"Certainly. Uh, well, our move from New York was rather sudden, and we hadn't made arrangements with the schools up here yet. Mark needs to be tested to find the proper grade level for him, and we may need to arrange for a specialist to help him in some of his more challenging areas—math in particular. Mark seems to want nothing to do with math, which makes the challenge all the greater."

"I see."

"And uh…there's another problem."

At first Mom looked like she didn't want to say more, and was even surprised that she'd said anything, but as Mr. Hawkins waited patiently, she must have changed her mind.

"...And we are trying to figure out how to deal with it. That is, my husband and I are trying to figure it out. It has to do with a troubling fascination of his."

Right there she stopped and didn't say another word, and I knew right away it was because of me. She looked around the room and leaned out of her seat to see if I was nearby. As soon as I saw her do it, I pulled my head back and down into the chair and looked out over the side edge instead where she definitely couldn't see me.

Turning back to Mr. Hawkins, she said, "He always finds a way to listen. He understands a lot for a child his age."

Mr. Hawkins smiled and nodded.

To my surprise and shock, Mom pointed toward the fireplace and said in a whisper. "It has to do with that."

Mr. Hawkins turned in his seat to look and I got the feeling by his "uh-huh" expression that he understood quickly it wasn't about the fireplace but about fire.

I got worried she was going to start blabbing about all the trouble I got into playing with matches and lighting the trash on fire in the basement. Not only would it really embarrass me, but I worried it might make Mr. Hawkins change his mind about me because I would be a bad influence on him.

I watched him lean over the side of his wheelchair and look around. I knew he was trying to get an idea of where I was. Not seeing anything, he looked back to Mom and shrugged.

"You seem to be implying a fascination regarding incendiaries. Would that be an accurate assessment?" he said.

Mom smiled and nodded. She seemed impressed with Mr. Hawkins. "You are very astute, Mr. Hawkins."

"Why thank you, Mrs. Leonard."

Mom nodded and continued on. "And the result was, uh—uh, how do I say it?—a separation from the institution of learning, if you know what I mean."

"Oh, my! And I do, indeed," said Mr. Hawkins nodding. "That

would explain his earlier question to me."

"To you?"

"Yes. He asked me if I had ever been suspended. Seems to be heavy on his mind."

"My goodness," said Mom. "I had no idea. He shared that?"

Mr. Hawkins just looked at her. For a time he said nothing, as if giving Mom extra time to think it over.

"Tell me, if you would, and if I am not being inappropriate— what does your husband think?" he asked.

"My husband?" repeated Mom.

Mr. Hawkins again waited without answering.

"I suppose the fairest way to say it, is that he and I don't always see eye to eye on everything—the present situation included. In this situation, he has a rather set way of believing, and he is not a believer in 'headshrinkers' as he puts it. I'm not saying he's closed-minded, but…well… that's how it is. A confrontation about it, particularly now, doesn't seem like it would be in anyone's best interest. Lately he has been talking about requiring..the..uh subject person to write down a long, anti…uh… incendiary paragraph 20 times a day. It is well intended, but I have my doubts."

"Hmmm. Yes. I understand."

I was getting so frustrated and mad because of the way they were using their phony language. And yet there was nothing I could do. I knew they were going to keep talking like this and Mom was probably going to tell Mr. Hawkins every embarrassing thing in the world about me since I was born and also about my "fire problems" and school problems and everything else. Not able to stand it for another second, I got off my chair, pushed open the glass doors, stepped forward and pushed open theirs as well before putting my hands on my hips and saying to Mom, "When are you leaving, Mom?"

Mom looked surprised at first, but then she made me madder by smiling in a sweet way while Mr. Hawkins sat there without saying a word.

She didn't answer, but at least it made her get up. She turned and looked back at Mr. Hawkins. "Mr. Hawkins, once again, I want to thank you for your…friendship…with Mark. And thank you so much for taking time to speak with me. You've been very helpful."

"It has been a pleasure, Mrs. Leonard. I'll look forward to the next time when perhaps we might chat a bit more."

"Yes," said Mom, "I would like that. Until next time, then."

When Mom finally left, the day with Mr. Hawkins started to get better right away.

For a while me and Mr. Hawkins pretended to be guys from the The Bridge on the River Kwai in the backyard. I acted the part of the super-mean Colonel Saito, and Mr. Hawkins was the good British commander who wouldn't make his officers work on the bridge even though they were all Colonel Saito's prisoners. Just like in the movie, I made Mr. Hawkins go into the shed as my prisoner and we pretended it was the metal oven torture room from the movie. Then I shouted at him through the open window to the shed. "All British soldiers and officers must work!" I used a Japanese accent, saying 'solyers' instead of 'soldiers' and sounding almost insane with anger like Colonel Saito did in the movie.

Seated inside the shed, I could see through the little window that Mr. Hawkins was shaking his head just like the brave British soldier in the movie. "I won't," he said. "And my officers won't." He added a really nice touch when he began whistling the tune from the movie from inside the toolshed to show me his spirit wasn't broken.

Later on, Mr. Hawkins wheeled himself back to the sitting room and invited me to come in and sit in the same big chair near the fireplace that Mom had been in. When I got there, he slowly made his way out of his wheelchair. Using his cane for support, he reached down and managed to pick up a piece of firewood and throw it on the pile that was already burning. I watched as lazy red and orange flames got stronger and began to dance all around the new piece of wood. Then, every so often, little chunks of wood from the old piece of wood underneath it would fall into the ash below and glow for a while before turning gray. It reminded me of a bright eye getting sleepy and finally closing.

"Yesterday you asked me if I had ever been suspended, remember?" said Mr. Hawkins.

Although I heard him, I guess I didn't react very much, since I was still in a sort of trance watching the flames sway and dance.

"Yeah," I said finally, forcing myself to look up at him. When our eyes met, he waited a few seconds before speaking. His face looked peaceful and kind. "Once again," he said softly, "I don't wish to embarrass you in the slightest, but I would like so very much to ask you a question or two. Would that be possible?"

I nodded.

"I get the feeling you were suspended from school because of something to do with fire. Would you be willing to tell me what happened?"

I thought about his question while my head turned back to the fire. I stared for a while, and watched for a time as a log caved in and fell below the iron platform holding it. Then I heard myself begin to speak. "Me and my friend Stuart were pretending to be good guys shooting down kamikazes. I lit matches and threw them down the stairwell to make it look like kamikaze planes were on fire like in the newsreels. A girl in the fifth grade told on us and Mr. Washington suspended me. He said I shouldn't feel bad about it. Later that night, Stuart's mom called up my Mom and told her she didn't want me to ever play with Stuart again because I was a bad influence."

"Oh, I see," said Mr. Hawkins thoughtfully.

I finally turned away from the flames and looked at him. At first, he just looked back at me. But after a while, he began to nod as if he understood it. It made me feel like I was right to trust him.

"And, uh, what do you think about everything now?"

"Now?"

"Mm-hmm."

"I don't know. Everyone got mad at me. Stuart can't be my friend. I didn't even get a chance to say goodbye to him. I got suspended and everything got bad."

"And you were only trying to..."

At first I shrugged my shoulders, but Mr. Hawkins' words helped me finish the sentence.

"...do something interesting. I wanted to show Stuart something cool. He was my best school friend, and I didn't have any others."

"I see. So you were actually trying to do something good, but it went terribly wrong somehow."

"Yeah, it went terribly wrong somehow."

Mr. Hawkins put on a thoughtful face. But it was a kind face.

"I wonder. If you could do it all over again, what would you have done differently?"

I thought about his question. I liked it for a lot of reasons. I tried to imagine all of the things that happened because of what I'd done.

"I guess I wouldn't have thrown the matches down the stairwell, and I wouldn't have lit the trash in the wastebasket on fire."

"Hmm. I didn't know about that second one."

I looked at Mr. Hawkins and was glad his face stayed calm. It felt good that I could talk to someone about it.

"Tell me, why did you light the fire in the trash can?"

I shrugged my shoulders, uncomfortable and not sure if I wanted to continue.

"Were you pretending when you did it?"

"Yeah," I said. "I pretended I had a special weapon that could put out fire and save the Allies."

"I see. Just trying to do something good again, eh?"

I nodded. I expected at any time Mr. Hawkins was going to tell me how dumb it was to do what I did, but it never happened.

"Want to know what I think?" he said.

I nodded.

"I think maybe pretending and fire aren't such a good mixture."

"Yeah," I said, thinking about it more and more.

"Something to think about maybe."

"Yeah. Something to think about maybe," I said, and noticed

that it meant a lot to me that Mr. Hawkins didn't seem to think I was bad.

Back in the game room, while working on the jigsaw puzzle, Mr. Hawkins began playing a bunch of different records he said were classical music. After a while he helped me recognize the sounds that came from each instrument by pretending to play them. He imitated plucking strings from a harp, and a while later wiggled his fingers as if playing a trumpet. By the way he did it, I got the feeling I might even know what the instruments looked like.

"Listen to that cello," he said at one point while leaning over the side of his wheelchair, eyes closed and plucking imaginary strings. And when the violin played, it was so beautiful and sad I could feel it moving my feelings all around. "Ah yes," he said sorrowfully, "Do you hear those woeful violins?"

Even though the classical music didn't sound as good as Buddy Holly, it had its own way of making me have a lot of feelings. At times, without even expecting it, I would find myself bouncing in my seat and waving my arms, while at other times I found myself just swaying back and forth to the different rhythms. Sometimes Mr. Hawkins would say the name of the guy who wrote the music, the composer, and I would try to remember which music they composed. My favorite composer of all was a guy named Beethoven. His stuff was unbelievable.

A while later, we finally took a break from classical music and Mr. Beethoven. Things got really quiet and it seemed like a good time to ask Mr. Hawkins a few questions. One question that had been on my mind ever since my dad first mentioned it was the first to come out of my mouth.

"Mr. Hawkins, what's overtime?"

Mr. Hawkins bent his head and looked up over the top of his glasses and smiled. "It's when you work more than you're supposed to."

I thought about his answer and I liked it. He had a way of making things sound simple.

"How much are you 'supposed' to work?"

"Most people work eight hours a day, five days a week."

"Is that called 'supposed to' time?" I joked.

"Very funny, Mr. Joker," he said with a smile. "Not exactly. It's called straight time."

Still smiling, I joked, "Is there anything called 'crooked time'?"

I knew because of a tiny smile that Mr. Hawkins got my jokes and liked them. But to my surprise, this time his expression got very serious and I didn't know what he was thinking until he said in a strong voice, "Yes, but only for crooks."

I got it right away, and his delivery was so good that it made us both start to roar with laughter. When we finally quieted down, he asked, "So where did you hear that word?"

"Do you mean about crooked time?"

"No, I mean about overtime," he said.

"Oh, I heard Dad say it to my uncle."

Mr. Hawkins nodded. "Do they work a lot of overtime?"

"Yeah. They leave early and come home late from their plant."

"Let me see now. So what you're saying is that they are the owners of the business, not the workers. Is that right?"

"Yeah, they're the owners. They sell brass tubes."

"I see.

"Is overtime good or bad?" I asked. "It sounds like it's bad when Dad talks about it."

Mr. Hawkins tilted his head from one side to the other considering. "I think a little overtime is good maybe, but not too much."

"How much do people get paid for straight time?" I asked.

Mr. Hawkins closed his eyes. "I think perhaps I have lost track. It used to be around one dollar an hour."

"Wow! That's a lot of money."

"Yes, to many people that is a lot of money."

"Mom told Dad she's working as much overtime as he is but that he still won't buy her a new washing machine."

"You don't say," he said.

"Yeah, I do."

There was a long pause. Then another question popped into my mind.

"Mr. Hawkins, what's time-and-a-half?"

Mr. Hawkins slid his glasses down his nose a bit as he thought. "It's an extra amount of money that you get for working more than eight hours in a day. It's like a special bonus for working so hard."

I listened carefully. I was getting pretty close to understanding this whole thing. "How much would the special bonus be?"

"Well, time-and-a-half is when you take the amount of money you are getting and you add half of that amount again to get the total."

That almost made sense to me, but not exactly, and so I didn't ask any more about it because I hated being confused, especially about adding and subtracting numbers.

"Dad doesn't know what he should pay the people who work for him. He says he needs something called an 'inventive' but that he doesn't know what it should be."

"An inventive?" repeated Mr. Hawkins. "Do you mean 'an incentive'?"

"Yeah, maybe. He says the polishers should go faster, but he doesn't know if that's right."

"I see."

"Yeah, it makes him sad— his problems at his business, I mean. His biggest problem is about overtime. He said he would be happy again once he figured it out."

"Uh-huh."

"He moved his whole business away from New York, so he's happier than before, but he's still not as happy as he was before he started this new business. We used to have more fun."

"You must miss having good times with him, I suspect."

"Yeah, I do," I said. "I do a lot."

CHAPTER 23

The next morning I woke up with the idea that I would eat a good breakfast, get cleaned and dressed, run down the street, and knock on Mr. Hawkins' door, and a few seconds later Tilden would let me in.

I guess I was being too sure of myself because when Mom told me at breakfast that I couldn't go over there because she didn't want me to 'wear out my welcome.' At first, I went into shock. A moment later, acting like someone who was about to die, I shouted, "I hafta go! Mr. Hawkins wants me to come over." But it didn't work. She just kept shaking her head. So I got louder and pleaded even more. "We have to do the puzzle and hear Beethoven and talk about Ted Williams and have a burping contest and make an ant farm. Don't ruin my life!"

"Listen to me," she answered while pointing a finger. "I don't care if you don't understand. Fish and guests smell after three days, and that's all I am going to say about it."

I didn't want to figure out what that meant, although I had an idea. All I wanted was to go. "Mom!" I yelled at the top of my lungs. "Don't say no! Call Mr. Hawkins yourself and see if he wants me to come over. I'll bet you a thousand million dollars he'll say yes."

"It doesn't matter what he says. I say no."

Things were going very badly and I knew I desperately needed to figure out something that had a better chance of working than begging and shouting. It came to me, somehow, an instant later. Acting very calm, I put my hands on my hips and faced her. "I don't think this is your department," I said.

Usually, I didn't mind if Mom reached over to kiss me, but this time, seeing her coming at me made me so mad I pulled away. Somehow she got a hold of my head anyway and gave it a big, yucky kiss.

"You are going to be someone great someday. Do you know that, Mark Lemon?" By the way she was smiling and her eyes were twinkling, and by calling me Mark Lemon, I could tell she loved me, and it felt kind of good. Still, I made sure to wipe off her kiss right in front of her as if it were disgusting grease. I didn't know how to get rid of my anger about not being able to go. I was thinking about kicking stuff around because I knew Mom hated when I did that. But just then, the most amazing miracle happened. It was the kind of thing that was so amazing it made me think God might be real after all. The phone rang and Mom picked up the receiver and said hello. A few seconds later I heard her say, "Oh, Mr. Hawkins, Mark and I were just talking about you." There was a long pause and then Mom said, "You're sure about this?" After listening further she said, "All right, Mr. Hawkins. I'll leave it in your hands. I'll rely on you to tell me if and when you are tiring or need a break."

Mom turned toward me, gave in to a smile, and winked.

"Yes!" I said, exploding with joy. I put my arms out, puffed up my cheeks and made the sound of a roaring engine and raced around the room like a fighter jet.

When I got to Mr. Hawkins' house, Tilden invited me in, just as I figured he would, and stuck me in the puzzle room, where I fixed the phone books on Mr. Hawkins' old wheelchair. As I climbed up on top of them and began to work on the puzzle, I heard Mr. Hawkins' voice coming from his study. He was on the phone talking.

"Tom! John Hawkins here. How have you been? Myself? Well, you know how it is—what's the expression? 'Getting old ain't for sissies.' I think that probably covers it. Tom, the reason for my call—are you still teaching the course on time and motion studies—the one for non-engineers? You are? Excellent! Tell me, will it cover how to calibrate a worker's productivity to his compensation?"

There was a pretty long silence, but then I could hear Mr. Hawkins begin to speak more excitedly.

"This sounds exactly like what I need. Are classes still at the community college? Gee, that's terrific. What a stroke of luck. What's that? No, not for me. My glory days are over by a long shot, but I may have someone for you. So good to speak with you again...yes...yes...bye."

I heard the sound of desk drawers opening and closing while Mr. Hawkins' whispered to himself. "Where on earth is my silver-blue stationery? I had it a second ago, and now... oh yes—on the shelf where I left it, no doubt."

I kept working on the puzzle, figuring that Mr. Hawkins would join me at any moment, but when he didn't, it came to me that maybe Tilden had forgotten to tell him I was in the game room, because a little later I couldn't hear Mr. Hawkins at all. I wheeled myself out of the room to go look for him when I was struck by the mouth-watering smell of freshly baked apples and cinnamon. I followed the scent all the way to the kitchen. When I got there I saw Rosa looking out the window into the backyard. Through the window I could see Vincenzo holding a hand drill in one hand and dragging a board with the other. I watched as he adjusted the board in such a way that he was able to free his right hand. With a shy look on his face, he waved to Rosa, who smiled, slowly lifted her hand, and waved back.

I guess it shocked her that I was in the room with her, because when she saw me she just about jumped through the roof.

"Qué sorpresa!" she said. "Oh, el Senior Marco. El Señor

Hawkins is on patio. He say you come when you here and I bring you manzanas...I mean apples and crisp."

I wheeled myself out to the patio where I saw Mr. Hawkins sitting. When he saw me he smiled, but it wasn't his regular, real smile. It was a kind of fake smile, like the kind my teachers used on parents' night. I wondered about it as I wheeled closer to him.

"Are you sad?" I asked.

He turned toward me, with a half of a real smile and began to nod slowly. "Perhaps a bit."

"Why?" I asked.

Mr. Hawkins took a deep breath and let out a sigh. "I suppose I miss my children, for one thing. It would be nice if they visited more often, especially because I would like to see my grandson. But they have their own lives to live and so perhaps I am not being entirely reasonable."

"How old is your grandson?" I asked, fluttering my legs.

"He is five now."

Mr. Hawkins pointed to the birdfeeder. "See the cardinal? She's the brown one. The male is bright red. He should be along any time now."

For several seconds neither of us spoke, until Mr. Hawkins said, "And the other thing is that I have a bum ticker and it puts a bit of a shiver into me from time to time."

I didn't understand what he meant about his ticker since I thought it meant he had a clock or something, but the more I thought about it, the more I realized it must mean something else. I got the feeling he didn't really want to talk about it, so instead I asked, "Mr. Hawkins, how did your legs get hurt?"

He looked at me and then back out toward the yard. "In an automobile accident many years ago. Now they're worse from age."

"Oh," was all I could think to say.

Rosa appeared carrying a tray. On it were forks, napkins, a covered dish, tall glasses already filled with ice, and a pitcher of juice. She smiled and placed the tray on a rolling, metal patio table that she wheeled closer to the stone table at Mr. Hawkins' side. As she scooped out the steaming apple crisp onto Mr. Hawkins' plate, she looked at him for a sign of when to stop serving. When there was a good-sized mound on his plate he raised his hand and said, "Es bueno. Suficiente!"

Rosa turned to me and began scooping some onto my plate. When it got full enough, I raised my hands just like Mr. Hawkins and said, "Es bueno."

Rosa laughed and headed toward the kitchen. The smell of the apple crisp was so wonderful we dove into it without another word. As some of the cinnamon on the apples dripped down my fork and onto my wrist, I forgot my manners and licked it.

Mr. Hawkins thought it tasted great too.

"My Lord, this certainly is wonderful," he said.

I watched his eyes close and his whole face twist up like he had never tasted anything better in his entire life.

"Is the Lord the same as God?" I asked.

Mr. Hawkins looked across the table at me and put down his fork. "Yes, I suppose they are synonymous," he said.

"Syn...?"

"Uh, the same. Yes. I think both words have more or less the same meaning."

I waited before asking my next question, thinking maybe it was somehow not right to ask, but I wanted to know.

"Mr. Hawkins, do you believe in God?"

Mr. Hawkins seemed startled by my question. After studying me for several seconds, he bent his head and unconsciously began to feel his legs while he thought. He thought for much longer than I ever would have imagined. Finally, looking up, he said very softly, "I'm not sure."

It was an answer I would never have expected. Mr. Hawkins didn't seem like the kind of guy who was unsure about anything.

"Do you think when I'm old as you, I'll be sure?" I asked

He looked at me and then out onto his land and nodded. With a voice that sounded very serious and kind of far away, he said, "I hope so. I hope so."

"Mr. Hawkins, do you ever pray?"

Mr. Hawkins seemed to be thinking seriously about my question.

"I…uh…do have a prayer that I say…uh…once in a while."

"Just one prayer?"

His head swayed back and forth just a bit as he seemed to weigh my question. Then smiling, he said, "Sometimes one is all you need."

"What do you pray for?" I asked. "Do you ever pray for your legs to get better?"

He cleared his throat. "No. I don't."

"How come?"

He was smiling now, I think because I asked him so many questions in a row.

"Because I know they won't."

"Oh."

"What about you, my curious friend? Do you ever pray?" he asked.

I thought about his question. "Yeah. Sometimes."

"And what do you pray for, may I ask?"

"Um, different things I need. Or to get out of trouble. But mostly for Dad to be happy again like he used to be."

Mr. Hawkins nodded, saying only, "I see."

"And what about you?" I asked, remembering it was his turn.

Mr. Hawkins bent his head and seemed to think for a long time. It was like we had a kind of deal to tell each other the truth, the whole truth, and nothing but the truth like on Perry Mason. He spoke slowly and carefully.

"I pray for the serenity to accept the things I cannot change, the courage to change the things I can, and the wisdom to know the difference."

I could hardly move. Even though I didn't know what the "seren-something" word meant, I think I understood what the whole idea of the prayer was. It meant like trying to be satisfied with what you have and to be smart about appreciating it. It was such a simple prayer and yet so grown-up sounding.

After a while, we both went back to our apple crisp and the delicious taste made us begin to moan all over again. At one point we began to moan extra loud, trying to outdo each other. When we'd laughed ourselves out, Mr. Hawkins looked like he was feeling better. With a new burst of energy, he cupped his hands and called out toward the house using his serious business voice.

"Tilden! I need to see you."

"Follow me, Mr. Mark," he said turning the wheels of his wheelchair and calling over his shoulder. "Right after I speak with Tilden on a business matter, we'll have some fun."

He went so fast, by the time I caught up with him he was in the foyer, already speaking with Tilden.

"First, try the public library," he said. "Look up everything that you can find on the—" For some reason Mr. Hawkins stopped and then looked in my direction and hesitated before continuing. But then in a kind of code he finished by saying, "…uh…on the aforementioned subject. Also, look into any other related disorders, and see if they lead to an abnormal interest in…eh…the previously described. Make sure to check out the reference library as well. Speak to Jane Simmons there and get her help if you get stumped. She should allow you to take out any reference books that you need. Just sign for them. If she tells you they can't be removed, have her call me. I want anything and everything she has on the subject."

I watched Tilden take a few notes in his appointment book.

"Yes, sir. I will attend to it right away."

"Thank you, Tilden."

"Certainly, sir."

Almost as soon as Tilden left, Mr. Hawkins asked me if I wanted to play Monopoly. When I said yes, he asked me if I wouldn't mind playing with two pairs of dice instead of just one. He said it made the game much better and everything went faster and you could get around the board and pass Go and collect $200 quicker. I could see his point, so I went along.

Adding up the numbers on all four dice was hard at first. I was used to adding up to twelve, but now there could be as many as four sixes. When I asked Mr. Hawkins how much it was, he told me to add it in my head. He also said he had an extra rule he liked to use whenever he played Monopoly. The rule was you had to add up the total of the dice correctly, or the other guy could challenge you and make you pay a fine of $5 of your Monopoly money if you got it wrong. If you lost a challenge twice, you had to give the other guy $10, and so on up to $500. To me, it was a silly rule, but Mr. Hawkins liked it so much I decided to go along with that one, too, so I wouldn't disappoint him. At first I had to work hard counting up how much extra the other two dice were and adding it to the amount I already knew, but after a while it got easier. Something else that was kind of odd was that he asked me to make change a lot, even when he didn't really need it. Like this one time, when he landed on one of my properties and had to pay rent of $27. Even though he had the exact amount, he gave me a $50 bill and asked me to give him the right change.

"Your change is $23," I said.

"Sounds right," he said. "Your turn."

This new way of playing Monopoly was a little hard in the beginning, but after an hour or so, I saw patterns I had never seen before. Like, if two dice added up to nine and the other two added up to eleven, I could add them together and say, "Twenty." There were even a couple of times when Mr. Hawkins added up his numbers wrong and I called him on it. He acted a little surprised, and said, "No, that can't be right. Let me see. Oh yes, you are right once again," and again he paid me the fine.

I began to notice how I was getting really quick at adding the dice and making change. It helped that Mr. Hawkins was a good sport when he lost, because he lost both games that afternoon.

That evening at dinner, as Mom shoveled piles of food onto all our plates, I thought about what a great day it had been. To top it off, Dad had dinner with us and was in a good mood and made an effort to talk to all of us. Ever since the big argument with

Mom, he'd been very quiet and seemed to be thinking a lot. I didn't know what he was thinking about of course, but I was feeling less scared around him. I think everyone else was feeling that way, too. A really good sign was that on the couple of nights during the week when he managed to come home at his regular shift time, he wanted the rest of the family to eat with him. He just ate slowly, and let everyone chatter as much as they wanted. That's why, when he said to me, "So what did you do today, Zeendala?" it was great to hear and I was happy to tell him.

"Played with Mr. Hawkins," I said. "Also, Tilden."

"Tilden?" Dad asked.

"He's the servant," said Mom.

Dad nodded. "Mom says you do puzzles and play Monopoly with Mr. Hawkins. Do you do that all day long?"

"Yeah, and we play sniper and watch movies and have jousts and make up characters and stories about Knights of the Round Table. And we listen to Beethoven and Bach and shoot Nazis and eat apple crisp."

Dad went from a grin to a bigger grin, and soon he was even laughing. "Is that all?"

I had a feeling he was joking, but seeing him so happy made me want to go on anyway.

"We have wheelchair races, but only when Tilden's not around. And, uh, we eat spaghetti 'mit' a meat a ball. We say it that way because Vincenzo says it that way and it makes us laugh. We play German tank commander. Mr. Hawkins is the commander and his wheelchair is his tank. He sticks his head through a hole in a tarp Vincenzo cut for him that covers his whole wheelchair. He uses a cardboard tube Vincenzo got from the dump to be his pretend cannon. Tilden pushes Mr. Hawkins all around in it. Tilden is a little skinny, but much stronger than I thought. I blow him up sometimes when I blow up Mr. Hawkins with rotten tomatoes from the garden. Sometimes we sing 'The Star Spangled Banner'. Rosa has a good voice. Everyone likes to sing except Tilden. Mr. Hawkins is teaching me Spanish. He and Rosa speak it. Rosa likes

Vincenzo, I think, and I'm pretty sure he likes her."

"Who is Vincenzo?" asked Mom.

"He works on the lawn and fixes stuff in the house. He speaks Italian. It's hard to understand him."

"What else do you do at Mr. Hawkins' house?" Dad asked.

I thought I'd already told Dad a ton of things, but I guess he was interested to hear more, so I went on.

"We have burping contests. We drink root beer first to help make 'em be louder and longer. The loudest and longest one wins. Is it disgusting to burp?" I asked.

"Yes!" Mom said.

"Well, it depends," Dad said.

"Mr. Hawkins said that in some cultures it's a sign of a good appetite." I paused for a second. "What's a culture?" I asked.

"It's hard to explain," Mom said smiling and laughing.

Dad looked on quietly. I knew he couldn't explain it either.

"Anything else that you do?" he asked.

I got the feeling Dad might be trying to find out something in particular but didn't want to actually ask. After telling him about so many different things, I figured it should be enough, but since he wasn't yet satisfied I went on.

"Sometimes we take a snooze and sometimes we eat cookies for our sweet tooth."

"Where do you take a snooze?" Dad asked in a slightly different tone.

"On the couch or in the game room or the sitting room. Wherever I fall asleep."

"And Mr. Hawkins, where does he snooze?"

"Upstairs or in his wheelchair."

Dad was quiet after that. It was as if he found out something he had been concerned about and now he wasn't.

I had nearly cleaned my plate when I asked, "What's a bum ticker?"

Mom and Dad looked at each other. Finally, with a voice that was serious and had a twinge of sadness in it Mom answered. "It means a bad heart."

"Oh," I said as I thought about some of the things Mr. Hawkins had said and done and started to put the pieces together. Then I said 'oh' again and began thinking more and more about it.

After dinner, I went off and started playing by myself with my army guys. I made up different battle scenes and imagined what would happen. I wondered how many casualties there would be for the good guys and bad guys and I wondered how it would look with dead bodies everywhere, like in the movies. But for some reason I was distracted the whole time. No matter how many times I tried to concentrate, my mind kept wandering back to Mr. Hawkins. I wondered if he was awake or asleep? Was he looking at the puzzle and planning what we should work on together, or was he figuring out something completely different to do the next time I came over? I wondered if he might want to see me as much as I wanted to see him. I wondered if he was thinking about how much fun we had, like I was thinking about it. That's when I realized I had to go over there tonight, even if it just meant being nearer to him and his gigundo house. I knew it was too late to knock on his door, but still, being closer to him seemed like the only thing on earth that I wanted to do. It was like when I once heard Dad say to Mom that I was "obsessed" and I figured out what it meant by the words around it. I think he was talking about Coney Island and how, after going on all of those great rides I asked Dad if we could please, please, please do it again the next day.

Since it was dark out and I knew Mom and Dad would never give me permission, I decided they might go easier on me if they found a note explaining where I was and why I went there.

I sneaked into Bonnie's room and ripped out another sheet of paper from her notebook and wrote: "Dear Mom and Dad, I got obsest and went to see Mr. Hawkins. I will come home prity soon. Luv, Mark".

I wrote the letter in my best penmanship, hoping it might help me if nothing else did. With a quick, last-minute prayer, I grabbed my Yankee cap and a sweater and sneaked down the stairs in my socks. When the coast was clear, I put on my sneakers, slithered out the front door, and raced down the street to get closer to the place where all the fun in my life was coming from.

I figured out that if I went to the house next to Mr. Hawkins' I could sneak into the back yard and climb the wall more quickly. And in less than a minute, that's exactly what I did. Lying flush against the flat bluestone surface atop the wall, I felt happy as I scanned the darkness. The flowers were especially beautiful because of the way the garden lighting hit them. The sky was filled with stars and the night air was cool and crisp and I didn't care at all that I was alone. I just looked all around and remembered all the things me and Mr. Hawkins did earlier in the day. I must have been there for at least ten minutes thinking about it, when I was surprised by sounds coming from one of the second story rooms not too far from me. A few seconds later a light went on and it made me shrink back into the darkness where I could more easily stay hidden. I watched as a tall, thin man came out carrying a lantern, which he put on a hook over the balcony. His movements were stiff and familiar, and even before he turned his head, I knew it was Tilden.

He went back and forth three times, each time bringing more things. By the end of his third trip he had set up a small table, rocking chair, two wine glasses, and an ice bucket with a bottle of wine in it. He fidgeted with everything several times until finally it was set in a way that satisfied him. A minute or two later Mr. Hawkins appeared and wheeled himself onto the balcony.

From where I was, Mr. Hawkins and Tilden seemed almost "lit up" like the way people are when they are on a bright stage. Most surprising of all, though, was how clear their voices were. It reminded me of this lake I once went to where the water was very still. I could hear people talking as if they were right next to me even though they were far away.

Mr. Hawkins was wearing his favorite old, loyal sweater and what looked like his favorite old, loyal, beat up Boston Red Sox cap. He turned his head and looked at Tilden.

"Ah, Tilden. What have we here?"

Tilden took the bottle from the bucket and handed it to Mr. Hawkins. "A nice ten-year-old Beaujolais, sir, the type you are most fond of. I was told it has a nice bouquet and a smooth texture—yet a tad on the sweet side."

"Ah, yes," said Mr. Hawkins. "A good choice. Especially for a crystal-clear night like this. By all means, let's have at it."

Tilden paused briefly. "Sir, can we agree on a two-glass maximum so as not to disregard Dr. Reed's instructions entirely?"

Mr. Hawkins nodded. "Indeed we can, my friend."

I watched as Mr. Hawkins turned and stared out over his yard. He was quiet for several seconds until he finally said, "All my life I have had things pretty much my own way. Would you agree, Tilden?"

Tilden thought for a time and then nodded. "Yes, sir. I would have to agree."

"Do you know, Tilden, at one point, when production was peaking during the Great War, I had 850 workers in my employ?"

Wow, I thought. That was a lot of workers. I felt a tiny piece of jagged cement under my arm and carefully adjusted myself so I could brush it aside without making a sound.

"No, sir, I didn't. That is an admirable workforce by any standard."

"Yes, Tilden. Eight hundred fifty-three to be exact—according to the payroll records."

Tilden listened carefully as his hands worked on the bottle, eventually prying the cork loose with some kind of metal thing.

"We were making helmets and shell casings by the millions for the armed services, using a new process that none of our competitors had caught onto yet. We were the first to use pressed steel instead of the traditional materials that were hard to work with and far too heavy. In retrospect, I can see that I had great foresight and great courage to invest in the equipment that we used. Each piece of heavy equipment cost a fortune, but I could see the potential when no one else seemed to be able to. Do you know why that was, Tilden?"

"No, sir. I do not."

Mr. Hawkins took the glass Tilden poured for him, sniffed it, and swished around the liquid. Then he took a sip and put down the glass on the little table between them.

"Because I had imagination! I could envision and imagine what was coming."

Tilden took a sip. "Yes, sir. I think I understand."

There was a short period of silence as they sipped and looked around the yard.

"I never had imagination, sir," said Tilden. "In fact, to be perfectly candid, I find the very concept difficult to understand. Certainly, if I were to see a child sitting precariously on a swing or a jungle gym, I would have concern as to what might follow. But that forward look is about as far as I seem to be able to see. For better or worse, that it is the true extent of my imagination. In fact, it is feasible that what I have described is not imagination at all, but rather, a certain wisdom gained from experience."

Mr. Hawkins nodded thoughtfully as Tilden continued.

"My inherent nature seems to have suggested that I pursue a life of service, wherein I could accommodate my desire for precision and order. I seem to find more reward in such efforts than most people."

Mr. Hawkins adjusted himself and looked back at his friend. "You have done it admirably, Tilden. Very admirably indeed."

"Sir, did I ever tell you that my mother once confided that I was born precisely on my due date?"

Mr. Hawkins laughed. "No, you never told me that."

"It seems my sense of order, which includes punctuality, precision, and exactitude, was evidently apparent on the first day of my life. I must say, they are traits I value and hold dear to this day."

"Precision and exactitude, eh?" repeated Mr. Hawkins with a nod.

"My mother once expressed to me and her other four offspring that I was a child who naturally took to making my bed and cleaning my room without ever being told." Tilden paused for a few seconds to sniff the wine and take a swallow. "Of course, such praise was too much for my fellow siblings to bear. As a result, they set about to ravage and plunder my room and belongings without end in an attempt to 'normalize' me."

Mr. Hawkins smiled. And for a while the smile lingered. But as time went on and no words came from either of them, a more serious, thoughtful look came over Mr. Hawkins. I heard an owl hooting in the distance and watched Mr. Hawkins put down his glass. He turned, looked out onto his land and said, "I have been fearful lately."

Tilden put down his glass. "Fearful of what, sir?"

Mr. Hawkins took a few seconds before turning back to Tilden to look at him directly. "Feeding tubes, Tilden. And those obnoxious-looking bags that the hospital gives you when you can't get up and go on your own. Truth be told, they are but symbols of something far more ominous."

"Sir?"

Mr. Hawkins' head turned again ever so slightly as he looked to a distant part of the garden and continued to speak. His words seemed to be directed to the land as much as to Tilden.

"My dreams have become uncomfortable. The common theme in all of them is a sense of lost control. Each dream, in its own way, says that I'll no longer be able to have things the way I want them—or the way I've always had them—that I will no longer be able to call the shots— be independent and make my own choices."

Tilden listened without moving.

"You know, Tilden, it isn't the end that I fear or even the pain that most certainly accompanies the final journey. It is much more about the inability to control the 'when' and 'how' that bothers me. Having always had it, I fear the loss of choice more than anything. These days they let you linger in the hospital long after you're ready to throw in the towel. I think it's wrong, and I don't want that kind of ending to a life that has been as full and rich as mine."

Some time went by and they each sipped their wine. Mr.

Hawkins lifted his glass of wine and put it right in front of his eyes as if to study it up close. Then he put it down again, took a deep breath and blew it out.

"I came to terms with my limitations long ago when circumstances put me in this chair in the first place. It was a difficult time. I had lost Katherine and was a broken man. I believe I told you. Yes, I am sure I did. I don't know how, but I resolved to play the hand I was dealt and carry on. Yet, even that decision was not without a hefty dose of doubt. The doubt, you see, was whether to go on at all."

There was another long pause.

"In the end I chose life. I did so because I could see that even from a wheelchair I had the means to positively impact the world—or at least a small part of it…while… perhaps…making amends for past sins. And, although my body would not be able to do what it once could, there was enough left of me spiritually, emotionally, and financially, to make the case that life could still offer meaning to a man like me. That is why I carried on, Tilden, and that is why to this day I know I made the right decision."

Mr. Hawkins turned away again and looked out over the land and spoke to it.

"But the world has shifted. What lies ahead is much less clear and far less certain."

His face winced as if his words caused him a sharp pain.

"I find it worrisome to consider that I might linger after a stroke or heart attack, and that in such an enfeebled state I might not have much of a say about anything—worse still, that I might become a burden to one or more of my children. They have suffered enough from my actions. It is not how I have lived my life and it is not how I wish to end it."

There was another long pause, and I found myself wondering what Mr. Hawkins meant when he said his children had suffered enough from him. It didn't seem possible that such a good person would make anyone suffer, especially his own children.

"Do you know what else, Tilden?"

Tilden looked straight at Mr. Hawkins but said nothing.

A smile came across Mr. Hawkins' face as he spoke. "I am keenly aware that this imagination of mine, so beautifully rekindled in recent days, will not, and cannot, sustain itself indefinitely. Imaginative thoughts, like beautiful, blooming flowers, all have their season. And in this season, it took an eight-year-old boy with an exceptional imagination to scale ten-foot walls and reignite something in me that I thought was long gone. You know, Tilden, there is a place in my heart that keeps telling me that it was as if our two imaginative souls needed to find each other, and because of my difficulty going outside these walls, he had to find his way in."

I remained still, but the joy I felt inside was like nothing I'd ever felt before. It made me want to sing. I had no idea that just by being who I am, that it could make someone like me so much—especially someone who was becoming more and more important to me. I could feel tears in my eyes.

Mr. Hawkins looked up at the sky. "My little friend will grow up, Tilden. This is but a brief interlude in his life—a brief intersecting of our paths. He has much to do and many mountains to climb. This glorious state of unfettered imagination that we are treasuring together will soon be forced to give way. When that time comes, Tilden, he will be gone and I will be back on my own. And this time around, I am less certain about my will to manage it."

There was a long silence. Finally, Mr. Hawkins cleared his throat and switched over to a very business-like way of speaking.

"Tilden, you know I have named you as the executor of my will, do you not?"

"Yes, sir, I do."

"And the money put aside for you in trust— I take it you are satisfied that it will provide a comfortable retirement and more?"

"Yes, sir. You have been most generous, extraordinarily so, in fact."

"Good. Tilden, I would like you to prepare the paperwork with our attorney to provide for Rosa and Vincenzo as well. They've been here long enough to deserve it. Give them each three months' pay for every year served, and put aside the same amount again for any health-related needs that might arise. This should be done regardless of where they may choose to be re-employed. Can you see to this, Tilden?

"Yes, sir."

"Good," said Mr. Hawkins.

There was another unusually long silence, this time broken by Tilden. "Sir, if I may be so bold?"

The old man nodded.

"Well, sir, I mean, after all, what is the urgency?"

Mr. Hawkins looked serious as he met Tilden's gaze.

"You never know, Tilden. It's not only important to look forward and see what might be approaching, but to pay heed also, to how fast it is moving."

I stayed low in the same position for several minutes before sliding back down the wall and heading home, my head filled with a thousand thoughts and my eyes blurry from so many different feelings.

CHAPTER 24

The next morning, the first thing to greet me was the smell of Mom's banana cake. The second thing—and I really don't know why, were the words Tilden used when he talked about living a life of service so he could pursue precision and order. I found myself trying to say the whole sentence again and again while looking in the mirror. I wanted to see if I could get the words to roll out as if I really knew what I was talking about.

Downstairs, Dad and Bonnie were almost finished with breakfast, and Bonnie was beginning to collect her books for school as I sat down.

With a potholder in her hand, Mom opened the oven and took out a second banana cake.

Dad noticed it right away. "Bea, why two cakes?"

"I'm going to give one to Mr. Hawkins," she said, placing it on the stove top.

"Hmm. Lucky him," said Dad.

"Lucky us," Mom corrected. "It's like having our own nine to five babysitter."

"And you don't think our boy is wearing out his welcome going over there every day and staying until suppertime?"

Mom thought a bit before answering. "No. I've had more than one conversation about it with Mr. Hawkins and each time I mention it, he insists it's not a problem at all."

"And, uh, you trust the man?"

Mom seemed to give extra thought to Dad's words, but then spoke with certainty, "Yes. I do."

"It doesn't seem at all odd to you? You know, the two of them spending so much time together?"

Mom hesitated for only a second.

"No. And don't get me wrong. I've thought about it. But no, it feels genuine. I met him, we spoke, and I'm satisfied. I had my doubts at first, just being a mother, but no, he's a fine, intelligent, well-meaning man and I'm not worried."

Satisfied, Dad went back to his breakfast, ate a few more bites, and then for some reason continued to stare down at his plate. It didn't take long for everyone to notice. But then, to everyone's surprise, he slowly picked up his fork and knife, placed it on his plate, and walked over to the sink with it. Mom's expression of shock was unmistakable. And Dad was careful not to look at her. It was as if he were trying something out and wasn't sure yet how he felt about it or what to say about it. I guess he broke a thousand years of tradition or something, and that was why it was such a big deal to her.

"Uh, what was I saying? Oh yes—" she said, stumbling over her words. "I, uh, told Mr. Hawkins, uh, that it won't be much longer before Mark is back in school."

"Good," said Dad. "Sounds like you have the bases covered." He looked down at his watch and over at Bonnie. "Bonala, time to go."

After they left the house, Mom remained very quiet, but nodded her head to herself over and over again. It was obvious to me that what Dad did made her happy, so I decided it wouldn't be that hard to do it, too. So I did. A second later, she grabbed me and planted a big kiss on my head, and that's how I knew it was something she really liked.

"Is bringing our dishes to the sink someone's department or everyone's department?" I asked.

Mom smiled again and kissed me again for some reason. Then she said, "I just need to put in a load of laundry and I'll be ready to walk you down the street and bring the cake to Mr. Hawkins. Watch Arlene for me, okay, sweetie? Aunt Jenny should be here anytime to babysit her while we go to Mr. Hawkins' house."

In no time at all we were down the street and ringing Mr. Hawkins' doorbell. Just like on the other days, Tilden answered, and welcomed us in. Soon I was in the game room, sorting out straight-edged pieces that helped to make the outline of the puzzle, when I heard Mom and Mr. Hawkins begin to speak.

"Oh, this is so very kind of you," he said. "And the aroma is magnificent. But isn't it I who should be welcoming you into our neighborhood with such a lovely gift?"

"Mr. Hawkins, you have already done more than I could have ever asked for. You took our lonely boy and filled him with excitement. It has been a wonderful help for him. It's been very hard, losing all his friends—and on such short notice."

"Ah, yes. That is difficult."

I got down from my chair and went into my spying position so I could see everyone. Just then, Tilden came back into the room and looked to Mom and then Mr. Hawkins. "Would either of you care for some tea?"

"Oh, thank you, but no," said Mom. "I will only be staying for a very short time. I really only stopped by to leave the cake and say thank you."

Mr. Hawkins looked up at Tilden and shook his head. Then he motioned to the cake and Tilden picked it up and started toward the kitchen with it. Calling after him, Mr. Hawkins said, "And don't eat the whole thing yourself, Tilden—be considerate of others."

Mom got the joke right away and began to laugh. It made Mr. Hawkins laugh too. Tilden called back, "I had in mind selling it on the black market, sir, where I am certain it will fetch a better price than the appalling wages you pay me."

Mom laughed again even harder, as Mr. Hawkins called back, "Good one, Tilly. That one goes in your column. Very good."

I was smiling, too, as I watched them.

"I had been meaning to call you, Mrs. Leonard."

"Me?"

"Yes. I thought you might be interested in the results of some of our research. That is, research conducted by Tilden and me."

Mom looked surprised.

"Last time we spoke you imparted a number of concerns about a certain issue. The, uh... incendiary issue, I believe."

Mom didn't say anything. Mr. Hawkins hesitated. "Shall I go on?" he asked.

Mom thought about it for a second or two. "Yes, yes, please go on."

Mr. Hawkins smiled. "I took from our last meeting that you were concerned about a certain person's troubling fascination with incendiaries."

Mom nodded unsurely.

"Yes, well, I hope you don't mind, but Tilden and I took it upon ourselves to do a little reading on the subject, to see if we might broaden our understanding of it."

Mom looked stunned.

"We checked out a few different possibilities, including, eh, hem, 'Romania', as in 'pyro' as well as other so-called fascination disorders." Mr. Hawkins stopped speaking and looked to Mom and waited."

"Please go on," she said.

"I felt that given the constraints you were facing with your husband, that such information might be helpful. I hope you believe the sincerity of my intentions."

Mom nodded. "What did you find out?"

"Well," said Mr. Hawkins clearing his throat a bit, "'Romania' as in 'pyro' is a compulsive disorder that has at its core an irresistible urge prior to acting. Most...eh... 'Romanians' seem to have clearly identifiable mental illnesses or some type of obvious impulse control disorder."

Mom looked worried. "So are you saying, that—what? Is this our...?"

"On the contrary. And please don't be alarmed. The individual previously referenced exhibits none of these characteristics. Perhaps one could argue weakly that there was an impulse disorder in the mix, but it is far more likely typical of his age. I have...come to know the individual well enough to be rather sure of that."

"But you are not a licensed psychiatrist?"

"That is correct."

There was a long pause. "Mr. Hawkins, do you have children?"

Mr. Hawkins seemed surprised by her question, but after a few seconds he smiled.

"You are wise to ask. Our children are no doubt the dividing line between theory and practice. But, more to your question, I have two sons and a daughter. My daughter, the youngest, and a great blessing for me in my later life, is scheduled to come up with her husband and my grandson next week to visit. They live in North Carolina and only get up this way once a year or so. My middle child, a son, was married previously, and my oldest never did. He is a paleontologist and I hear from him once in a while, usually by phone. My younger son helped run the business after I retired, but after a time he decided it wasn't what he wanted to do with his life. There were some issues between us, but nothing I thought to be insurmountable. I confess it would be nice to see him a bit more often."

"I'm sorry. Thank you for your candor," Mom said softly.

"Of course."

"Mr. Hawkins, I cut you off regarding your...eh...research. Was there more that you wanted to say?"

"Yes. A bit. In our readings, we came across a few papers advocating personality-modifying medications or some other rather bizarre behavioral modifications. These papers are not credible to either Tilden or myself, and I mention them only because it was

listed as an option for those unfortunates who might be more
troubled than our...eh...subject. Beyond that, there seems to be
very little on the subject at this time."

"So, what do you conclude?"

"I believe what you are seeing at work, is the innate curiosity
of one who is quite gifted. This 'someone' needs to quench a type
of thirst— a thirst born of imagination and creativity. In searching
those limitless boundaries, the line between reality and fantasy is
sometimes blurred, as in this instance where the favored prop and
its dangerous nature, are not fully understood."

I didn't understand most of what Mr. Hawkins said, but Mom
seemed to.

"What are you suggesting?"

"Well, I'm not licensed to do that, but I can give you my
opinion."

Mom nodded.

"I believe you have a very normal, healthy, eh, situation...and
that time will prove to be a great ally. I expect this plant will outgrow
its pot. However, because we are speaking of one so imaginative,
the challenge might at times be greater than for others with less
imaginative proclivities."

I loved Mom and really liked Mr. Hawkins, but I hated their
stinky code. I couldn't understand any of it, and yet I somehow had
a feeling it was about me.

"Go on, please," said Mom.

"There isn't a lot more. It is probably true that the cat's
fascination with the ball of yarn might continue for a while, and
then, perhaps, when he has played with it enough, he might not
find it as interesting as it once was, especially if it were possible to
remove the taboo nature of the experimentation."

Mom's eyes narrowed as she stared at Mr. Hawkins.

"The only other thing I would add," he said, "is that the
curiosity part of this equation might reach saturation faster if more
experimentation was allowed rather than less."

Mom squinted as if she couldn't quite believe what she was

hearing. "I was with you until this second. Are you saying that I should involve the...uh...cat with the yarn more often so the cat tires of it rather than remove the ball and provide a different plaything?"

Mr. Hawkins leaned forward in his chair as if to get close enough to deliver an important message. "Ah, but this is the cat's favorite plaything, and it is what it needs to understand, not something else, or it would have been solved a while ago and much more easily, I suspect."

Mom looked interested but unsure.

"What I am saying, Mrs. Leonard, is that, if the cat is going to be involved with the yarn and has a strong urge to do so, wouldn't it be best if you were nearby at such times? That way, if the cat knots up the yarn you will be in a position to untangle it. And if the cat is, say, curious, and needs to experiment until the curiosity is satisfied, doesn't it amount to the same thing? In any case, anticipation and preparation would seem to make sense. As I see it, the alternative is random experimentation without supervision. And in that scenario there clearly is risk, perhaps even substantial risk."

Mom looked as if a part of her wanted to run out the door while the other part wanted to stay and listen. After a while, Mr. Hawkins said, "A penny for your thoughts?"

"My thoughts?" she said, looking in my general direction before looking back to Mr. Hawkins. "I only know if I can get through this—if he can get through this—I will throw my hands up to the heavens and thank almighty God."

Mr. Hawkins didn't say another word, but instead nodded ever so slightly.

"Thank you, Mr. Hawkins. Each idea you have given me is like an extraordinary gift, given at a time when I am truly desperate for support and direction." Mom took a few steps toward the door before turning as she remembered something. "Mr. Hawkins, the next two days are Jewish holidays so Mark will be busy with our family. Then we have plans to visit a school, so it may be a while before he can see you. However, if I know my son, he will want to see you as soon as possible, and may nag me to the point where I will want him to visit you for my own survival. That's why you will forgive me if I ask you again if you're tiring of his visits. If you are—"

"I am not tiring at all, Mrs. Leonard. It has been a great pleasure getting to know Mark." He leaned toward her, "Also, I take naps during the day and that keeps me sharp. I look forward to seeing him whenever it is convenient. In the meantime, have a happy holiday."

"Thank you. If I don't see you before their visit, please enjoy your time with your daughter, son-in-law, and grandson."

"Yes, I will, indeed. Thank you. And to you and all of your family, may I wish you a L'shanah Tova. I believe that is the correct expression. Yes?"

Mom smiled. "Yes, it is," she said. "That is it exactly. Thank you."

CHAPTER 25

A little while after Mom left, me and Mr. Hawkins sat down to play Monopoly. Right away he asked if I wouldn't mind playing with six dice this time instead of our usual four. It sounded crazy, but because it was something Mr. Hawkins wanted to do, I said okay.

As the game went along, I noticed I was getting very, very good at adding up the numbers. When the dice were rolled, I could just look at them and know how much they added up to. And making change was so easy I started doing it in my head. After about an hour, Mr. Hawkins said, "Well, you seem to be pretty good at adding and subtracting. You sure are able to add single numbers and make change quickly."

It was all true, even though I never thought about it as adding and subtracting. What was important to me was whether I won or not. That was when Mr. Hawkins said, "Would you like to learn more about math? Like how to add and subtract double digits?"

So far, everything Mr. Hawkins had ever suggested turned out to be fun, so I felt confident his idea to teach me about double digits might be fun, too, even though it sounded like something teachers in school would try to make me learn.

"Okay," I said, shrugging.

"Excellent!" he said.

For the next hour, Mr. Hawkins taught me about adding and subtracting numbers in a way that was as much fun as playing Monopoly and as interesting as I could have ever imagined. I was feeling great about everything he'd taught me, and I had a lot of math questions I wanted to ask him, but he must have gotten pretty tired, because just as I was about to speak, I heard him say, "snooze," and without so much as another word, his head bent forward and he began to snore. I found myself looking at him and thinking about what kind of person he was. I wondered if he knew how much he helped people, and I wondered if the people he helped appreciated it as much as I did. I thought to myself that when I got to be a grown-up, I would try to help tons of people, just like he did.

I must have fallen asleep right after him, because the next thing I knew I was looking at a wide-awake Mr. Hawkins sitting up in his wheelchair and I was the one just waking up.

"Did you have a good nap?" he asked.

"Yeah," I answered groggily. "Did you have a good snooze?"

"Yes," he said. "'Twas a short one but a good one."

"Is it lunchtime?" I asked.

"It is," he answered as he sniffed the air. "And I smell something good. Let's find out what Rosa is up to."

He wheeled himself toward the kitchen and I wheeled myself along right behind him. By the time we got there, the wonderful smell of fried fish was making my mouth water. When we started eating, I noticed Mr. Hawkins liked to dip his French fries in ketchup and roll them around until they were almost covered with it, just like I did.

Using ketchup reminded me of the time me and Jeffrey pretended ketchup was blood. We smeared a bunch of it on our faces and pretended we were bleeding while we made lots of different faces in the mirror. Of course I couldn't show anyone in my family because I knew Mom would probably say something in Yiddish that meant "God forbid" and Dad probably would say something about how it was a sin to play with food and a waste of money, and Bonnie would probably put it on her list for Judge Copperbrain. But here, in Mr. Hawkins' house, I felt free enough to do just about anything. That's why I took a chance and let some of the ketchup from my fries smear along the side of my mouth while I called out to him, "Mr. Hawkins, I've been shot."

Immediately turning toward me, he said, "My heavens. What shall we do?" When he turned away from me, I thought maybe he was going to pretend to be a doctor or something to help me, but when he turned back around I saw he'd put ketchup all over his lips and chin too. It looked so funny it made me cry with laughter. Making it even funnier was the way he sounded when he cried out. I grabbed the ketchup bottle and tried to pour as much out as I could, hoping to have blood all over my face and not just on the side of my mouth. That way I could make my fake wounds seem even bigger.

Mr. Hawkins motioned for the bottle and I gave it to him. He started slapping the bottom of it with his palm, while speaking. "We've got to get some...squeeze bottles or little packets...so we can have this blood when we need it...Don't you think?"

That was exactly what I thought. Blood was a good prop to have because, whenever you got shot or stabbed or blown up, you could make it much more realistic if you had something that looked like blood oozing out from somewhere on your body.

Just then, Tilden called over to Mr. Hawkins in a tone that sounded alarmed. "Sir, we seem to have a veritable invasion of youthful trespassers on the back lawn."

Mr. Hawkins put down the ketchup bottle and rolled toward the window to see what Tilden was talking about. I followed him. Sure enough, three kids were in the backyard, just like I had been on the day I first arrived. One of the kids was none other than little, round Anthony. And one of the others, who looked a lot like him, had to be his older brother. The third kid, whom I'd never seen before, was carefully walking on the back lawn and looking all around. A second later a fourth kid, as if falling from the sky, landed on the lawn also. All of them had on parts of military outfits and I realized that word must have gotten around that this was a great place for imaginary games and battles. I guess Anthony couldn't stand it anymore and was finally ready to start pretending.

"Sir," Tilden called. "I think two of these fellows are Vincenzo's boys. The other two I do not recognize."

"Yes," said Mr. Hawkins, looking through the windowpane. "They look prepared for battle, wouldn't you say?"

"Or mischief," replied an annoyed Tilden. "They are going to traumatize the lawn and garden, sir. Shall I evict them?"

"Not at all," said Mr. Hawkins as he turned to Rosa. "Do we have enough fish for these boys and lots more fries? I want to invite them in."

"Señor, tengo un monton de peces. Además, tengo otra cosas."

"Good," said Mr. Hawkins. "Let's see if we can have a little party. Tilden, invite them in."

"All of them, sir?" said Tilden unhappily. "Dirty boots and all?"

Mr. Hawkins scowled. "Of course all of them. Have them take off their shoes when they enter the mudroom."

I could see Tilden through the door, straightening up and turning down his collar. As he rose, he brushed off his waistcoat and trousers and adjusted his gray tie. Exiting through the sliding-glass doors, he moved toward the small band of boys, stopped in front of them, and without a single hand movement or gesture, explained Mr. Hawkins' invitation to them. Minutes later, like little ducklings waddling behind their mother, they followed him inside. I heard the clunk of many shoes hitting the floor, and soon four boys were led into the kitchen. Mr. Hawkins smiled and motioned for them to take a seat, and with wide eyes they all sat down.

"Now tell me your names, mates, so that I won't have to point at you. Also, please forgive me when I forget your name, since that is what happens when you get old. By the way, this is my good friend Mark from right down the street. He has recently moved into the neighborhood, and I can tell you with certainty, he is a nice, fun fellow. I would make a special effort to get to know him if I were you."

Boy, did those words make me feel good. I looked around at the other kids, and they looked back at me. During the next few minutes, each new kid introduced himself, with some help from Mr. Hawkins, and soon after we all ate fish and chips, drank root beer, and burped as loudly as we could as if we'd been friends forever.

Mr. Hawkins looked around at all our hopeful faces. "I have the movie Sahara with Humphrey Bogart. Should we watch it and act it out afterward? It has some good battles in it. I love it. And I've seen it at least ten times."

"You have the movie—really and truly?" said one of the kids.

"I do indeed. Now let's go downstairs to the movie room and I'll get it set up. Now make way for my wheelchair, lads."

In the movie room, Mr. Hawkins got up from his wheelchair to get the reel of film from a special cabinet. I could see it was very hard for him. Even with his cane to help steady himself, the look on his face told me it hurt to walk. Still, he managed to collect the big reel of film and bring it back to the projector, where, breathing a little heavier, he began to thread it.

For the next two hours, Humphrey Bogart and his band of soldiers from different countries, who were outnumbered by evil Nazis, hypnotized us all.

When the movie was over, we all rushed out into Mr. Hawkins' backyard and started shouting out the names of who we wanted to be. At first, we weren't very organized, but after a while things started to improve. One kid went to the birdbath where the water was trickling and said, "This is the water hole, but you can't see it, OK?" Since no one was against the idea, it became the water hole. Mr. Hawkins became the tank commander because his wheelchair was already covered with a tarp and he had his cardboard cannon sticking out of it.

Mr. Hawkins was great at making props. He had Vincenzo hook up a speaker outside to play music during the battle. He played a record that had a lot of July 4th fireworks sounds, like missiles and rockets firing, and it really helped to make things more realistic.

Late in the afternoon, Mr. Hawkins told Tilden to play taps over the speaker to let all of us kids know the battle was over and it was time to go home. Exhausted, we all cleaned off our boots in the mudroom and talked about what a great day it had been. As Tilden held the door open with his right hand to make it easier for everyone to file out, I felt a tap on my shoulder and was surprised to see it had come from Tilden. "Mr. Mark, before you go, Mr. Hawkins would like to see you. Please follow me to the game room."

When the front door closed, I followed Tilden, wondering what it could be about. When I got to the game room Mr. Hawkins was sitting next to the record player. In his hands was a big, black record that he was being extremely careful not to scratch. He held the outer edges with his fingertips and blew on it gently to get any tiny pieces of dust or lint off before finally placing it on the turntable. He didn't bring the needle over to it, though, and instead just kept it resting on the little stand off to the side. When he looked up, he smiled and motioned for me to come closer. When I did, he raised a hand and put two fingers in front of me and said,

"Two things. Remember when we did math this morning with double and triple-digit numbers?"

I nodded, and wondered where this was going.

"How did it make you feel to be able to do those problems?"

I didn't have to think for long. "It felt good," I said. "I think I like math now."

"Good. I am so very glad to hear that."

He leaned down and pulled out a book from a bag by his feet and showed it to me. I could see right away it was a book of math exercises. He flipped through the pages and spoke, occasionally pointing to different parts of it.

"The first chapter is all about addition and subtraction, and the next chapters are about multiplication. Because I think you have the hang of addition and subtraction, I want to talk about multiplication next. We'll work on it the next time you come over, but I wanted you to see some examples first. These," he said, pointing, "you will have to memorize."

Then, leaning down again, he took out a silvery-blue envelope from the same bag and held it out for me to take.

"And secondly, now might be a good time to give your father this envelope, since your holiday is coming. Perhaps he will have some time to look at what I have written down for him. It is something that might be of help to him in his business. Your concern for your father is why it has come about. You should be proud of what a good son you are."

Feeling indescribably happy and proud, I put the envelope in the workbook and put the workbook into the paper bag. After smiling at me, Mr. Hawkins looked at his watch. "My, but it's getting late. We better get you home before supper, or your mom is going to worry."

"Mr. Hawkins," I said, sliding off my chair, "are there other things you can do with math?"

Mr. Hawkins hardly moved, but his expression told me he was glad I asked that question—maybe even very glad. He considered for a long time until finally he said with a voice of wonder and a slight shaking of his head back and forth, "There is no limit. With math, you can count the stars."

I thought about his words for a moment and then another and another until I felt my jaw drop. It was as if I were unable to move. I wanted Mr. Hawkins to tell me everything he ever knew or heard about math and the stars and I wanted him to never stop. Mr. Hawkins must have noticed because he watched me and barely moved himself. A moment later, without a word, he looked over to his record player, turned it on, and moved the needle onto the first song.

I don't know if he had been planning to play it for me all along, or if it was a coincidence. All I know is that a choir began to sing so loudly and powerfully that my feelings started to jump all around.

The word Hallelujah rang out again and again until my eyes unexpectedly began to fill with tears, even though I was as happy as could be. I knew right then and there, something wonderful was happening to me, something I couldn't even begin to explain. Somehow, I felt sure what Mr. Hawkins said about math and the stars would stay with me for the rest of my life. Maybe that's why, with my mouth still hanging open I remembered again how Dave-the-Brain had told me that there were more stars in the universe than there were grains of sand in the whole world. And now, Mr. Hawkins was telling me that someday, somehow, maybe I could count them.

Dazed, I walked home. But I didn't remember any footsteps or the growl in my stomach until much later. The only thing I wanted to think about was the stars. I wanted to know how to count them, visit them, know how far apart they were from one another, and someday how many of them there were. The idea that there was a way to do that, using some kind of math completely fascinated me. Imagine, finding a number that was so big it would be as much as all the grains of sand in the world and all the stars in the universe.

CHAPTER 26

The next morning was Rosh Hashanah. My mom draped my holiday clothes over the chair facing my bed. Light gray pants, white dress shirt, gray striped tie, and shoes as shiny as mirrors, were all part of her way of reminding me what day it was and making sure I didn't forget to put the right clothes on. Clothes had to "go together" for her to be happy. She would say things like, "I like the tie because it brings out the gray in the suit jacket." Of course she would never dream of letting me decide what to wear on my own, because she was afraid someone in the synagogue might think someone from our family was a slob.

Before going downstairs, I took time out to tie one end of the tie around my neck and hold up the other end above my head while looking in the mirror. I pulled up on it a little extra and made choking sounds to help imagine what it might really look like to be hanged to death. I even drooled a little out of the side of my mouth to make it seem more realistic. Afterward, I went downstairs and ate a mound of pancakes. I knew there wouldn't be any food or fun or happiness to look forward to until services were over at around one o'clock. As hard as it was going to be to get through Rosh Hashanah, I knew it would be even harder eight or nine days from now (I could never remember exactly how many days), when Yom Kippur came, because Yom Kippur is the strictest, most serious holiday of all. The only reason I thought about Yom Kippur in advance was because it was kind of like the finish line of a Jewish holiday marathon and I was anxious to cross over and be done with it.

Kids in Bayside called it "Young Kipper", and so that's what I called it. When I found out I was pronouncing it the wrong way, I still said it the wrong way because Young Kipper is easier to say than Yom Kippur, and it sounds nicer, sort of like a baby fish. I learned in Hebrew school that Rosh Hashanah is the final period of what is called "repentance"—a time when you admit to God what you are sorry about and promise to do better next time to make up for it. Repentance lasts for eight days. During those eight days, God is supposedly deciding once and for all whether He will let you live for another year or not, but also, what will happen to you if you do live. I think the way it works is, if you are sorry enough and show it by praying extra hard, He might let you live. On Young Kipper, God makes His final decision. That's the last chance you get to have your name written down in The Book of Life. That is why Young Kipper is so holy. Once Young Kipper is over, that's it. The Book of Life is closed and everything that is going to happen to you for the next year can't be changed. Of course, God is the only one who has the book, so nobody can sneak in and change it.

I kept hoping that when we got to synagogue, Dad would let me take breaks and go outside, or at least into one of the other temple rooms where I could try to make friends with other suffering kids. Suffering kids were easy to spot because they all did crazy things the second they got out of synagogue, like tearing at each other's clothes, or wrestling on the grass while still in their sport coats and ties, or throwing a rubber football at each other as hard as they could, or stealing each other's yarmulkes right off each other's heads and running away with them.

Dad always brought along an old wristwatch and gave it to me to wear. He usually allowed me 20 minutes before I had to come back into the service. He must have realized that if it were up to me I'd never come back. I had to check it a thousand million times to make sure I didn't go over the limit, since I knew my dad was strict about being in services and I didn't want to give him any reason to be mad at me.

I figured out it would probably be okay to bring along the math book Mr. Hawkins gave me and to practice memorizing some of the multiplication problems. I kept my fingers crossed that Dad would let me, since it was one of the few ways I had to fight the boredom. I brought along a pencil, even though we weren't supposed to do any writing because of a rule that said writing was like work, and no work was allowed on a High Holy Day like Rosh Hashanah.

When we finally got to synagogue, I was surprised at how nice and new the place was. The main room where people prayed, called the sanctuary, had super-high ceilings and lots of glass to let light in. The seats, walls, and carpeting were different shades of light colors, like the colored chalk the girls in Bayside used when they drew hopscotch squares on the sidewalk. The cushioned seats were the kind you had to push down and hold for a couple of seconds because as soon as you let go they would spring back up. The rabbi and the cantor did their speaking and singing in the front of the sanctuary on a kind of stage. Next to them was the bimah, the special table where the rabbi and cantor put the Torah when they were reading from it. On High Holidays, like Rosh Hashanah, no matter what synagogue I ever went to, there would always be tons of extra people. In this Beth Israel place, they opened huge doors that connected to a great big space that was usually a "reception area" for parties and celebrations. But on Rosh Hashanah, when millions of people came to the synagogue, they opened up the reception area and filled it with long rows of extra seats for the people who only came on the High Holidays. As Dad and I looked around, it was easy to see the best section in the front was already completely filled. That's when I realized we would be sitting way in the back on the crappy metal folding chairs on a tile floor instead of the cushiony, carpeted front section.

It was always easier to imagine stuff when it was quiet. Unfortunately, when the rabbi, dressed in a white robe and a white yarmulke, moved forward and began to speak, his voice sounded like it was coming from every corner of the synagogue. That's when I looked up and noticed all the loudspeakers everywhere and realized I was completely trapped. The synagogue people had thought of everything.

In a way, it reminded me of Smelly Pelly's class when I had to sit in one place and be as bored as can be with no hope of escape. I pictured her evil face and beady eyes in my mind when my thoughts were interrupted by the sound of the rabbi's voice.

"Please rise and turn to page blah, blah, blah and read responsively," he said.

It seemed like a thousand people got up, and I could see and hear the swish of pages being turned throughout the synagogue. A moment later, the voices of the entire congregation reading together made the whole synagogue sound as if it were humming. A long, long time went by until finally the rabbi said, "Please be seated," and everyone sat down. A little while later the rabbi said, "Please rise now for the blah, blah, blah," and everyone got up, just like he asked, and began reading again. I could never understand why everyone did it. Stand up, sit down, read, be seated, rise—the whole thing drove me crazy. I wondered, for a second, if the rabbi said for everyone to stick their pinky finger in their nose and jump up and down if they would do that too. I bet some people would.

To get away from my suffering, my mind drifted to something Mr. Hawkins said to me while we were doing the puzzle the other day. He'd said I was the type of person who needed proof before I would believe something. I think he was right. I think it's why I had such a hard time believing anything would ever come from all these prayers. Some of them were thousands of years old. Also, even though I could sound out Hebrew letters and some words I'd been taught in Hebrew school, I didn't know what they meant. It made me wonder again: if there was a God, was He going to be happy with me saying words of praise to Him that I didn't even understand?

When I looked over at Mom, I could see she wasn't interested in praying either. She was all dressed up as if she were in a fashion show and that's what really interested her. She wore a fancy hat that had a lot of fake flowers on it, and she had an open prayer book, but hardly looked at it. She was more interested in what other women were wearing.

A lot of ladies wore the stupidest hats. They were either crazy shapes or had huge brims or giant feathers sticking out of them. Some of them were so big they hogged space from people who were next to them or in back of them, who were just trying to pray. Almost all the women wore high-heel shoes, which made them all walk funny and make a lot of clop-clop sounds. None of them would be able to go very fast if there was a fire drill. The men didn't seem to care about the fashion show or even know it was going on. They all wore plain blue, black, or gray suits and black ties and white shirts. Some of the older men had their tallit draped over their heads and rocked back and forth while chanting Hebrew prayers.

It wasn't long before I started to get bored. That's when I remembered I'd brought along Mr. Hawkins' math book. No one had noticed a thing until I placed the workbook over my prayer book and began working on memorizing the multiplication examples. I started at 2 x 2 and quickly got up to 12 x 12 before Dad looked down and noticed me.

For a second I worried I might be in trouble, but then he whispered, "Where did you get that?"

I searched his face for any sign of trouble. Seeing none, I whispered back, "Mr. Hawkins gave it to me."

"The man down the street?" he asked.

I nodded.

Dad looked down at the book and then to me, before lifting his head to rejoin the congregation. Mom, who was on the other side of me, noticed Dad looking and got curious herself. After reaching over and flipping through the pages, she began to nod.

"Mr. Hawkins gave you this?" she whispered.

"Yeah."

As my eyes met Mom's, I felt something drop out of the book and onto the floor. I looked down and saw the silver and blue envelope Mr. Hawkins had given me to give to Dad. I quickly picked it up, got back in my seat, and touched Dad gently on the arm that was covered by his tallit. "Mr. Hawkins told me to give this to you."

"To me?" he whispered.

I nodded and handed the envelope to him, noticing the words "For Mr. Leonard" on the outside. Dad looked at it, turned it over a few times, and put it in his suit pocket.

I couldn't believe he wasn't going to open it. I would never have been able to do that. I would have ripped it open in a second, like birthday-present wrapping paper. But as I thought about it, it occurred to me that maybe Dad didn't want to think about anything else on Rosh Hashanah, or maybe he didn't want to break some rule about opening it during services.

A whole hour went by and I was starting to go crazy. I needed a break, so I asked Dad if I could have one, and I could hardly believe it when he said okay. I took my workbook and walked out of the main area, through the lobby, and out onto one of the grassy spaces surrounding the synagogue. Breathing in fresh air, I thought about how great it felt to be free. I stayed outside for the whole 20 minutes before going back inside. When I sat back down, I looked up at Dad.

Amazingly, he was looking down at me and smiling. And even more amazing, he asked, in a whisper, "How much is seven times seven?"

I couldn't believe my ears. He was going to play with me during services. Smiling with delight, I wiggled in my seat, cupped my hands over my mouth, and whispered, "Forty-nine."

He barely nodded. "What about eight times twelve?"

"Ninety-six," I said in a flash.

He nodded again and smiled.

"What about eight times eight?"

"Sixty-four," I said confidently.

He put the back of his hand to my cheek as if to feel it and gently stroked it back and forth.

"I'm proud of you. Keep up the good work."

I felt electricity run through my whole body. I never knew there was a way to make Dad be proud of me. I didn't even know I was supposed to try to make him proud of me. But somehow, by accident, I had made him say the words, "I'm proud of you." To me it was almost as good as hearing him say "I love you."

CHAPTER 27

Dad stayed in synagogue until the very end. But amazingly, he let me and my sisters and Mom go home at around noon so Mom could make us lunch.

I was so glad to be able to finally change into play clothes and run around in the backyard, and yet my mind couldn't help but wonder what was going on at Mr. Hawkins' house. I tried asking if I could maybe just go over for a while until my cousins came over, but Mom told me "no" in a voice that was very close to being angry. I think it was because this morning I asked her and she told me not to ask again.

Looking around at what else I could do while I waited forever for my cousins to come over, I decided to climb the crab apple tree. When I got as high up as I could, I looked all around and noticed there wasn't anyone in our neighbor's backyard. I also noticed that on the ground in our backyard there were tons of little ugly crabapples and tons more still hanging from the trees. I decided it would be cool to pretend that the neighbor's yard was full of Nazis and that I could blow them up using crabapples as pretend hand grenades.

I climbed down and began lobbing them by the handful over

the fence into the next yard. I pretended to pull out the firing pin with my teeth like the GIs did in their battles in the Pacific. Then I fired some crab apple mortar rounds, pretending to slip the shell into the mortar cylinder before squatting down and covering my ears with my hands to protect my eardrums from bursting. With each imaginary explosion, I opened my arms wide and made the sound of it the best I could. Every now and then, I threw some apples at the hollow metal incinerator barrel next to the garage and imagined it to be a direct hit by my anti-tank shell against an armor-plated enemy tank.

The shelling of our neighbor's yard was going along fine, the battle definitely helping the Allies, when I noticed Mom looking out the back door at me. For some reason she seemed distracted and didn't smile even though she was looking right at me.

She went down the back steps and made her way over to the side of the house by the water faucet that connected to the garden hose. Then she turned the knob and waited for a surge of water to rush out. She fiddled with the sprayer part and aimed it until she was satisfied it was coming out in a long stream. I thought it strange she didn't spray any plants. When she began to roll up the bulky part of the hose, she took extra time to make sure it wasn't tangled and could unwind easily from the hose reel. Appearing satisfied, she walked back up the stairs into the house.

I went back to bombing the neighbor's yard but was startled by what looked like a thick green snake slithering in the grass. A second or two later I realized it was only the other garden hose moving away from me, and sure enough it was Mom again, with a serious face, fooling around with the nozzle like she did with the hose on the other side of the house. The only thing that seemed dumb to me was that she didn't bother spraying any of the flowers or bushes. Instead, she just went back inside.

I decided to go inside and maybe grab something to eat since all of my bombing and blasting was making me hungry. When I did, I saw Mom bent over, looking like she was about to throw up. It was a scary sight, especially after seeing her feeling fine just a little while ago. I moved to the platter of vegetables on the counter and took a few slices of cucumber, but I kept my eyes on Mom. My eyes flicked to the kitchen counter, where the Worcester phone book was opened to a page with a list of emergency numbers. I thought for a second maybe Mom was getting sick and had called someone about her sickness, but then I saw a circle around the words Worcester Fire Department.

"Mom," I said softly, "are you all right?"

She nodded slowly.

"Why are you all bent over? Are you going to throw up?"

Still bent, she put a hand on my shoulder and said between breaths, "Sometimes when a person is about to make a hard decision, it can make them feel sick."

She lifted her head and managed to give me a kiss on my head and a pat on my shoulder. "Why don't you go back outside and play. Are you bombing the neighbors?"

I felt better as soon as she said it. "Yeah, I'm shelling them with grenades and mortars and rockets. I'm doing the battle of Stalingrad."

"Good," she said softly. "Go back outside and keep playing."

"Okay," I said.

I turned and slowly went out the door and down the stairs and started up the battle again. But with each cluster bomb I hurled, I found my thoughts going to Mom. I wanted to be sure everything was okay. Everything seemed okay. She even said so. So maybe it was.

A few minutes later she must have recovered completely because I heard her loud piercing voice from the back step, "Mark! Come here!"

From my place near the crab apple tree, I saw her holding two paper trash bags filled to the brim with trash. She had a bag in each arm and something small she held tightly in her hand.

I got down and went over to her. When I was right in front of her, she pushed the two bags of trash into my chest and said, "Go burn these in the trash barrel." Dazed, I put my arms around them and waited for her next command. A second later, she opened her hand and showed me a book of matches. "Here," she said, shoving the pack into my right hand. "Come inside when you're done. I have to finish making lunch." She turned and went back inside.

I stood there stunned. My mother had just told me to burn the trash! For several minutes with my arms hugging two bags of stinky trash, I tried to gather my thoughts. I wondered why she did it, and whether she might change her mind. She didn't seem crazy like the crazy people I'd seen on TV or in movies, but her words and instructions seemed crazy. I waited. And I waited some more, conscious of how stupid I must have looked standing there with two full trash bags that seemed almost as big as me. Finally, hearing and seeing nothing, I went to the trash barrel and dropped the two bags inside while wondering what would happen if Dad came home right now. I realized with excitement that I would be able to tell him Mom told me to do it! I could even tell him that I was doing her a favor! And if the police came, I could tell them the same thing. Even if Bonnie's evil, secret Judge Copperfield came, I could tell him I had Mom's permission! I realized for the first time that having permission was a great feeling, and it made almost all my guilty feelings disappear. I was free to pretend with the best prop in the world, and as long as I did my pretending while I was over the barrel, it seemed like no one would mind and everything would be okay.

I struck the first match and watched it flare up. With my thumb and pointer finger I moved the match through the air, making the sound of a plane as it dive-bombed, just as I had with Stuart over the stairwell back in Bayside. I had to remind myself again and again I wasn't going to get the strap for this and no stupid girl was going to come out of the bathroom and snitch on me. And also, Mom and Dad weren't going to have a big fight about it either— all because I had permission!

My burning Japanese Zero touched down onto one of the bags, but because I let it burn down so low it went out. I struck another match and watched it flare. I was thinking how I could keep doing this, how I could keep experimenting, and how it was all up to me. I hesitated for a second as I realized Mom might ask me why it took so many matches to get a bag of trash burning. But my answer would be that she never told me I should only use one match, which was the truth. The way I figured it, if everything I burned was being burned in the barrel, nobody could complain about anything or blame anyone or be mad at anyone. And that's exactly what happened. I burned the trash and watched it and imagined until it burned down to mostly ashes. Then I put the lid on the barrel and made my way into the house. The first thing Mom said after sniffing the air was, "Oy vey. You stink from smoke. Go upstairs and change your clothes. Your cousins will be here any minute."

I started up the stairs to do what Mom said but when I got to my room, I was horrified by what I saw. My army guys were scattered all over the place. A few hours earlier I'd set them all up in my blankets as if they were soldiers on a mountainside. I put special sniper guys and bazooka men and grenade throwers inside each little crease and crevice of the blankets on my bed and set up about a hundred other infantrymen to stand guard all around it. But now, the blanket was off the floor and all my best guys were scattered, or missing or lost under the bed, desk, and radiator. I knew it was evil Bonnie's work, and I decided right then and there I needed to give her a good punishment to get even. In an instant I decided to kidnap her favorite doll, the one she called Serena Sweet Eyes. It had big blue eyes, blond pigtails, and a pink dress. Even though Bonnie was twelve and almost never played with dolls anymore, I knew she still loved Serena in the same way I loved Blackie. So when no one was looking, I went into her room, kidnapped Serena, and took her up to the spooky old attic. I tied Serena's hands behind her back, taped her mouth shut, and tied her to a rotten old rocking chair. Then I raced back downstairs to complain.

"Mom!" I screamed. "Bonnie knocked over all my guys that I spent a year setting up."

"Bonnie!" called Mom, moving to the stairs. "Get down here now. I want to talk to you."

About a minute later, Bonnie came down the stairs slowly, like on the show Queen for A Day, with a fake smile meant to tell me she wasn't worried about anything. In her hand was a hairbrush and a piece of white paper. She sat away from me with excellent posture. She was wearing one of her frilly, pink dresses, the kind she might wear to a party. She made sure to hold out the piece of paper so I could see it. It was the first time I had ever seen the paper that might be the dreaded list of my infractions.

"What are you going to do about what Bonnie did?" I demanded.

"First," said Mom, "we're going to find out if she did it. What if you're wrong and it happened some other way?"

As angry as I was and as sure as I was that it was masterminded by evil Bonnie, I was willing to pause, because, just like with pretend rules, you had to be fair.

"Bonnie," said Mom, "did you knock over Mark's army men?"

Bonnie cleared her throat and sat a little straighter. She looked away and began to run the hairbrush through her hair in long strokes as if to say she wasn't concerned about anything. She smiled in a really phony way, while fidgeting with her stupid charm bracelet. "I may have done it accidentally when I was vacuuming."

"And what were you doing vacuuming Mark's room?" asked Mom.

Bonnie kept her perfect posture and made the strokes through her hair last longer. "I was vacuuming the whole upstairs for you. Remember, Mom?"

Mom paused. "Do you mean about an hour ago when you volunteered to vacuum the hallway and the carpeting?"

"I wanted to be helpful since our cousins were coming," said Bonnie putting down her hairbrush and adjusting the ribbon in her hair. "The light must have been off in his room and so I might have knocked over some of his army creatures without knowing. If I did, I'm sorry."

I knew instantly she wasn't the least bit sorry. The way she said it reminded me of Eddie Haskell, the guy on Leave it to Beaver who was a real phony.

"What a liar!" I shouted. But Mom silenced me with a pointing finger. I bit my tongue, watching and waiting to see what Mom was going to do. A second later the finger pointed to Bonnie.

"I don't want you to go in his room ever again. Do you hear me?" said Mom in her warning tone.

"Not even if he lights a fire in there?" Bonnie asked while holding out her hand to examine her long, painted fingernails. "Wouldn't you want me to pour water on it?"

She glanced at me and I knew she was laughing inside.

Mom touched Bonnie on the shoulder and said, "Look at me."

Bonnie looked up and I knew Mom had her attention.

"Not ever. Do you understand?"

Bonnie shrugged her shoulders. "Okay, but don't blame me if the house burns down."

"Never mind that. Do not go in his room!"

Bonnie didn't answer. Instead, she went right back upstairs with her brush and piece of paper.

That was it? Just a promise not to do it again? It wasn't enough. She had knocked over and scattered soldiers from the United States of America, and all she was going to get was a warning? It was completely unfair, and that's why I decided to sneak into her room and borrow a couple of her records that she had told me not to ever, ever touch. I stuffed them into a small paper bag and hid them at the bottom back of the front closet, figuring I'd bring them over to Mr. Hawkins' house the next time I went over there.

When my aunt, uncle, and cousins arrived, the house became a busy beehive with people doing stuff and conversations going on all over the place. Mom went into the kitchen and started talking to Aunt Jenny about cooking and recipes while Dad and my uncle sat in the living room and talked about business. Bonnie was in her room showing our cousin Sheila all about nail polish and makeup, and my boy cousins were busy playing board games. I moved from one room to another listening to pieces of different conversations. After hearing all about how you can make a good casserole from my aunt and Mom, I made my way into the living room and listened to my dad and uncle as my uncle spoke.

"...I know we have a lot of expenses, but when you make a move like this, there are bound to be hidden costs. Even so, even with all of it, I like our chances with this new building and workforce," said my uncle.

The smell of coffee and cake made my uncle gesture to my dad that he was going to get some and would be back soon. As he got up and moved toward the kitchen, Dad put a hand in his pocket and felt the envelope I'd given him at the synagogue. Looking down, he turned it over several times before finally opening it and reading it. Then looking up, he took a few steps toward me.

"Mr. Hawkins gave you this?"

I nodded.

Dad's face was curious but he was also smiling a little bit. "He seems to know something about our business. Do you know how he knows?"

I shook my head.

"Maybe your mom knows." He walked toward her. Dad showed the note to Mom and asked if she knew anything about it, but she read it quickly and shook her head.

"Mark said he didn't know anything about it," said Dad.

"He probably doesn't even know he told him. Or maybe Mr. Hawkins figured it out from something Mark said. The man is very bright. Also, he's very giving that way. He went out of his way to do me a favor already, and invested a lot of time to—"

But Mom stopped short, remembering I was in the room.

"I think if he stumbles onto ways to help people, he acts," she said. "It appears to be what he likes to do."

Dad put the note down on the counter behind him and I picked it up, curious about what was going on. I opened the note and read it:

"Mr. Leonard, I understand there is an evening course being

offered at the Quinsigamond Community College on the subject of time and motion studies, an effective tool for establishing production norms and incentive plans. It begins this week. My good friend and associate Dr. Thomas Dixon will be teaching the course. Best of luck. Enjoy your holiday—John Hawkins."

I couldn't understand it all, but I got excited when I saw the words "incentive plans" because I realized what Mr. Hawkins was trying to do and how he got the idea. But mostly, I was very excited because he was trying to help Dad!

That's when I remembered. "Dad, I did tell Mr. Hawkins about a problem in your business. Was that bad?"

Dad smiled at me and gently pinched my cheek. "No. I'll bet you were trying to help me."

I nodded excitedly, feeling incredibly glad he understood.

"Zeendala, what exactly did you tell Mr. Hawkins that made him think to write this note? Do you remember?"

I answered excitedly. "I asked Mr. Hawkins what 'overtime' meant. He told me about what straight time was and how overtime was like straight time but with some extra money for doing more than the regular amount of work. I made a joke and asked him if there was anything called 'crooked time' and do you know what he said?"

Dad smiled and shook his head.

"He said, 'Yeah! But only for crooks.'"

Dad was smiling a lot now and his eyes twinkled as he continued to look at me. My heart skipped a beat and I felt like I was swelling with happiness. I realized this was how I wanted him to be forever.

"Anything else?" he asked.

"Yeah, I told him you didn't know what to pay your workers because you thought they should go faster but you didn't want to make them nervous. You were trying to figure a better way to pay them. I heard you tell Uncle Al about it."

Dad seemed just short of amazed. "I had no idea you could be such a good listener. Who'd believe that those ears of yours were working overtime?"

"Overtime?"

Dad had said it on purpose to make me laugh and it worked. Then he ruffled my hair. "Did I help?" I asked hopefully.

Dad nodded. "You may have helped a lot. We'll have to see, but regardless, thank you. I should probably give your friend a call and thank him myself."

CHAPTER 28

The next morning, before going to services for the second day of Rosh Hashanah, Mom cleared away a little space for me at the kitchen table and Dad even stopped by for a while to look at the math book with me. Later, from upstairs, he started calling out multiplication problems as he dressed to go to synagogue. He tried to be funny by always making up word problems instead of just numbers.

"If seven soldiers each have seven mortars, how many mortars do they have all together?"

I gave him the answer with confidence and happiness mixed together, yelling back, "Forty-nine!"

"Forty-nine what?"

"Forty-nine mortars!" I chirped back with delight.

"Excellent! And if Mickey Mantle hit six home runs a week for six weeks, how many home runs would he have hit all together?"

I liked Dad's examples.

After synagogue, I went home early with Mom again. We sat down at the kitchen table, had cocoa together, and went back to work on multiplication problems. I was surprised at how much quicker I was able to get the answers, but also how good Mom was at it.

"Mom, why didn't you go to college?" I asked.

"I didn't realize how important it was," she said, sounding a little sad. But her tone changed quickly. "But you'll go. You're smart enough, and with a little help from your dad and me, you'll do great things."

"Really?"

"Really."

"Do you think I'll be able to do math in college?"

"Why not?"

"Do you think I'll be able to do math to figure out how many stars there are?"

Mom seemed both pleased and surprised by my words and maybe that's why she stared at me for a while. "You'll need to study hard and learn a lot of different subjects, but yes, someday you'll be able to."

"I think there's a gazillion billion trillion quazillion of them," I said excitedly.

"Is that what you want to know someday?"

"Yeah, and I want to know how far away from each other they are, and how long it takes to get from one to another and how big they are. That's what I want to know. I want to know all about the stars and space, like that Jewish genius guy Einstein. You know, the dead guy—the one you said didn't comb his hair right?"

"I said that?"

"Yeah, remember? You said his hair looked like he got an electrical shock. You said maybe he got his finger stuck in an electrical socket and that's why it looked that way. Also, you said he should get a wife to nag him to comb it better. Don't you remember?"

Mom wore a big smile. She bent over and kissed me on the head and said, "Yes, now I remember, Mark Lemon. And yes, his mother should have taught him how important that was."

We both started laughing.

Later on, Mom told me I had to hang around so we could have

family time together. She said Dad had been missing us all from working so hard, and Rosh Hashanah was a chance for everyone to relax and be together.

I decided to go to the backyard until she called us all in for lunch. I climbed up the crab apple tree and looked around again for someplace to bomb. I was getting ready to unleash another crab apple rocket attack on our other backyard neighbor when Mom's voice called out once again. "Mark! Time to burn the trash!"

I climbed down the tree and headed toward the back steps of the house just like the day before. And just like the day before, she had trash in brown bags in her arms. I wondered why Mom was giving me this job a second day in a row. It made me wonder if she was planning to make it one of my new everyday chores.

"Here," she said, again handing me a book of matches.

I took them and went to the metal 55-gallon drum and dropped the three bags into it. I leaned back to peek around the edge of the garage and see if anyone was coming. Seeing no one, I took a few steps back so I could see the back stairs. They were empty, too, so I knew I was in the clear.

I lit a match and then another and another, pretending a whole bunch of kamikazes were coming down from the sky in flames after being hit by anti-aircraft guns. One after another, they fell into the barrel followed by trails of smoke.

After a while, when it seemed like nothing much was happening, it came to me that it might be more interesting to do a new experiment. I thought back to the time Vincenzo had gotten a few heavy cardboard tubes from the dump with the idea of choosing one to be a pretend cannon for Mr. Hawkins' wheelchair. Vincenzo had chosen one and put aside the rest. I overheard him say he was going to be taking the leftover ones back to the dump in the next few days. For some reason, I began to wonder how long it would take to burn up one of them and how much ash would be left when it was all done burning. The more I thought about it, the more curious I became. Not long after, that old, familiar obsessed feeling kind of kicked in and soon I was on my way down the street to Mr. Hawkins' house to get one.

CHAPTER 29

I was so glad Rosh Hashanah was finally over and I could get back to my normal life. I just about jumped out of bed and raced down the street the next morning. As usual I knocked on the door, got let in by Tilden, and got stuck in the game room, where I took a seat and waited for Mr. Hawkins to join me.

But right away I noticed that something was different. The old table, with the puzzle on it, had been moved into a different corner of the room and a new bridge table had been set up. The new table was covered with newspaper. On it was a tube of glue, some little jars of paint, two tiny paintbrushes, tissue paper, and a jar with some water. There was a box with a beautiful color picture of a U.S. aircraft carrier at the center of the table. I knew right away it was a plastic model with parts inside to be glued together.

I wiggled into a comfortable position at the table, opened the box, and took out the big paper diagram that showed where all the parts were supposed to be connected. It opened like a great big map and had arrows pointing all over the place. The first pieces I saw were the largest—the hull and deck, followed by a whole bunch of smaller pieces wrapped in clear cellophane.

Mr. Hawkins appeared and wheeled himself into the room. "Ah, I see that you have already seen my plan for today. Do you like plastic models?"

"Like them? I love them!"

"Good, good," he said.

"We'll still do the puzzle, won't we, Mr. Hawkins?" I said. "It's been loyal to us, kind of. Know what I mean?"

"Indeed we shall. And yes, it has. I suspect that this entire aircraft carrier model can be done before the afternoon is over. I thought it might be fun for a change of pace. The next time you visit—tomorrow—hopefully, we can continue with the puzzle. How does that sound?"

My eyes opened wide and I nodded excitedly.

"Excellent!" said Mr. Hawkins.

Mr. Hawkins let me put most of the pieces together while he carefully painted the parts with a small paintbrush he dipped into tiny jars of paint. I asked for his help at times because some of the things in the diagram were hard to understand. Other times we worked together without talking. After one particularly long silence, I got an urge to ask Mr. Hawkins some questions.

"Mr. Hawkins, what do you like most about doing models?"

He thought for a while. "I like the decals and the painting. I like putting finishing touches on things. What about you?"

I snapped a small piece into place and was happy to realize I'd figured out where it went on my own.

"I don't know. Everything, I guess."

Mr. Hawkins scratched his head for a second. "Mostly I like seeing the progress, and finishing it, and feeling proud of what I accomplished."

I nodded because I felt that way too about models. "What's your least favorite thing about models?"

"Let's see…my least favorite thing…that would have to be putting everything away and finding out that some of the glue leaked on me. I can't stand when that happens. And what about you?" he asked right back.

"Um…the same as you, I think. I hate when the glue drips."

I thought some more and after a while asked, "Mr. Hawkins, what is your favorite thing in the world and what is your most unfavorite thing in the world?"

Mr. Hawkins took the flag bridge part of the model and held it carefully in one hand and turned it around to see where he should paint. He moved his glasses down a bit and looked into them, flicking his eyes at me for a second.

"To tell you the truth, I don't have only one favorite thing. I have many, because the world has so many good things in it, like flowers, music, good food, entertainment, and the pleasures of knowledge. I like good books and movies and the good feelings that come from doing something admirable. I could go on and on, I suppose."

I liked his answer. After hearing it, I could see how it would be hard to choose only one thing.

"What about your most unfavorite thing?" I asked.

"Let's see," he said, thinking for a while. "That would have to be cod-liver oil. Yes, that would be pretty accurate, I think."

"What's cod-liver oil?" I asked.

"Oh, my goodness, cod-liver oil is the most dreadful-tasting thing that ever was. Or pretty close to it," he said, still concentrating on the part he was painting.

"Then why did you eat it?"

Mr. Hawkins adjusted his glasses again and turned the tiny part that he held between his thumb and finger and put it aside. Then he dunked his brush into the water a couple of times to get out all of the red color. He dried it by pressing it against a white cloth, first one side and then the other, before changing over to blue.

"My parents made us have it whenever we got a cold or a fever or indigestion or almost anything. My mother and father made the three of us swallow a spoonful or two of that God-awful stuff even though we all hated it."

"Did you have brothers or sisters?"

"Yes, I did. One of each."

"Was your sister older than you?"

"Yes. She was four years older."

"Did you hate her as much as cod-liver oil?"

Mr. Hawkins put down his paintbrush and slid his glasses down a bit so he could look at me over the top of them. Finally, he said, "We fought for a long time like cats and dogs."

"Yeah," I said as I glued in the railing to the main hangar deck. "My sister and I fight like cats and dogs too."

"And why do you think that is?" he asked.

"'Cause she writes lists about me."

"What kind of lists?"

"Lists of my infractions."

"Infractions?" He laughed. "Now there's a word."

I didn't know why Mr. Hawkins thought my most hated word in the world was funny, so I told him what I thought. "I hate the word 'infractions,' don't you?"

Mr. Hawkins considered this. "Well, yes. I could see how that could be a devilish word."

"Yeah," I said. "It's devilish." I noticed just thinking about Bonnie pointing her finger and saying that word got me worked up.

"What else does she do to make you dislike her so much?"

"She tries to get me in trouble whenever she can. She orders me around when she babysits me and my little sister. She wrecks my army men and figures out ways to get me really mad. She wishes I'd never been born."

"Oh, my goodness! What makes you say that?"

"I heard Mom tell my aunt that Bonnie hated me when I was born because everyone started to like me more than her about a minute after."

Mr. Hawkins nodded, smiling. "I see. Just one minute after you were born, eh?"

"Yeah."

"That must have been pretty rough on her, I suspect."

"On her?"

I was surprised for a second time, because again it sounded like he was taking her side. But as I thought about it I guess I could understand that it must have been a bad feeling to get "pushed aside" the way Bonnie did. Still, all I had to do was remember when she vacuumed my room and knocked over all my army guys, and my sympathy was gone.

Mr. Hawkins picked up the entire hull of the plastic carrier and seemed to be checking along the side of it to figure out where the decals and paint might go, when out of nowhere he said, "Of course, sisters make great allies."

His words shocked me so much at first I could hardly believe they had come from him. That's why it took me so long to speak. "What do you mean?" I asked finally.

Still looking at the hull and turning it, he answered casually, "Oh, I just mean they can be quite helpful when they're on your side."

I didn't want to be disrespectful to Mr. Hawkins even though I was pretty sure he was confused. After all, he had never even met Bonnie. But I wanted to be polite so I didn't make a big thing about it. "Yeah, well, I guess, but she will never be on my side. We hate each other too much."

"I see. That can make it more difficult. Still, though, they can be the best."

Now he did have me curious, because he was continuing to believe something I couldn't understand or imagine.

"How?"

"Oh," said Mr. Hawkins, yawning. "They seem to have their own special ways of doing things that can make them pretty good to have when you're in a pinch."

For a few seconds I was like a dinosaur fossil with my mouth stuck open. I watched Mr. Hawkins put down the hull and reach for the paint again. Picking up a decal, he placed it in the water dish and shifted it back and forth until the decal began to loosen from its backing.

"You don't know my sister. She wants me to get the electric chair. I know it."

Mr. Hawkins peered at me over his glasses again. "That would be shocking!" he said, and it made me laugh even though I had been trying to be serious. Soon after, he was laughing too.

Going right back to what he'd said, I asked, "But how can someone you hate be your ally?"

"An excellent question."

For a time, I thought our talk would stop there and I wouldn't get an answer. But then he put down everything he was working on and looked right into my eyes. "You've got to find a way to shock her," he said.

"What?"

"Shock her."

"Like with the electric chair? I don't know what you mean."

"No, no, no, not like that. With a good deed! When she least expects it. Just when you think she dislikes you the most, shock her with an act of kindness or do a good deed. Then see what happens. Oh my, it can be such fun."

This all sounded completely wrong. Mr. Hawkins didn't know how rotten Bonnie could be or how mean I could be back to her. It had been going on all our lives, since the minute I was born, and if that was why she hated me, how could it get better? I can't say I was losing respect for Mr. Hawkins, because I liked him too much for that, and I knew he was very smart about almost everything. But it did come to my mind that maybe, in this one particular situation, he might be a teeny, tiny, little bit dumb.

"Is that what you did with your sister, the one you fought with like cats and dogs?"

"Yes, indeed. That's how I learned this trick."

"What happened?"

Mr. Hawkins closed his eyes and tilted his head back as if to ask the ceiling to help him remember.

"Let's see. I think we fought a lot because we used each other's things—often without permission—and didn't always put them back where they belonged. You know, the stuff that kids do," he said winking.

I winked back at him because I knew I was one of those kids he was talking about. "Like what?" I asked.

"Well, if I remember correctly, my bicycle had a flat tire, and so when my sister, Francine, wasn't around I borrowed hers. It got scratched because I liked to do wild things with bikes, and when I finally got home I left it behind our garage and forgot about it. It rained, and when she found it some weeks later, it was all rusted and looked awful."

"Did you try to wreck her bike?"

Mr. Hawkins became thoughtful. "I think I did. But I'm not sure. You see, I was upset with her for borrowing my crayons and sketching pads. She would take them and not return them—no matter how many times I told her not to. So, it is reasonable to presume that once I got on her bike, something devilish might have overtaken me."

"And then what happened?"

"Well, after my tire was fixed, someone left my bike out in the rain, even though I was quite sure I had put it away."

"Was it devilish Francine?" I asked, on the edge of my seat.

Mr. Hawkins thought for a few seconds and nodded. "I am fairly certain it was. Especially when dinner time came and she asked me if I'd been on any bike rides lately. I think it was her way of 'turning the screws,' so to speak."

Just hearing what Mr. Hawkins said made me slap the table with my free hand. "That sounds exactly like Bonnie! She does annoying, sneaky, rotten things like that all the time— like asking a question when she already knows the answer. So what happened?"

"Oh, it went on like this for a while, our parents scolding both of us— my father punishing me, and my mother punishing Francine, and everyone shouting and crying."

"And then what? Did you shock her?"

"Oh, I see. You want to get to the 'shock' part, do you?"

"Yeah," I said, fluttering my feet and bouncing around in my seat.

Mr. Hawkins leaned back, reached behind him, and filled the glass that rested next to his pitcher. I watched him take a long sip and swallow before putting the glass down.

"I don't even know how to explain it, but I got it in my head one day that maybe I should try something nice to see what kind of an effect it would have. When I thought about doing what I had in mind, it was kind of nice thinking how I might feel afterward. Once I figured out that I would feel good about doing something good, even to one so devilish, I realized that I couldn't lose, not even if she didn't appreciate it."

"But what did you do? How'd you shock her?"

Mr. Hawkins leaned toward me and looked all around as if to check and see if someone else might be listening. Then, as if he were going to tell me a top-level military secret, he put a hand to his mouth and whispered, "I used up most of my savings and bought her a new bike—an even nicer bike than the one she had."

"You did?" I asked in disbelief, unable to hide my disappointment. "Then what?"

"I asked her to come to the garage because I told her I had fixed up her old bike. When she agreed to see what I'd done, I opened the garage door and showed her the new bike."

"Is that how you shocked her?"

"Yes! That's how I did it! Oh, my, you should have seen her face. She couldn't believe it! She looked at me as if I were from another planet. She had no idea what to say or do. She thought maybe it was a trick, and she even asked me if I'd stolen it from a store. To her, stealing it was more probable than the truth. She thought there had to be a catch. But of course there wasn't. There was nothing at all but the good deed itself," he said with his arms raised in triumph. "It was great fun."

"Did she become your ally?"

"Indeed she did—straightaway. She never took another crayon from my room or borrowed another sketch pad from me without asking."

"How did she show you she was your ally?"

"Well, there were a lot of ways, too many to recall, but she definitely surprised me to no end by what a good, strong ally she became. And she remained so for the rest of her life."

"She died?"

Mr. Hawkins closed his eyes and nodded his head slowly. I could tell thinking about her made him sad. "She died many years ago from cancer. I do miss her terribly."

After that, things got quiet and I found myself thinking a lot about how Mr. Hawkins shocked his sister and how he believed the most important thing was to feel good about what he did.

As we made more progress on the model, I broke the silence once again. "Mr. Hawkins? When your dad punished you and your mom punished Francine, was that because of whose department it was?"

"Pardon?"

"Did your dad punish you because it was his department?"

Mr. Hawkins' face squinched up a bit as if he'd bitten into a lemon. "I'm still not certain I get your meaning, but let me say, when it came to discipline, my father was the one who dished it out to the boys."

"What were the punishments you got?"

"Oh, they were all different, depending on what I did."

"Yeah? Like what for doing what?"

"Oh, he'd take away things, or give me extra chores, or make me say I was sorry if he thought it was appropriate. Once, I even had to clean out the pigpen every single day for two weeks straight. I didn't care for that one at all."

"Did he ever give you the strap?"

At first, Mr. Hawkins didn't answer. But when he did, his voice sounded unsure.

"The strap? Do you mean like a belt?"

"Yeah. It's a belt."

Again, Mr. Hawkins didn't answer right away. Instead, I found him looking into my eyes. The creases in his forehead showed he was thinking hard. "Uh, no. My father never gave me the strap," he said finally.

"Mine does...well, he did...I don't think he will again—but he might. If I'm really, really bad, I think he might. But maybe not."

"I see," he said quietly, barely nodding.

I looked down at the hull again and then a few seconds later I looked up and noticed him still studying me, barely moving.

"I've never had cod-liver oil, but I think I would rather have it than the strap," I said, while picking up a small piece that looked like a flag and searching the big diagram to see where it was supposed to go.

I glanced up and saw Mr. Hawkins looking thoughtful and maybe even a little sad.

"Does...your mom...give you the strap too?" he asked.

"No, only Dad. She stopped Dad the last time before he got to do it. She was like Superman. She threw her ring at him and I had to crawl under the couch to find it. It was a mess, with everyone screaming and crying like in your house with Francine and you."

Mr. Hawkins didn't say another word for the longest time. At first it looked like he was just concentrating extra hard on a single piece, but after a while it seemed too long for him to be painting the same little piece he was holding up in front of his eyes. That's when I noticed his eyes looked kind of glassy, even watery.

"Mr. Hawkins, are you crying?"

He put down the piece, reached into his back pocket, took out a handkerchief, removed his glasses, and began to dab his eyes. "No, no, no," he said. "It's...allergies. Never know when they're going to kick up."

Even though he said it, and I doubted he would ever lie to me, it felt fake. He must have noticed me staring at him, because he used a grown-up trick to distract me and get me thinking about something else. I'd caught Mom doing it a hundred times. He pointed toward the bag I brought over and said, "Hey, what have you got in the bag there? I see you've brought something over."

Even though I was still a little dazed because he changed

subjects so quickly, I was happy to answer because I knew it would lead us to another good thing to talk about.

"Elvis Presley and the Everly Brothers. Have you ever heard them?"

Mr. Hawkins dabbed his eyes a few more times. After several more deep breaths his allergies seemed to get better. "Is Presley the one that does all that wiggling with his hips?"

I nodded.

"Well, what are you waiting for?" he joked. "Let's have a listen. Maybe we can even get stiff old Tilden in here to listen, too," he said with a laugh. "He may like them since the Everly Brothers have a lot of precision and exactitude."

"Yeah," I said getting ready to try and repeat Mr. Hawkins' giant word. "Yeah, they have a lot of exact..a.."

Mr. Hawkins laughed again. It was a funny laugh, though, because his allergies made it seem like he was laughing and crying at the same time.

CHAPTER 30

I thought about shocking Bonnie every step of the way home from Mr. Hawkins' house. I had ideas like maybe sticking her finger in an electrical socket or accidentally throwing all of her dolls into the trash and lighting them on fire. But then I thought about how Mr. Hawkins said I also had to be proud of whatever I did and that sort of changed things.

That night, with my stomach growling, we all sat at the dinner table and waited for Mom to serve us. Dad's head was down and he didn't seem to notice any of us as he flipped through a business magazine. When Mom's wonderful plate of broiled steak, mashed potatoes, and gravy arrived, I saw she had also made steamed summer squash in tomato sauce as the vegetable of the day. The second I saw it, I knew there would be fireworks with Bonnie, since vegetables as squishy and slippery as this one were one of Bonnie's worst nightmares.

As soon as Mom put down her plate and Bonnie saw the squash, she made a sour face and leaned back as if to get away from it. With a "yuck" expression plastered on her face, she poked the squash with her fork and lifted a piece with an expression that showed she almost expected a family of cockroaches to come running out. I glanced over at Mom, whose back was turned while she worked at the stove. Meanwhile, Bonnie placed her elbow on the table and put her head into her open hand as if to think about all the misery that was in her life.

It was at that moment when an idea overtook me. I took my fork, and like a silent kamikaze streaking out of the sky, dove my fork down onto Bonnie's hated squash, stabbed three pieces, and lifted them off her plate and into my mouth before I could even figure out what I did or why I did it. In shock, Bonnie looked down at her plate and then up at me. And that's when I saw it! It was just like Mr. Hawkins had predicted. She was in "good deed" shock!

I chewed and swallowed quickly while Bonnie looked on. I knew she was wondering if I was so hungry I wanted to eat all her vegetables, as well as my own, or if by some miracle, I was trying to help her. She glanced over at Dad's bent head and Mom's turned back and then slowly turned her plate so the squash would be closer to me. I got her message and followed up with yet another dive-bombing run, until there was just enough squash left to give the impression to the secret police of our house that she had made a good squash-eating effort.

I wondered for a second if what I did might be a crime instead of a good deed because of how sneaky it was. But then I reasoned if it was going to bring peace to the table, that alone was enough for it to be considered to be a good deed. Also, as much as I loved Mom, I knew she was a bit nutty about Bonnie's bad eating habits. So, in thinking more about it, I decided for sure that it was, definitely, positively, a good deed. And Bonnie's look of complete shock was something that, true to Mr. Hawkins' prediction, was definitely worth seeing.

That's when another amazing thing happened. Bonnie made a tiny smile, leaned toward me, and whispered in a sweet, unphony voice, "Thank you."

CHAPTER 31

The next day, Sunday, Mom drove me to a big, red three-story building called the Mason School. It was a private school and Mom said we might not be able to afford it. Even so, she said it was worth seeing this school before seeing the public one, because it would give her and Dad more choices. To me, it was dumb to have to go to an extra school and waste a beautiful day. But there was nothing I could do about it since I was only a kid and kids almost never get a say about anything, but especially school things.

Soon we were walking on shiny brown, waxed floors down a large corridor.

I could tell right away it was a serious school. The lockers in the hallway didn't even have any dents or scribbling on them. We came to a door that read "Headmaster". Minutes later we were being guided down the corridors by a tall, thin man in a white shirt and red tie. He was named Mr. Adams, and he was the headmaster of the Mason School.

His face had a kind look that wasn't phony, and I was glad to see it. Faces with small beady eyes, big reddish-purplish noses, or teeth that looked like fangs were bad signs. I didn't usually trust those people. I decided if everyone in the school had a kind face like this Mr. Adams guy, I might be okay. Principals and headmasters should never hire weirdo teachers who looked mean or didn't like kids.

"Mr. Adams, I want to thank you for seeing us on a Sunday and agreeing to test Mark. I didn't mean to interfere with your weekend plans," said Mom.

"Not at all," said Mr. Adams. "We are a small school. At the Mason School, all our staff and faculty are on call at all times for students and their parents. I'm glad to be here today to meet you and Mark and perhaps get to know you better. I believe that test scores are only part of the picture when it comes to students. I thought we might move to the teachers' lounge."

We moved past an orchestra room, a study hall, and the gymnasium.

"Mr. Adams, you mentioned that the test results could be sent to the public school in our district, which I believe is Midland Street School, in the event we decide to choose that alternative for Mark."

Mr. Adams nodded. "Yes, that's correct. We're happy to share results with public schools to avoid the necessity of testing twice, if that is your wish. I believe you said there might be an issue of expense in considering Mason."

"Yes, that's true."

"Private school is quite expensive and no doubt, not for everyone. We hope the testing will help Mark find the best alternative for him, wherever that may be. I want to apologize for the confusion over getting Mark started. We had difficulty securing Mark's records from the school in New York, and when we finally received the transcript, there were a number of missing components. We had to go back to them several times and then incredibly, they sent it to the public school instead of us. However, I think now we are finally all straightened out."

Mom nodded. I could tell she liked this Mr. Adams guy.

"That's all right, Mr. Adams. As it turns out, he has been getting some tutoring, which I think has made a big difference. And to tell you the truth, with the Jewish holidays upon us, we thought it better to start after they were over rather than face interruptions."

Mr. Adams nodded. A few seconds later, he opened the door to the teachers' lounge and we went in. The seats in the room looked more comfortable than the straight chairs that most schools had. I sat in one and since my feet didn't touch the ground, I kicked my feet back and forth as I waited for the next thing to happen. Mr. Adams and Mom took a seat near me.

Mr. Adams smiled at me. "So, Mark, I understand that you originally lived in New York and have recently moved to Worcester?"

"Yeah, I lived on 211th Street."

"Two Hundred Eleventh Street?" Mr. Adams asked.

"It's in Bayside," said Mom. "On Long Island."

Mr. Adams nodded. "What kind of things do you like to do? Do you like sports?"

I nodded. "Yeah, I like the Yankees and Mickey Mantle and Whitey Ford and Yogi Berra."

"Oh, yes. That makes sense. Well, you may find most people in Worcester are Red Sox fans. Their hero is Ted Williams."

I looked at Mr. Adams and my face kind of pruned up. Ted Williams again, I thought. I knew he was a good hitter and everything, but I didn't think he should be in the same conversation as when we talked about Mickey Mantle—the greatest player that ever lived.

"What other things do you like to do?"

I thought for a while and was about to say I liked to burn the trash, but something inside me told me that even though it was true, it might not be a good thing to talk about. I thought about his question until so much time had gone by, I was afraid I might seem stupid if I didn't say something, so out came what was on my mind. "I like to play war."

"War?" You mean like with toy soldiers?"

"Yeah, mostly with army men, but sometimes with cowboys and Indians. Also with tanks, Jeeps, bazookas, and mortars."

"I think I know what you mean."

I noticed Mom bending her head downward. She put her head in her hands and slowly shook it back and forth. I would have worried she was getting sick or something, but then I noticed she was smiling. For a second I thought maybe I'd said the wrong thing, but since no one stopped me or seemed upset, I went on.

"Yeah, in Massachusetts, they have a lot of crabapples that I pretend are bombs or hand grenades or rockets or mortar shells. I throw them into the neighbor's yard to kill the Nazis there."

Mr. Adams nodded. He looked interested. "Uh-huh," he said.

"I got rid of the Nazis from one backyard, but they moved into the other backyard, and so I bombed them with a rocket attack and killed most of them. The first backyard was France and had French people living there. Now that they're free they can go back to making French fries and French toast and other French stuff. They don't have to worry. I freed them."

Mom shook her head more and more.

"Well, you have done a great deed, and I'm sure that the French people appreciate it," said Mr. Adams with a smile.

Even though I could tell Mr. Adams said what he did to be nice, I knew it was true also, because I'd once seen newsreels showing American tanks rolling into Paris, and tons of French ladies climbing onto the tanks to hug and kiss the soldiers because of how happy they were that their country got rescued from the Nazis. I remembered feeling really proud to be an American, and more than once I'd imagined myself sitting on the side of one of those Sherman tanks in army gear, holding a rifle, a belt with a canteen, and a few grenades on it. The only bad part was the kissing stuff. If I'd been there, I wouldn't have minded if the French ladies threw flowers at me, but that's all—no kissing.

"Hey, Mark," said Mr. Adams, "what do you say about taking a test for us so that we can see what you know and what you might like to learn?"

"Sure."

A few minutes later, I was in a different room by myself. Mom waited outside in case I needed her. I was given a little booklet and told the test took 45 minutes. After reading the booklet, I was told to answer questions about what I read, and in the second section there were a whole bunch of addition, subtraction, and multiplication problems.

I got right down to business and went through the test booklet pretty quickly. The second part, which had all math problems, seemed really easy. I even had time to go through it a second time—something that had never happened before. I was thinking about it as we said goodbye to Mr. Adams, who told Mom the results would be ready in a few days and he would call to share them with her.

Mom was happy after we left the school building, so happy, in fact, she took me out for my almost favorite food in the world—a hamburger with French fries and a root beer float at the Hamburger Express. She told me I had done well and had been polite. She said she was proud of me even though she didn't know yet how I'd done on the tests.

When we got home, wouldn't you know the first thing she did was hand me the matches and the usual two bags of trash.

"Burn this for me, sweetie," she said, as she leaned over and gave me a kiss on the forehead.

After lighting the two bags without any problems, and after waiting and watching for ten minutes or so, I stepped away from the barrel and looked at the back door as well as at both sides of the house to see if anyone was watching me. I had had a creepy feeling, from the very first day, and every day since, that someone was watching me even though I couldn't see who or from where. Just then, Mom came to the back door and said, "Are you done burning the trash?"

I put my hand up to my forehead to try and block out the sun. "Yeah, why?"

"Because," she said.

"Because why?" I asked.

Mom and I had had this conversation a thousand times.

"None of your business," she said.

"I hate it when you say that."

"I have to run over to Aunt Jenny. I'm completely out of milk and the stores aren't open today. Dad's at the plant. Do you want to come with me, or do you want to stay home with Bonnie? It will take half an hour."

"No, I'd rather stay home and play." Mom knew I hated running errands with her and that's probably why she gave me a choice.

"Okay, but Bonnie's in charge as usual—agreed?"

"Yeah," I mumbled.

"I can't hear you," she said as if singing a song.

"Yeah, yeah, yeah—agreed."

"Is the trash burned?"

"Yeah, I said I was."

"Okay. If you're smoky, make sure not to sit down on the living room couch or it'll smell from smoke, okay?"

"Yeah, Okay."

She disappeared back into the house, and a few minutes later I heard the car start up and pull out of the driveway. I looked all around. It was a beautiful day and everything was quiet and peaceful. Bonnie was in the house somewhere and I was all alone. That's when it sort of popped into my head that it might be a good time to burn up the big, heavy cardboard tube I'd taken from Mr. Hawkins' house the other day. I knew Mom had asked if I was done burning the trash and I had said yes, but she never asked me anything about burning any extra trash.

I went into the garage where I had stored the tube and dragged it out and rolled it over to the incinerator barrel. It had taken a lot of effort to get it down the street from Mr. Hawkins' house because it was too heavy to carry for very long, and I had to drag it and roll it down the street and push it every which way before storing it in the garage.

When I was pretty sure no one was looking I began to lift the tube a little at a time until I was able to rest one end of it on the rim of the metal drum. Then I got under the rest of the tube so I could lift it up and slide it into the barrel. I noticed once it was in the barrel it stuck out over the top quite a bit, like a straw leaning against the edge of a soda glass. Maybe even by as much as Mom is tall, except not counting her head. The tube opening was large enough to roll a basketball down.

For a while, I just watched, wondering if the little flames from the red ash below would be enough to light a tube made of such heavy cardboard. At first it seemed like it might be too thick to catch fire since the ashes around it just sort of smoldered, but after waiting a little longer, the tube began to act like a chimney as more and more smoke began to come out of the top. Looking over the edge of the barrel, I could see small flames beginning to make their way up the outside of the tube, and in no time at all, a lot more smoke began to pour out of the top. Soon, I realized by the smoke and flames starting to shoot out of the top that the fire must have been racing up the inside of the tube much faster than I ever would have imagined. Then I saw that the top of the tube was much too close to the garage overhang and the flames were acting more and more as if they were being shot out of a flamethrower. I realized for the first time that I couldn't control what was going on. "Oh, God," I heard myself say with increasing horror. "Oh God."

I looked up and saw the underside of the garage overhang. It was covered with black soot, a sure sign the fire was heating the wood underneath it even though the flames weren't touching it yet. I had this awful feeling I was going to have to choose between getting the worst punishment in the world if I ran inside to tell Mom or getting thrown in jail by the police and firefighting people for burning down our street. Then I realized I didn't even have the first choice, because Mom wasn't home. If the garage caught fire and the flames acted the way the tube monster was acting, it would light other houses on fire, too, unless I called the fire department. I had a feeling it would take too long to get the fire department and so I raced to the side of the house and turned on the water. In a panic, I started to drag the hose to a fire that was more and more out of control. "Oh, God! Oh, God!" I said. Having trouble with the handle, I finally managed to squeeze it, but the water came out as a useless fine spray. With growing panic, my tense fingers twisted and turned the nozzle as I struggled to get a stronger stream of water. The area on the garage that had been painted white was now black and beginning to blister.

"Oh, God, it's going to catch on fire," I said as I continued to fumble with the nozzle. Finally, I got a stream of water to shoot out and I aimed it at the top of the tube, where flames and smoke were pouring out—but it did almost nothing. I changed direction and shot the stream of water at the inside of the barrel but had to switch back over to the roof of the garage, where the painted wood continued to blister and smolder. The battle was unbelievably exciting, but way too scary to enjoy, because it was real and not pretend. And that's when I remembered Mr. Hawkins' words that pretending and fire weren't a good mixture. I had agreed and nodded my head, but still somehow, I was in this situation. Fearful thoughts raced through my mind. I didn't want to light the city on fire, and I didn't want to get hit with the biggest strap in history by Dad, or make Dad sad for the rest of his life, or make him not love me for the rest of mine, and not visit me while I was in prison on death row.

I kept hearing myself praying and I thought of how I was saying those words even though I didn't know if I even believed in God. I had a bad feeling the flames were too strong for only one garden hose.

I wondered what I would do if Mom came home early. I didn't know if that would be a good thing or a bad thing, since I didn't know what she would do. I could only imagine her running outside to scream at me, or maybe the fire department would come because of a call from a worried neighbor. Maybe they would bring the police and arrest me and call Dad. These were the longest seconds and minutes of my life and I just kept whispering, "Oh, God! Oh, God! Oh, God!"

That is when He answered me! And it was in the strangest way imaginable. A stream of water appeared alongside mine. As

I followed it down to the head of the hose to the holder of the hose, I saw it was Bonnie. Of all the people in the world for God to send to me, He chose Bonnie. She held the hose from the other side of the house and sprayed while I sprayed. In her eyes I could see the same fear I was feeling—and a sense that even the two of us might not be able to defeat the flames, even with two hoses. But she stayed with it, and stood right alongside me. I called to her in a quivering voice. "Keep squirt...ing the... top where my wa...ter is going. I'll do the bot...tom."

She moved her spray to the rim of the garage that was covered in soot, and to the boards under the roof that were black, blistered, and steaming from the heat.

Without a word, and like the best friend I'd ever had, she stood there with me. There was no look on her face that said she couldn't wait to add this to the list of infractions or anything else. There was only the look of a helper. I drove my spray toward the bottom of the barrel while Bonnie drenched the top part. Seconds turned to minutes, and still we sprayed and sprayed and sprayed while feeling the radiating heat from the barrel and the tube monster.

Finally, the miracle we needed happened. The tube monster suddenly caved in on itself as the bottom part turned to ash and collapsed. Right away I could see it made a big difference in our battle. I started to feel a tiny bit hopeful as our twin sprays began to take a toll on the angry flames that seemed once again to have Dad's angry face in them.

I went from fearing the whole neighborhood would catch fire, to simpler worries about Bonnie and the mess I was in. It was way too early to know if she had acted this way to help me, and been the best ally of my life, as good as Mr. Hawkins' sister, or if it was just a brief break before returning to her devilish ways. There was no way to know.

As grayish-black smoke rose into the air, another section of the tube collapsed back into the barrel, and Bonnie and I breathed a sigh of relief at the same moment. I took the poker and the metal lid, and poked and pushed the rest of the nearly burnt tube back into the barrel. Bonnie kept on with the hose, and although the spray hit me here and there, I didn't mind or complain. When finally it was done, I got the lid on the barrel, stepped back, and took my first real breath of fresh air. Bonnie looked straight ahead and kept spraying. I checked all the edges of the overhanging part of the garage that had been near the flames, and even though I could see there were a lot of places where the paint had peeled off and left black, steaming blisters, nothing had caught fire. Finally, Bonnie stopped spraying and began to breathe more deeply, too. For the first time since she got there, she looked at me. Without a word, or a question, or an accusing finger, or a "ha-ha" look that would have meant it was going to the top of the list, she rolled up her hose and disappeared behind the house.

No one came. Not the police, the fire department, or even a neighbor. I rolled up the hose on my side and ran around the yard stupidly hoping to be rid of the smell of smoke on my clothing. I went into the house and, not seeing Mom, raced upstairs to take a shower. From the sound of the water, I knew Bonnie was in the bathroom, but for the first time ever, instead of pounding on the door like I had done a hundred times before to annoy her, I went back to my room, took off my clothes, and sat on my bed wrapped in a towel and waited for her to finish. The whole time, I thought about everything that happened and what might have happened had it not been for Bonnie. I realized if Mom had come back from Aunt Jenny only five minutes earlier, I would have been a goner. It made me wonder how it all happened. For the first time, I had a new thought about it. The tube monster wasn't really a monster. It was a tube. And it was my imagination and pretending that made me think of it as a monster. Mr. Hawkins' voice echoed again: "I think pretending and fire aren't such a good mixture." It was almost as if he were here reminding me about it right now, and it made me think for a very long time.

Supper was a chance for me to calm down and try to forget my worries. As I looked around the table at Dad and Mom and Bonnie and Arlene, I realized how lucky I was. Things could have turned out a lot worse.

Dad looked at his watch and began to eat faster. Mom noticed it right away.

"What's the hurry?" she said.

Gulping an oversized forkful of potato, he said, "I've got to get back over to the library before it closes. I need to research something for the class before Tuesday. I just realized I need to be out the door in ten minutes."

"I had completely forgotten. How many nights is it all together?" Mom asked.

"Just Tuesday and Thursday. But I might stay in contact with the instructor. He impressed me when we talked by phone."

I was eating Mom's veal cutlets like someone who hadn't seen food for a week. Boy, did she know how to make them taste great.

Dad pointed his fork in my direction while chewing a mouthful. "As soon as I can, Zeendala, I'm going to stop in and thank your friend Mr. Hawkins in person for putting us in touch with Mr. Dixon. Judging by my long phone conversation with him, I think he can really help us."

It made me very happy to hear, even though I was still thinking about my life-and-death battle just an hour earlier.

"How did Mr. Hawkins help?" I asked.

Dad chewed as fast as he could without talking, but he showed everyone by waving his fork and knife that he was going to say something as soon as he finished swallowing. "Mr. Hawkins has a great deal of experience in business, and he knew some things we didn't know. He pointed us in the right direction and told us that there was a class I should go to if I wanted to learn how to improve my business—a special class to help me with a special problem. It's being taught by a very smart man with a lot of engineering experience."

"Thanks to you," said Dad looking directly at me. "You are a good son to care about your dad's business so much, and you were smart to be able to tell Mr. Hawkins about such a grown-up subject in a way he could understand."

My happiness at hearing Dad's words made my chest swell. Dad had never, ever given me such a compliment before. And it was all true. I had cared enough to talk about his problems and look what happened. And Dad even said I was smart.

At that moment, the phone rang and Mom walked over to pick it up. Dad put on his coat and took a last sip of water.

"Hello?" said Mom. "Oh, yes, Mr. Hawkins. How nice to hear from you. Thank you for calling back."

After a pause Mom said, "Yes, my husband is here and wanted to speak with you." Dad waved to get Mom's attention while gesturing he wanted the phone. In that instant I knew it was a perfect chance to help pay my huge debt to Bonnie. My fork did another dive-bombing run. This time it was onto Bonnie's green beans and I stabbed, scooped, and swallowed all the evidence. I felt especially glad to do it for her. She looked over at me and then down, turning her plate as she had last time.

"Yes, Mr. Hawkins?" said Dad as he took the phone. "I wanted to thank you for the excellent contact you provided me. I only wish I knew how to repay the favor."

After a pause, Dad began to almost laugh as he spoke. I noticed it right away, because I couldn't remember seeing him laugh in the longest time.

"Well, okay. It's a deal. One banana fruitcake coming up," said Dad. "I'll ask my wife if she can make another, and if for any reason she can't, I'll make it myself."

There was another pause.

"I'd like that, Mr. Hawkins. Perhaps when I bring the cake by, we could spend a few minutes chatting."

There was another silence.

"Yes, sir. I'd like that. I'd like that very much," Dad said.

Dad hung up the phone and looked around at all of us, still smiling. He leaned down and gently pinched my cheek. Then, he did something I don't remember him doing since I was much younger. He put his whiskery face into my neck and cheek and gave me a great big sniff. It was the kind of thing Sephardim allowed between dads and sons, and I couldn't help but think it had a kind of "I love you" feeling to it.

CHAPTER 32

The next day I was right back where I wanted to be—at Mr. Hawkins' house sitting in the game room with him and working on the puzzle. "Mark, can you see it?" he asked. "It's coming into view. The sunset is the hard part, still, because of all the different shades of yellow. But look at the glow of the thatched roof of the farmhouse. Isn't it just beautiful?"

Mr. Hawkins chose a record, and put it on the turntable. For the first minute or so, I hardly noticed the music at all, but then, little by little, it began to make my feelings grow in a way that's hard to describe. I looked over at Mr. Hawkins and saw his head bobbing and realized mine was bobbing too. Soon after, I was bouncing in my chair so much it was hard to concentrate on the puzzle and find good pieces.

"Ah," said Mr. Hawkins, "Beethoven the magnificent!"

Not satisfied to just pretend to play instruments as before, Mr. Hawkins started waving his hands around like an orchestra conductor might have, shaking his head and moving his arms wildly. I joined in and started waving my hands, too, also doing my best to impersonate a crazy conductor. Mr. Hawkins picked up a wooden ruler from his desk and began waving it. I was pretty sure he'd heard this music before, because he knew exactly when to wave his arms this way or that way when the music changed. With his white hair flying all about, he raked it back with his free hand while looking silly and out of control. I began to laugh.

It all would have gone on much longer had it not been for Tilden, who marched into the room, went directly to the record player, and, without saying a word, lifted the arm and stopped the music cold. But the biggest surprise of all was Mr. Hawkins' reaction. Looking like an embarrassed little boy, he said, "Okay, okay, 'twas only a little fun, Tilden. No need to go overboard."

"Hardly," said Tilden, obviously annoyed. "This and your occasional joust is as much fun as a heart attack, no doubt."

"Oh, baloney, Tilden. I know my limits," said Mr. Hawkins.

"Yes. You seem to know it's time to quit when your heart stops. I prefer a slightly earlier indicator."

Mr. Hawkins put down his ruler and raked back his white hair again. "Very well. I suppose you deserve a thank you. You are a good friend, Tilden. I shall take greater care in the future." Then he couldn't help but add, "Mind you, though, if I feel the glory of the music pumping through my veins again, I may summon Satan and take what comes without interference from you. After all, there is no way to listen calmly to a masterpiece like that and sit idly by. To do so is more like the end than any end you are worried about." To my surprise, Mr. Hawkins turned to me and said, "Isn't that right, Mark?"

I could only shrug my shoulders since I didn't really understand what everyone was talking about.

Tilden continued, "Sir, I wish to take your blood pressure now."

"Very well," said Mr. Hawkins with a scowl.

Tilden wheeled Mr. Hawkins out of the room. As he did, Mr. Hawkins called to me, "Try to work on the sunset pieces. They're yellow and gold mostly. I'll be back in about ten minutes."

I watched Mr. Hawkins and Tilden leave the room and I kept looking in their direction long after they were out of view, thinking about both of them and how they cared for each other. When Mr.

Hawkins returned, we started on the puzzle again, snapping pieces into place a lot faster than before. After a while, in the mood to talk about something interesting, I looked up at him and asked. "Mr. Hawkins, do you like war?"

Mr. Hawkins didn't look up right away. Instead, he put his fist under his chin and his elbow on the table. "I like pretending about war," he said. "I think there is great glory in it. Real war, however, is a different story. Real war is a terrible thing."

"But don't we need war to kill off all the bad guys?"

"Maybe so. Still, the face of war is unimaginably terrible."

I wondered what Mr. Hawkins meant by "the face of war", but before I could ask, a different question sort of moved in front of it. "Were you ever in a real war?"

Mr. Hawkins shook his head. It seemed like he was choked up or something.

"Which war was your favorite war?" I asked.

Mr. Hawkins looked at me with a half-smile before looking away. When he looked back at me he spoke very slowly. "Well, I wouldn't call any war a favorite, but I guess I was most involved in the Great War, which is often called World War I. My factory made many things for the war effort."

"Wow," I said. "Who were the good guys and who were the bad guys?"

Mr. Hawkins shook his head in an odd way, the way people do when you can tell they're confused. "It was hard to tell," he said. "Each country fought for their own reasons. The United States was on the side of the Allies. On the other side were the Central Powers of Germany, Austria-Hungary, Turkey, and Bulgaria."

"Who started it? The Japs?"

Mr. Hawkins paused before speaking. "You may wish to refer to them as Japanese. The word you used is considered a slur."

"What's a slur?"

"It's a way of saying something that isn't nice."

"But the Japs—I mean the Japanese— weren't very nice to us. They bombed Pearl Harbor, didn't they?"

"It's true. But trust me, eventually, everyone will call them by their proper name, and it will be best if you are not among the last to do so."

I couldn't follow it all, but I decided to just do what he said, since I trusted him and knew he wanted the best for me. Also, I didn't want to be someone who did slurs now that I knew it made people feel bad.

"But to answer your question, it all began when the Archduke was shot."

I began to feel excited to learn about this other war—a war I knew nothing about. A war that was big enough to get its own name: The Great War or World War I. It seemed like no one knew anything about it, maybe because only really old people remembered it. Mr. Hawkins told me that it lasted from 1914 to 1918 and that nine million people were killed and 20 million were wounded.

"More people were killed in World War II than in World War I," I said, proud to show off my knowledge. "I heard on the newsreel at the movie theatre that 50 million people were killed in World War II."

Mr. Hawkins answered, sounding sad, "Yes, it's true."

"But if World War II killed more, how come they call World War I 'The Great War'?"

"Because it was the biggest war that had ever been fought at the time. No one knew there'd be a bigger, more horrible war coming."

"Oh," I said, thinking. "Can you tell me about it?" I had no idea where I would be able to find out about World War I if not from Mr. Hawkins. Not even my friends in Bayside, including Dave-the-Brain, ever talked about it.

"Perhaps, a little at a time."

"Okay," I said. "A little at a time."

Mr. Hawkins started talking about World War I and I was immediately hypnotized by it. It was so complicated because so many countries were involved, and every country had different people who made decisions to do this or that, and the different countries made all these alliances, which meant if one country attacked another country a whole different country would attack them. Pretty soon, every country was at war. Mr. Hawkins told me a lot of countries started off thinking it was fun and exciting but by the end of the war, hardly anybody still felt that way.

Mr. Hawkins knew absolutely everything about the Great War. He showed me pictures from his books and maps of Europe. He told me what kind of clothes the soldiers wore in battle and how guys lived in trenches for months and ate out of tins. He told me that there was barbed wire everywhere and terrible weapons like mustard gas that blinded people and burned their throats. He said there were bombs that made a whizzing sound when they were in the air and a huge bang sound when they exploded, so they got to be known as "whiz bangs", and everyone in the trenches was terrified when they heard one coming. He told me about the soldiers who went crazy and couldn't stop shaking because their nerves were ruined from all the bombs. He told me how men went deaf and blind and how they would charge their enemies and get mowed down by machine-gun fire. The tank was invented during this war. At first they were big, clunky, slow-moving things, but after a while they started making them better and better.

After talking a lot, Mr. Hawkins got strangely quiet. When I told him I was glad he helped so much, he barely nodded.

Mr. Hawkins looked at his watch and then up at me. "Anthony and Sonny's cousins are in from Italy, and Ted and the other fellows you met have all been asking me about having the next big battle. What do you think?"

Wide-eyed and excited, the answer seemed right in front of me. "How about the Great War?"

Mr. Hawkins looked at me and our eyes seemed to lock on to each other's. "World War I?" he asked.

I nodded.

Mr. Hawkins started thinking, but before he could answer, Tilden unexpectedly entered the game room.

"Sir, may I see you?"

Mr. Hawkins wheeled himself out of the game room and Tilden closed the glass doors behind him, which was a little silly if he did it so I wouldn't hear, because I could easily hear through the glass. Like a lot of grown-ups, Tilden didn't realize what good hearing kids have. That's why, even though he whispered I could hear everything.

"Sir, I just noticed in the obituaries that your dear friend Herman Bloom passed away. I'm very sorry."

Mr. Hawkins looked up into Tilden's eyes but seemed unable to say a word.

"There is a funeral tomorrow, sir, and a notification that any gifts be given to the Beth Israel Playground Fund. I believe it was Herman's latest philanthropic endeavor, if memory serves." Mr. Hawkins nodded but still could not speak. Finally, with great difficulty, he managed a few words.

"Life is frail, Tilden. He and his firm served our company as an auditor and accountant for 40 years, and then, just like that, he's gone. Such a wonderful, honest, truly good man."

It took a while, but eventually Mr. Hawkins turned his wheelchair in the direction of the game room. Tilden opened the doors for him and he rolled toward me. He stopped, cleared his throat, and gently put his hand on my shoulder and spoke in a voice heavy with sadness, "Mark, tomorrow I must attend a funeral in the morning and it might run into the afternoon. During the two days following, my daughter, son-in-law, and grandson are due in from North Carolina, so I will be spending time with them. I'll let your mother know."

I looked back at him and my eyes must have told him that, although I understood, I was disappointed I would have to wait so long to see him.

He looked back at me in a way that told me he had not forgotten what we were talking about.

"After all, if we are going to have this war, it should start on a Saturday when all the kids are out of school, don't you think?"

I was happy about Mr. Hawkins' idea about a big battle on

Saturday, but I was very unhappy I wouldn't be able to see him for the whole rest of the week. I knew I was eventually going to go to school and it would mean most of our fun would be coming to an end. That's why I felt like I had to get in every second I could, playing with him and learning from him. Not seeing him till Saturday made it seem like an impossibly long time.

Mr. Hawkins must have read my mind, because he called Tilden and asked him to bring in some books about the Great War. He sorted through a few and then chose one and wheeled closer and put it on my lap. "This is an excellent one," he said. "It shows the dreadful conditions soldiers lived and fought in. It includes maps and a lot of other excellent information. There are lots of pictures. This should keep you going until we meet again."

I flipped through the pages while Mr. Hawkins looked on. It was a strange and fascinating book. It showed soldiers in trenches, behind machine guns, and wearing gas masks. It showed a smoking battlefield with hundreds of dead bodies. At first Mr. Hawkins explained a lot about it to me, and I thought he was even getting excited as he turned the pages and pointed out different things. But the whole time I could also see he couldn't keep his concentration, because his friend, Mr. Bloom, had died.

CHAPTER 33

The next day I got an amazingly lucky break. Dad came home early from work and decided to stop off at Mr. Hawkins' house to give him the thank-you gift he promised—Mom's banana fruit cake. I asked Dad if I could come along and he said, "Okay" but reminded me he wasn't planning on staying very long. Dad had called ahead and Tilden said Mr. Hawkins was back from the funeral and looking forward to meeting him. It was super exciting to think about Dad and Mr. Hawkins meeting each other for the first time.

When Tilden let us in, Mr. Hawkins was already in the sitting room next to the fireplace poking a few of the logs with a poker. He looked distracted and I wondered if he was still thinking about his friend Mr. Bloom, especially since he had gone to his funeral today.

Between that and the crackling sound of the fireplace, it must have covered the sound of me, Dad, and Tilden as we entered the room, because when Mr. Hawkins finally turned to face us he seemed surprised. Tilden stepped forward and began to introduce everyone.

Mr. Hawkins put out his hand and Dad came forward and

shook it. Dad smiled and held tightly with his other hand to a brown bag with the cake in it.

"A thank-you from me and Mrs. Leonard," said Dad, as he looked for a place to put it down. "You've been so generous with all of us."

Mr. Hawkins looked up from his wheelchair and smiled. "Not at all. Not at all. You are entirely welcome." Mr. Hawkins glanced at Tilden, who stepped forward and offered to take the bag from Dad.

As he did, Mr. Hawkins leaned over and gave the cake a big sniff as it went by his nose. "This is such a treat," he said. "On my honor, I have never tasted anything quite so delicious. If you don't object, I shall ask Mrs. Leonard for this marvelous recipe so that my cook, Rosa, might try her best to duplicate it. I ask you first, because if I knew of such a recipe, I might be very protective of it."

Dad smiled and nodded slightly.

"Please thank Mrs. Leonard for indulging me a second time."

Dad nodded again, and I could tell by the way he did it, that he was sort of looking over Mr. Hawkins to get more of an idea about him. It probably looked like Mr. Hawkins wasn't a very serious person by the way he was carrying on about a silly old cake. But it had an interesting effect on Dad. He appeared to be more relaxed.

No one was sure what to do until Tilden eyed Mr. Hawkins and Mr. Hawkins nodded to him ever so slightly. I knew then that Tilden was going to seat Dad and send me to the North Pole. Sure enough, Tilden made a sweeping gesture toward one of the comfortable chairs near the fireplace to Dad. A second later he turned to me and before he could say a word, I said, "The game room?"

Tilden did a teeny, tiny thing with his lips that I swear looked almost like a smile. "Perhaps your father and Mr. Hawkins would like to chat in private for a while."

I knew it would be useless to resist, so I went without a fuss and tried my best to work on the puzzle, thinking I might get a chance to spy on them a little later. But then Tilden closed the double doors to the game room as well as the doors to the sitting room where Dad and Mr. Hawkins were. To make things worse, Dad and Mr. Hawkins seemed to be speaking in a whisper or at least very softly. For the first time, I was really and truly shut out of the conversation and there was nothing I could do about it without being really obvious. Some time went by and I decided I would just have to ask my dad later on what he was blabbing about and hope he would tell me. I knew it was mostly about business stuff, and things that I didn't really know too much about, so maybe it was all right that I didn't hear every word. A half an hour must have gone by before I noticed Dad knocking on the door to the game room to let me know he was leaving. His expression was calm and relaxed, and it reminded me of the way he often looked after praying in synagogue. He smiled, waved goodbye, and indicated by a hand motion that it was okay for me stay. I guessed he was leaving it up to Mr. Hawkins when to send me home. I waved back and smiled and a minute later he was gone.

Mr. Hawkins wheeled himself into the game room, smiled, and moved to his regular place near the puzzle. We worked on it without a word for quite a while until Mr. Hawkins finally spoke. "Your father is a fine man," he said.

I smiled, feeling proud and glad that Mr. Hawkins seemed to like my dad.

"Yeah," I said, not knowing what else to say.

"Your dad mentioned that he goes to synagogue from time to time. I was wondering if it was the Beth Israel synagogue right up here on Baker Street."

It seemed like a funny question, but since I knew Mr. Hawkins had guessed right, I nodded. Still, I had to ask, "How come you want to know that? Are you going to convert?" I asked hopefully.

Mr. Hawkins gave me a big smile. "Well, no. But I had a dear friend who often went to synagogue and I was wondering if it was the same one."

"Oh, was it Mr. Bloom?"

Mr. Hawkins' eyebrow went way up and I realized that my

question was something I had learned while spying.

"Yes, it was," he said. "It was indeed."

Mr. Hawkins and I worked on the puzzle and told jokes to each other and laughed at the good ones while all around the house we could see Rosa buzzing from one room to the next and chattering. She came by the game room, pushed the doors open, and spoke to Mr. Hawkins.

"Estoy muy occupado preparando para mañana."

We both put our pieces down and wheeled ourselves into the foyer. From there, looking into the dining room, I could see that next to one of the table settings was a brand-new, red, toy fire truck that Rosa had begun to wrap.

"Rosa!" called Mr. Hawkins as she whizzed by, "Please remember to tell Vincenzo not to cut any geraniums. Richard is allergic."

"Si, señor. I me-rember."

"Good," said Mr. Hawkins, as he broke from me and began to wheel about cheerfully. "And you will be making Alice's favorite cinnamon apple pie, yes?" he said excitedly.

"Si señor. Tengo manzanas. I bake tomorrow. It be ready."

"Good, Rosa. Good. Alice remembers it from a year and a half ago. She still talks about it."

I began inching my way toward the door, feeling like I might be in the way, when the phone rang and I heard Tilden pick up.

"Hawkins' residence. Tilden speaking… Yes…" There was another short pause and then I heard, "And it is good to speak with you, Alice. We are looking forward to your visit. Please hold on and I will transfer the phone to your father."

Tilden walked across the room. "Sir, it is your daughter, Alice," he said.

"Very good," said Mr. Hawkins.

"Hello, Alice?" said Mr. Hawkins, sounding happy. And right away I could tell there was a strange pause. "What is it, darling?" Then there was another pause. "Yes… Uh-huh…"

Rosa looked on from the kitchen and I could tell from her

expression that she was happy for Mr. Hawkins and excited to make the visit with his family something special. But the mood in the house started to change.

"A cold? Just a cold?" Mr. Hawkins said. "The plane ride wouldn't be too bad for that, I don't think. We could keep a close eye on it while Matthew is here. Don't you think?"

Mr. Hawkins sounded like me when I begged Mom and Dad to go to Coney Island.

"Uh-huh...Well, how much school would he miss?—I mean if you have to go back later, you have the whole weekend. Darling, is there something you aren't telling me?"

There was a long pause.

"It's all right, darling. Everything will be all right. Tell me, though, does this have anything to do with Richard?"

Mr. Hawkins must have asked the right question.

"No, you don't have to answer."

There was another pause, the longest so far.

I felt so sad for Mr. Hawkins I wanted to cry.

"Yes, it is very disappointing. I was looking forward to it. We were all looking forward to it. I was certain that we would all have a wonderful time. Rosa baked three pies. Two are your favorite apple and one is a..." he said with his voice cracking. "And New England is beautiful this time of year. I thought we might all drive north a bit and see the foliage."

There was another pause.

"Alice, I can't help but think this is happening for some other reason than Matthew's cold or Richard's ambivalence."

There was a long silence and I wished I could figure out what was being said on the other end of the line.

"Darling. You must forgive. I say it not so much for me but for you. There comes a time or it may haunt you forever."

There was another long pause.

"Yes. Well, perhaps. Perhaps I am jumping the gun. Perhaps Thanksgiving, then?"

Vincenzo came into the house through the back door. Seeing

Rosa with tears streaking down her cheeks, he took her hand and began to listen.

"I see... Any chance for Christmas?" Mr. Hawkins asked.

There was a pause that made everyone in the room sad.

"Well, 'hopefully' will have to do, then. We all have to do what is best for us, don't we darling?...No, I'll be fine…The heart?...Oh, you know...same old, same old. Do what you need to do, darling. Take good care of yourself, Matthew, and Richard too."

Mr. Hawkins hung up the phone and looked up with weary, watery eyes. I glanced at Tilden and even he seemed to be wilting from the disappointment. It was almost as if he couldn't stand as straight as usual. The room remained stone silent. Finally, bravely, and fooling no one, Mr. Hawkins clapped his hands together and said, "Let's all have some apple pie and add some vanilla ice cream! Rosa, dinner is still for four—the four of us—tomorrow night, as originally planned."

CHAPTER 34

The first thing on my mind when I woke up the next morning was Mr. Hawkins. I was still feeling badly for him, and I wanted to see if I could cheer him up. I thought if only we could play together, we might be able to find a couple of really funny characters to pretend to be and that might help get him out of his bad mood. But I also had the feeling it was going to be much harder than that because sometimes grown-ups, and even kids, don't want to pretend at all when they are really sad. I wondered if Mom and Dad might change their minds and let me go visit Mr. Hawkins since his family wasn't going to be visiting. The idea was good but risky, especially because Mom and Dad had made such a big deal out of it, saying I was not to go over there, or even ask to go over there, under any circumstances.

After dressing and eating breakfast, I went back up to my room and rolled onto my back and looked at the ceiling while I tried to think about something that would be interesting to do. The Great War came to my mind first, and I took out the book Mr. Hawkins had given me and went through it page by page. I wondered what it must have been like to be one of those soldiers. I thought about the mud and barbed wire. I thought about the soldiers who charged each other and got mowed down by machine-gun fire. It even made me wonder what it would be like if a real mortar shell blasted through the ceiling of my bedroom right now. But a different bomb—the sound of Mom's voice calling out to me— shattered my thoughts. "Mark! It's time to burn the trash!"

I noticed how I was beginning to find her calling on me every single day to burn the trash really annoying.

I got up and walked toward the doorway. Looking up one last time, I imagined that a giant mortar shell had blown a hole in the ceiling of my room and that it was so big I could see straight up to the sky. I imagined all my windows shattered and my bed and dressers blown to bits with fire smoking in a couple of corners of the room. I didn't have time to imagine who the enemy was yet or what to do back to them, since Mom's nagging voice meant I needed to come now and not later.

When I got downstairs, Mom was waiting with two bags of trash and a book of matches, just like the day before and the day before that. I took them and walked out of the back door and down another set of steps. After plopping the bags into the barrel, I lit a match, touched the bag with it, and stepped back. I watched the fire take hold, and for a time it was interesting, but my mind strayed to the pictures of the battlefield in the book and to Mr. Hawkins' disappointment about not getting to see his grandson.

Maybe it was because of my life-and-death battle with the tube monster, or maybe it was something else, but today I was only in the mood to get the bags lit and hang around long enough to watch the paper begin to turn to ash. And that's exactly what I did, plopping the vented lid back onto the barrel before leaving to go to my room to read more of the Great War book.

Once upstairs, I began looking through the book again, but I couldn't really concentrate because my mind kept wandering to Mr. Hawkins' house and figuring out a way to get out of my promises. By late afternoon I'd managed to figure out something. My promise had been to not bother Mr. Hawkins, but no one ever said I couldn't go near him.

I began to think again about that lawyer guy on TV, Perry Mason, and how he always wiggled out of stuff. I remembered how Brian McBride once explained to a few of us kids on 211th Street about something judges called "reasonable doubt." It had to do with being really sure someone was guilty if they were accused of a crime. From what I remembered, if there was even a little doubt, a reasonable doubt, the judges couldn't put you in jail because it would be against the law.

It came to me that just about every grown-up I ever knew, knew I could get obsessed about certain things. Dad had said as much himself. It made me wonder if I might be able to use it as a defense somehow.

I began to think, between reasonable doubt and being obsessed, I might have a chance not to get punished if I got caught trying to wiggle out of my agreement. I'd have to tell Dad that punishing me when there was reasonable doubt or when I was obsessed was against the law, and although I could see he might not go for it, I had to at least give it a try.

For a few minutes, I was feeling hopeful there might be more good defenses than I first thought. But as the minutes passed, I realized a lot of my defenses were kind of stupid and probably wouldn't work, especially with Dad. For a minute or two, I thought about just being a good son and doing what I agreed to, but my need to go over to Mr. Hawkins' house was becoming so strong I had the feeling I wasn't going to be able to control myself. In a way, it kind of proved I really was obsessed.

I waited until well after dinner. With Mom exhausted in front of the TV and Dad downstairs at his workbench fixing something, I knew it was now or never. I took a couple of deep breaths, grabbed my jacket and Yankee cap, looked up at the ceiling and prayed all my defenses might save me if nothing else did, and slipped out of the house.

The chilly night air smacked me in the face like a blast from a great, big air conditioner. I zipped up my jacket, raised my collar, stuck my hands in my jacket pockets, and ran down the street. I

was just about to cross the neighbor's front lawn and make my way
to the back to scale the wall when I leaned around the corner to
take a last look at the mansion from the front. To my surprise, I
noticed a bright light coming from the downstairs basement area
of the mansion. Quickly changing plans, I moved closer to the light
and recalled that the movie room, which was in the basement, was
on the side of the mansion I was closest to. The light was actually
coming from that very room, and the window Mr. Hawkins said
needed to be open for "proper ventilation" was still open now.

I squeezed in between the shrubs and the open window until
I could feel my back pushing right up against the row of jagged,
twiggy bushes. Many of the twigs felt like little daggers, but I
managed to accept the pain and only move slightly to adjust to
them. Craning my neck slightly, I was able to see the entire room
without anyone in it being able to see me.

Mr. Hawkins was sitting in the center seat in the front row of
his tiny theatre with his head tilted back staring up at the ceiling.
His wheelchair was off to the side and his arms were spread wide
as if he were putting them around people next to him on both
sides. For the longest time he didn't move. Only the rise and fall of
his chest told me he was breathing. Everything else was strangely
silent. Tilden stood nearby in silence too. Finally he leaned
toward Mr. Hawkins and spoke. "Sir, would you care for some hot
chocolate?"

Mr. Hawkins seemed not to hear him.

When Rosa arrived at the entrance, Tilden turned to her.
"Rosa, would you be so kind as to make enough hot chocolate for
the two of us. I should like to join Mr. Hawkins now."

"Entiendo. Lo tendre en un momento," she said with a bow.

Tilden took a seat near Mr. Hawkins, leaving one seat between
them, and leaned toward him.

In a voice that was hoarse and defeated, Mr. Hawkins said, "It
has been an emotional day."

"That it has," said Tilden nodding. "The loss of a dear friend, a
disappointing phone call, and the absence of your little friend have

conspired against you today, sir."

Mr. Hawkins nodded.

"I used to think Alice's husband, Richard, was behind this kind of thing. It made sense to me because of his negative beliefs about my life in industry and the war materials we made. It fit his profile to not want to have anything to do with me, and to use my daughter and grandson as a lever to punish me, even though to this day I bear him no ill will."

"I didn't know, sir."

"I can't be sure of course, but the message seems to be crystallizing. And the more it does, the less likely it seems that it is originating from him, and the more likely it is that it is coming from Alice herself."

Tilden's expression changed ever so slightly to one of curiosity. "Sir, if I am not intruding, I wish to understand this better."

"I don't know that there is anything to understand."

"What is your daughter's or son-in-law's real complaint? Why are they restricting their travel here?"

Mr. Hawkins tilted his head back and seemed to once again be speaking to the ceiling.

"My daughter is at a stage of life when she misses and needs her mother. It was one thing for Alice to grow up the better part of her youth without one and have only a preoccupied father who appeared to love his factory more than his children. But now it is like a second blow to be denied her mother's involvement and joy as a grandmother. And if so, Alice is right, for if Katherine were alive today, I have no doubt she would have been an active participant in all of it."

Tilden just listened.

Mr. Hawkins let out a long, emotional sigh. "Perhaps today is a good day for old dark secrets to finally meet the light of day."

Tilden looked on without moving and so did I.

"I have few regrets in my life, Tilden, but the two I have I've carried around for a very, very long time and the weight of them has finally become too much. Perhaps now, this very night is the time to unburden myself."

It was so quiet it was as if someone had turned off all the sounds in the world. Mr. Hawkins let out another long sigh and spoke slowly and softly. There was great sadness in his voice.

"The first of these secrets, known only to my children, is that on the night of the auto accident that claimed Katherine's life and left me without the full use of these legs, I was …it happened because…I was… intoxicated. The press never found out and it remained within the family."

There was another long silence.

"You see, Tilden, it was I who killed Katherine, just as certainly as if I had done it by design. My children know it and I know it. For them, the loss is, in some ways, as fresh and painful today as it was back then."

I watched as Mr. Hawkins seemed to be overcome with emotion. To my surprise, he bent his head and spoke his prayer in a whisper. "God, grant me the serenity to accept the things I cannot change, the courage to change the things I can, and the wisdom to know the difference."

I was frozen, listening to every word, when Rosa entered the room carrying a tray. Instinctively, I pulled back a bit, shocked by her sudden arrival at such a serious time. I felt a branch stick into my back and although it felt like a dagger until I adjusted myself, I didn't make a single sound. Rosa set down her tray in the silent room, smiled to no one, and left quickly. Both men slowly picked up their mugs and began to sip.

They were silent for a long, long time until finally Tilden spoke.

"And I, too, have a confession."

Mr. Hawkins looked up at Tilden with an expression of complete surprise.

"It is that I have always known."

At first, Mr. Hawkins didn't say a thing or move, like he was trying to figure out how Tilden had kept such a big secret from him for such a long time.

"Sir, I hope you will forgive me, but I have lived here a long time. Little has escaped me."

Mr. Hawkins nodded over and over, as if to say it all made sense.

"It is not up to me to judge," said Tilden. "All I know is that you have paid a terrible price for your mistakes, sir. Secondly, you have dedicated your life to helping others, and I cannot begin to count the number of those who have been the fortunate recipients of that aid. It is very much the reason why I am still at your side."

Mr. Hawkins, near tears, looked at Tilden. "Loyal friend, it appears tonight, that no matter how many people I may have helped, they cannot make up for the ones I've hurt."

There was such a long silence that I really didn't think anybody was going to say anything more. They looked like a lot of those movies when at the end they just close the curtain or freeze the picture. But then, Tilden spoke.

"Sir, if you are up to it, I recall you saying there were two things. This comes as a surprise to me, because I know nothing of another secret."

"'Tis true."

Another impossibly long silence came, and I wanted to shake someone to get them speaking again. Of all my spying missions, ever since I was little, I don't think I ever managed to get information as interesting and top-secret as this was. I was hungry to hear more.

Tilden looked as frozen as I must have, as he prepared to hear Mr. Hawkins' next words.

"Yes, the second thing," said Mr. Hawkins. "I will tell you something now, Tilden, that I have never told any man."

Even though I was being a great spy, a part of me wondered whether it was right for me to be here listening to such big, grown-up secrets.

"Every day during the Great War, I carried a sense of guilt with me—every day, mind you. And not because of the fortune I earned. With every shell casing that came off the production line, I felt it."

"Guilt for what, sir? Certainly you are not saying that you were thinking like Richard."

"No. I am not."

"Then what, sir?"

Mr. Hawkins tried to speak, but he had trouble getting the words out. "I felt guilty that I was never in the trenches with our boys, doing my part there."

Tilden's expression showed surprise but not sympathy.

"Sir, need I remind you of what you did do? Need I remind you of the accolades and dinners and awards as a captain of industry that you received from all corners of America?"

"I know, Tilden, I know. But it doesn't change a thing. I know it isn't entirely rational either. Nevertheless, there is a part of me that wished, and still wishes, that I had been in there with my brothers and fellow soldiers, even if it meant dying with them. I was never able to fight with them, to save them, or to die with them, because I was considered more valuable to the country as a manufacturer of war goods. I was already 37 when the country entered the war, and perhaps I wouldn't have even been able to pass the physical, but it hardly matters. Somewhere along the line I lost touch with my brothers, and it has always haunted me."

"I would like to understand, sir, but at present I am unable to."

Mr. Hawkins shook his head as if trying to get rid of a memory. "The men who died in the trenches, who were blown up, lost limbs, or were blinded, made the ultimate sacrifice. I read about them at night while I lay in a steaming tub, washing myself with scented soap, or after eating a full, hot meal. I thought about them when I rested my tired body on a large bed with a firm mattress, between clean sheets under warm, woolen blankets. I thought about them when I awoke and had my scrambled eggs, always the way I wanted them, with tea and biscuits and the newspaper, which was brought to me each day. Yes, it's true that I felt the glory of running a factory at full capacity and seeing more than 800 men and women bustling about. And yes, as I watched boxcar after boxcar of our products leave the factory loading docks, I marveled at what it meant to our already swollen bank accounts. But I never forgot the soldiers, Tilden. I never forgot that there were real men using our materials and real men suffering in a way that I would never have to. They used our cookware, shell casings, and steel helmets and did the heavy lifting to win a war. All I could do was promise not to forget them. Thus far I have not. Still, at times, it hardly seems like enough."

Tilden cleared his throat. "Sir, I read somewhere recently that it is not uncommon for survivors to be burdened by the guilt of having survived. Could that be what you are speaking of?"

Mr. Hawkins considered Tilden's words carefully. Then he began to nod. "Yes, Tilden, an astute observation and quite interesting. Nevertheless, I'd like this kept between us."

"You have my word," said Tilden with a slight bow.

"Thank you, my good friend. As always, you are a most helpful sounding board." He reached out and touched Tilden's arm.

"Sir," said Tilden, "the timing is poor at best, but if I may…"

"Go ahead, my friend. What's on your mind?"

"Well, sir, you must have noticed the front doorbell ringing quite a lot lately."

"Yes, I had been wondering about that."

"Yes, well, a virtual torrent of young boys have come to the door to ask when the next battle will be. I have never seen so many faces. Word seems to be spreading."

Mr. Hawkins managed a smile. "Ah, yes, I see. And you are not sure what to tell them, I take it?"

"Precisely."

Mr. Hawkins' smile returned and grew. "You can tell them all that they are invited, and that the battle will take place on Saturday, when everyone is out of school."

"Not happily, but I will nevertheless tell them, sir. Shall I mention a time?"

"Yes, Tilden. Tell them to come at two p.m."

Mr. Hawkins got a faraway look on his face, and then his smile began to grow and I could see by the way he closed his eyes and went inside himself that he was back in his imagination again, perhaps doing what I told him—being someone else

CHAPTER 35

It took me till the next morning to fully realize how much trouble I would have been in if I had gotten caught sneaking out. Dad might have gotten so mad it would have erased all the good feelings we were starting to have and ruined everything. It was even possible he'd be tempted to use the strap on me again. The feelings and thoughts about it were so scary I had to block everything out of my mind and pretend it would never happen. I took a deep breath and let it out and thought about how great it was to see a sunny morning.

As I began to dress, I noticed that my sneakers were caked with mud. Mom had told me a thousand times to wipe my feet on the mat before coming in, and the last time it happened she'd yelled at me in her worst, screechy voice that almost busted my eardrums. But that wasn't the thing that began to worry me the most. I realized if there was mud on my sneakers from last night, there must be a trail of it starting at the doorway, and that meant if Mom or Dad noticed it, there would be questions—lots of them. Like where was I last night, and where did all the mud come from—and then questions about our agreement and my promises. I felt panic and moved down the hall to the top of the stairs to see if there was a trail of chunky mud anywhere like the kind that was on my sneakers. But when I looked down the stairs I saw to my amazement that Bonnie, of all people in the universe, was vacuuming like mad to get rid of the muddy evidence. I watched in disbelief as her long sweeps of the vacuum cleaner gobbled up the dirt and mud, forever concealing the truth of my crimes. I wondered, too, about how she wasn't even asking for a single thing in return.

In many ways, it was the final proof of how much she wanted to get along with me. Imagine doing good things for me without even letting me know and not putting it on the Master List. It was truly amazing.

It made me think long and hard once again about the way she helped me defeat the tube monster and how steady she had been at my side. It reminded me of what Mr. Hawkins had said about sisters, and how they made great allies, and how I thought he was wrong at first. But now here it was. More proof that he was absolutely right. I thought about Bonnie for a long, long time. In many ways I was seeing her differently than ever before.

No longer did I see her as my super-brat sister. Instead, I was beginning to see her as more like one of the soldier heroes in the movies, when they fought at your side and were willing to give up their lives for you and you were willing to give up your life for them. I thought about it all during breakfast, only glancing at Bonnie from time to time. But then, I caught a look from her that told me she was full of hope. Our eyes met, and I could sense it was up to me to say something, especially because she'd done more things for me than any sister alive.

I waited until Mom turned her back. The water from the sink was running and I doubted she could hear a thing. I leaned toward Bonnie and put my hand to the side of my mouth and cupped it so only Bonnie could hear.

"Want to be allies?"

There it was. The biggest honor a kid could give a sister. It was like asking another country to be your ally, whether in war or peace.

To my surprise, she nodded almost immediately.

I thought there should be some kind of ceremony for such an important treaty. I decided our own special salute would be to touch our elbows together. I lifted my elbow and motioned she should touch it with hers. Bonnie knew I had a whole special world of stuff like this from my imagination and she seemed happy to be part of it. A second later our elbows touched, and it was done. It was sealed. We were allies.

About an hour later, after Bonnie and Dad left the house, I remembered that Serena Sweet Eyes was still bound and gagged in the attic. I guess I was lucky Bonnie had so many dolls lined up against the wall in her room that she never noticed Serena was missing and had no idea that she was bound and gagged and being held captive in the spooky attic. But now, everything had changed. I didn't want Serena or Bonnie to suffer. I wanted them to be happy. So the first chance I got, I raced up to the attic and untaped Serena's mouth. Then I freed her hands and arms and brushed her off, being extra careful not to get her dirty before putting her back in Bonnie's room. I even said "sorry" to her as if she were real.

With only Mom and I left at home and a whole new day in front of me, it seemed like it might be a good time to try to convince her to let me go to Mr. Hawkins' house. It seemed especially possible because Mr. Hawkins' daughter and her family weren't coming to see him like he'd planned. But I wasn't supposed to know that, so I couldn't mention it. I was still under orders not to ask no matter what, because of how I'd promised not to ask them under any circumstances. I was trying to figure a good way out of it, at times racking my brain to think what Perry might do in this situation and how to wiggle out, when the phone rang and a miracle happened. It was a miracle that could have only come from God.

"Hello?" said Mom.

The next thing I knew I was hearing the magical words of a true miracle as they came tumbling right out of Mom's mouth.

"Oh, hello, Mr. Hawkins, how are you? Oh, well…yes. He's here…oh, my, I'm sure he'd love that…my, that is quite an invitation, but I was under the impression that your family was visiting."

After a short pause, Mom said, "Oh, how unfortunate. I'm so sorry. You must be so disappointed. Oh, I am so, so sorry."

I was down the stairs and in the doorway of the kitchen in a flash.

There was a long pause and then I heard, "In an hour? Yes, that could work. How nice of you and Tilden…I am sure he will absolutely love it. And thank you again." She turned to me with a big smile. "How would you like to go with Mr. Hawkins and Tilden to Mr. Hawkins' factory?"

I couldn't believe it. Not only were we going to play, but we were going to start off the day in his factory! "Wow!" I said, exploding with excitement. I quickly finished my breakfast, showered, and put on a cleaner pair of pants and nicer shirt because Mom said I had to look nice. And even though Mr. Hawkins said for me to come in an hour, I raced down the street and rang the bell 15 minutes early. When Tilden opened the door and saw me, he said, "Mr. Mark, you are early. Mr. Hawkins is with a guest in the garden. Do you wish to come inside or would you prefer to wait on the step?"

"Uh…the step," I said, knowing instantly that I was going to spy on Mr. Hawkins and his guest as soon as I could.

As soon as Tilden closed the door, I went around to the other side of the mansion and squeezed through a weak spot in the gate by pushing aside one of the bars that had come loose. Mr. Hawkins was at the stone table, sipping tea, but his guest to the right of him was farther back in the shadows and out of view. I could hear their voices though, and to my surprise the voice of the guest sounded strangely familiar.

"Mr. Hawkins, this is an extraordinary gift," said the mystery guest.

There was a pause and Mr. Hawkins said, "It is what Herman felt passionately about. It seems like the least I can do to honor such a fine man and friend."

"Indeed. Yet it is most generous, sir, and frankly, coming from someone outside our faith makes it even more so. This check will be enough to complete the entire playground and perhaps even add an extra swing set or two—both of which had not been part of the original budget."

"I'm very glad to hear it, Rabbi. As for being outside your faith, it seems secondary. It is for children, after all."

Rabbi? I thought. What was Mr. Hawkins doing talking to a rabbi? It occurred to me maybe he was thinking about changing his mind and converting after all. If it was true, it would be really cool having him be Jewish since he was easily as good a person as Einstein and Salk. Also, I bet Mom would love it.

"Mr. Hawkins, in your attached note, accompanying your check, you asked to see me in person. Is there something else I may do for you at this time, perhaps some way of acknowledging this generosity?"

There was a long pause.

"As far as acknowledgement is concerned, it would please me and his family if you acknowledged Herman. After all, he is the one who championed this philanthropic endeavor and he deserves the credit. As far as something for me, well, there is one thing…"

There was a silence and I knew the mystery rabbi was waiting just like I was.

"Yom Kippur is coming very soon, is it not?"

"Yes, it is."

"Rabbi, the little I know about Judaism I learned from Herman, but if memory serves, Yom Kippur means Day of Atonement, does it not?"

"Yes, it does."

"And have you planned your sermon?"

The rabbi didn't say a word for the longest time. I realized this conversation wasn't about Mr. Hawkins converting after all.

"I have. It is nearly complete."

"And if I told you that the addition of a few, gentle words to your sermon might very well heal the heartache of an entire family, would I be out of line to inform you of those words and ask that they be woven in?"

The rabbi was listening, just like I was, as I wondered who the family might be. Finally he spoke.

"Well, let me see. Without even knowing the words you have in mind, or having had any time to think this over, I come to the natural question of why you would be choosing such an unlikely avenue of communication."

"Well, Rabbi, given the nature and circumstances of the people I am thinking of, words from your lips, in this one instance, are likely the best avenue of all."

"I will think on this," the rabbi said. "I promise."

CHAPTER 36

Excited as I could be, I found myself in a great big black car. Tilden helped Mr. Hawkins into the passenger seat and I went into the back seat. Mr. Hawkins adjusted himself and turned around to look at me.

"Hey, my friend," he said, as he put out his big hand to shake mine.

I didn't know how to shake hands with a grown-up, and I wasn't sure about how hard to squeeze and everything, so I just put my hand in his as if I were handing him a dead fish and hoped for the best.

As Tilden drove off, I was amazed to hear how excited Mr. Hawkins was. "Tilden, did you set a meeting at the factory with Alex Stafford?"

"Yes, sir. I did."

"Does he recall the location of the little building within Building C?"

"Yes sir, he does."

Without hearing Tilden's answer, he began to speak the way people speak when they are amazed about something.

"There is a little building in the plant where Katherine kept a number of my finest purchases. Many are museum-quality pieces that I haven't seen in years; too many to remember them all. I'd almost forgotten about them until…"Turning his head and looking back at me with a smile, he said. "Until you, Mr. Mark, mentioned the Great War."

We drove up a long, winding road to an old, reddish brown, brick factory building surrounded by a chain-link fence. At the top of the fence was barbed wire.

The building's windows were tall and dirty and looked like they hadn't been cleaned in years. Some window areas had been bricked over. It was a pretty ugly place, and the buildings themselves seemed dead. As we came up to a more modern, small, flat building, I noticed it had a sign that read "Security." In the distance was a great big sign the size of a billboard that read, Home of Hawkins Steel.

A few minutes later, after a call by a security guard, a thin, handsome man who looked to be about my dad's age came toward us in a little cart, like the kind people use when they play golf. The man wore a black sport coat with a red tie. His shoes were shiny and black. As he came closer, he smiled at Mr. Hawkins and showed a lot of nice white teeth. There weren't any warning signs about him, like beady eyes, fangs, or a reddish nose, so I liked him right away.

The cart had two seats in front and two in back, and it came to a stop in front of us. The man got out and went over to Mr. Hawkins and shook hands.

Mr. Hawkins smiled.

"Good to see you, Alex. It's been too long."

"It has, Mr. Hawkins, it has," said Alex.

"Alex, this is my good friend and assistant, Tilden. I believe you met once before, long ago, and this is my new friend, Mark, a fine lad from our neighborhood. He is visiting with us today."

When Alex finished shaking Tilden's hand, he put his hand out to me. I squeezed it and tried shaking it the way I thought I was supposed to, when I heard Mr. Hawkins say, "Tilden, Mark, this is the president, Alex Stafford."

What he said confused me because I was pretty sure Mr. Eisenhower was the president, but then I figured out what Mr. Hawkins meant in his next sentence.

"Alex has been the president here at Hawkins Steel for, what now, eight, or is it ten years?"

"Eleven," said Mr. Stafford.

"Now you see? That's what I mean," said Mr. Hawkins, shaking his head. "The older you get, the faster it all goes."

Mr. Stafford and Tilden helped Mr. Hawkins from his chair and into the passenger seat of the cart.

We were all seated and Mr. Hawkins' wheelchair had been folded and placed on the flat back part of the cart, when Mr. Stafford got into the driver's seat, put his foot on the pedal, and the cart began to move along silently.

We rolled along for a while and then into a gigantic space. I looked up at the ceiling and could see a whole bunch of dirty, broken, and cracked windows. On the cement floor, millions of tiny pieces of metal and metal shavings were mixed in with little pieces of glass that seemed to twinkle like sand at the beach. In some places, paint and oil had spilled and had never been cleaned up. The only thing left in this giant building was a row of grayish-black steel machines that towered over us like iron monsters. Every machine had a giant wheel made of steel. Sticking out of the wheels were tooth-like things that went into other smaller wheels that also had teeth. The iron monsters looked like steel T-Rexes. I wanted to get off the cart and walk around them like I did with the giant jousting horse in Mr. Hawkins house, but the cart kept moving and so I had to be satisfied to just imagine they were steel fossils.

"A bygone era," said Mr. Hawkins in a whisper.

Mr. Hawkins pointed toward the empty space and, for a few seconds, he half smiled. "I remember a time when every press was in operation, and a dedicated auxiliary man was feeding every machine. There were floor operators and supervisors, material handlers, and the fellows from the tool shop. It was a breathtaking time. I can still hear the racket like it was yesterday. Can you picture it, Tilden?"

Tilden cleared his throat. "No, sir. As we have discussed, I can neither picture it, hear it, nor imagine it."

"Oh yes. My mistake," said Mr. Hawkins flashing a smile at Alex.

The cart took a whole bunch of right and left turns and finally came to a small brick building with a single front entrance surrounded by a chain-link fence. Mr. Hawkins stared at the little building for a time as if all alone and gazing out onto the ocean.

"This is it—the artifact storage room. We kept our records in here. Many of them date back to the turn of the 20th century."

Mr. Stafford and Tilden helped Mr. Hawkins get off the cart and into his wheelchair while I twitched with excitement.

When we got to the fence, I watched Mr. Stafford reach into his pocket and take out a giant ring of keys that must have had about one hundred keys on it. Finally, he found the one he was looking for. He put the key into the lock, turned it, and the lock clicked open.

Mr. Stafford pushed the fence gate forward and took hold of it so it wouldn't automatically close again. Tilden pushed Mr. Hawkins through the entrance and Mr. Stafford moved forward to the door of the little building, where he selected another key and tried to turn it. But it wouldn't turn.

Mr. Stafford went back to his briefcase and took out a jar that contained a grayish powder. He opened the jar, dipped the key into the gray stuff, put the key back in the lock, and turned it all the way to the right. When it clicked, Mr. Stafford leaned against the door with his shoulder and jiggled it a few times until at last it swung open. Mr. Hawkins looked at Alex. "Alex, if memory serves, there should be a string hanging from a light switch somewhere near the entrance," said Mr. Hawkins.

"Yes, sir, I see it," said Mr. Stafford.

He pulled the chain, and a dim bulb helped break through the darkness.

Mr. Hawkins wheeled himself forward a bit and then called back to Tilden.

"Tilden, I'll take my cane for this."

"Are you sure, sir?"

Mr. Hawkins nodded and Tilden went back to the cart and got the cane. When he brought it over, Mr. Hawkins said, "Stand by if you would, Tilden."

Held up partly by Tilden and partly by his cane, Mr. Hawkins moved ahead in the dim light and I followed. Boxes and boxes filled with papers, much of it bulging out of the sides, were stacked along the back wall. But what grabbed everyone's attention like metal to a giant magnet was the clothing, boots, and tools that sat silently on heavy wooden shelves. It was all stuff from the Great War and it left me and Mr. Hawkins with our mouths hanging open.

Mr. Hawkins slowly moved forward and began to touch things on the shelves. In a whisper, he spoke as if telling about a secret that had been a mystery since the beginning of time. "Here they are," he said, "all my old friends."

I stood perfectly still as he gently touched different items. "Look," he whispered, "a Prussian iron cross. And here is a British officer's compass. There must be two dozen gas helmets here! And look! A German medical orderly's pouch."

Moving a few steps to the right he continued, "Look! Almost a dozen British dummy rifles—the kind new recruits used. And look! German Mauser and British Enfield rifles! It's all coming back now. Yes, I remember buying these."

With the help of his cane, he stepped carefully to another part of the room where a large storage locker stood. It looked a lot like the one I'd seen at my Grandma and Grandpa's house. They kept a lot of their winter clothes in it and it always smelled like mothballs. Mr. Hawkins started to unzip the plastic covering, when Alex, seeing Mr. Hawkins struggling a bit, came to his side and took over. Mr. Hawkins looked on breathlessly. When Alex pulled back the covering, there before us were a couple of dozen uniforms just like the kind I had seen in Mr. Hawkins' Great War book. They were lined up like my dad's suits at the dry cleaners. Mr. Hawkins seemed to be in a trance as he moved closer and reached out to feel the fabric. He was so choked up at one point I thought he might cry. Speaking in a whisper he said, "German, French, and American infantry—and haversacks—like the ones soldiers used in the trenches to hold their soldier's kit." Inching forward, he motioned for Alex to help show what was under the uniforms. As if pulling back a curtain, Alex showed an even clearer view of the uniforms while Mr. Hawkins whispered in amazement. "And here is the basic soldier's belt, complete with canvas extensions. And look!" he said. "It has everything a combat-ready soldier might need—a fork, spoon, razor, shaving kit, bootlaces—everything. It's all here."

Barely catching his breath, he continued, "Tins with tea and stock cubes and others that were for 'bully beef.' Look how well preserved they are." He motioned toward the floor. "Two convalescent carts for the wounded. Oh my, yes, I remember buying them in near-perfect condition."

With Tilden's help, Mr. Hawkins stood looking into a corner of the room at two objects, each about two feet high and covered by dusty sheets. He moved uneasily toward them a step at a time before reaching out and pulling back the sheets with his free hand to reveal two brand-new, shiny, machine guns.

"Oh, my lord! I had forgotten about these! British Maxim Mark Three machine guns." He touched them ever so gently and stroked them with his fingertips. "Look! They're as new as the day they were made. Everything is here," he said, like a grateful person whose prayers had been answered. "It's all here."

I couldn't believe I was looking at two machine guns used during the Great War. In a way, it was like going back to that time and being part of it.

"Can I touch them?" I said in a whisper.

Mr. Hawkins nodded, and I reached out my fingers and touched different parts of one of the guns as gently as I would a newborn baby. I ran my fingers along the barrel like Mr. Hawkins had.

"Holy cow," I whispered, wishing I could stare at them for another hour.

Mr. Hawkins' legs began to shake a little and he seemed to be trying to catch his breath. He motioned to Tilden that he wanted to move back out of the room and into his wheelchair.

Together, Mr. Stafford and Tilden moved Mr. Hawkins from the room to the cart, where they got him seated. Mr. Hawkins looked tired and a little pale, but oddly happy as Mr. Stafford went over to the driver's side and hopped up onto the seat. He was about to start the cart when Mr. Hawkins put his hand on his wrist.

"Have this all delivered to my home today, Alex. Can you do that?"

"Yes, sir, I can."

"Tilden," said Mr. Hawkins, "Have Rosa do the alterations on as many of these as she can into extra smalls. Small enough to fit a boy."

"It will be done sir," said Tilden.

"Good," said Mr. Hawkins still trying to catch his breath. "Good."

Far away in thought, Mr. Hawkins forgot to give a last wave goodbye to Mr. Stafford as we pulled out of the driveway and headed home.

CHAPTER 37

O n the way home, Mr. Hawkins couldn't stop chattering. "Tilden, on Saturday when we have all of the boys over, I want the place to have the look and feel of a real war reenactment."

"Yes, sir."

"Tilden, what is the expected head count for Saturday?"

"Including all the members of Vincenzo's family and all the other boys from the neighborhood, I would estimate between 15 and 18."

My eyes opened wide. I had no idea there were that many kids in the whole state.

"Sir," said Tilden, "Vincenzo wanted me to convey that his entire family is looking forward to Saturday. He wished to know if his sister-in-law, I believe her name is Marie, can participate?"

"Yes, of course," Mr. Hawkins said. "She can be a nurse with Rosa. They can take the wounded off the battlefield and restore them to health. They can use the convalescent carts. After they fix up the wounded on the side path by the shed, they can re-enter through the back gate. Tell Rosa she will need a Red Cross flag."

Maybe Tilden had no idea how Mr. Hawkins could give so

many orders and keep everything straight in his head, but I did. The trick was to just picture it all in your mind. In that way, all a person had to do was describe what he or she was seeing, instead of having to remember a long list of things.

"Tell Rosa it will be her job to keep the soldiers well fed. Get pizza and drinks enough for all. The battle will be starting at two o'clock on Saturday afternoon and go until evening. We must make absolutely sure no one gets injured."

"Yes, sir."

For a while it appeared Mr. Hawkins had run out of things to say. But then he started again, whispering in a strange, solemn tone. It reminded me of synagogue and how people read the Mourners' Kaddish, praying for the people they loved who had died.

"Did you see those uniforms? Each one, as new as the day they were made needing only good, strong, bodies to fill them—to be ready for battle and ready to meet their fate. None of those men ever knew if they would fall dead in the mud in some foreign land, forgotten by all but the families back home that missed them so..."

Mr. Hawkins was so far into his imagination it was like he wasn't in the car anymore. I knew how it felt to be like that, so I was careful to be as quiet as I could.

"Tilden, this is important. Have Vincenzo make up at least 20 rubber bayonets to replace the steel ones that have already been removed. Have him make sure that they fit over the dummy rifle ends."

The big black car pulled into Mr. Hawkins' driveway. Tilden beeped once. Vincenzo came out of the backyard with his overalls full of dirt and a rake in one hand. He met Tilden at the van, ready to help.

"Ah, yes. Vincenzo, Tilden," said Mr. Hawkins, looking at each of them. "For Saturday, helmets are mandatory. I don't want anything hitting a boy's unprotected head. We will need an additional speaker hooked up. Make it bigger than the other one if possible. I want to play the fireworks album and I want it, on occasion, to be loud. Can you do all that, Vincenzo?"

Tilden concentrated on getting Mr. Hawkins into his wheelchair, and he pushed him along a path on the side of the house that led to a ramp into the mansion. As he walked alongside, Vincenzo looked concerned.

"Sir, not to be a disrespectable, but you're not worried about your flowers and bushes and bird feeders with all of these kids running around?"

"No."

"You're not worried about so many kids digging up the place with their boots?"

"No."

Mr. Hawkins turned and looked at Vincenzo. "Saturday we are going to use fireworks. They're not legal up here, mind you, but I don't expect the neighbors to complain. Still, I will need you to tell them that no one will be harmed."

Vincenzo nodded.

Tilden pushed ahead into a part of the house I had never seen before, and we came to a little elevator only big enough for Mr. Hawkins, his wheelchair, and Tilden. There was no door on the front of it. I waited outside and soon it was rising ever so slowly toward the second floor.

Mr. Hawkins called down as it rose, "Vincenzo, I want you to push a mound of dirt up against the front wall and also behind it, so that the kids can come over the wall easily and run down on the battlefield without entering the neighbor's yard or coming through the house."

"Sir, you want me to get a big a mound of dirt and make a big a mess in front of the house?"

"Yes, exactly, a huge mess," yelled Mr. Hawkins, now out of sight.

"Mark! Tilden will come down for you. Come up! I want to talk to you about something."

The lift came down again and I stepped onto it. As the lift began to rise again and Vincenzo and Rosa were half out of sight, Tilden called down to them. "Rosa, Vincenzo, I would recommend getting started as soon as possible. Years of experience with our fearless leader tells me that these are not the last instructions we shall hear."

On the second floor were a few old paintings on the walls and suits of armor standing like guards to the upstairs part of the house.

Tilden wheeled Mr. Hawkins down the main hallway and motioned for me to follow.

"Where are we going?" I asked.

"To Mr. Hawkins' room, where I trust he will take a nap," said Tilden. "It has been a long day for him."

Mr. Hawkins didn't argue. I walked alongside him. Mr. Hawkins took my arm and leaned over toward me. "What other props should we have to make the battle more realistic?"

I thought about his question until I had a picture in my mind, and then I described it. "Our bombs should be crabapples, water balloons, and tomatoes. There's a million crabapples in my backyard, on the street, and in practically everyone's backyard. Can we take the squishy tomatoes off the vine and use them as grenades too? Or maybe they could be mortar rounds."

"Yes," Mr. Hawkins said. "But we need to remember that everything has to be lobbed, not thrown. Throwing could be dangerous and we don't want anyone getting hurt. Not anyone. Do you know what a lob is?"

"Yeah, I know how to lob. It's like with my army grenade guys. It's like this," I said, showing the pose of one arm cocked behind me and the other one out in front for balance.

"Yes," said Mr. Hawkins. "That's it exactly."

He turned to Tilden. As he spoke, I noticed he was having trouble catching his breath. "Tilden, make sure Vincenzo tells every boy the lob rule,...and add anything you can think of to prevent...real injury. Tell Vincenzo to think on it as well."

"Yes, sir," said Tilden.

"What else?" Mr. Hawkins asked me.

"Can we fill balloons with water and make up ketchup packets for fake blood?"

"Yes. Rosa can help with that as well."

"Can I use one of the gas masks on Saturday?"

Mr. Hawkins' eyes sparkled with excitement. "Absolutely!"

Mr. Hawkins looked tired and was even more out of breath than before. Yet he went on whispering to himself. "Comrades in arms... huddled in trenches...mortar attacks at any time...the wetness...the misery, the cold... and the dream of a hot meal...but only tins of bully beef. Machine-gun fire...and the fear...palpable fear."

At that moment I got the sense that something was very wrong. Mr. Hawkins' breathing became heavier and it even made it hard for him to talk. I looked at Tilden, who immediately noticed it too and began feeling for something near Mr. Hawkins' chest pocket. Tilden's face, especially his eyes, showed more worry than I was used to seeing, but he stayed calm and his hands remained steady. He spoke to Mr. Hawkins, but Mr. Hawkins either couldn't or wouldn't speak back.

"Sir!" Tilden said, bending down alongside of him. "What is it, sir?"

Still, Mr. Hawkins did not answer.

Tilden pulled a small silver tin from Mr. Hawkins' shirt pocket and took out two little pills. Then, he seemed to almost pry open Mr. Hawkins' mouth and slip the tablets under his tongue.

"Mr. Mark," said Tilden, pointing, "in that room on your right is a sink with a glass on it. Fill the glass halfway with cold water and bring it to me at once."

I raced over to the sink, filled the glass with water, and brought it back as quickly as I could. Tilden put the glass up to Mr. Hawkins' lips and I could see Mr. Hawkins was only able to drink a few sips from it. A few seconds went by and I couldn't really tell if he was better or worse. But then, slowly, his breathing got better and he began to look around. His eyes met mine and he smiled weakly before turning toward Tilden, who was now kneeling beside him. He began to nod his head and his breathing got even easier, but I knew it had been a close call. Mr. Hawkins looked over to Tilden.

"Tilden, my life just flashed before me. I need you to do something for me."

"Yes, sir," said Tilden.

Still struggling, Mr. Hawkins spoke in a way that gave my whole body chills.

"Alice may never forgive me, Tilden, and my sons may not either, but they must know that my caring and concern for them remain unconditional. And it shall remain so, whether I am alive or not. If she falters or has regrets, Tilden, show her the letter— the letter I will ask you to write—to reassure her of my caring, my commitment, and my faith in her. Tell her that imperfect fathers, like me, still care and still feel deeply for their children. I have forgiven myself and I am at peace. Tell her I am accepting the things I cannot change, and I have wisdom enough to know the difference. Can you compose such a letter for me, Tilden? I will do my best to sign it, if I am able."

Tilden bent his head slightly and then lifted it. "Yes, sir. It is done."

I stood there frozen. It had been more serious than I wanted to believe. Tilden took hold of the wheelchair and pushed Mr. Hawkins down the hall toward his room while I trailed behind. When Tilden got him settled in bed, he looked at me and took me aside.

"Perhaps, Mr. Mark, it might be best for you to return home now. I think Mr. Hawkins might end up sleeping through the night."

"Those pills you gave Mr. Hawkins worked really good," I said hopefully. "He got better fast. Were those some kind of magic pills?"

"Yes, you could say that," said Tilden.

CHAPTER 38

As soon as I got to the breakfast table the next morning, I got bad news. Mom turned to me and said, "Zeendala, Tilden called while you were upstairs. He said that Mr. Hawkins will be resting and that it would be best if you didn't go there today."

My heart dropped. "He did?"

I felt myself growing sad when Mom's cheerful voice chimed in. "Zeendy, I got a call this morning from school. Do you remember the nice principal we met a few days ago, Mr. Adams? Well, he gave the results of the test to the public school principal, Mr. Rand, who called today and said you can start school this Monday. Daddy and I decided that you'll do fine in public school."

"Oh," I answered, barely listening.

"Know what else?"

I shook my head.

"You're going to be in the third grade and you can tell everyone your real age. No one around here will know anyway. And Dad and I are going to help you with homework every night."

This all sounded okay, good even, but I was so disappointed about not seeing Mr. Hawkins, I didn't care.

"And do you know what else?"

Usually, I would feel curious and excited because Mom sounded excited, but I couldn't feel a thing.

"What?"

"Mr. Adams says you are very good in math and you will probably be ahead of most of the kids in your class. He said very few kids have ever finished the whole test section or had such a high score. Can you believe it?"

I could believe it, because I felt pretty good about how I could add, subtract, multiply, and divide after playing Monopoly with so many dice and doing the workbook and getting help from Dad with funny word problems. I knew it made Mom really happy and I was glad, but I was still so disappointed I couldn't sound excited. All I could think about was Mr. Hawkins and getting ready for the big battle tomorrow. I felt like tomorrow couldn't come fast enough and I had a hard time thinking about or appreciating anything else. I spent most of the day that way, until my imagination got going and I pretended to be a whole bunch of other people. That carried me into the late afternoon when, for some strange reason, my dad came home.

I was so surprised and happy to see him that when he went into the kitchen I followed him. He said hello to Mom, gave her a kiss, and she kissed him back. It was probably one of the only times I was glad to see them kiss because, even though it was a disgusting habit, it was a good sign that they liked each other again. Dad sneaked a piece of orange banana cake from Mom's dessert tray, loosened his tie, and went upstairs to his bedroom to change. A few minutes later, he came down in his favorite old worn clothes and headed for his workbench in the basement. As I followed him there, I asked a lot of questions about the Great War to see what he knew. He was about to tell me about a cousin of his that was actually in it, when we were interrupted by the horrifying sound of Mom as she yelled down the stairs. "Mark! Time to burn the trash!"

My first reaction was to feel really annoyed. I was beginning to hate the sound of her sharp, screechy, hyena voice right in the middle of whatever I was doing. I wondered if, now that we were allies, Bonnie might burn the trash once in a while since she never had to do it. But Bonnie wasn't even home from school yet and also, she didn't like to get smelly because she was a girl. I guessed it would still be my job for the rest of my life or at least until I grew up and got married and had kids of my own or something.

I had no choice but to go upstairs and do it. Out the door I went, with two bags of trash and the book of matches. I touched a match to the bags of trash and stepped back and watched them burn. I stood there a while longer, but after only a few minutes I stepped back farther to avoid the smoke and waited for the flames to catch on. When they did, I put the ventilating lid over the barrel and went back inside the house through the back door. Mom looked surprised to see me come in so soon and pulled me closer for a sniff. Sticking her nose in my chest, she said, "Not bad. Did you burn the trash?"

"Yes," I said, wiggling away. I went to my room and pushed my rocking chair closer to the window, spread out the Great War book in my lap and began to read. But before I got very far into the book, the sound of Dad's electric shaver noisily buzzing away got me thinking. It struck me as odd because the only time I ever heard Dad shaving was in the morning—not in the middle of the day and never at night. Something wasn't quite right, and a feeling of worry I can barely explain came over me as I walked to Dad and Mom's bathroom. Adding to my confusion was that he had changed into a white shirt and tie. It made me ask, "Why are you shaving, Dad?"

He gave my cheek a gentle pinch and said, "I don't want to look unshaven in synagogue."

Synagogue, I thought? "But why are you going to synagogue at night?"

"It's Kol Nidre."

I had heard those words before, yet something about it was troubling. Something I couldn't quite put my finger on. I knew it was a Jewish holiday but wasn't sure exactly which one.

"Isn't Kol Nidre the one that's part of Young Kipper?"

"That's right. It's the night service before the main day service."

"Isn't Young Kipper on Sunday?" I asked worriedly. "Tomorrow is Saturday. I thought it was on Sunday."

"It starts tonight," he said, splashing on some aftershave lotion. "I have to eat quickly and get going. I'm running late."

My eyes were wide open. My heart skipped a beat.

"But isn't it supposed to be nine days after the second day of Rosh Hashanah?"

"Nine days after the first day of Rosh Hashanah," Dad corrected.

"Are you sure?"

"Yes, I'm very sure," he said with a smile.

I nodded, bent my head and began to think as a river of worry flooded my mind. I had completely forgotten about Young Kipper and that it was tomorrow, the same day as Mr. Hawkins' World War I battle. I had been sure Young Kipper was going to be on Sunday. My heart skipped another beat as I put everything together in my mind. Mom had already started her giant cooking time, and she had begun to clean everything extra in advance. I just hadn't noticed or given it much thought, since she seemed to always be cooking and cleaning. Still, I dared not believe it, because if it turned out to be true, I knew Dad was going to make me stay in services all afternoon, and possibly, since I was older than last year, the whole time, until it ended at sundown. If that happened, I would miss the whole battle—the whole entire battle! I began to panic. My heart thumped. This couldn't be happening. How did everything get so confused and mixed up?

"Oh no! Oh no!" I said under my breath. I knew I had to do something. But what? I began to walk in circles thinking and thinking of a way out.

I heard Dad eating and talking with Mom in the kitchen and soon after, I heard the sound of the front door closing. I raced downstairs to see Mom, who was pulling out a tray of candied sweet potatoes from the oven with a potholder. She looked up at me and before I had a chance to say a word she said, "Oh, good. Zeendy, be a help and baste these like you did last year." She handed me the baster and I knew candied sweet potatoes were a bad sign—a very bad sign.

"Mom, Mr. Hawkins is having a World War I battle at his house tomorrow and I really, really want to go to it. Do I have to go to services?"

"Of course you have to go to services. Tonight starts Yom Kippur."

"But, Mom, I can't miss Mr. Hawkins' World War I battle. It's going to be fantastic." I was twitching and moving from side to side. "There are going to be a lot of kids there. I told him I was coming. I can't lie."

"Nice try," Mom said.

"But, Mom," I said, feeling myself getting more itchy, hot, and upset by the second, "it's super important."

"It's out of the question. I don't want to discuss it. I have a lot to do to get ready."

"But, Mom! It's really, really important. It's the most important thing of my whole life."

Mom turned to me and smiled a partly sympathetic smile. "Sorry."

That was it? "Sorry" was all she was going to say, even after I told her how important it was? I could feel my stomach turning into knots and my face flushing.

I hated Young Kipper. It was always the strictest holiday in the world. You couldn't eat. You couldn't turn on lights or watch TV, and you couldn't ride in a car or on a bike. There were a million rules that didn't make any sense. Now it even looked like Young Kipper was going to take away my most favorite thing in the world—my imagination time with Mr. Hawkins and a whole bunch of kids and a battle that was going to be the best battle that any kid had ever known.

Giving it one last try, I went up to her, nearly in tears and pulled on her apron. I could feel my face turning red. "Pleeeeze!" I pleaded.

Mom turned to me and yelled, putting her potholder down and removing her apron. "It's out of the question! Do you hear me? And that's final."

I burst into tears, ran out of the room, and screamed at my mother like never before. "I hate everyone in this stupid family! I hate you, and I hate stupid Young Kipper, and I hate services, and I hate everything. I might go and kill myself too. That's how mad I am."

"Don't you talk like that!"

"I'm going to fast until I die. I'm going to write a note to the newspaper and tell them that I died because of Young Kipper and that my parents made me fast until I was dead. Then everyone who reads the newspapers will know you and Dad did it."

I guess Mom thought what I said was funny. I could hear her snickering under her breath. It made me even madder that she thought any part of what I said was funny, because my problem was bigger than the most gigantic mountain in the world that was about to have an avalanche at any second. But what could I do? The only person in the world I could think of that might be able to fix such a big problem was Mr. Hawkins. But even that was blocked because I couldn't even call him, because of another stinky Young Kipper rule: No phone calls on Young Kipper.

I raced upstairs, jumped on my bed, grabbed Blackie, and cried into my pillow. My life was over. From now on, everything was going to be bad, boring, sad, stupid, stinky, and dumb.

Mom came upstairs and knocked on my door. I screamed at her to go away. When she didn't, I screamed at her again as loud as I could. "You interrupted me in the middle of killing myself, and now I have to start all over again!"

I thought I could hear her laughing on the other side of my door and it made me even angrier.

"How long have you been killing yourself?" she asked.

I was furious that she thought it was all a big joke. I screamed at the top of my lungs. "Go away! It's none of your business. You'll find out in the morning when it's too late and I'm already dead. You'll have to go to jail for letting your only son kill himself while you laughed the whole time."

I heard her footsteps as she left, and I hiccupped and cried for a few more minutes before calming down. I looked through the window and out into the darkness and thought about running away from home instead of killing myself. I reasoned it might worry Mom and Dad more to have me missing because when you're dead, they don't have to go looking for you, but when you're missing, there is more to worry about, maybe. Then an even better idea came to me. As soon as the coast was clear, I was going to sneak out of the house, run down the street, and see Mr. Hawkins. If Mom and Dad wondered where I was, well, too bad for them. If Dad wanted to give me the strap for it, well, I would just have to run away before he did. But he shouldn't, since what I was planning wasn't as bad as lighting fires or playing with matches. Anyway, things were too confusing and I didn't want to think about it. But I did anyway, just seconds later. I was going to leave when it got dark, and I wasn't even going to leave a note. They didn't deserve a note.

I waited almost a whole hour. As the clanging of Mom's pots and pans continued, I put on an extra sweater, an extra pair of socks, and my Yankee cap. When the coast was clear, I went downstairs and peeked around the banister to make sure Mom was still busily working in the kitchen. I slipped out of the house and carefully and quietly closed the door behind me. Once on the street, I pounded my hip like the Lone Ranger hitting his trusty horse, Silver, to go faster. At a gallop, it only took a few seconds before I was in front of Mr. Hawkins' house. The mound of dirt that Mr. Hawkins had told Vincenzo to get was exactly where Mr. Hawkins told him to put it, directly in front of the right front wall of the house. As I moved closer, I saw a small sign stuck in the ground that read: Enter Here. It had an arrow pointing toward the mound.

It was cool to think about climbing over the wall to get to

the battlefield without having to first go into the house. It made it seem much more realistic. I wondered if I would have to drop down ten feet on the other side once I got to the top.

Out of breath, but wildly excited, I began to climb the mound. When I got to the top, which was level with the flat bluestone top of the stone wall, I looked down to see another mound also pushed up against the wall from the other side, making it easy for soldiers to slide down and enter the battlefield. But at that very moment something else grabbed my attention and would not let go. It was so unbelievable, so incredible, it nearly turned me to stone. It was the yard. The magnificent yard everyone loved, where shrubs and flowers had once bloomed, was now just overturned earth and rocks. The whole backyard looked as if it had been hit by a hail of bombs. Off in the distance, it looked as if a big trench had been dug. A giant piece of construction equipment with a huge steel shovel stood still in the middle of the backyard. I could hardly believe my eyes as I stared out at the ugly mix of mud, dirt, rocks, and overturned earth.

In the distance I could see an outline for another trench on the opposite side of the lot where no earth had yet been turned. The two trenches faced each other, the distance between them as large as part of a football field. Many small craters, big enough for two or three kids to fit in, were scattered around the yard. Each one looked as if it had come from an explosion of a bomb or missile.

I could see stacks of crabapples and a sign that read: Lobbing Only! Also, the two prized machine guns were at opposite ends of the field of battle, one positioned over the trench and the other for the trench still to be dug. I could not help but think of how huge a sacrifice Mr. Hawkins had made to make this the best war battle of all time.

Stunned, it took a while for me to notice a faint light coming from the far side of the yard. It appeared to be coming from inside the trench. As I slid down the mound of dirt, I imagined myself to be a spy who was going to report what he saw back to his commanding officer.

I moved toward the trench slowly until I was near enough to look down into it. Down below, I saw Mr. Hawkins holding a lantern with his free hand while leaning on his cane with the other. I guessed he was ten feet below me. Boards had been built into the earthen wall behind him forming a kind of seat and back support, and I knew right away it was Vincenzo's work.

Mr. Hawkins sat down, put down the lantern, and began to touch the soil of the trenches with his hand to smooth it over. What he was doing didn't make a lot of sense, but I couldn't hold back my curiosity another second.

"Mr. Hawkins. It's me, Mark," I whispered.

Startled, he jumped a little. Then he turned his body and held up the lantern. I could see under his robe he was wearing pajamas. On his feet were slippers and on his head was his favorite Red Sox cap. At first, the light from the lamp blinded me, so I put my hand up to shield my eyes.

Mr. Hawkins looked strange, as if stunned or something. His white hair was a wild-looking mess. There were smears of dirt and mud on his face.

"Oh, yes... Mark," he said looking up at me.

A moment later he looked down as if searching for something that had fallen out of his pocket. Confused, he tried to use his cane and the wall for support while looking all around to locate it. Finding nothing, he looked up at me with a boyish expression.

"Magnificent, isn't it?"

I nodded. "Yeah."

"Down here it looks incredibly real."

Mr. Hawkins moved toward another part of the trench and looked up at me. "I fear Vincenzo may never speak to me again. He resisted me mightily. In fact, he almost refused to do it. I can hardly blame him. Tilden, too, was madder than a hornet, angrier than I've ever seen him. But I know him. He'll come around."

He looked around. "Men stayed in these things for months. They ate together and told stories of their lives and their loved ones back home."

Just then he looked up at me.

"Tilden says I've been strange lately. He thinks I should go to a physician because I've been a bit short of breath and had a little chest pain. But I refused. I told him I'd go after the battle, on Monday maybe. In the meantime I promised him I would take my pills."

He made a peculiar face, like a little boy who liked the idea of causing trouble, but didn't want to get caught.

"Let's keep our voices down. Tilden doesn't know I'm out here."

Some time went by and there was hardly a sound until Mr. Hawkins said, "None of the soldiers ever knew when a bomb or enemy shell would land right in here with them. Or worse still, a canister of mustard gas and other horrors too ungodly to mention."

He let out a big sigh. "I let Rosa cut as many flowers as she could before digging it all up like this. It helped a bit."

There was a moment of silence, so I took a chance to say something. "The book you gave me said the gas burned the soldiers' eyes, faces, hands, and throats."

Mr. Hawkins turned away. Then he turned back around and nodded. "Yes, men huddled together, never knowing when they would share their last breath together."

I was completely fascinated. No book could compare with what he was saying and the way he was saying it.

"Vincenzo promised me he would finish the job tomorrow morning and would also participate with his sons in the battle after returning the backhoe to the rental company. I told him, again and again, it could all be put back together. I think it helped to satisfy him somewhat. At least, I hope it did."

As I shivered in the cold night air, Mr. Hawkins must have noticed my teeth chattering.

"Why don't you come down here, Matthew, and I'll give you a nice, woolen blanket. I have a whole stack of them."

Matthew? Wasn't Matthew his grandson's name? "Mr. Hawkins, I'm Mark. You called me Matthew."

Mr. Hawkins paused for a second and, as if he were confused, answered, "Oh…yes. Yes, of course. I meant to say Mark. Slip of the tongue. I have a grandson around your age. He's Matthew. Oh yes. I told you. Yes. The names sound alike somewhat, don't you think? Not to worry. I know who you are, dear friend. Forgive me."

I nodded. Naturally, I forgave him. I would forgive him for anything in the entire world.

By now I was getting colder, but I didn't want to go home yet, so I went to the edge of the trench and slid down into it until I was right next to him.

"Aha!" he said with a laugh as I arrived. Taking a fresh, new, woolen blanket, he leaned forward and carefully laid the blanket over my shoulders and wrapped it around my chest. As he did, I noticed the smell of liquor on his breath.

"Have you been drinking liquor, Mr. Hawkins?"

He seemed surprised by what I said. But then he made a slight nod of his head. "Yes, I have. A lot of men drank from the depression that overcame them, because of the dark, the cold, the fear, and the danger. Liquor helped them survive. So long as you weren't on guard duty. Get drunk on guard duty and your own men might shoot you." When he paused, it was as if the whole world had become silent.

"How do you like it down here?" he asked.

"It's totally neat!" I said.

Mr. Hawkins nodded and smiled. "I want to show you something. Now move over here so you can get the best view of the sky." He pointed to where he wanted me to sit.

I squeezed into a hollow part of the trench and sat down. Mr. Hawkins moved alongside me. He took a woolen blanket for himself and he began to search the sky. After looking all around for a minute or so, he finally called out, "There! See there, Matthew!" he said pointing upward.

I decided to ignore his confusion about my name.

"Mr. Hawkins? Didn't you say people got shot by their own soldiers if they were drinking liquor when they were on guard duty?"

"Did I say that?"

I nodded.

"Well then," he said, "I won't go on guard duty tonight. How's that?"

I nodded. It made it more okay, but still I would rather he didn't drink that smelly liquor stuff at all. He looked at the sky again and after a while pointed upward.

"I don't know what you're pointing at," I said.

"I am pointing at the Big Dipper. It's made up of seven stars. If you connect them, they look like the outline of a saucepan or a dipper."

I looked around, but there were so many stars, big and small, dull and bright, I couldn't see any pattern. Mr. Hawkins looked back and forth between me and the sky to see if I had seen it, but I still couldn't. He took a twig that was sticking out of the ground and drew seven points in the dirt on the side of the trench. Then he connected them. "This is what you're looking for."

It took a while, but after going back and forth between his drawing and the sky, I finally saw it. "I see it!" I exclaimed. "I see it!" My imagination wanted to leap out of my body. I wondered if the Big Dipper was like some kind of island in the sky you could jump off from and see other stars and planets. I wondered how far away each star was from the other, and how long it would take to get there in a spaceship. My mind flooded with possibilities as me and Mr. Hawkins just looked and stared and said nothing. I could have done it for hours, and would have, had the subject of my greatest fear not risen to the surface.

"Mr. Hawkins," I said, "tomorrow is Young Kipper. My mom and dad are going to make me stay in synagogue all day until the night when it gets to be sundown."

Mr. Hawkins immediately understood what it meant. "Oh, my heavens, what an unfortunate surprise."

"I don't want to go," I said, holding back tears. "This is going to be the best battle in history, and I hate services. I shouldn't have to do anything I hate, instead of something I love. Isn't that right?"

"This is a tough one. I guess we didn't plan it exactly right. Sunday's no good. Church and such for the other soldiers. Hmm, this is a tough one."

"Could you talk to my mom and dad about it? They think you're smart and you helped everyone in our family, and you're the only one who knows how important this is to me and you."

Mr. Hawkins looked sad and a little confused. He bent his head and thought. His expression said he understood and wished he could help, but soon he knew, and then I knew, he was not going to do it. He raised his head, looked into my eyes, and gave me the words. "This I cannot do."

At first I thought I should try begging, arguing, throwing a fit, or having a tantrum, but somehow I couldn't. I knew if he said something, after giving it so much thought, it was the end of it.

Mr. Hawkins reached over, gently took my face in his hands, and kissed me on the top of my head like Mom sometimes did when she wanted to help me with my sadness. I knew then and there that I loved him. He wasn't Jewish. He wasn't Dad or my uncle or my grandpa, and he even wore a Red Sox cap, but still, I knew what I felt way down deep inside.

"Maybe you'll get lucky and get out early," he said. "If you can make it, I'll have a French infantry uniform and some weapons for you on the front porch. You can put the uniform on over your clothes. It's a small size. Rosa said it will fit you."

I thought about his idea of getting out of services early, and in no time my imagination was working like mad to find a way to have hope. Maybe, just maybe, if I showed Dad I was praying harder and faster than any Orthodox Jew alive, he might agree. Maybe I could even find one of their big black hats somewhere and wear it. I would. And if somehow, some Orthodox kid, or even an Orthodox grown-up for that matter, got lost on their way to the stricter religious synagogues and ended up at Beth Israel, I would battle them to the death in a Hebrew praying- and-mumbling contest. I was ready to do anything, anything, to show Dad I deserved to get out of services early.

When I got home, I slipped in the door just as I had slipped out. The noise of the dishwasher helped cover any sound I may have made, and in a second I had sneaked back upstairs. But all I could think about was tomorrow's battle and whether I would get to be part of it.

I thought about my time in the trench with Mr. Hawkins and how he showed me the Big Dipper and the star-filled night. I thought about everything we talked about and the times we didn't even say a word. But I also thought about how Mr. Hawkins was sad part of the time and had been drinking and sometimes had been trying to catch his breath. And I couldn't get away from the fact that he'd called me Matthew at two different times. I hardly slept the whole night.

When the sun came up the next morning I was tired, which was the worst thing to be on Young Kipper because I knew I would still have to go to services. It meant I would not only be bored and miserable, but tired too.

When Mom came to the doorway to my room I remembered to still be mad at her from the night before because of all the mean, rotten jokes she made and from laughing at me. I decided to get even with her a little by telling her what I did last night, but also to see if she even cared whether I was dead or alive.

"I ran away from home last night. You probably don't even care. I came back because I didn't have any good place to go. But I'm still mad at you, and when I find a good place to go, I'm going there without even telling you. I know you don't even care if I die. I know you probably think what I am saying is cute or funny and that only makes me madder, so I will never come home once I leave. Never!"

There was complete silence. I thought for sure I was going to get yelled at, but instead, she looked at me with a loving look and shocked me with her words. "It wasn't right to laugh at what you said. I apologize and I'll try not to do it again."

Somehow, with that apology, I didn't feel as angry as before.

"You know," she said, as she came in and sat down on my bed, "according to Jewish law, when someone asks you for forgiveness on Yom Kippur, you have to forgive them if you believe they are truly sorry."

"Really?"

Mom nodded.

It was one of the first Young Kipper rules I ever heard that made sense.

"Does that mean that if I ask you to forgive me for something, you will?"

Mom nodded again.

"Can you be forgiven for more than one thing?" I asked hopefully. "I think I have a lot of things."

She nodded again and patted my head. I liked the feeling but I didn't want her doing it while I was seriously thinking of stuff to get forgiven for, so I wiggled away.

"Does the forgiver have to really and truly forgive and not just say it so they can get you back later?"

"Yes, it has to be genuine. You have to mean it."

"Okay," I said. "I'm sorry I lit a fire in the basement and used matches at school."

I stopped there for a second because I knew I had to sneak in my latest fire story and get it forgiven before she could even think about it. If I could sneak it in and get it forgiven, I'd really be in the clear. I saw her nodding as if she were ready to forgive any little extra things troubling me when I saw my opening.

"And I'm sorry that I lit one in the trash can in the backyard that almost caught the garage on fire. Do you forgive me?"

She winced when I mentioned it, and I knew my eyes were sort of bulging a little, but it was my best chance to get everything forgiven at once. Also, I figured out that since nothing was on fire right now, it would be much easier for her to forgive me. Things that "almost" happened were definitely easier to forgive than things that actually happened.

She closed her eyes and took a deep breath and let it out. "Yes. I forgive you."

Wow! I thought. The Young Kipper rule was really neat.

I began to wonder if I might be able to use the rule with Dad. If I had known about it before, I might have tried to light all my fires on Young Kipper and get forgiven as fast as possible before anyone knew what I did. But I had a feeling part of the rule must be that a person couldn't do something with a plan to get out of it. Also, I knew, without even checking, there had to be another rule to keep the first rule from getting used the wrong way. There always was. Also, I knew if a rule fell on the Sabbath or something, there would be another handy third rule to replace the second rule.

"You look tired," Mom said. "Why don't you rest for a while before you get up and get ready for services?"

It was the best idea of that morning.

CHAPTER 39

Time dragged on in synagogue, and by what would have been lunchtime I was as hungry as a lion. I hadn't eaten a thing since the night before, and I was pretty sure I was about to drop dead from starvation. Still, I tried to fast as long as I could, hoping Dad might think of me as a really good son and let me out early.

But for some reason, Dad seemed far away in thought and unusually quiet. Mom noticed it, too, and for a while she asked me to switch seats with her so she could be next to him. When she could see Dad had a lot on his mind, she was very good at getting him to speak, without making him feel like she was being pushy. I could tell he liked the feeling of being in synagogue. For him it was relaxing and it made him feel closer to God, I think.

Mom nudged closer to him. He was sitting in the aisle seat. To her right were me and Bonnie. Mom gently pushed her elbow into his ribs and it made him smile. It was a joke between them. She would do it whenever she wanted him to come out of a trance and talk to her.

Seeing that there was a recess and a mass of people moving all around, he said, "Do you remember the conversation I had with our neighbor, Mr. Hawkins?"

Mom nodded. "You didn't say much about it. Only that it was useful."

Dad nodded. "I've been thinking about it every day."

Mom nodded again.

Dad began to speak, but it was different from the way he normally spoke. It was as if he were filled with a lot of different feelings and had to work to make his way through them.

"There is a guy at the plant—a new worker. To be honest, he has rather limited capabilities..." Dad paused, like he wasn't sure if he was going to continue, but Mom took his hand for a second and it helped him go on.

"I don't think this fellow ever met someone Jewish before. He said as much, but he tried to say it respectfully."

There was another pause.

"Yesterday he wished me 'Happy holiday'. He actually said the words 'L'shana Tovah.' It turns out that he asked his son, who reads better than he does, to look up in the encyclopedia what a Jew was. That's where he learned the expression. He said he practiced saying it so that it would come out right. I think it was his gift to me for giving him a job—his way of saying thanks."

I could see Mom was moved by Dad's words and so was I.

"Every time I think about it, a word keeps coming to mind. It's the same word that Hawkins used over and over again—decency. I think this worker and all my employees for that matter only want a chance to work and be treated fairly—and with decency—nothing more and nothing less. When I think back on the situation in New York, I know the labor component was very difficult and very frustrating for us, but even there I would have done better to strive for decency and better working conditions than to resist everything tooth and nail."

I saw Mom rub the back of Dad's hand.

Dad got a little choked up but managed to go on. "Hawkins was right. He was absolutely right. Decency has to be part of business. And it costs very little to provide."

It made me very, very happy to hear Dad say what he did, mostly because I liked that he liked Mr. Hawkins just like I did. I also liked that Dad seemed pleased, almost happy. To know Dad was happy was worth the entire world to me.

Soon, people took their seats and the doors to the sanctuary closed. Mom leaned over and kissed Dad gently on the cheek and motioned she was going to go back to her old seat again. I moved back to the seat next to him. After settling in, my mind began to wander and I found myself thinking about the battle at Mr. Hawkins' house and how it was set to begin at any time. I thought about his backyard all dug up, and I wondered if any miracle could deliver me from here to there.

I also thought about how I got to be in Massachusetts after being a kid from Bayside, and it reminded me of what happened that time when the nice man almost ran me over. I remembered how I had promised myself to pray for him and his family and everyone important to him so he would have a good new year. I leaned toward Dad and whispered, "Dad?"

Dad tilted his head so that his ear was closer to me.

"What's the prayer you say for people to protect them and their families from bad things happening for the whole next year?"

Dad thought for a bit before turning his head and looking down at me.

"There are two. The first is a prayer to confess your sins and the second one asks God for forgiveness."

"Does that get you into The Book of Life?" I asked.

Dad smiled a little. "Hopefully it does."

"Hopefully? You mean after all that praying you still can't be sure?"

Dad shook his head.

"What's the sin one?"

"Hmm?"

"The sin one—where you confess all of your sins?"

He looked down at his prayer book and flipped through a bunch of pages until he came to the prayer I was talking about.

He turned his prayer book toward me and I saw the page number and found the page in my own prayer book. As soon as I got there I saw the English translation of the Hebrew and could hardly believe my eyes.

"Wow! Look at all those sins, Dad! There's a million of 'em!"

I guess Dad thought what I said was funny because he smiled. "Well, they aren't all your sins. They're the sins of all of Israel. When you pray, you say you're sorry not only for your own sins but also for the sins of all of the people in Israel too."

I nodded as if I understood, but I really didn't. How could I be sorry for other people's sins? I had enough of my own sins to deal with, and the way I was going, I would probably be sinning more. Any regular person could see it was too much to be responsible for everyone in Israel. Also, I didn't know a single person in Israel or even where it was. Still, I kept nodding like I got it. I hoped that nodding like that, when I didn't understand, wasn't a sin also.

"What if I want to pray for someone who isn't from Israel?"

"You could say his name to yourself or add it to your prayers."

"Will that get him into The Book of Life?"

"Hopefully."

Hmm. Hopefully, again. I decided I would just have to count on "hopefully" since Dad couldn't be more definite than that. I closed my eyes and whispered quietly "God, please protect the nice man I scared to death, and not only him but his whole family and his pets and everything he cares about. It wasn't his fault he almost ran me over. It was my fault. So forgive me, too, for what I did, and even though I don't understand all of these words like lewdness, and immorality, and coercion, and impurity of speech, and desecrating the divine's name, please put me and him in The Book of Life. I promise to try and be good and not burn anything down."

The rabbi took his place at the bimah and looked out onto the congregation. From our seats he looked to be about a mile away. Looking like a king in a flowing white robe with his tallis, prayer shawl, and white silk yarmulke, he cleared his throat and began to speak.

"Welcome, members of congregation Beth Israel. As we gather here today in our beautiful synagogue, I am reminded of…"

Using all my powers of imagination, I tried to block out the rabbi's next words and fly off to someplace wonderful. I felt a desperate need to break free and get away with not only my mind but my body too. All I could think about were the trenches, kids, uniforms, machine guns, and crabapple grenades. I knew the kids in the neighborhood must be going nuts because of everything Mr. Hawkins had done.

"…Yom Kippur is not only the Day of Atonement, the most sacred of the Jewish holidays and the Sabbath of Sabbaths, but it is indeed the final day of the ten-day period of repenting…"

I'd bet anything Rosa was cooking up something great for all of the soldiers playing there now. Food was on my mind a lot, since I was starving to death from fasting.

"…According to ancient scripture, as most of us know, God spent 30 days prior to Rosh Hashanah deciding the future lives of all mankind. But the God we worship is a merciful God and thus it is said and thus it is written, that God has granted us a ten-day reprieve for our many sins…"

The rabbi's voice became more serious and I realized it was the same voice I had heard at Mr. Hawkins' house that time. This was the rabbi who was in the shadows. It was the very same guy who had talked about the playground and Mr. Hawkins' friend Mr. Bloom. I was almost certain it was him, but because he was so far away because of our crappy faraway seats, I still couldn't be absolutely, positively sure.

"My fellow Jews and congregants, the last ten days of this reprieve ends this evening at sundown, at which time the Ark will be closed, and The Book of Life will thus be sealed. Yom Kippur is a solemn day and it is, in a sense, a last chance to do right by ourselves and the people we may have injured…"

I looked at the rabbi way in the distance because what he said interested me for a moment and took me away from my thoughts of trench warfare. The whole thing about God closing The Book of Life was imaginative, and I wondered if an ancient kid about my age made it up.

"As we read our ancient biblical teachings and pray for God's forgiveness, it is also a time to include the unfinished business of seeking out those whom we may have harmed or injured in some way. To these people, Jew and Gentile alike, we should undertake acts of repentance. If we have sinned—if we have injured them, what better time is there than now, to be strong enough in spirit, and righteous enough in heart, to acknowledge these sins and ask for forgiveness."

The rabbi cleared his throat and almost seemed to lose his place, but then he recovered and went on. "Even our own children deserve such consideration. Often powerless and misunderstood, we must ask, too, if they are they not entitled to an apology for the errors of our ways. Are they not entitled to be heard more, to be better understood, and to be given the benefit of the doubt? And should we perhaps reconsider the ways in which we seek to discipline? Our ancient religion does not fear change, and if times are changing, perhaps, so must we. This is all part of atonement. And it is all part of Judaism at its finest."

A shiver went up my spine. All at once I became very interested in the rabbi's speech, surprised that it had something to do with kids. Best of all, he was making sense. I also liked that he said "Jew and Gentile alike." That was the one thing I thought should be different in the world. I thought people everywhere were mostly the same, like the nice man who almost ran me over and all the popcorn people. They all believed that, if a dumb little kid got run over, it would be a terrible thing. It didn't seem to matter to any of them whether I was Jewish or not, just that I was all right.

I thought about Stuart and how I'd gotten him into trouble. He deserved an apology from me and it made me kind of sad I never had a chance to say, "I'm sorry," in person. I decided to include him in my list of apologies and everyone else I could think of. I tried to count them: the popcorn people, the motorcycle guy, and all the people who cared about me. Even my ally, Bonnie, and Arlene and my whole family and all my uncles, aunts, and cousins. I whispered "sorry" to myself about 25 times and pictured each one of them appreciating my apology. But just as I was finishing, the most amazing thing in the entire universe happened. It was more unbelievable than the Red Sea parting or the Jews leaving Egypt to be free from slavery. My very own dad leaned down toward me, turned his head, looked straight into my eyes, and whispered, "Zeendy, what I did was wrong—very wrong. I know that now. I've been thinking about it a lot and for a long, long time. I would like to ask your forgiveness. Do you think you can?"

I felt a feeling similar to when I bumped up against the fast-moving car that almost killed me. First, there was shock, and I had trouble believing what had actually happened. Then, my heart started to pound a million beats a second. As I looked up into Dad's eyes, I saw in them, and in his expression, that it was not a joke or my imagination playing tricks on me. He meant it. And I knew for sure, it was about the strap. It had to be. After all, there was nothing else he would have ever needed to ask me to forgive. He was an excellent dad in every other way.

It came to me that he was the one choosing to wait this time, just like when us kids have to wait for grown-ups to decide what they are going to do to us.

My heart kept pounding as if that bongo drummer was in my chest again. Still, something inside kept me from uttering a word. I only knew I needed to say more than "okay." Somehow, I knew a time like this might never come again, and so I had to be sure to make the most of it. My eyes were watering so much and I was fighting so hard to hold back tears, my vision was getting blurry. I was so afraid I would cry and lose my best chance ever to tell Dad what he needed to hear and what I needed to say. Finally, it poured out.

"Do you promise never to use the strap on me ever again?"

Unbelievably, tears filled his eyes, and I knew it wasn't from any allergies. At last he nodded. I could see he was choking on his feelings, just like I was on mine.

"I do," he said finally, his voice steady and certain. "I do."

I kept looking at him through tear-filled eyes and did my best to give a tiny nod to let him know he was forgiven. A nod was all I could do, since I was too choked with feelings to speak. There were so many feelings in the air I guess it made Mom notice. She leaned over, looked at me and then at Dad, and with the rabbi's words still echoing in all our ears, she seemed to understand what had happened. She stretched her arm past me and put it on Dad's arm. Tears were in her eyes too.

"You're a good man, Irving. I'm prouder of you today than I've ever been."

Dad closed his eyes, bent his head, and nodded repeatedly. He covered his face with his hand and moved his pointer finger as if to scratch his forehead, but we all knew he wasn't. After a lot of deep breaths, Dad looked more or less like his regular self again, calm, quiet, and listening to the rabbi's words.

I thought about Dad and the kind of man he was. I thought about how he was not the type of guy to go back on his promises. He was strong and good, like the heroes in the movies, ready to give his life for what he believed in—the kind of guy who would fight and die for you. I thought about how he had given his word, and how I could rely on that forever and ever and ever. Most importantly, although he didn't know how to say it, I felt sure he loved me.

The rabbi's sermon went on forever and he talked about all sorts of different Jewish stuff, like about Israel and giving to charity and something that Moses once said. When it was finally over, the praying started again and although I tried my best not to show it, my urge to somehow get out got stronger and stronger, because all I could think about was Mr. Hawkins' house and his Great War backyard. And even though Dad's promise was as good as any miracle, and was the best thing I could have hoped for, other than having him be happy from now on and for the rest of his life, the truth was, I was still stuck in services with no way out. I realized my only hope was God. I decided if ever there was a time to prove to me that He was real and could do miracles, now was the time. I closed my eyes and made up my own silent prayer.

"God, you and Mr. Hawkins are the only ones who know how important this battle is to me. Mr. Hawkins said he can't help me and that means it's up to you. I prayed hard and asked for forgiveness like the rabbi said I should. I even forgave Dad for the strap. I did the right thing for the man who almost ran me over and all the popcorn people who looked on. What I mean is, I think I shouldn't have to stay in services anymore because I'm dying in here. Can you please, please, please do a miracle and help me find a way to get out? Amen."

At that exact, precise instant, my father looked at his watch and then at Mom. Seeing him look at his watch, she leaned over and whispered, "I have some preparation to do at home, and I think the kids have had enough of fasting. Why don't I take them back? We'll be ready for you when you come home at sundown."

Then the miracle happened. Dad nodded and said, "Okay." He looked down at me and rubbed my head. "You can eat whenever you want. You did very well."

I couldn't believe it! There was a God! And sometimes He answered prayers right on the spot. Of course He was always clever the way He did it, like now, using Dad and other people to do the miracle for Him, but I didn't care so long as it got done.

When we got outside I began jumping all around, itching to race home. Mom saw I was bursting with energy and insisted I stay close to her so I didn't accidentally run out into the street and get hit by a car or run over.

When at last we were home, my legs were wobbly and my head felt woozy. Inside, Mom got Arlene settled and took out a platter of fresh vegetables and dip from the refrigerator so we all wouldn't drop dead from hunger. I knew the real meal, which would be warmed up at sundown, would be extra special, but right now my eyes were on the platter of food in front of me. With both hands I grabbed at slices of crunchy carrots, cucumber, and celery, dipping them in dressing as fast as I could and immediately stuffing them into my mouth and wolfing them down. I was still hungry and chomping when I ran upstairs and changed into comfortable play clothes. On my return trip I slid down the banister, grabbed another fistful of veggies, and raced out the back door. I was down the steps and halfway across the yard when the horrifying sound of Mom crying out reached my ears. "Mark!" she shrieked.

I stopped and looked back. To my horror, I saw her on the back porch holding two full bags of trash with her left arm while showing me a book of matches with her right hand.

"No!" I screamed as if it was the end of my life. "I have to go!"

She shook her head. "You have to do it."

"It'll take too long," I screamed, nearly popping a vein in my neck. "I'm in a hurry. I have to go see Mr. Hawkins."

"You have to do it. It's your job."

"Who said it was my job?" I shouted loud enough for anyone in the neighborhood to hear.

"I said."

"Well, I can't do it today! Get someone else to do it! What about Bonnie?" I roared.

"No. It's your job."

"I don't want to do it anymore! I'm sick of it! Every day! Every day! I always get smoky and it smells, and I don't like being interrupted every single second of every single minute of every single hour of my life. Can't you do it for once?"

For some reason Mom's expression changed ever so slightly. I don't know how to describe it, but it was as if she had been holding her breath for a very long time and had finally released it. Still she waited as we kept trying to stare each other down.

"You still need to do it," she said.

"No!" I yelled. "I'll do double trash tomorrow."

"No good." She shook her head. "You've got to do it every day or it will smell."

Desperate, I decided to call on God one more time and say another silent prayer. "Please, God, it will take up too much time. Tomorrow I will burn double or even triple trash if you will please,

please, please let me go. Set thy people free, oh Lord. You are the only one who knows how important this is. Blessed art thou who convinces Mom that I shouldn't have to do the trash today. Amen."

Mom's eyes and mine stayed locked and it was looking more and more like she wasn't going to budge. And that was when I got an idea that no doubt came right from God Himself.

"It's Young Kipper!" I declared. "It's Young Kipper!" I said again, shrieking with glee. "No burning trash on Young Kipper!"

Mom didn't want to smile, but I could see she couldn't help it. She kept looking at me and her smile got bigger and bigger, and I knew all over again what a great mom she was. She was going to be a good sport about it and not throw a tantrum just because her kid outsmarted her.

She put the bags down and waved me off with a sweep of her arm. "Go!" she shouted. "But come home at sundown. Don't keep Dad and me waiting."

"I won't!" I yelled over my shoulder as I raced off.

I must have gone halfway down the street when I realized I wasn't wearing my lucky Yankee cap. I immediately stopped, spun around, and headed back toward the house. As I crossed the lawn to the backyard I was thinking about a million different things. But they all disappeared when I saw Mom with her back to me still up on the porch above me. For some reason her arms were lifted as high as they would go and were spread apart. It looked as if she were looking toward the sky and praying, or maybe, thanking the heavens for something. She stayed like that for a long time, and I watched without moving as her feet began to move in a kind of graceful dance step like the kind people do at weddings and Bar Mitzvahs, except she seemed to be doing it in slow motion, bending her knees and gracefully putting one foot in front of the other and then back again. Curious, but silent, I watched her for a while longer before deciding not to disturb her. Instead, I turned around and raced back down the street, remembering I wouldn't need my Yankee cap anyway, especially after I put on my Great War helmet and the rest of my battle clothes.

CHAPTER 40

When I got to Mr. Hawkins' house, I heard fireworks over the loudspeakers and boys yelling and shouting. Dozens of footprints were already in the mound. I raced to the front porch and found the cardboard box Mr. Hawkins told me would be there and sure enough, there it was with my name on it.

The uniform inside had been shortened and fit almost perfectly. I hurriedly put on two extra pairs of heavy woolen socks to help fill up the extra space in the boots before lacing them up. I put on the steel helmet and crisscrossing belts, slung the sack and duffle bag over my shoulder, grabbed the wooden French Lebel rifle, and raced back toward the mound.

When I reached the top of the mound I saw the other trench had been dug. The backhoe was gone and wire fencing—the kind people use to keep little animals out of their garden— was rolled up like barbed wire near both trenches. Seven or eight boys in the trench closest to me had on German helmets and infantry uniforms. Anthony, his brother Sonny, and some other boys were huddled down in the German trench. Dressed in a German infantry uniform, Vincenzo looked through a telescope toward the trench on the opposite end of the yard. Some of the boys were playing cards with others munching on slices of pizza, when a boy looked up from the German trench and pointed at me.

"Frenchy!" he yelled.

Two other boys immediately stopped what they were doing and reached for crabapples and began lobbing them my way, calling out, "Get him! Enemy soldier!"

I ran to the other trench across the yard as fast as I could while tomato and crabapple grenades exploded all around me. When I got near the Allied trench, someone acting as the lookout yelled, "French soldier approaching. Hold your fire!"

I quickly sat down, hung my legs over the edge, and tried to slide down when I felt the hands of other boys helping to ease me down.

"Quick, my friend," said one of them. "Don't let them get you with a grenade."

When my boots hit the bottom of the trench, water splashed and mud splattered and I caught sight of a hose with running water. Holy cow, I thought, Mr. Hawkins even arranged to make mud so we could know how it felt in the real trenches of the Great War! As I got up, a crabapple landed less than a foot from me. When I felt the splash I made an explosion sound with my mouth and felt my wound. I began to fall to my knees when the same boy pulled me up and spoke to me as if I had been his friend in combat forever. His lip and front teeth stuck way out, and he had trouble making his words clear. When he spoke, tiny drops of spit flew out and spattered my face.

"It wasn't a direct hit. You don't die unless you get hit three times," he said. "Each time you get hit you should whack yourself with the fake blood packets. Do you have any?"

I shook my head.

"Here." He gave me a handful of them. "All you have to do is whack yourself with one in the face. The red blood stuff comes squirting out. It's the honor system. You die for a while and it looks neat. They cart you away and the Red Cross ladies fix you up, and you can come alive behind the shed and get back into the battle."

I looked around. Mr. Hawkins sat at the end of the trench on wooden planks specially built for him. In his hand was an unusual-looking lookout's rifle that had mirrors attached. He looked happily lost in his thoughts and didn't even notice me.

I stepped up on a crate and looked out over the edge of the trench to the battlefield and watched as Rosa and another woman, whom I figured out was Vincenzo's relative, Marie, waved a white flag. They helped some of the wounded into the convalescent carts and bandaged them with gauze.

Finally, Mr. Hawkins turned his head in my direction and noticed me. But he appeared so dazed and reacted so slowly, I wondered if he was okay.

The hand that had been shaking when I last saw him was even worse, but he managed to call me over with a motion of his head. When I was next to him he looked at me through glassy eyes and put a hand on my shoulder. Then, breaking into a smile, he said, "I see you made it after all."

I smiled and nodded and we sat without saying a word until his voice broke the silence.

"The battle has been raging here since two o'clock this afternoon. Most of the soldiers are firing randomly and hurling grenades. The Germans attacked once and we repelled them. There were lots of dead and wounded."

No sooner had he spoken than puddles all around us began to splash from a hail of crabapples and tomato bombs. After pressing our heads against the earthen wall for protection, Mr. Hawkins went on.

"Last night, after you left, I wrote a script for the whole battle! It just came to me! I pictured the whole thing in my mind and wrote it down. I gave it to Tilden, and he's been reading pieces of it over the speaker. Tilden is in the officers' quarters. Over there." He pointed. I looked over and saw a dim light coming from the sunroom.

"I put notes in the margins of the script and told him to play the music and read it aloud. I think the boys are quite taken by it. He's been playing the fireworks records and they sound beautiful, even frightening. You can hear the bombs bursting and the sound of thundering rockets. We've been huddled together down here, me and the Doughboys and French troops. Tomato and apple grenades are coming over all the time. Watch out. Stay low."

Tilden's voice came over the speaker. As I searched, I saw him in the distance looking down at something and turning pages as he spoke into a microphone.

"On February 21st, 1916, Germany launched a massive attack against the city of Verdun near the border of France and Germany. After many hours of artillery bombardment, the German infantry advanced…" said Tilden into the microphone.

The entire battlefield grew quiet as every kid in our trench hung on each word. "…The French were caught off guard and were temporarily thrown back, but when summer came, their resolve grew stronger and they reclaimed all their lost territories. Fierce attacks and counterattacks were launched by both sides."

When Tilden finished reading, a spooky quiet returned to the trench. Soldiers backed away from the walls of earth and relaxed. Others played cards and talked softly. I moved about the trench, looked at all the new faces, and settled on one in particular who was dressed in an American uniform and speaking to Mr. Hawkins and a few of his mates. He started by saying "Back in Iowa," and then he went into this long speech about how it was to be away from home. He talked about dairy cows and sheep and his dog named Crusty. He talked about how his mom would always make flapjacks for him in the morning after he milked the cows and fed the chickens. He said the roosters crowed at sunup and the morning mist burned off and made the air so fresh. I knew this kid wasn't from Iowa. In fact, I was almost sure he lived around the corner. But he was so convincing that after a while, I started to feel bad he had to leave Iowa and be stuck in a trench in the middle of the Great War. I found myself hoping he would someday get back to Iowa to be with Crusty and have flapjacks again.

Mr. Hawkins patted him on the shoulder. "I hope you make it home, soldier."

As other kids talked and made up stories about the battle, it had a funny effect on me. I started to understand how lonely life in the trenches must have been. Like a lot of those trench soldiers, I lost track of time. My only sense of time came from the early evening shadows that were all around us.

Just then, the silence was shattered and I heard the lookout shouting, "German attack! Heavy infantry coming this way!"

Everyone scrambled into position, aimed their rifles, and fired. It looked like an all-out attack as the Germans poured out of their trench with their rubber bayonets. Darting from side to side, they stormed ahead, many being hit and dying on the battlefield as our guys lobbed handfuls of crabapples, tomatoes, and water-filled balloons at them. Still, some got through and two even made it down into our trench and bayoneted two of our guys before they were shot dead.

The classical music coming through the speaker was filled with trumpets, horns, and clashing cymbals. During certain moments I actually felt fear as I imagined what it must have been like to be charged by someone with a real bayonet at the end of a real rifle.

When it was over, we patched up our dead guys, gave them new life, and put everything back the way it was. Some guys began playing cards again and making up stories. The kid who said he was from Iowa even improved on his story and I found it hard to believe he'd ever lived anywhere else.

Every few minutes, I glanced at Mr. Hawkins, and could not help but notice that he didn't seem like himself, even though I could tell he was trying to be. There were creases on his face that I'd never seen before, and his shaking hand had to be stopped by using his other hand to silence it.

I looked into the evening shadows, knowing somewhere in the back of my mind that I had something to do or somewhere to be, but for the life of me I could not remember where, when, or why.

Even though I didn't want to get out of pretend, I felt I needed to tell Mr. Hawkins one more thing from my real life, something I thought would make him happy, so I sloshed through a mud puddle and went close to him.

"Mr. Hawkins?" I whispered.

He turned slowly and looked at me, perhaps surprised I was getting out of my imagination. Smiling, he leaned closer.

"I got into school. I'm going to go to public school. I start on Monday. Maybe you can come sometime and see it," I said.

Even though I felt sure he heard me, it took him a long time to answer. When he finally did, it was with a forced smile and a nodding head, but there were no words.

"Also, the principal said I'm good at math."

He nodded his head some more. I could tell he was pleased, even as his hand began to shake again and he struggled to catch his breath.

"Mr. Hawkins?"

I waited.

"If I go to school all day and have to do homework after and have to go to Hebrew school, when will we be able to play?"

He hardly moved after I said it. His head remained bent like he was thinking. Finally, after what seemed a long time, he looked up and gazed at me. I was surprised to see how bloodshot his eyes were. He put his hand gently on my shoulder and whispered, "Don't worry. You will make many, many new friends. I promise."

Maybe it should have made me happy to hear him say that, but it didn't. Instead, it had a kind of weird and scary feeling to it. It was not like him to answer that way. He always had helpful things to say—and smart things. He knew how to figure stuff out. I didn't want or need other friends to replace him. Even if I made a thousand friends, none of them could ever be as good a friend as he was.

He moved away from me and plopped down against the far trench wall where there was more of a seat for him. I watched him put out his hand and curl his right pointing finger, a sign he wanted me to come closer. I went over right away and sat next to him.

"In my script, I told Tilden to play Beethoven's Symphony Number 9, Ode to Joy. I told him to turn it way up and not to turn it off until the song was over. It should start soon."

I watched as Mr. Hawkins took deeper breaths like people do when standing on the end of a diving board before they make a scary, serious dive. It was like he was getting ready to do something that called for courage and strength.

When the music started again, it quickly grabbed hold of my feelings. There were violins, horns, clarinets, and cymbals mixing and crashing together in a way that could only have been made by Mr. Beethoven. I liked that it made me feel...bigger. It must have made Mr. Hawkins feel that way, too, because soon after, he began to use his cane to stand. He closed his eyes and breathed deeply once again. Finally, he stood up and appeared to be very short of breath. I watched as every one of our trench soldiers turned to watch him. Then, all at once and to everyone's surprise, he called out for everyone to hear.

"Soldiers of the free American and French forces, our time has come."

My first reaction was to feel excited and happy, but it became less so when I saw him remove a flask from his pocket, unscrew the top, and take a big swallow. After wiping his lips with his sleeve, he took hold of his cane and rifle and using them like crutches, he struggled to move his feet to the edge of the trench wall. After signaling, two boys got behind him and began pushing him up. Soon a third and then a fourth joined in. In a matter of seconds he was up and out of the trench with his back to the enemy. We all looked on spellbound as he worked one leg and then the other to free himself from the trench completely. After leaning on the butt end of his rifle as if it were a second cane, he gave a final mighty shove until he was at last standing on his own two feet. From where I was, way down in the trench looking up, he looked like a giant oak tree, solid and powerful, that had been planted above us.

I watched him look all around the battlefield as if gazing

onto something beautiful and amazing when he paused, turned, and looked back down at me. He had a happy look on his face. It was then I realized he'd been wanting to make me understand something and had been waiting for just the right moment. In that one look were all the things we felt for each other. Our eyes lingered and then the moment was gone. I knew a split second later, when he raised his head high and looked away from me, he was going to go into his soldier's role completely and was not going to come out. I remembered what I had first said when we had first met. "If you're sad, just be someone else."

I knew he had not forgotten my idea and my advice and was taking it seriously. That "someone else" was the leader of other Great War soldiers—men he'd spent months with, in the misery of the trenches and in the horror of battle.

I watched him turn and face the entrenched enemy in the distance. Not a single soldier from the German side shot at him. It was as though every soldier realized the man in front of them was special—one deserving special respect and treatment.

Supported only by his cane and rifle, he took a wobbly step forward. With each movement, he twisted sharply to the left or right, as if in reaction to stabbing pain, while the music ramped up like nothing I'd ever heard before. Mr. Hawkins turned each twinge of pain into another step forward until he'd gone almost 20 feet. Stopping, he reached into the pocket under his infantryman's coat and took hold of something small and silvery. It looked a lot like the container of his magic pills, but I decided it could not have been because of what he did next.

With a great sweeping motion of his arm, he sent the silvery object flying into the evening shadows and a moment later, he did the same with his cane, launching it high into the air, bottom over top, rising farther and farther as if sent there by a circus juggler.

Now with only his rifle for a cane, he forged ahead, advancing a dozen more steps before panting and finally stopping. Looking back over his shoulder, he waved his arm in a way that made it clear to everyone he was ordering us all to follow.

I felt the music overtaking me, making my heart pound and my blood race through my veins. Everyone fixed their rubber bayonets and tossed their gum out of their mouths and spit one last time as they prepared for an all-out assault. The music burst with cymbals as the Allied soldiers streamed forth out of the earth like fierce army ants released from underground tunnels. Everything seemed to cross over from pretend to real and I couldn't tell where the line between them was. In fact, I was no longer sure about anything.

With my chest heaving, I followed the lead of the other boys who scrambled over the top. Others went around and up the wooden steps on the side built into the earth. With fixed bayonets, we all raced forward, even as Vincenzo hurled over a package of newspaper and wax that smoked like crazy. Someone called out, "Mustard gas," as it landed and the smoky cloud choked the last tinge of late afternoon light as some of the boys acted out the terrible death and blindness that would have come if the smoke were a gas instead. Others, like me, ran around the poisonous mist and kept our eyes on Mr. Hawkins, our glorious commander, who struggled onward, one step at a time. For some reason, without ever having planned it, we all began to scream and shout as we charged.

I ducked and dodged a hailstorm of crabapples, water balloons, and tomatoes that fell all around me until finally I felt the ping of a crabapple hitting me on the neck. I reached for a blood packet and slapped it against myself, making the red liquid ooze.

Mr. Hawkins was still out in front of us, having covered more than half the distance to the enemy trench when me and a couple of other infantry soldiers caught up to him. That's when I saw up close how heavily he was panting. On his face and around his cheeks and jaw I saw tense muscles that even his helmet could not hide. Yet, in spite of his pain, he was smiling and looked satisfied. It was as if he were having a really good dream and didn't want to be awakened, no matter how much it hurt to stay in it.

I heard a door slam. It was from the sunroom. I looked over my shoulder and watched Tilden step onto the battlefield and nervously look about. Mr. Hawkins was now only 20 feet or so from the enemy trench. Tilden usually walked as if he were forever in some kind of ceremony, his head high and his steps just short of a march, but now he sprinted with astonishing speed toward his friend at the far end of the yard.

As Mr. Hawkins moved through a wall of heavy machine-gun fire, his smile remained. Even as gunfire ripped into the Allied forces and fireworks lit up the sky, his smile remained a part of him.

I could feel everyone's emotions going higher and higher as members of the Allied forces dropped down into the German trenches and went into hand-to-hand combat. Soldiers on both sides were bayoneted and blown up, stabbed, and shot, as blood packets were ripped open by the dozens and their red liquid streamed from the wounds of every soldier. One soldier, caught in barbed wire, screamed as if in a terrifying nightmare while others, blinded by gas, groped their way in the dark and howled in agony. Boys with fear in their eyes bayoneted other boys with anger and revenge in theirs. Cries of pain and suffering rose into the air.

Mr. Hawkins fell to a knee and then crumpled to both knees, and clutched at his chest, unable to stand any longer. It looked like he was going to fall face first into the enemy trench. But in that instant, Tilden dove into the trench and used his own body to shield Mr. Hawkins' head from hitting the ground. Mr. Hawkins collapsed with a thud into Tilden's outstretched arms and both of them fell down to the muddy bottom. Tilden worked his way out from under Mr. Hawkins, carefully supporting his head in his lap as the battle raged around them.

I was the first soldier to break the rules by not dying after being hit by a barrage of water balloons and tomatoes. Dazed, wet, and splashed with tomato, I walked around in a kind of circle, as I looked down at Mr. Hawkins and Tilden.

"This is the face of war," I heard myself say. The screaming and suffering and dying and the faces of the soldiers in a fight to the death made me realize that even though it was glorious to pretend, war was a terrible thing, just like Mr. Hawkins had once said.

I began to think about everyone who ever had a friend or brother or father who died in a war. But before I could think more, a German soldier, pointing a finger at me, shattered my thoughts as he yelled to his friends. .

"He's got shell shock. Leave him alone and get the others!"

They were talking about me and the dazed look on my face. It was true. I was in a kind of shell shock.

Tilden raked back Mr. Hawkins' white hair with his fingers and I saw that Mr. Hawkins looked terribly weak. Breathing very fast and hard, his hand went over his heart, his eyes closed, and his body went limp. All around, kids were still acting out their fighting and dying, but I could only look at Mr. Hawkins, and what I saw made me want to throw up.

I tried telling myself maybe Mr. Hawkins had figured out a new way to look when he pretended to die. I wanted to believe, I tried to believe, that maybe, just maybe, Mr. Hawkins was faking being dead, like he had a hundred times before when we would pretend to fight and die. But the longer I stared, the less likely it seemed. With his body still, Tilden began a frantic search of Mr. Hawkins' clothing. Whatever it was he was looking for, he couldn't seem to find it. I heard Tilden call out to Mr. Hawkins almost angrily, "John! John! Where the hell are the nitro tablets? For God's sake!"

Mr. Hawkins couldn't answer. The expression on Tilden's face made me worry even more, as he frantically searched every pocket on Mr. Hawkins' haversack and every other small pocket in his belt and coat. Finally, frustrated, his voice boomed. "The damned tablets, John! What the hell did you do with them?"

Tilden's eyes looked wild now. I knew he was more nervous than at any other time I'd known him. I studied Mr. Hawkins for any sign of life—a fake frown, wink, anything that would show he was okay and only pretending.

Tilden turned to Vincenzo, who was still deep into the battle and shouted at him. I knew right then, just by the sound of Tilden's voice, he was thinking of everything as a life-and-death situation. Vincenzo stopped what he was doing and Tilden barked orders to everyone. At first I could only see his mouth moving because the noise of the battlefield drowned out everything else. But then people began to realize that there was something wrong. Rosa and Marie stopped what they were doing and, with confused looks, began to follow Tilden's orders. The outside lights came on and Tilden, Vincenzo, and Rosa whisked everyone away.

"No more war today! Time to go home!" shouted Tilden, from down in the trench. "Everyone out! Out!" He pointed to kids as he saw them. "You! Out! Now!"

The battlefield fell quiet as confused kids looked about. I began to panic. My mind started to churn out questions I could not answer.

Could this be about Mr. Hawkins' bum ticker? If the silver thing he threw away were the magic pills, why did he do it? Were those the same pills Tilden was looking for? I looked back behind me. It was impossible to see anything so small and silvery in the evening shadows. I tried anyway, hoping it might jump out at me. But all I saw was mud and rocks and overturned earth covered in darkness. I went back toward Mr. Hawkins, anxious to help. When I got to the top of the trench and looked down, I saw him. His eyes were closed and his head was in Tilden's lap. Tilden spotted me and pointed at me and then yelled at me in a way that scared me half to death. "Go! Everyone! All of you! Go now! Leave!"

Kids started taking off their uniforms and putting down their weapons and moved toward the dirt mound. Some looked back toward the trench where Tilden, Vincenzo, and Rosa knelt near Mr. Hawkins. But even after Tilden's loud, scary, shouting voice reached my ears, I could barely move. Instead, I stood as if frozen, looking down in the trench, waiting for Mr. Hawkins to smile or pop up as if he had fooled everyone. But new, unwanted thoughts raced through my mind. This wasn't supposed to happen. This was too real. Mr. Hawkins looked very sick and wasn't moving. In fact, he looked so sick I thought there was even a chance he might…

"Leave! Now!" shouted Tilden.

This time I obeyed, backing away toward the dirt mound. Without even thinking of taking off my uniform, I started up the mound backward, using my hands to feel the dirt as I did. Once at the top, I slid down the other side to the outside of the mansion. To my surprise, many of the kids were joined by their parents and curious neighbors. They were all looking at the great mansion and its ten-foot walls and chattering quietly. My body shook from a thought that wouldn't go away. I had to face the truth no matter how scary it was. Mr. Hawkins might die. A voice in my head began to repeat it over and over again. Mr. Hawkins might die. Close to crying, I started to shake. This was not the way I ever wanted war to be.

Just then, from out of the dark shadows, Mom appeared. She put her hands on my shoulders and centered herself in front of me. "It's sundown. You have to come home right now and wash up and get changed right away to break the fast when Daddy comes home."

"Oh God!" I cried out, not hearing her. "Please don't let Mr. Hawkins die!"

"What?" she said.

I remembered how I called on God earlier to get out of services and He made a miracle happen. I remembered how He helped me figure out how to get out of burning the trash. That was a miracle too. And that's when it came to me: my last, best, and only hope—The Book of Life. I looked at the surrounding darkness and realized I had very little time.

I turned to Mom. "I have to go!"

"What?"

"I have to get Mr. Hawkins into The Book of Life!"

I looked around and could see only a tiny sliver of light from a sun that looked almost completely set.

"What?" Mom repeated.

"I have to go!" I said as I moved away from her.

"You can't!" she said.

"I have to!"

I took off down the street, turned the corner, and headed toward the synagogue, wondering why I had forgotten to pray for Mr. Hawkins to be put into The Book of Life. "Why?" I kept asking myself. If I hadn't forgotten, I'd bet it would have been a snap for God to give such a good person another year.

I heard Mom calling over my shoulder, but I ignored her. Instead, my mind centered on my greatest fear. Please, God, don't let there be any Jewish people coming my way because that means the service is over, the Ark is closed, and the fate of everyone in the world is sealed.

With my Great War rifle still in my hands, I raced up the street. Every street I passed on my way to the synagogue took away more and more of my breath and left me panting harder and harder, as I remembered how desperately far away it was.

With a sharp pain in my chest, I was forced to stop running, but I kept on, walking as fast as I could, panting with each step. Finally I was five blocks away, then four, then three, and I felt the hopelessness of what I was doing, knowing if I asked a thousand people all at once, right now, if it was sundown, that every single one would probably say, "Yes." Only two blocks from the synagogue, I saw what I had hoped so much not to see: a family of five people in holiday clothing, slowly walking in my direction. The father of the family had on a yarmulke.

"Are services over?" I panted.

The man looked me over, probably wondering who this strange little French infantryman was. But he was polite and answered with a nod, "Yes." Then, with a friendly smile he offered, "L'shanah Tovah."

"Is the Ark closed?" I asked, afraid to hear the answer.

"Yes, the Ark is closed."

I fell down to my knees, threw down my rifle, and raised my head toward the sky. Like the man who almost ran me over, I began to rock back and forth and sob. I didn't say the "Our Father" prayer like he did, because I knew it wasn't a Jewish prayer, but for a second, as I looked up at the night sky, I thought between hiccups and sniffles and crying that I might say it, if I knew it would work. I just wouldn't tell any rabbis or cantors what I did. But it was all in my imagination. It was all a bunch of nothing.

The father of the family kneeled down and placed a gentle hand on my shoulder.

"Are you all right?"

Between hiccups and tears I managed a nod, though I wasn't all right at all.

The whole family stayed near me. They were probably wondering why the news of the closed Ark had caused me to cry.

Out of the darkness, Mom appeared, a confused look on her face. "Mark," she said in a whisper loud enough for everyone to hear, "what are you doing? What's going on?"

I couldn't answer.

She squatted all the way down to get next to me. With her voice softening, she said more calmly, "Let's get out of the street. Let's move over by the grass and you can tell me what's going on."

The family, now that Mom had things under control, walked around us and offered to her, "L'shanah Tovah."

"L'shanah Tovah," Mom said in reply.

We moved to the synagogue lawn at the edge of the parking lot. I looked up at the sky and back to the street and back up at the sky again. I thought about the time I asked Mr. Hawkins if he believed in God and remembered he'd said he wasn't sure. I felt now was God's one and only chance to prove once and for all He was real and could hear prayers. Without saying anything Mom could hear or know, I closed my eyes and made a special prayer. "God, I promise not to ask for anything else for a whole year or even forever if you do this one thing and let Mr. Hawkins live. No one will have to know you did it after The Book of Life and the Ark were closed. You could open the book and scribble his name down really quickly and shut it real fast. And since you are the only one with the book, no one will ever know you did it after the sun went down. It could be between just you and me. I would never tell anyone."

Throughout my silent prayer, Mom sat alongside me, stroking

my head and back. I took longer breaths and my whimpering and hiccupping lessened as I felt Mom tug on the sleeve of my uniform to take it off me. I held out my arms like I always did when I was little, when she could see I was so tired I was about to fall asleep in my clothes if she didn't manage to get them off me.

She helped me take off the infantry coat, one sleeve and then the other, and then my haversack and helmet. I felt glad to be done with the weight of them. I didn't want to do war anymore, maybe even for a long time. There was too much sadness in war. There was only killing and wounding and hurting people. People everywhere had people who loved them, like I loved Mr. Hawkins, and whenever someone died in a battle, it meant people somewhere would cry and be sad like I was. And for what?

I remembered the ants my friends killed in Bayside and I knew now it wasn't right. Even though it wasn't against the law, I was pretty sure ants had feelings just like people. And wasn't that what mattered? Wasn't killing wrong, especially when it was for no reason?

With my boots and coat and all my wartime tools removed, and Mom sitting beside me stroking my head, I took a few more deep breaths. I was glad she was going to wait before asking me a million questions. It's how she always proved she knew me and cared about me. She knew there would be plenty of time later for me to tell her everything. Finally calm, after about a million tears, I put my head straight back and looked up at the enormous sky in the falling darkness and said, pointing, "Look, Mom. That's the Big Dipper."

CHAPTER 41

I tossed and turned the whole night remembering the look on Mr. Hawkins' face and the way his body hung limp across Tilden's legs after clutching his chest. Still, because I had never seen a real, live, dead person to know for sure what they looked like up close, a tiny part of me thought there was a chance Mr. Hawkins had miraculously survived and maybe even recovered. I couldn't bring myself to make up a pretend story about how he made it through the night and was going to be there when I went to see him the next morning, but I still had a tiny bit of hope.

When the first light of morning finally came, I went downstairs as quietly as I could and made my way down the street. When I got to the mound in front of the mansion, there was a handwritten sign stuck into the ground that looked like the kind of signs people put up when they want to sell their house. It read: There Will Be No More War.

I knew it was Tilden who made the sign, and I knew it was meant to stop all kids from coming to the house, and I was sure it would.

At the front steps, I noticed the door wasn't completely closed.

I thought about ringing the doorbell, but something told me not to. Instead, I gently pushed the door and stepped inside. The house was as quiet as could be and seemed deserted as I walked a few steps and looked around.

I heard the sound of glass touching glass and I knew immediately it was coming from the game room, so I followed it. When I got to the doorway I saw Tilden sitting in Mr. Hawkins' seat at the puzzle table holding a piece of the puzzle in his hand, looking down at the nearly finished picture. He had a half-full bottle next to him and a glass filled with a brown liquid. He looked un-Tilden-like, his hair uncombed, like messy Einstein, his shirttail sticking out as if he had been up all night. As I touched the glass doors leading to the room, they made a slight squeaking sound. Tilden slowly turned and faced me. His eyes were glassy and not able to focus until at last he spoke to me.

"I…apologize…for having raised my voice at you last night. I had no right to do such a thing. Mr. Hawkins would not have approved. I…beg your forgiveness."

I nodded to Tilden and whispered, "It's okay."

I realized I had been lucky to know Tilden because he was such a good person. I mean, how many grown-ups were there in the world who would bother apologizing to a kid after they did something wrong?

"He's gone," he said, sadly.

His words took me by surprise, and I nodded as if I already knew. But there was a bigger part of me that wanted desperately to escape Tilden's words or at least change their meaning. Maybe "gone" meant only for today, I thought. Maybe Mr. Hawkins was on a trip. Maybe "gone" was a tricky word that could mean a couple of different things. I began to imagine "gone" could mean he went to a place like the North Pole because it would be better weather for his bum ticker. If that was what happened, I knew it would be okay with me. In fact, I would make a deal with God right now, this very second, that he could stay there a whole year as long as God would promise me he was alive. As I hoped and prayed for it

I could even see it. He could make new friends that were Eskimos and live in an igloo and ride cuddly white polar bears all over the place. He could build great big snowmen and do tons of ice fishing while playing classical music. I would be okay with that. I really and truly would. I wouldn't be jealous that he'd made a new friend, and I would promise never, ever to complain.

But even my best imaginings couldn't win out against the truth I saw in the deep creases of Tilden's forehead.

"He's at the funeral home," Tilden said. "He will be buried in a couple of days."

My world of pretend shattered like glass and my heart sank as I realized it was all over. Mr. Hawkins had died. He didn't make it into The Book of Life and God had not rescued him or answered my prayer.

Tilden turned away from me and went back to the jigsaw puzzle. There were fewer than 15 pieces left. Numb, I climbed up onto Mr. Hawkins' loyal old wheelchair and sat down, propped up by phone books as I had done with Mr. Hawkins so many times before. In silence, I picked up a piece and began to search for a fit.

Tilden also held a piece out over the table to see if it matched any of the shapes.

"John would have wanted this finished," he said. "He always wanted things finished if he had put effort into them. It was his way."

There was a long silence.

"He left me a note, you know. I should like to read it to you."

I lifted my head up and looked at Tilden.

"It was at the bottom of his instructions about last night's music. I didn't read it until it was too late. He intended it that way. It was his choice. John valued his freedom of choice above everything. Last night he made a choice too. I must honor it."

Tilden picked up the paper next to him and cleared his throat.

"It reads, 'My dear, dear, friend, all that needs to be said, has been said. Please forgive me. This journey must be traveled alone—John'."

A shiver went through me as I watched Tilden cradle the letter like he cradled Mr. Hawkins' head on the battlefield.

"You know," he said clearing his throat again, "he said to me many times that I was among his very best friends. Though employed as a servant, I was his confidant, advisor, friend, and protector. I spent the larger part of my life with him, and I shall not ever regret a minute of it."

The pieces snapped into place like magic and soon there was but one. I let Tilden pick it up and click it into place. The picture looked like last night's sunset, though neither of us wanted to talk about it.

Tilden lifted his glass of brown liquid and gently swirled it around as he and Mr. Hawkins always used to do together. After bringing the glass to his lips, he took a sip and gave me the closest thing to a smile I had seen him give anyone, ever.

"In all the time I knew him, he never had occasion to use the word 'love'. Perhaps he thought I would have felt awkward with such a word. Indeed, I think I would have. Perhaps in silence he thought it and felt it about his children, but for the life of me, it was a word I never heard uttered from his lips. It just never came up. Imagine that! A man with as big a heart as his, who served the people around him so steadfastly, never had occasion to use such an important, powerful word."

Tilden paused, took another sip, put his glass down, turned, and looked directly into my eyes. Then, very softly, he said, "No, indeed. That was a word he reserved for you alone."

All kinds of feelings crashed into me like an unexpected wave at Rockaway Beach. I could feel my eyes watering as I remembered Mr. Hawkins telling me about all the good things in life—so many he couldn't choose just one. I remembered how he talked about nature's beauty, and the joys of living well, and the pleasure he got from doing admirable things. My eyes welled up and soon it became hard for me to sit there without crying.

"Tilden," I said. "I have to go home now."

Tilden nodded and his expression showed his understanding.

"Of course, Mr. Mark. Do come by sometime."

I nodded as I got up from the table, thinking to myself that I truly would visit Tilden sometime and would always think of him as a friend. I made my way down the hall and out the door with a mixed-up bundle of feelings I hardly knew what to do with. I started down the street toward home with my head down, looking at the cracks in the cement, when I sensed someone coming toward me from up the street. I raised my head and saw it was Dad. His face was sad, and I knew his sadness was for me because I had lost such a good friend. Closer and closer he came and I could see in his eyes and sense in his heart that it was as open as mine. A second later, I saw something I hadn't seen for the longest time and had longed for, seemingly forever. His arms opened wide as if calling me to run into them. And so I did. As fast as I could. As if shot out of a cannon, I launched myself into his powerful embrace and felt him lift me high above him before bringing me down so that my face was touching his. I felt his kisses, and scratchy whiskers and the scent of his aftershave as it overwhelmed me with sheer joy. My tears burst forth and I heard myself say while trembling,

"Tilden said...that Mr. Hawkins said he loved me."

Kissing me again and again, on my cheeks and on my head and pressing his nose into my neck, he said with his voice cracking, "I love you too. I love you too."

ACKNOWLEDGEMENTS

I wish to acknowledge and thank all of those wonderful early readers who provided me with the feedback and encouragement I needed during this great, sometimes exhausting, journey. Every writer needs such people—those willing to slosh through our crude workings and endless drafts in the name of friendship or plain old curiosity. To Jordan Carter, and Neal Grace, my lifelong friends and soul mates, I thank you. To Linda Leyden Illiano, thanks for taking a chance with my manuscript and providing me with validation and encouragement when it was in short supply.

Thank you, Charles Evan, who waited with his lovely late wife Melissa for each week's work to be read before the football game on Sundays. I am forever grateful for those special times, now fixed in my memory as the magical period of creation, encouragement and feedback.

To my sister Bonnie Fins Stoddard, what a surprise to find an editor travelling incognito in my own family. How wonderful it was to experience your intolerance for the extraneous, and witness first hand your slashing pen, until my novel was trim and fit and half its original size.

Editors one and all, I thank you for services rendered, skills imparted and encouragement delivered. Thank you, Michael McIrvin of A-1 Complete Writing and Editing. Thank you Jessica Keener, author and enthusiastic supporter. Caroline Leavitt, Lauren Baratz-Logsted, Sue Rasmussen, Becky Tuch, and Diane Giombetti Clue—each of you can see your influence within the pages of this work and is thus forever linked to it. I am grateful to have known you, and proud of your contributions as much as my own.

Barbara Ballinger, the highly accomplished author of more books and articles than I can count, who took it upon herself to help this crude storyteller for little more than his heartfelt thanks. You committed yourself to this work as if it were your own, day after day, week after week, and through its toughest times and rewrites. You saw within my hieroglyphics a story that you believed in. As my constant email companion, editor, reader, and friend, you picked me up more than once with encouragement that I could— and must—do better when I had lost my way and feared I might not make it to the finish line.

Thank you, Joanna, my love and partner, for being you.

There are many others who made this journey wonderful, and I hope all that I have omitted will forgive me.

Lastly, I want to thank Mom and Dad. Dad, thank you for a lifetime of support and encouragement to speak my truth honestly and openly. Mom, I will always remember how you waited with the greatest of expectant smiles for each new chapter to be read aloud to you right up until your dying day on July 30, 2012.

29741985R00205

Made in the USA
Middletown, DE
02 March 2016